Portable Magic

The Authors First Anthology

Edited by Lou Aronica, Aaron Brown, Allison Cronk, and Nora Tamada

THE
ST●RY
PLANT

"Books are a uniquely portable magic."
– Stephen King

Studio Digital CT, LLC
PO Box 4331
Stamford, CT 06907

Story Plant Print ISBN-13: 978-1-61188-213-1
Fiction Studio Books E-book ISBN-13: 978-1-936558-65-0

Visit our website at www.thestoryplant.com

First Story Plant Paperback Printing: July 2015
Printed in the United States of America

Contents

Ellen's Lake
By Nina Boyd
◄═►

NINA BOYD has been writing for as long as she can remember, a passion second only to studio art. The best entertainment for her has always been taking a stack of blank paper and a good pen and creating an entire world as real as the one around her. She relishes the moment when her characters come to life and start telling their story on their own. She enjoys the fantasy/adventure genre in particular, in which anything can happen and often does. There is no better world for her characters! She lives in California with her husband, three cats, and piles of projects. Here's what she wrote about "Ellen's Lake":

> "Ellen's Lake" developed from a culmination of things. I had just gotten back into writing after my dad passed away, and I was starting to take it more seriously, going to and forming my own critique groups and things. Most of my stories since my dad's passing have had an element of death in them, but "Ellen's Lake" is special to me for another reason. During my time as a teacher, I've come to see that there are so many kids out there like Jesse, dealing with problems the adults in their lives can hardly imagine. Sometimes the adults are the problem. Often those kids have built entire worlds grownups know nothing about, although we used to live in similar ones when we were their age. Jesse's story, like all coming-of-age stories, is an important one. I hope

it makes older readers think back to their own teenage days and young readers consider their present from a new perspective. I hope it makes them realize that childhood and adolescence are harder than we'd like to admit, but all the painful experiences are worth something. They make us who we are.

⟨⇒⟩

"It's almost spring," I say, leaning down to brush the wildflower blossoms with my fingertips. Their stems bend slightly in the breeze, letting the new flowers catch the sunlight that streams through the fields.

"The winter's been short this year," Ellen agrees. "Soon it'll be warm enough to go swimming in the lake again."

"That's all you care about." I laugh at her. "It's just water, El."

"I love the lake." She frowns, as she always does when I tease her too much.

"I'm sorry," I say swiftly. "The lake'll be nice. You're right."

"I'll race you to it," she challenges, my teasing already forgotten.

"All right."

"One, two – hey!" she shrieks, scrambling to catch up to my head start.

"Slowpoke!" I call to her over my shoulder. Laughing, I turn back to the path ahead, cut through the long grass, and fly past the trees. I make it to the lake just seconds before Ellen.

"You cheated!" she accuses, panting.

"I only do it when it doesn't matter," I tell her, reaching over and brushing some leaves out of her hair.

"It always matters," she says, and steps away from me.

I roll my eyes and look instead across the lake that we've come to so many times. A wind picks up around me and sails away, gliding over the green depths of the lake and flowing towards the forest on the other side. For a second, or maybe an hour, I forget where I am. My skin prickles. Something is pulling me away. Something in that forest . . .

"Jess!" Ellen calls.

I shake myself and turn toward her.

"We've got to go back," she says.

"All right."

The setting sun glides over the path, lighting it up.

I try not to look back at the forest.

<=>

Mid-spring sunlight streams in through my window. I hear a soft tapping at the glass.

"Jess," Ellen whispers in the morning stillness, "the lake looks perfect; come outside and see!"

I get out of bed, stretching. I strip off the shirt I've fallen asleep in and drop it over the back of my chair. Before I can reach for another, the window creaks open wider behind me. I hear Ellen's feet hit my bedroom floor.

"El!" I hiss, jumping several feet. "You can't just come in here!"

She drops her bag on the floor, wrinkles her nose at my shirt, takes it off the chair, folds it, and puts it neatly on the seat. "Why not? I always have."

But something is different now. I don't know what.

"Come on," she urges me. "We can eat breakfast on the way."

"What did you bring this time?"

"Apples," she answers, reaching down to pull one from the bag.

"Apples!" I scoff. "That's not enough."

"You aren't supposed to eat much before you swim, anyway," she scolds, hands on hips. We both laugh at her bossiness.

"You've already been swimming in the lake today," I accuse.

"How do you know?"

I step closer and lift a strand of her long damp hair. I hold it in front of her face and shake my head solemnly. "The evidence doesn't lie."

She laughs and pushes me away. Something in me jolts at the touch of her hands on my bare skin, but she's already across the room again, fiddling with the window.

"Come on, slowpoke," she says, half smiling over her shoulder. She pushes the window open wider and jumps through. Her hair swirls around her.

"I'll show you who's slow!" I call after her, jogging across my room and vaulting through the window too.

The fields are full of light. Long spring grass brushes my legs as I dash after her. The smell of wildflowers fills the air.

A sudden wind surrounds us as we run. I remember the other breeze, so similar, from those few weeks ago when we raced to the lake, and how it had glided its way to the forest . . .

We've almost reached the lake. Ellen still flies ahead of me. I see the grass waving in her wake She pulls her clothes away from her bathing suit as she runs.

"You're so far behind!" she yells back.

I raise my eyebrows at her challenge and burst into a sprint. I catch up to her easily. She shrieks and tears through the remaining stretch of grass. She jumps, making a perfect arc over the small hill dividing grass and sand, and wades into the lake.

She walks backwards in the water, watching me run towards her. I cut through the grass and take a flying leap over the ledge, landing on the sand with a thud. I recover, stumble into a run and splash through the knee-deep water, getting closer and closer to her.

"I've already won," she tells me, shaking her head.

"Only because I didn't cheat this time," I say breathlessly.

"You cheat too much," she says. "It's good you didn't today." She leans back, turning her face up to the sun, and floats. Somehow she is completely calm, not breathless at all. Her hair drifts around her, up and down in the waves we've created.

She looks sideways at me, squinting as the water laps against her face. "Why are you just standing there?" she asks. "Swim. We came all this way, didn't we?"

I shrug and start swimming around her, going farther and farther out each time around. Sometimes when I turn my head to breathe I glimpse the forest across the lake.

It's always dark there.

When we were younger, I told Ellen stories about the forest to scare her, stories I'd heard around campfires from the older kids.

None of us had ever been in the forest, of course. But it was fun to pretend.

Back then, the forest had been far removed from our lives, untouchable. We had been safe from it. An understanding existed: no one should or ever would go in there.

Now . . .

Now the forest is calling to me, and the scary thing is, I don't think I can stop myself from answering it. I don't think I *should* stop myself. I can almost feel it, something like a heartbeat, vibrating from the opposite shore and coming at me, riding the waves across the lake. The distance between the forest and me seems to stretch and bend, bringing it closer.

There's a small splash behind me as Ellen stands upright again in the water.

"What are you looking at?" she asks, swimming towards me. She follows my gaze toward the dense, black wall of trees.

"Nothing," I say, shaking myself.

"You're looking at the forest," she says nervously.

I know we're both remembering those old campfire stories.

"Remember what the older kids used to say about it?" I say in a low voice.

"Don't talk about it," she begs.

"They used to say that people get lost in there and never find their way out. That something in there . . ."

"Jesse!" she says sharply.

"Something in there calls to them, and traps them there."

She glares at me and tries not to look at the forest.

"Let's go back," she says.

"Ooh, are you scared?" I tease, pushing her lightly.

"Yes!" she snaps, glaring at me. "It's not funny, Jess!"

"It's just a bunch of trees," I tell her. "You don't have to be scared of them."

"It's not the trees that scare me. It's what they're hiding."

"Woooo," I imitate a ghostly voice. "Ell-e-e-e-n! We're the spirits of the forest! You can't see us but we're he-e-ere!"

"Shut up!" she cries. "I told you it isn't funny!" She turns her back on me and swims towards the shore, leaving me behind.

"Hey!" I call after her, but she doesn't answer or even look back.

She's been mad at me before like this, lots of times, but she's always gotten over it.

"Ellen!" I yell. "Come on!"

She wipes her wet feet on the grass and keeps walking.

I run after her.

"I'm sorry," I say, pulling on her shoulder to make her turn around.

She pointedly looks away from me.

"No, you're not," she accuses. "I told you not to talk about it, and you did it anyway, on purpose."

"I won't ever do it again. I promise."

"It was mean," she replied, but her eyes flick in my direction and I can tell she's giving in.

"Come on, it'll be a long walk back if you stay mad at me."

"Oh, all right," she says, sighing and facing me again.

"So you don't hate me?"

"No, I don't hate you." She shakes her head and finally smiles.

I can always get her to smile.

She looks so different, suddenly, standing in front of me, with the water still dripping off her. She's been shorter than me for a while. I noticed it in my bedroom, and I notice it more now.

She's still smiling at me.

Without knowing why, I lean toward her.

"Jesse!" she jumps away from me. "What are you doing?"

"I – I don't know."

"You're acting so weird today." She laughs uncomfortably.

I want to say something to fix the moment. I want to apologize, but I'm not sure for what. The sun shines directly overhead now, and the water drops on her shoulders sparkle.

"Don't forget your clothes," I tell her, mostly to fill the silence.

She stoops down to pick up her shirt and shorts from the sand.

We walk back through the fields quietly. Ellen pulls her shirt back on over her bathing suit.

"Wait a second." She stops in the middle of the path. She steps into her shorts and buttons them up, then bends down to fix her shoe.

A faint ringing pulls my attention away from her and back through the fields the way we had come. There's something back there by the forest, something that wants my attention. Something that sparkles . . .

Ellen straightens up and looks at me. "What?" she asks strangely.

"Nothing. Come on, let's go. I'm hungry."

⟨⇒⟩

I return to the forest on my own that evening, away from Ellen's accusing eyes. I have to know what's over there.

A light breeze sends ripples over the lake, again pulling me over to the dark forest.

I'm not scared. Not exactly.

The air is cooler on this side of the lake. The forest stands behind it, very dark and very quiet.

I see one bright thing, though. Close to the ground, as though it's growing right out of the dirt.

I stoop down next to the bright thing. It's something sparkly. Something unusual. There's more than one; I can see that now. Growing just at the border of the forest.

I've never been this close to the edge.

I take out my pocketknife and cut one of the sparkling things away from the rest. It's surprisingly difficult.

I feel the forest's stillness shift, as if it knows what I've done.

I hurry back home.

Once I'm alone in my room with the sparkling strand, I lay it out on top of my desk to examine it. Under my desk lamp, its sparkle is even more obvious. It looks like a twig with flowers attached – except instead of blossoms they're more like diamonds. The thing is about four inches long and moves like a fragile thread when I pick it up. But as frail as it appears, I cannot break or stretch it.

I hold the diamond-like strand between my fingers and walk slowly around my room, looking for a good place to keep it. I suddenly want to make sure it's safe. But each corner I try seems to leave it much too exposed. Finally, I put it carefully away in an old pencil box. I try to lie down and sleep, but I keep opening my eyes to check on the box. Should I leave it on top of my desk so I can see it, or in a drawer so it's hidden?

I get up and grab the box. It'll be safer next to me.

In the morning, I take the sparkly thing out carefully and look at it. I can't take my eyes off it.

The days pass in a blur. The sparkly thing never shows any signs of wilting. In fact, every time I look at it, it seems to shine brighter than it had that first day. After a week, it's still as clear and bright as ever. I breathe a sigh of relief on that seventh day. It had been growing out of the ground, after all. Suppose it had withered and died like an ordinary plant after I'd cut it?

My stomach growls.

The sound pulls me out of my daze. I can't remember the last time I ate. I force myself to close up the box and tuck it safely away in my desk drawer. Not a moment too soon. I hear Ellen tapping at my window.

I push the window open and stick my head out. The sunlight hurts my eyes.

"You look terrible," she says. "I knew it. I figured you must have been sick and that's why you've been away for so long." She waits for me to move so she can climb into the room. But I don't.

"Aren't you better yet?" she asks uncertainly.

"I wasn't sick," I tell her. Instantly, I regret not going along with the much simpler lie.

"Oh," she says in a small voice.

Still neither of us moves.

"Then, why haven't you come by?" she asks tentatively.

I shrug uncomfortably. "I don't know."

I look away from her hurt expression.

"Well," she says, clearly trying to figure out my behavior, "why don't you come outside now? All the trees are blooming and the fields are so full of wildflowers you can barely even see the grass."

The mention of wildflowers reminds me of our last time at the lake, and takes my mind back to the hidden pencil box.

"Come on," she says, mistaking my silence for reluctance, "you'll feel better if you come outside with me." She attempts a smile.

"I told you, I'm not sick."

"Well, you've been inside too long," she says firmly. "Now come on. I'm not leaving without you."

"Fine," I say impulsively, "let's go to the lake then."

Her face changes and she backs away from my window. "Oh no, Jess, let's not. I'm not sure I like the lake anymore."

"You've always liked it," I argue.

"I've never been afraid of it before." She rubs her arms as though trying to rid them of goose bumps. "I've never felt that way at the lake. I mean, I know everyone tells stories about the forest, but this is the first time I've – "

"All right, fine. We won't go to the lake," I break in irritably.

"What's wrong with you?" she asks sharply.

"Nothing," I lie, glancing compulsively at my desk.

"I can always tell when you're lying, Jesse Miller," she presses.

"I'm not lying."

"I know you are!"

"Well, you have to be wrong sometimes, don't you?" I snap.

"I don't think I want to spend the day with you after all," she says quietly. Her calm, low voice is worse than an argument. "Maybe I'll see you in a few days." She turns to walk away.

"Wait," I call after, shoving my pride aside. Maybe if I let her see the sparkly thing, she'll understand. "Just come in. I want to show you something."

She's never been as curious as me, and I can see her deliberating whether whatever I have to show her is worth backing down for.

"All right," she agrees finally, coming back to the window. I pull her up and walk over to my desk.

"Look," I say, handing her the pencil box.

"I knew you were hiding something!" she says triumphantly.

"Open it," I tell her. My heart starts to beat faster, anticipating her reaction.

She lifts the lid with a soft click and pulls out the sparkling strand. But she doesn't gasp in delight or exclaim over its beauty. Instead, she just stares at it, puzzled. "What is this?" she asks, turning it over in her hands. She's not handling it carefully at all.

I take it from her and put it neatly back in the box. "I found it out by the lake."

"Where by the lake?" she asks suspiciously.

"At the edge of the forest." I shrug.

She frowns. "Why are you so obsessed with that forest?"

"I'm not," I say impatiently. "Come on, just look at this thing."

"I've never noticed anything like this by the lake before," she muses. "It looks like some old glass or something. Are you sure it's not just trash from someone's camping trip?"

"Trash?" I sputter at her. "This looks like *trash* to you?"

"I don't know," she answers, shrugging. "I can't really tell what it is."

"Don't you see the sparkle?" I demand. "I've never seen anything like this before! Look how shiny it is, even out of the light! How could you think it's trash?"

"I guess it's kind of pretty," Ellen says, raising her eyebrows at my intensity.

I try to calm down a little.

"I thought you'd like it, is all," I say. "I know you're scared of the forest. But it can't be that bad if something this pretty is growing right next to it. I just wanted you to see it."

Her expression softens. "It is interesting," she admits. "Thank you for showing me."

"You can have it, if you want," I say on impulse, holding the box out to her.

"Oh no, I couldn't," she answers, shaking her head. She pushes the box back at me. "You found it. And besides, you – " She stops herself mid-sentence.

"What?"

"Well, you seem to want it more than I do, anyway."

"Oh."

"It's all right, keep it," she says. "Now, come on, let's go for a walk. You've been stuck inside for too long."

"I can get more of them," I say, and now that the idea has come to me it seems so obvious. "You can have this one. I'll just get some more. I can probably get a lot more, actually."

"What do you mean?"

"I can just go and cut some of the rest, can't I." I turn away from her and start opening and closing my desk drawers, looking for a safer place for the pencil box.

"Maybe you shouldn't," she says. I can feel her staring at me.

"Why not?"

"It was growing by that forest."

"So?"

"So I don't care what you say about it, there's something dangerous about that place." She reaches out and pulls at my hand. "Come on, a walk will be good for you."

I shake her off. "I am going for a walk, to the forest. You can come if you want."

"Jess, no," she protests. "I don't think you should cut more of these."

"Why not? Maybe I can sell them or something."

"Sell them?" she repeats. "Why would you want to do that?"

"I might as well. I bet if I go to the right people, I could get money for them."

"Since when do you care about money?"

I pull out my pocketknife and start cleaning it so I don't have to look at her. "In case you haven't noticed, Ellen, I don't have much of it. That's not going to change if I just let things carry on as they always have."

She stomps across the floor and crosses her arms. "You've never let that bother you before. And you've never ignored me when I've tried to talk to you, either."

I keep polishing the knife and don't answer.

She tries to snatch it out of my hand, but misses. I jerk the knife away from her. She grabs for it again, and it flips out of my hand, too quickly for me to catch it. In a silvery flash, it slashes her hand, slicing her palm right down the middle.

She cries out and presses her other hand to the wound. The knife clatters to the floor.

"Let me see it," I order her, kicking the knife aside and moving closer.

She shakes her head. Tears form in her eyes.

"El! Let me see it!" I try to pull her hand away. "I have to bandage it for you. Come on!"

"I can do it myself." She sniffs, backing away from me towards the window. She glances at the drawer where I put the box. "Get rid of that thing, Jess. There's something strange about it. I don't like the way it's making you act."

"You can't just walk home like that," I tell her, ignoring her remark. I stretch out the bottom of my shirt and try to tear it, but she's already boosting herself up on the window-sill one handed.

"Don't be an idiot!" I yell at her, exasperated. "Let me wrap it up at least!"

She drops clumsily over the side and starts to walk away. "Take your own advice," she shouts back. "Take that thing back to the forest. And don't you try to follow me, Jesse Miller!"

Her steps fade away until I can't hear them anymore.

I fling the edge of my now misshapen shirt back down and stoop to pick up the pocketknife. Drying blood coats the blade. I swallow hard and remorse pushes me to go after her, despite what she'd shouted and despite my stubbornness – but I ignore the impulse. Let her go, then, if she's so convinced she doesn't need me.

I clean the knife on the edge of my shirt, then pull the shirt off and drop it in the trashcan on my way out.

In the room down the hall, my father never stirs from his stupor. I've stopped tiptoeing around him. He rarely wakes up anymore.

The air outside is fresh and cool. I think begrudgingly that Ellen was right; I already feel as though I can breathe easier again.

I glance behind me in the direction of her house but I don't see her.

She'll be fine, I tell myself savagely.

I turn my attention to the path ahead, and my footsteps quicken. I fiddle with the pocketknife as I walk, flicking the blade open and closed.

She'll be fine.

As I approach the forest, my heartbeat speeds up. The ground sparkles in the late morning sun.

Is it just my imagination, or are there more strands now than a week ago?

I reach down and cut one of them away from the grass. It's harder to cut than the first one. Now that I'm looking closer, I can see lots more budding. Have they always been there?

I cut another, and another. I can't stop now. Could I take all of them? Why shouldn't I?

I reach for the next one, and the next. The sun slides lower in the sky.

It's nightfall before I leave the edge of the forest, my pockets full of the sparkly strands. As far as I can see, I've managed to cut away every last one.

I trudge home, letting the door slam loudly behind me, but I might as well be alone in the house for all the reaction it produces.

I stow the strands carefully in the larger drawer of my desk, behind a stack of papers. The moon climbs in the sky outside my window. I drop into bed, exhausted, and immediately fall asleep.

I awaken what feels like only a couple hours later, to the sound of my window creaking slowly open.

I move my head slightly so I can see. Moonlight shining in through the window highlights the silhouette of my visitor: tall, but not as tall as me, thin, but no longer straight-down thin like me, with a cloud of wavy hair floating around her as she moves toward my bed.

"Jess," Ellen whispers, "are you awake?"

I lie as still and quiet as I can.

Ellen sits next to me on the edge of the bed. I carefully open one eye to see if she's looking at my face. She's gazing out the window, seemingly lost in thought, so I look down at her hand. A tidy bandage wraps it now. From the professional appearance, she'd gone to the expensive clinic on the edge of town to get it treated.

I think of my bloody shirt in the trashcan, and how that had almost been her bandage. I wonder if she told anyone at the clinic how she was injured.

"I can't tell if you're awake," she finally says. She pauses for a moment, then drops her hand lightly onto my back. I hold my breath and wait.

"I went to the lake before I came here," she says. "You were there today, weren't you?" She pauses again as if expecting me to answer, but I lie quietly and wait for her to keep talking.

She sighs. "I can tell where those sparkling strands were. You cut them all, didn't you? They were growing right on the border of the forest. Now the grass there is all torn up. It looks so mangled . . ." She trails off. Her hand hasn't left my back. "Why did you do it?" she whispers. "Why do you want those things so badly, Jess?"

I can't hold my breath any longer, and try to let it out quietly. She peers closer at me, but she seems to know I won't give myself up now.

"Well, if you're awake, come to my house tomorrow morning, okay?" she asks. "Come by and we'll just spend time together." She stands up and adds, "I miss you."

She seems to be waiting for something. When I don't stir, she sighs and moves back to the window.

But just when I think she's left, I hear her cross the room towards me again. She leans down. Her face is so close to mine that I feel her breathing. In that split second, she kisses me.

Then she's gone.

⬳⬲➤

I wake up later than I ever have the next morning. I think back to Ellen's late night visit and her invitation, but I can't go to her house. Not now.

I pull some of the sparkling strands out of my drawer and put them carefully into a smaller satchel. I'm not exactly sure where to sell them, but I have some idea.

I've been down to the old hardware store a couple times to pick up tools for repairs on the house. Years ago, I bought the pocketknife there. Each time I've gone, a handful of old men have been sitting around outside the store, with nothing better to do than pass the time on one of the slowest street corners in town.

I swing the satchel back and forth from my wrist thoughtfully as I walk down the street, eventually leaving the dirt paths of my neighborhood for paved sidewalks. Slow moving cars pass me. Just a kid with a toy, they might think.

I jog across the street toward the hardware store. As usual, an assortment of older men crowds the wooden steps leading to the shop door. Most of them have rocking or folding chairs. In some cases, it's hard to tell which got there first, the men or the chairs.

I walk casually up the steps, nodding hello to them. I lean against one of the pillars holding up the sagging overhang and start swinging the satchel again.

At first, the men pay no attention to me, and the two that had been talking when I'd approached continue their conversation.

I open the satchel and pull out one of the strands. As I planned, it catches the light perfectly.

"What's that you've got there, son?" one of the men asks wheezily. He leans forward in his folding chair and peers at the strand.

"I found it," I tell him. "I'm not sure what it is."

"Let's have a look at it," he urges, holding out his hand.

"I don't know . . ." I answer slowly, pulling it closer to me. "I didn't find that many. I think it's really rare. I kind of don't want anyone to touch it."

"That's Tom's son," another of the men says in a not-so-hushed voice. "Probably the only nice thing he's got, and he just found it by accident, didn't he?"

I feel my face grow hot, but it can't be helped. Their pity will make the sale easier.

"I found it yesterday," I say, passing the strand back and forth between my hands.

"How many did you find?" the first man asks, in a less sympathetic tone than the second. "You said you didn't find that many. How many was it, exactly?"

I think fast. There are four men.

"Three," I say.

A small note of tension hovers in the air.

"Three," the first man repeats. He's watching the strand closely. I can see the desire in his eyes.

"I really only need one for myself," I go on.

"Poor boy, he should keep all of them," a third man interjects from a chair that's creakier than his voice. "Don't make him give them up, Carl."

"I just thought it'd make a good present for my Annie," Carl answers. "He does have three, after all, and he says he only wants to keep one."

"That's right," I answer casually.

Carl squints at me, finally tearing his gaze away from the strand. "I'll give you twenty dollars for it," he says.

"Now, Carl," – the second man laughs a little – "it's just a bit of string with some shiny things attached. Why don't you get your wife something at the jewelry store down the street?"

"This is rarer than anything he could find at the jewelry store," I argue.

"Well, let us look at it properly, then," he says, also holding out his hand.

I glance around at all four, who now give me their rapt attention. "Promise not to take it?" I ask, slowly pulling the strand back towards me just enough so they all lean forward.

"We promise," they say.

"All right." I hand it to Carl first, and he admires it in the light before passing it to the next man.

"It's not really string," I say as they pass it around, each admiring it for several minutes. "It's stronger than any string I've seen. And I don't know what those shiny things are."

"Diamonds?" Carl guesses.

"Glass?" another asks.

"Quartz?" says a man back in the corner.

"I don't think it's any of those things," I tell them. "All I know is, I found three of these things when I was out walking. I don't remember where. I wish I did. But all of a sudden, I looked down and there they were, on the ground."

"Maybe someone dropped them," one of the men says.

I'd rather have them believe that than discover that the strands were growing out of the grass.

"Maybe," I agree. "But wherever they came from, I only have three. And I've never seen anything like them."

"I'll give you a fifty for one of them," the man in the corner pipes up.

The strand has been passed completely around now and Carl hands it back to me solemnly.

"All right," I agree. I walk over to the man, who smells like dust and sweat, and trade him the strand for the cash.

The other men watch the transaction intently. I feel them calculating. Two strands left, and one of them mine. What's the last one worth?

"I'll give you sixty for the other one," Carl says.

"Why should Jake's be fifty and Carl's sixty?" the second man demands.

"I didn't even want to sell them," I tell him. "They offered. I don't have any price in mind. I guess it's just whatever it's worth to you."

"I'll give you two hundred for the last two you've got," the fourth man says.

"I'm not selling both of them," I tell him. "I want to keep one for myself."

"Two hundred twenty for the last one," the second man counters suddenly.

My stomach drops. Two hundred and seventy dollars is more money than I've ever seen at one time, let alone had.

"Done," I say, pulling it out of my satchel.

"Now, hold on a minute," Jake says from the corner. "It was Carl who originally wanted to buy one."

All of the men turned to look at him.

"I can't do more than sixty," he says simply.

"Two hundred twenty," the second man repeats firmly.

Jake shakes his head, pursing his lips and glancing at Carl. But I need the money.

"Done," I say, trading the strand for the cash.

I try not to hear the grumbles from the old men as I put the money in my pocket. They can sell to each other if they want to, can't they? Carl just didn't want it badly enough.

I walk back across the street, my pocket full of cash. I clutch the satchel holding my one remaining sparkling strand. I feel a sudden panic. Of course I have the whole drawer of them at home, and I've only sold two, but I already feel that I've let too many of them go. I have the only ones in the world, after all, and who knows if any more strands will ever grow out of the grass?

I walk faster down the street. Two hundred and twenty dollars for one, when the first had gone for fifty. I'd made out better than I had expected.

Much better.

I'd come out of it far too well, actually. I've never carried this much money around in my life.

Had anyone else seen me selling them? Suppose they followed me? Suppose they tried to steal my money from me? Or tried to steal the last strand?

I look over my shoulder a few times, but no one is behind me.

I shut myself back in my bedroom as soon as possible. My heart is already returning to normal.

I open the drawer where I've hidden the sparkling strands. They seem too exposed, suddenly. I look around my room for something else to put them in. My eyes land on a rough canvas bag with drawstrings.

That'll work.

I pull out the drawer and dump all the strands into the open bag. I didn't know I'd brought home so many. They almost reach the top of the bag.

I cinch up the drawstrings and sit back to consider my options.

I'd told the men I'd only found three, so I couldn't sell to them again . . . unless I tell them I'd found more. That was believable, wasn't it? Or I could try to find different people to sell them to.

I finger the cash in my pocket. It had been so easy to get it...

But what if I ended up selling all the strands? Sure, I'd keep one for myself, but would one really be enough?

Suppose word got around the town, and people came to me to try to take them by force? I'd seen the glint in the eyes of those men. I'd played off their desire at first, definitely, but there was something unnerving about it. They had wanted these threads of strange diamonds, perhaps more than they'd ever wanted anything.

I put the cash in the satchel and hide it in the back of my desk drawer.

A shadow falls over me.

After so many weeks of silence in the room across from mine, I almost don't realize who's casting it.

"Whatcha got in the bag, Jesse?" my father asks from the doorway.

I stare up at him in disbelief. I can't remember the last time he's gotten out of bed during the day.

"Stuff," I answer evasively, moving slightly so I'm standing between him and the canvas bag.

"What kind of stuff?"

"Nothing important."

"Important enough to tie up tightly," he observes, nodding at the drawstrings. "Must be worth something." He comes all the way into the room and looms over the bag curiously.

"Keep away from it," I say sharply, pulling it closer to me.

"Don't you order me around," he snaps, glaring at me. "What's in there? A present for your little girlfriend?"

"Leave her out of it," I tell him. My heart starts to pound, reminds me of things I've tried to forget.

"She hasn't been around lately," he goes on, sensing he's hit a nerve.

"What do you care?"

"Pretty little thing," he says thoughtfully, and I feel the same twinge of fear I'd felt years ago, when Ellen had run into him in the hallway one night.

"She moved," I say desperately.

He shakes his head. "I know when you're lying, Jesse Miller," he tells me and, crazily, I remember Ellen saying the same thing.

"She moved," I repeat. "Ask anyone." Then, on sudden inspiration, I add, "This is just a bag of books she left me."

"Hmph," he says, looking at it doubtfully, but seems to decide that I couldn't possibly have anything that's really valuable. He lumbers back to his room.

I make myself wait until I hear him lie back down before I run to the door and lock it.

⟨⇒⟩

That night, I look for a place to hide the bag. It has to stay in my room, but there are no secret corners, no places he won't look if he wants to find it badly enough. I don't want to risk hiding it outside, but it's not safe inside now that he knows about it. I don't trust his sudden loss of interest, either. He's come back to things before when I thought he'd had enough of them.

I slam the closet door in frustration. *Why* did he have to wake up then, of all times? The closet door shakes and comes loose from its frame. I glare at it and struggle to shove it back on the sliding track.

Suppose I sell more, somehow. Could I earn enough to leave, really leave? I push the hope from my mind. No one would let a fourteen-year-old live on his own. And anyway, even if I made a lot of money selling the strands, it would only last me so long – and he would come looking for me long before that.

Suddenly, unbelievably, I hear a tapping at my window.

I glance quickly at my bedroom door, which is still closed and locked against him. I listen carefully for any sounds of him stirring in the next room.

Only silence.

I move quietly over to the window and let Ellen in, taking care to open the window slowly enough to keep it from creaking.

"Hurry up, silly!" She laughs at me, but I jump at the sudden loudness of her voice, and clap my hand over her mouth. "Shh!" I hiss at her, glancing again at my bedroom door.

Still, thankfully, there's no sound from the room across the hall.

Her confused eyes meet mine. I put a finger to my lips and take my hand away from her mouth.

"What's going on?" she whispers.

"My dad got up today," I tell her quietly. "He came in my room. He – tried to take something."

She looks at me intently for a moment. "Those sparkly things?" she finally asks.

I sigh. "Yes."

She narrows her eyes at me, but she doesn't move away as I expect. "I hoped you'd get rid of them," she says.

"I couldn't."

"Why not?"

"They're too valuable, El." I sit down on the bed, careful not to let it creak, and she does the same. "I sold just two today and I made almost three hundred dollars. I have to keep them. It's my way out, don't you see?"

"Almost three hundred . . ." she repeats. "But you don't know anything about them. And your way out of what?"

"You know what."

She's silent for a moment, staring at the bedspread.

"He didn't actually see them," I continue. "All he saw was the bag I've been keeping them in. I told him something else was in the bag, something he wouldn't care about. He went back to bed. But if he starts to think I lied or if he decides I actually might have something worth some money, he'll come after me. I can't stay here."

She looks up at me in alarm, and I see her struggling to disagree with everything I've said. But the rules that make sense in her easy world don't work for mine.

"So don't sell any more," she says. "Don't give him a reason to care about them. Just get rid of them. Put them back by the forest, throw them in the lake, bury them somewhere. You made a bit of money out of them. Get rid of the rest before something terrible happens."

"I can't give them up," I tell her. "I'm too close to being able to leave this house. Think what I could do, where I could go! I wouldn't be stuck here anymore. I wouldn't have to hide or leave anymore when he wakes up. I wouldn't have to worry about –" I break off. I don't want to finish that sentence.

"Worry about what?" she asks.

"Nothing."

"What?" she demands, her voice finally rising above a whisper.

"Shh!" I order her, again looking at my door. "He's dangerous, all right? Now that he's gotten out of bed again during the day he'll do it more often. He's not as out of it anymore. And he mentioned you today. If he ever found you here when he's conscious, he'd – try to do things."

"What things?"

I feel my face flush, even though it's not me I'm embarrassed for, and I'm glad it's so dark.

"Come on, Ellen," I say uncomfortably. "Don't make me say it. He's not a nice guy. There's something wrong with him. Everyone says so."

"You don't have to listen to what everyone says –"

"They're right," I tell her fiercely. "They're right and it's not safe for you here now that he's waking up again. You can't keep visiting me here, not anymore."

I look down at the floor. I can't look at her now, not after I said all that.

"Come stay with me," she suggests in a small voice.

"You know that won't work."

"Well then, where will you go?"

The idea has come to me as we've been talking, and I'm not sure how, but it seems so obvious I can't believe I haven't thought of it before.

"Into the forest."

"What forest?" she asks sharply.

"The one you don't like."

"Jesse," she breathes, "what are you talking about?"

"It's the only place he won't follow me. And you know if I leave and try to stay someplace in town, or with you, he'll find me and drag me back here. He won't let me leave that easily. He'll look for me all over town if he has to, including at your house."

"You can't go in the forest!" she says desperately.

"I have to."

"How is that any less dangerous than staying here?"

"Maybe it won't be that bad. Do you know anyone who's actually been inside the forest? Maybe all the stories make it sound worse than it really is."

She shakes her head. "Come stay with me," she says again. "Even if my parents say no. We can hide you. We can figure something out."

"It won't work," I tell her. "I have to do this. I have to go."

She nods in defeat. She looks so sad that I have to tell her. I have to at least tell her before I leave.

"I was awake last night when you came in my room," I say. "I should've known you wouldn't give up on me."

"You were awake?" she repeats.

"The creaky window woke me up."

She laughs. "I can't believe you were awake that whole time!" She puts her hands on her hips and glares at me. For a moment it's as though the past few minutes never happened, and we easily might be going to swim in the lake in the morning.

It could be the last time I see her in a while. Who knows how long?

I lean toward her and she leans toward me, and we're kissing, and I don't have to pretend to be asleep for it. Everything about her is soft. She smells like the wildflowers outside.

A loud bang shakes my bedroom door. "Jesse!" my dad bellows from the other side.

I break away from Ellen and push her toward the window. I fling it open, no longer caring about the creaking.

"Who are you talking to in there?" he demands, now kicking at the door. "I heard you! Who do you have in there?"

I boost Ellen up onto the windowsill. "Run!" I urge her.

"What about you?" she asks, her eyes wide with fright.

All I can see is my father crashing into the room, finding her there, and I hear the gossip of the village in my ears: the reason he lost his job, the things he did. She has to leave. There's no time for goodbyes.

I shake my head at her. "I'll be right behind you," I say. "Just go!"

She jumps over the side and starts running through the grass.

I grab the bag from the corner of my room and pull some clothes out of the closet quickly. My bedroom door rattles on its hinges. I throw the clothes into the bag; grab my pocketknife and the money from my desk. Toss the bag out the window. Vault over the side after it.

I grab up the bag and take off running, but not after Ellen. I go in the opposite direction, toward the forest. I hadn't planned on going at night. But there's no way around it now.

I frantically hope that if Ellen turns around and sees me, she'll keep moving, and that she won't call after me.

She doesn't.

I keep running, feeling oddly free. He won't follow me to the forest; I know I'm right about that. Too many things about it frighten him.

I tear through the fields, down the dirt paths. The cold night air stings my cheeks, but I'm moving too fast to care.

I reach the lake.

It's still and dark, reflecting only the moon.

The forest doesn't reflect any light.

Swimming across the lake would be faster, but there's no need to let the only extra clothes I brought with me get wet, so I walk around the edge of the lake instead. I feel my heartbeat slow the closer I get to the forest. The familiar sounds of the lake soothe me: the frogs murmuring, the bugs humming, the light wind blowing through the reeds.

I can see the forest's grassy border now. The tired remains of the threads stick out every which way in the moonlight.

I shift the canvas bag to my other shoulder and approach the forest more slowly. It's right in front of me now, big and black and dense.

And silent.

I hold my breath and step over the threshold.

Even the grass there feels different.

I can no longer hear the frogs, the bugs, or the wind. It's as if I'm in another world, and the other has never existed.

But I don't feel shivery the way Ellen did.

I walk farther into the forest. There's no sign of any animals. The trees grow much closer together here. Their branches seem to curve upwards in a strange way, and the soil at their roots smells different.

I look all around as I walk, but still there's no hint of danger. Could everyone have been wrong?

I find a clump of three trees growing closely together. The bases of their trunks form a sort of two-sided shelter.

I remember building forts around trees like this with Ellen when we were younger. We'd go into her backyard, especially if we knew rain was on the way. We used to tie branches together to make walls and hide from anything we made up.

Back then, the dangers we tried to shut out were only imaginary.

I look around and set the canvas bag down. It's as good a place as any to try to sleep.

It takes me awhile to find fallen branches big enough, but eventually I collect a decent amount that I can use to construct another wall.

I wonder if he'll try to use Ellen to find me. I wonder if he'll go to her house and . . .

I push the thought from my mind. As long as her parents are there, she'll be okay. She'll be safe.

I weave the sticks together with some tall grass. It's no easier now than it was back then, but it gives me something to do and keeps my mind from torturing me.

After an hour, I've built something resembling a wall. It's hardly a real shelter, but it's the best I can do in the dark. A tiny caterpillar inches down one of the branches away from my hand, and I nearly drop the whole stack of branches from the shock of finally seeing another living creature.

He continues moving slowly but steadily away from me, probably hoping I'll just ignore him. Soon he's made it to the bottom of the branch and drops back into the soil, eventually disappearing.

If there are caterpillars here, maybe there are birds.

I look up into the trees for a moment, but all I see are branches crisscrossing the stars. It's still as silent as when I entered the forest.

I sigh and lean the second wall of branches against the tree trunk. It seems safe enough to sleep, and I can't keep myself from drifting off any longer . . .

A strange noise wakes me. I open my eyes to a faint tapping sound. It's sunny out now; somehow I slept through the whole night.

I still don't hear birds or anything that sounds like animals skittering through the woods, but the tapping noise persists. It's coming from the entrance to the forest, back where I'd first come in.

I follow the noise, but as I move closer to it, the sound suddenly stops. I jog to the border and across, but I don't see anything that could have been making it. Then, a few yards away on the ground in front of me, I see a bag. It's a paper bag, from a grocery store, and it was definitely not there last night. I look around again but see no one, so I approach it.

Inside is a collection of food, boxes of crackers and things that won't go bad being outside with no refrigerator. I can guess who left the bag there, but where did the noise come from? Then I spot a stick leaning against a tree trunk. Ellen must have tapped it several times to wake me up.

I look at the stick for a moment. I imagine Ellen walking out past the lake to the edge of the forest, maybe trembling, not wanting to go inside, to leave the bag there for me. She had just left, sometime between when the sound stopped and when I stepped out of the forest. She couldn't have gotten that much of a head start. I suddenly want to see her so badly I almost forget why I've come to the forest in the first place, and I actually walk a few steps toward the lake, back in the direction of her house, as though I can just visit her the way I used to.

Then I remember last night, and I instead pick up the bag and retreat back into the darkness.

I stow the bag in the small fort I've made. It looks oddly out of place in the midst of all the branches and dirt. Its presence makes everything seem a little better, somehow.

If I can go out to the border to get something Ellen left for me, why can't I go out for other things? I don't have to be completely stuck in the forest, after all. I can go swimming in the lake if I want to. I could maybe meet her there some-times. The dark shelter of the forest will always be waiting to hide me again.

The canvas bag has fallen open, maybe during the night when I'd used it for a pillow. One of the sparkling strands pokes through the top.

I could sell more of them, if I had to. Maybe on the edge of the forest. Maybe one day I could go back to the village, if I got enough money. But there were other ifs, things I couldn't avoid. If I went back, he'd find me, and he wouldn't leave me alone. No, running away last night changed things, and I couldn't return. At least for now, the forest was home, and I might as well explore it.

Trees tower over me in all directions, but I see over-grown paths between some of them. Before I start walking, I pull out one of the shirts I'd thrown into the canvas bag last night. I tie it high up on one of the branches, then step back a few paces. It stands out enough; I'm pretty sure I'll be able to see it to find my way back if I get lost.

I reach into the grocery bag and lift up a box of granola bars. A red apple rolls out from underneath it.

I smile and tuck it inside the box so it won't get bruised.

Not all of the forest is as dark as the area I'd slept in. As I walk, I see some clearings where the sun shines through pretty well. I still don't hear any animals, but the stillness is peaceful rather than spooky, and I'm starting to think maybe the forest isn't so bad.

A tiny stream flows next to me. Its gurgles and splashes are deafening in the otherwise perfect silence. I sit on some larger rocks and unwrap my granola bar.

She must be okay if she was able to come all the way out here. I can only hope she got back to her house safely.

The foil wrapper is blinding when the sunlight hits it, and it gives me an idea. I crumple it up and put it in my pocket, next to the money I'd grabbed from my desk last night.

The sunlight is already heating up the rocks, so I take my shoes off and stick my feet in the stream. I watch the water wash away the dirt. The current carries it downstream, further from the direction I'd come. I wonder how big the forest is. Maybe there are animals in it, somewhere, and I scared them all away.

Maybe there was a big cave somewhere, hidden away, that I'd been lucky enough to avoid so far. Maybe it was only a matter of time before I came up against a huge beast, some animal I'd never seen before, and I wouldn't be able to protect myself.

I reach into my other pocket and pull out my knife. The last time I'd held it, it had been an accidental weapon. Could I use it to kill? I've never killed anything before, except the little spiders that sneak through the cracks around my window in the summer.

I drop the knife back into my pocket and put my shoes back on.

My shelter is just as I left it. The canvas bag is undisturbed. I reach down and cut off a small piece of the drawstring. Then I take the granola bar wrapper from my pocket and crumple up one of the sides. I wrap the string around it, tie it, and then tie the other end to one of the tree branches. The silvery wrapper dangles in the air, twisting and turning like some strange Christmas tree ornament. It catches some of the rays of sunlight breaking through the trees.

When the tree is full of wrappers, it'll stand out during the day at least, and I won't have to worry about finding it. There's an odd prettiness to it now.

It's something Ellen would have done.

I want her to come back, and to know that I'll come out to see her this time.

I gather some sticks and go out to the lake. I poke them into the ground carefully, one at a time.

Finally, I stand back up to inspect my work. The sticks blend in with the dirt, but they form a clear path of arrows pointing towards the forest.

If she comes back, she'll see them.

<=>

After a few days, I've eaten everything but the last granola bar, and have given up trying to catch fish in the lake. I made a spear with a long stick and my pocketknife, but spearing fish turned out to be a lot harder than I thought. I haven't been able to start a fire anyway. All the plants in the forest have a poisonous look, and I've run out of ideas for food.

I'll have to go into town to get some. Maybe I can pull it off somehow without him finding out. He hasn't left the house in a while, after all. Just because he's taken to getting out of bed doesn't mean he'll suddenly be walking the streets.

Still, heading that far away from the forest seems crazy now. What if someone tells him I've come back? Maybe he's told people to look for me. Maybe he's just waiting for me to give in and return. He probably figures I'll come back eventually. What if he catches me before I can escape back into the forest?

But there's no way around it. I'll have to go to the store and come back as quickly as I can. I haven't seen any sign of Ellen. Maybe she's already forgotten about me. Or maybe someone's been keeping her from coming here. For a moment, I can't control my imagination, and I see her walking past my house, maybe on her way to the lake – it could have been yesterday – and my father wakes up . . .

I take a deep breath. Maybe I can ask about her at the store. They might not know anything, but it's worth a try.

I cross over the border. Now it's the other side that feels foreign to me. Everything is so bright and loud. I feel strange not bringing my spear. I left it by my shelter of trees. I carry it with me all the time in the forest now, but I shouldn't need it out here.

I try not to look at the tired threads drooping over the grass. No strands have grown back.

The corner store is pretty close to the lake, closer than the hardware store. It shouldn't take long to get there and back safely. I start walking, still adjusting to the noises. The birdcalls and the light breeze around me seem deafening.

The path back through the grove of trees is oddly dusty. Usually patches of mud cover most of it this time of year, but the skies have been clear for several days now and the soil is dry. I peer down the path, half hoping to see Ellen coming towards me, but it remains deserted.

The fluorescent lighting in the store, although dimmed by a layer of dust, is too bright after the dark shelter of the forest trees. I grab a plastic basket and squint as I walk quickly through the aisles, grabbing things at random. I suddenly feel uneasy being inside, with the walls around me, trapped.

I approach the counter and set my basket down in front of the cashier. He unloads my basket mechanically, running the packages over the scanner, not looking at me.

I watch him in silence, until I can't hold back any longer.

"Have you seen Ellen Thomas lately?" I burst out.

He finally looks up at me for a half second.

"You're covered in dirt," he comments. "You're a mess, even for being on break from school. What have you been doing today?"

"Playing outside," I tell him impatiently. "Have you seen her?"

"Who?"

"Ellen Thomas! You know, she's my age. Her dad is Jake Thomas. He runs the realtor office down the street."

"Oh, right, skinny blond girl." The man shakes his head and taps the screen with my total. I hand him some money. "Haven't seen her."

My stomach clenches, but there's no reason for him to see her, after all. It's not as if she'd come in here every day.

"Here you go," he says, handing me the bag.

"Hang on a minute." I reach into my pocket again and pull out more money. I can't shake this rising panic. "I need to talk to her. Can you get a message to her for me? Tell her to meet me at the lake today, before the sun goes down."

He shakes his head again. "You school kids and your games. I can't just leave the store to go deliver notes to your little friend."

I drop the stack of cash down on the counter between us. "It's not a game."

He looks down at the money and back up at me, the dismissive grin fading from his face.

"Go to her house. She'll be there. Tell her to meet me at the lake before sunset. Don't tell anyone else."

"Look, kid . . ." he starts slowly.

"Will you do it, or not?" I demand.

He looks back down at the money. "All right," he says finally.

"Don't tell anyone else," I repeat.

I leave the store with my bag full of food. I'm not even sure what I bought. Would he do it? I gave him enough money to make it worth his while. But what if he just took it and did nothing? I could try to see her, of course. But I'd already let one person see me in town. I couldn't tell if the cashier had recognized me or not. Would he tell my father I'd come back?

I look down the path in the other direction, toward the houses, toward her house. Maybe just for a few minutes . . . But if she saw me, she'd try to get me to stay, and it would be harder to leave.

I'd have to stay hidden.

I walk quickly down the path, feeling with each step that I've made the right decision. Luckily, no one else is out along this way, and I manage to reach her house unseen.

I set the bag down against the outer wall and peer into her window. She's not in her room, which is just what I was hoping. She could be in the bathroom, or in the kitchen, so I had to be quick.

I know her window won't be locked, and it isn't. I push it open and climb in. There's a pad of stationery on her desk, with a pen next to it. It's almost as if she put it out for me.

I scribble a note telling her to meet me today, before it gets dark. I think for a moment. Then I add, "Thanks for the apple." There's now a smudge on the paper where I've rested my hand. I guess the guy in the store was right about the dirt.

I hear footsteps outside the door, and I quickly jump back over the sill and close the window quietly. All I can do now is walk back and wait.

The forest welcomes me back. A breeze lifts in the air, waving the branches towards me as I return to its depths. I set the bag of food down against one of the trunks of my shelter and tear into a package of something salty and crunchy. Junk food, Ellen would call it. But it's delicious after the little breakfast I'd had.

As I dig into the bag, I notice the dirt under my nails, the not-so-thin layer of grime on my arms, and the smudges on my clothes. I'm pretty sure I hadn't remembered to buy soap, but at least I can swim most of it off before she comes. If she does.

I make myself eat an apple, which I somehow remembered to buy, and take another with me, along with my spear. I jump in the lake, creating a terrific splash that probably takes off the first layer of dirt. I swim down, down, past the muddy sides sprouting little plants and past the uncatchable fish. I can't see the bottom. Ellen and I could never swim down that far without coming back up for air.

I kick back up to the surface and drape my soaked shirt over one of the sun-warmed rocks, where I'd left the second apple – but I don't see it now.

"You need to work on your penmanship," Ellen calls from behind me. I whirl around. She takes a bite of the apple and smiles at me. "I almost couldn't read your note."

I'm so glad to see her, but I don't know what to do. It feels as if it's been years.

She finishes the apple and jumps in next to me, sending a wave of water over both our heads. She kicks back up to the surface and brushes her wet hair out of her eyes. "I haven't been out here in so long," she says. "There isn't exactly anyone else to go with."

"Well, I'm glad you came," I tell her.

She drops her gaze. "I wanted to come see you before. But . . . I didn't know if you wanted to see me."

"Are you kidding? You're the only thing I miss."

"Really?"

"Yes, you big dope," I say, pushing her a little. "How could you think I didn't want to see you?"

She smiles. "I don't know. I guess I just thought you'd want to be alone, and it would be easier for you."

"I didn't, and it wasn't. But I didn't want you to get hurt."

"Well, I won't get hurt here." She looks at the dark trees behind us. "What's the forest like?"

"Peaceful," I say truthfully.

"Then why do you need that?" she asks, pointing at my spear lying on the grass.

"I wanted to be prepared, just in case. I haven't explored the whole forest yet."

She looks into the forest thoughtfully. "It doesn't seem as scary as it did before."

"No."

"Are there any animals in there?" she asks.

"There's insects," I tell her. "But I haven't seen anything big yet. It's not like most forests. There's something special about it, but I don't think it's dangerous. I think it's easy to be afraid of it until you go inside. I bet all those older kids who used to tell stories about it have never been in there."

"What's different about it?"

I climb out of the lake and shake my hair dry. "Come inside and find out."

"I don't know . . ." she says slowly.

"Come on. I've been living in there for like a week and I'm fine."

"Oh, all right." She climbs out of the lake after me. Her long hair clings to her back, and her clothes drip as we walk toward the forest.

"You're sure there's nothing in there?" she asks nervously.

"Nothing that seems to care that I'm here."

I walk ahead of her, leaning on my spear like a walking stick. We pass the straggly threads growing on the border.

Ellen steps over the threshold after me. All the sounds from the lake disappear again.

"It's so quiet in here," she whispers. "Where are all the birds?"

"That's what I wondered."

She looks around, taking everything in. "It smells different in here."

"The dirt feels different, too."

"It's like a forest, but not a forest . . ." She goes on, "I mean, all the things to make a forest are here – but it almost doesn't feel real."

"It's real enough. I made a shelter out of the tree trunks and fallen branches. I sleep on the dirt. I walk on the paths."

"That's not what I mean. There's something different about it, you're right. It just seems like . . . Almost like it's from another world, you know?" She looks sideways at me. "Kind of like those strands of sparkly things you found."

"Kind of."

"Do you still have them?"

We've reached the shelter I made, and I point at the canvas bag. "They're in there, under my clothes. I kind of forgot about them, honestly." As soon as I say this, I realize it's true. They haven't seemed so important for a while now.

"You could just leave them here," she says, "and come back home."

"I can't live with my dad again, Ellen. And you know no one else would take me. I won't be able to come back unless he's gone."

"What do you mean, 'gone'?" she asks, sitting down and leaning against one of the tree trunks.

"I mean gone. Left town. Or maybe we'll get lucky and his liver will give out."

"Jesse!"

"I'm serious. What's going to happen to me if I come back? Nothing good. Not with the way things are right now."

"Well then, I'll keep coming to visit you."

I smile at her and she smiles back. The awkwardness is gone, out here in the woods, after the kiss in my room and everything else that happened. It doesn't matter now.

We walk through the forest. I show her all the places I've come to know: the creek, the sunny groves and the darker ones, the strange rocks and where the few butterflies live. It gets dark, and I know she has to leave, at least for today.

"I'll walk you out to the border."

I've been using my spear as a walking stick this whole time, and I keep hiking along with it all the way to the edge of the forest. We're still laughing about some joke we'd made earlier and, at first, I don't see him.

"Jesse," Ellen gasps suddenly, pointing ahead.

There, framed by the setting sun, stands my father, who has finally left the confines of the house and somehow forced himself into this world.

"So this is where you've been hiding," he says. "Well, I found you. I found you, and you're coming back to the house. Along with the rest of that money."

I grip the spear more tightly. In that instant I know that I never needed it for the forest. I needed it for this moment, which I realize I've been dreading.

"What money?" I say.

"Don't you play stupid with me," he says softly. "You sold something to those old saps at the hardware store. They told me. Everyone told me what I wanted to know. That's how I found you. You paid off that clerk in the store." He laughs harshly. "Not enough, I guess."

My heart is crashing against my chest. I push Ellen back, back towards the forest. He won't follow her in there. But I've called attention to her with that slight movement.

I've done it now.

"Don't send your little friend too far," he says suddenly. And when I see the way he looks at her, I know what I have to do.

"It doesn't matter that everyone told you what I did and where to find me," I say loudly. "You can't make me come back."

"You do as you're told!" he bellows. "The people in this town still respect me, damn it, and so will you!"

He charges at me, maybe to drag me back with him, maybe to hit me again – but it's what I've been waiting for. In a flash, I yank the spear out of the ground and aim straight for his heart.

But I hadn't counted on Ellen. Faster than me, she jumps in front of me to block him. What are you doing, I want to shout. Get out of the way. But it's already too late. Slowly, horribly, I see the spear pierce her instead. She lets out a sound that I'll never forget.

She falls to the ground. A dark stain slowly spreads on her shirt. Her eyes stare up blankly. I wait for her to blink, to gasp or cry for help, something. Anything.

My father is still standing in front of me, looking down at Ellen's dead body, maybe in shock. I can smell the alcohol now that he's this close. I know he won't be able to react in time.

He looks up at my sudden movement, but he's not fast enough. The spear goes where it should have, and I don't even feel my arm move.

Ellen's eyes stare up at the trees, as lifeless as the rest of her. I drop down next to her.

She'll get up soon, any second now, and I'll walk her to the clinic on the edge of town. Tomorrow we'll walk in the fields and look for signs of fall as we always do. She'll need time to heal, of course. Maybe the day after tomorrow we'll walk . . .

But I don't feel a pulse; I don't feel her breath.

I don't feel anything.

A wind picks up around me. Ellen's eyes stare up at the stars. She still hasn't moved.

I reach down and shake her. "Hey!" I whisper. "Wake up!"

She's not asleep, I tell myself. Her eyes are open.

"Ellen!" I say, and I shake her again. She doesn't move. And suddenly I'm shouting, yelling her name.

But she's not there anymore.

The branches of the trees above wave and creak slowly in the wind.

I'm the only one who can hear them now.

I stand up slowly. There is only blackness in front of me, and nothing behind me.

I walk toward the village.

In the hardware store, no one looks at me. I go to the back and pick up a shovel. I walk out with it. Someone might be shouting at me. I'm not sure.

Back in the forest, I dig a hole. It takes a while to make it big enough. I drag his body over to it and roll him over the edge. I cover him up until he's gone.

I pick up the canvas bag, remove my extra clothes. I carry it out of the darkened forest, carefully not looking at Ellen, and drop it on the border where I had first found the sparkling strands. The tired strands still droop over the grass.

I dig another hole, right in front of them. I drop the canvas bag into it. The sparkling strands clink softly. I shovel the dry dirt back into the hole.

It's darker now, which will help with the last hole I have to dig.

Some stars start to peek out above. The wind has picked up. It's rustling the grass. I make the last hole by the lake, on the side closest to the village. My arms are aching now, but soon I'll be finished.

I walk over to Ellen's body. Her fingernails are very white now, even whiter in the moonlight. The stain on her shirt has darkened and dried. Her hair is spread around her. It looks just how it used to when we'd lie in the grass, looking up at the stars.

She's heavier than I thought she would be.

I put her in the grave. That's what it is. Somehow, this lakeside has become Ellen's grave. I shovel dirt back over her slowly, watching it cover her. I remember her laughing with me in the forest only hours ago. I remember all those times we raced down the path from my house, through the grass, jumping into the lake. I remember how it felt to kiss her.

It's almost as though she's still here. Maybe she's standing behind me. She might be, as long as I don't turn to look . . .

The wind blows softly around me. I clutch the shovel tightly. If I let go, I don't know what will happen.

In the distance, I hear the low rumbling of thunder. The wind lets out one last sigh.

The rain finally comes.

The New Fenian
By B. Lynch Black
⬄

B. LYNCH BLACK, writer, artist, and out-of-work actor, born, raised, and still residing in the Bronx, New York, has written and published numerous short stories, essays, and reviews. Most recent short stories: "Eyes On A Distant Star," Hon. Mention *Future Writers of Earth* 2013 and winner of N3F competition; "The Gantlet," Circlet Press, 2008; "All of Me," Forbidden Publications, 2006; "Sitting at the Gate of the Temple," *Watching Time* anthology 2006. Poetry: "Rosh Chodesh," *Voices Israel* 2012; "Mincey Stew" *Voices of Our Mothers* 2010; "The Meaning of Coffee," *Portia Steele Poetry* 2007; "A Silver Hair," Winner, Green Rivers Competition, Animal poems, 2009. Black is currently writing an historical fantasy novel that received a research grant from the Ludwig Vogelstein Foundation. Here's what B. Lynch Black wrote about "The New Fenian":

> I am a lover of mythology and especially of Celtic and Norse stories and poems. My father, who is my hero, was a police officer. Rereading the story of *Oisín and Niamh in Tir na Og* gave me the idea to create a Celtic-style mythology around a police officer who had to complete three tasks. Heroic tasks are a common theme in all mythology and folklore.

⬄

For my Father, James Black.
One of the Good Guys.

◄⇒►

Part I

Chapter One

◄⇒►

A warm night for the time of the year and a full moon brought people out in droves. Which usually meant trouble. And in that respect the night was no different from expected. And in other respects it was like no other night before it.

I finished my last four-to-twelve and took myself to An Beal Bocht, my favorite café, to listen to the *seisún*. I had a three-day break coming up and wanted to unwind after a rough week on the shift: two DOAs – one a ten-year-old boy, the other a forty-year-old woman. The one killed by his mother; the other probably killed by her son. Three street fights and a mugging. Twelve arrests and tons of paperwork. All too typical of all my weeks.

Dermot pulled a pint with his usual good humor and Brenda put a ham sandwich together for me. I took a long grateful swallow from the pint and a big bite out of the sandwich. John, the accordion player, had just launched into a series of reels, and the guitarist and fiddler kept the tunes company.

The Beal is located in the middling reaches of the Bronx in a bit of a nondescript neighborhood. The architecture consists mainly of the once-desired "pre-War" style buildings. The residents are nondescript too for the most part. Not rich, not poor. Near a college, but not a big one. The Irish came there, but it wasn't an Irish neighborhood. The décor was eclectic – a cross between an old barn and your great-aunt's dining room. And the service was casual but friendly. It always seemed to me the perfect spot for those who belonged nowhere.

That night, the place was filled with the usual suspects: students from the nearby college talking about life as if they had actually lived it; musicians hanging around waiting for their turn at the set; a local acting troupe cutting up at the corner table by the window; the resident Poet, smoking his brains out, studiously writing the poems that would be featured at the weekly Tuesday night readings. I've been told the poetry read on those nights is good, but it always seems gloomy to me, with romantic notions of death. There's nothing romantic about death; I can tell you that. I fight to keep Death at bay and I pick up the pieces of his handiwork.

Sometimes I read my own poems on those nights but, strangely enough, morbid as they are, they aren't usually enthusiastically received.

Anyway . . . I was unwinding nicely, just settling into the post-shift blues, when *they* came in.

The café was already packed, every seat taken. You had to fight your way over to the coffee machine. Fortunately, I wasn't drinking coffee. There wasn't a chair to be seen, but within a minute of their entry a large table opened up as the college students went off to cram for exams.

All of them were dressed in dark pants or jeans and T-shirts, with a variety of haircuts, mostly long. It was difficult to tell the girls from the boys, until they shrugged out of their leather jackets. I glanced outside. There were as many motorcycles lined up as there were newcomers, though I hadn't heard the engines when they pulled up.

They weren't particularly raucous but their presence was felt. Especially the one who seemed to be their leader. She had a tumbling mass of pale hair and dark eyes. Jeans tight enough to have been painted on and her black T-shirt fit lovingly over her slender figure. There were other women in the room that night, but I couldn't stop looking at her.

Every time one of them talked or laughed, you could hear the sound of little bells. All of them had several earrings and each had a little silver bell in one of their ears.

Dermot came to their table, and I heard his transplanted Dublin accent across the room as he talked to them. "How'er yas? What'll yas have now? The usual?"

So. They were regulars of a sort, though I'd never seen them before. I'd have remembered. I watched them out of the corner of my eye, through the smoky haze that always hung about the room at that hour, despite air filters and health codes. Even when Dermot brought me a second pint – my taste buds had hardly registered the first – I couldn't take my eyes off them. Especially her.

And she looked at me. She'd catch my eye for a second or two, then her glance would flick away. Deliberately. Thoughtfully. Once, she nudged the young man next to her, inclining her fair head in my direction. He grinned while she fixed me with a stare.

Dark eyes held me. I was getting warmer, though I told myself that it was the beer and the closeness of the room. Little-bell sounds murmured across the room to rest in my ear.

After a while, I wandered to the tiny bathroom and, passing their table, again I caught her eye. And she smiled.

Back in my chair, glass in hand. The music filled the room, and the tinkling sounds of the bells drifted over the heads of the patrons, over the tune John was currently playing, above the crowd. One of the newcomers started playing a tin whistle and the Cape Breton waltz I always liked dissolved into a slow air called "Mna naEirenn." Women of Ireland.

I allowed myself to relax into it, let the music take me over. The sad, sweet strains touched the strings in me that resonated with the melancholia that had been my companion for years. "Chronic Work Identification Depression," a psychologist had called it and recommended prolonged therapy. But I have my own panaceas. I drink. I write gloomy poetry. And I listen to music.

All kinds of music – any kind of music, but most especially those long, slow Celtic airs, laden with sweet, sweet sorrow. I needed that. I craved it. Music was a drug for me. And just like a junkie craving the very stuff that will kill him, I couldn't live without it. Or without the way it reached down into the dark, mystical places in my soul. A part of me that only showed itself in somber, desperate and despairing moods.

It's those moods and the depressions that cost me every lover I've ever had, and most of my friends . . . and all of my ability to rest. The job was all I was now. The long hours, the variety, loving the adrenaline rush and yet hating the futility of it . . . all served to feed my dark habit – and music was richest food of all.

I thought of the dead boy and the dead woman . . . and they were just this week's toll. I didn't know how much longer I could go on with it – or how I could give it up. Sometimes, just casually, I wondered how long would it be until I went home one night after a shift, put on a CD of some Celtic music – melodious, evocative and sorrowful – and sat beside the window to look at the moon before I blew my brains out.

I was jolted out of my reverie when she left her table. The packed bodies seemed to move away from her graceful progress and there was none of the awkward jostling and shifting and involuntary rubbing of body parts so typical of a move in the café.

Then she was standing at my side, jacket slung over her shoulder. "Hello." Her voice was as musical as the strains of John's accordion. "May I join you?"

I cut my eyes over to her companions. "Your friend won't mind?"

She turned her head slightly and smiled. "Him? No, he won't mind. May I sit?" But she had already slid into the chair.

Up close, her body was not so much thin as willowy. Her hair seemed alive and electric – the ends of her hair seemed alive with light, shooting prism-like reflections off the glass beads and metallic ribbons woven into the small braids scattered throughout. It was impossible to determine the exact color of her eyes in the mix of neon and track lighting that barely cut through the smoky gloom of the café. But they were shining; I could see myself in their mirror-like surface. I didn't raise my hand but Dermot was there with a refill for me and a drink for her.

She told me her name, Neve McLear, and asked mine. "Connie O'Sheen," she repeated after me with a light laugh, then took my hand. There was both fire and ice in the sensation that shot up my body at her touch. She played sensuously with the ring that I always wore. To cover my confusion, I took another long swallow from my drink with my free hand. The sound of the accordion filled my head, my senses brimming. "The music makes you sad?" she asked.

"No." I shook my head. "Life makes me sad. The music just . . . puts a framework around it."

"Ah." She nodded. "But life is lovely . . . surely there's nothing to be sad about." She leaned toward me, fixing me as a dark reflection in her gaze. "I can show you there's nothing to be sad about."

I glanced over at her companions, but they seemed oblivious to us, laughing and drinking. The men were flirting with a few of the women waiting for the rest room. The women were focused on the musicians. I turned back to her, nodded once.

"Come on." Grabbing her leather jacket from the back of the chair, Neve swung her head toward her friends. She gave a slight gesture, and they all nodded at her. John was playing – a fixed expression on his face – and, with his accordion and the tin whistle leading the way, the rest of musicians sweated over a strange tune I never recalled hearing before. They didn't even note our exit. But Dermot did, giving us a momentary stare. Neve graced him with a brief nod and a cheery salute. "T'anks!" Dermot called as we left. "Be seein' yas!"

Outside, the night had turned cold and there was a breeze that swayed the branches of the stark and bare trees lining 238th Street. The full moon was starting to dip in the sky but was still brilliant as a silver mirror, hanging there. Rarely had I noticed how bright the moon could be in winter. I studied it for a moment, hesitant, uncertain of the next move. Neve seemed to be running the show. "Your place?" she asked.

Now, even though my emotional life was more than a bit of a mess, my apartment was always neat – compulsively so, I've been told. Going to my place was OK with me. Nodding, I gave her my address. She said she knew where it was and gestured to the last motorcycle in the row. It was bright silver, trimmed in black with sleek lines. Like her. My new friend swung her long, lithe legs over the saddle and gestured me to climb aboard.

"No helmets?" I queried.

"Live a little dangerously, *agrah*," Neve said, smiling.

"I'm a cop; I think that's generally dangerous enough." But I settled myself on the seat behind her and nervously circled my arms around her waist.

Neve turned the key and jumped on the starter. The motor purred into life and the cycle moved off from the sidewalk as smoothly as an ocean liner leaving the dock. She pushed into gear, and the force of the acceleration caused me to lean forward, clutching her, my face in her hair. The clean, fresh scent of her swept up through my nose and clouded my brain. She smelled of woods and apples.

The buildings and streets flew by us in a stream, like ribbons of shiny wet oil paint on canvas. It wasn't just the speed but the entire strange experience that was making my nerve endings dance. I rarely – no, make that *never* – was much of a one for "pick ups." And yet, here I was on the back of a motorcycle, with a woman I'd met only minutes before, racing toward my apartment. I barely felt the wind and cold, though I didn't have the protection of a leather jacket or boots. It was only a few moments before we pulled up in front of my building. She parked the bike and hit the kickstand.

I reached for my keys and suddenly Neve grabbed the front of my coat and pulled me close. In her boots, we were nearly eye-to-eye. "Don't be afraid," she murmured, "treasure of my heart. No harm shall befall thee . . ." I had just a moment to take note of her strange words when she kissed me. And her speech patterns went out of my head.

When we got to my apartment, things happened as you would pretty much expect. There was a lot of kissing and murmuring, pulling of clothing and fumbling with fingers and buttons. There was clumsiness and grace and laughter and caught breath. Now, I know that these kinds of experiences are always described with purple prose and romantic hyperbole. So I won't subject you to that. But I will just mention that her body was lovely: long and willowy, but properly rounded, her breasts like little perfect apples. In passing, I will say the color of her skin was like the moonlight: luminous, shimmering in my neat, orderly – and oh so spare – room. How her wild tangle of moon-pale hair enveloped me in a cloud of scent. And I will confess that I was swept away with an emotion that was stronger than lust, yet perhaps not quite love . . . an aching, a reaching – a *yearning* – that filled me more than the physical climax that swept over my entire body and left me near tears.

Afterwards, I lay beside her, the dark of my room relieved by the light from the moon and the street lamp outside, admiring her body and face. I couldn't stop stroking her and burying my face in her hair, inhaling her unique scent. I nuzzled the soft, tender spot behind her ear, pushing the little bell with my nose. She smiled and ran her fingers over my hair and face, kissing me, murmuring throaty endearments I couldn't make out but whose tone I wanted to hear over and over again.

Then she said, clearly enough to be heard, though her husky voice was low and soft, "Sleep a little while, and fear nothing..." And as if struck a blow from behind, I fell asleep all of a piece.

I slept, for once, without dreaming, and when I woke, the cold light of dawn was seeping through my window. Neve was standing over me, jacket in hand. "I must go."

I sat up. "Don't go! Come back to bed. Don't leave me..." Even to my own ears I sounded childish.

"I must, my treasure." She leaned over me and tousled my hair, then kissed me long and sensuously, her tongue flicking lightly at my lips. "But it will surely be that you'll see me again." She shrugged into her black leather jacket.

"When? How? Give me your number..." But she was already at the door.

"Soon..." And with a whispered sound of her bell, she was gone. I listened for the sound of a motorcycle from the street and could just barely discern it before crawling into bed and falling back to sleep.

<=>

The next week went by in the usual fashion. On my days off, I read and listened to music. Worked out at the gym. Wrote poetry. The only new activity was daydreaming about Neve. The rest of the time it was work, drink, sleep... and more work. I didn't go to any other cafés or bars, only to the Beal Bocht. But there was no sign of Neve.

Then, a few nights after Neve had gone, I saw the boy. (Well, more a young man, actually, but anyone under thirty was starting to look like a kid to me. When I think what a baby I was when I went on the job, I find it a miracle I'm still alive to this day.) He was sitting in the back corner of the Beal on poetry night.

Definitely one of Neve's crowd. I spotted him the moment I came in through the glass door, the cold and dank scooting in behind me. He was looking a bit ragged, but more than that, bewildered. Poetry night draws a good crowd, but the crowd it draws isn't usually made up of big drinkers, so Dermot had the time to pay a bit of mind to him. There was a sandwich and a drink sitting in front of him . . . but still, he was a study in wretchedness. I debated approaching him for the better part of an hour.

I had finally decided and stood to make my way over to him, drink in hand, when my name was called to read. His head came up sharply and he caught my eye, looking startled. Then a barely discernible smile lightened his face and he nodded, just slightly. The small silver sound of a bell drifted to my ear.

I took the mike and unfolded the piece of paper from my pocket, resting it on the music stand provided as a podium. I didn't need reading glasses yet, but a bit of distance helped.

Clearing my throat, I read:

> By the cold silver moon
> A treasure came;
> blown in on a warm wind
> That overlay the chill night.
> Delivered to me
> For that night's use.
> Laying her across my bed,
> I counted it out
> Finding more than I could hold.
>
> So, with a laugh she spilled
> Out of my hands;
> Running through the street
> To slip away in dawn light.
> Returned to sender

With my heart's mark.
Laying down across my bed,
I hoarded emptiness
Losing more than I could find.

Oh, treasure of my heart, should you return
You would find me full in my emptiness.
The moon-lit depression of my bed
Reflects the hollow bowl of my life.

(You don't have to tell me. I never said my poems were any good, just that they're as depressing as everyone else's.)

Anyhow, my work didn't exactly move the room to either applause or tears, and I stepped away to let the next fool get up and display their piece of soul to the world.

I went to sit with Neve's friend. He moved over on the bench, raised his glass to me. "*Slainté.*"

"*Slainté,*" I returned. We drank in companionable silence until our glasses were empty. "Connie O'Sheen." I held out my hand in introduction.

"Shoney." He grasped my hand with his – long and slender with a remarkably strong grip.

"Bit of a surprise to see you here. Is ... is Neve with you?"

His eyes clouded up, and he shook his head. The little bell rang, its tone dull. "I was having a bit of fun and didn't watch the time. I got separated from the group. I'll have to wait for them to come around."

Well, that aroused my curiosity. Call it a cop thing. I tried, er, *questioning* him. Where did he live? Was it far? Where was his bike? Maybe I could get him back ... But his answers were evasive and full of non sequiturs.

I was tired. I had an early shift the next day and had to get going. But somehow, I couldn't just leave him sitting there without knowing what he was going to do. "Have you got a place to stay? Where've you been sleeping for the last day or so?"

"Oh, I've been making out all right. Don't worry." But his smile had lost some of its cheer.

"Come on home with me." God knows what makes me say things sometimes. I surely don't.

His eyes brightened. "Are you certain?"

I wasn't. "Of course. You're more than welcome. You can sleep on the couch. So come on if you're coming, because I have to get some rest before work tomorrow."

While he was getting into his jacket, I went to pay Brenda for my beer and sandwich. Handing over a couple of bills, I said, "I'll get his too" with a gesture over my shoulder.

"*Arrah*, no." Brenda shook her head, all her little studs and earrings glittering. "His is all taken care of, Con, never fear. You gonna be lookin' after him for now?"

"Yeah." I shrugged. "For tonight at any rate."

Her head tilted a bit in his direction. Before I could say any more, she gave Shoney a little wink as he came up next to me. He smiled at her and made some sort of gesture or sign to her before he turned to me.

"My bike's outside. Do you mind riding pillion?"

"Uh, no." I couldn't understand how he could have his bike and still not be able to get home.

"Grand. Hop on then."

"Will you be able to hear me give directions?"

"Just shout and point. We'll manage."

And we did. He didn't drive at the same reckless rate of speed as Neve but still it took us only a few minutes to make it to my place.

He came up the stairs with me and once in my apartment looked around with great interest.

"Care for some tea?" I asked him, not because I wanted some so much as – tired as hell – I still wasn't ready to face the things that came with sleep just yet.

"Yeah . . . a cuppa'd be great." He held up a CD. "Mind?"

Shaking my head, I moved around in the kitchen, setting the kettle on the stove to boil. The music of Loreena

McKennitt filled my small apartment. *The Visit.* My favorite album of hers. And one guaranteed to feed my mood habit.

Shoney was leaning on the doorframe. "Can I give you a hand with anything?"

I handed him the sugar bowl and spoons, milk, and a box of cookies. When the kettle boiled, I rinsed out the pot, threw in the tea bags, and filled it up, bringing it out to the small table in the foyer.

The boy was leaning back in his chair, a dreamy look on his face. We didn't have much to say, but it wasn't uncomfortable, our quiet. We sipped our tea, ate our cookies, listened to the music and I started to unwind. I knew eventually I was going to have to go to sleep – or at least lie down. I had to be up by six and out by seven. And on the job by eight. And God, how I hated day shifts!

I pulled out linens from the trunk that doubled as a coffee table to make up a bed for Shoney on the couch. He watched me from his chair without a word. After I had cleaned up a bit, I dug out an old pair of sweat pants and a T-shirt and tossed them to him together with a towel. "The shower is yours, if you want it. I'll take mine in the morning."

"Ta." He made off for the bathroom. In the bedroom, I stripped down, got into my own over-large, stretched-out T-shirt and shorts, and got under the covers. I lay there, listening to the sound of the water running and wondered about Neve. Where was she? And then my thoughts wandered to Shoney. How had this boy gotten lost, and why wouldn't he tell me how to get him home? And why did I give a damn?

I heard the water turn off and a few moments later. The bathroom door opened. My door wasn't closed completely. I lay in the dark, too weary to think, but unable to get beyond the edges of sleep.

"Connie?" Shoney spoke from the living room couch.

"Uhm?"

"Not sleeping then, are you?"

"No . . . no, I can't quite sleep." After a long pause, I said, "Shoney, will Neve come back for you?"

"Oh, aye." He gave a long yawn, muting his voice. "No doubt of it. She and the rest. They'll be back."

"When?"

"In good time." There was a few minutes silence, then a light chuckle. "Don't worry, Connie; I think she'll come looking for you, I do."

I waited for more. From the living room there came soft shuffling sounds, and I thought Shoney was asleep. But a moment later, his shape appeared at my bedside.

"Connie . . ." His hand slid along my leg, shifting the covers. I grasped it.

"Ah, no, Shoney . . ."

"Not to fear. I'll just keep you company, so." I didn't fight him too hard. He moved the covers and cuddled up against me like an oversized cat. "Goodnight."

⇔

Another week went by. Shoney stayed. Sometimes he slept in my bed, sometimes on the couch. We watched old movies on cable, listened to my CD collection, drank – sometimes tea and sometimes beer – and waited. And there was no more discussion of how to get him home. There were lots of other discussions though.

For all that I couldn't elicit much information from him, Shoney was very curious about my life, though there wasn't much to tell. He could see how I lived, look at what books and music I had. And I was never one to talk about being on the job. At least not to "civilians." It was hard enough to talk about it with other cops.

Most cops I knew were good guys, who wanted to do – and did – their job the best they could before hurrying home to their wives, husbands, kids, and life. And there were those who used the job to get everything they could for themselves; used its position, its power and its authority to give some a kind of petty tyrant importance to their lives. And then there were those like me.

I can't exactly say the job was my life – after all, I had other interests. Poetry, music, drinking . . . old movies, new art. But somehow I derived my sense of self – my weight and impression in the world – from how I did my job. And how the job affected me.

As long as it depressed me, as long as I could feel despair and hopelessness and sorrow for the people I came in contact with, as long as I could feel anger and contempt for the lowlifes – and believe me, they *were* lowlifes – I knew I was alive.

Alive, but losing all the other bits of me. All the soft, disorganized, fuzzy parts. I was being pared down to my essential elements. Clean and pure and straight inside as a flame-forged, diamond-honed, unadorned steel blade.

Not a worldview one could share with a strange young man invited home. But maybe with someone I loved, someone who loved me. Neve . . . a hollow feeling around my heart.

Instead, I gave Shoney the funny stories. I told him about the amusing, harmless street characters: the flirtatious old people and those suspects who talked themselves out of arrests with bizarre tales. The pranks of kids, the eccentricities of higher ups, the practical jokes we cops played on each other and especially on the brass. These were the sops I gave his curiosity about me. The rest I kept to myself.

He asked me once about my ring – a large, dark reflective stone set into white gold, decorated with symbols of police life. It had belonged to my father and so I wore it for sentimental reasons. Or so I told Shoney. But there was far more to it than that.

I had adored my father, who was a cop before me. One of the good guys. He took a pride in the job and in serving the community that approached the religious. So I couldn't believe it when he and my mother had fits when I told them I was going to take the test for the department. "Connie, it's not the job it used to be," my father protested. "And in ten years' time, it will be even less so. It's not the place for you." My mother had wanted me to become a professor or a lawyer – other ways to serve the greater good. But from childhood nothing else had held the place in my imagination that being a police officer did. And when he retired and I went on the force, he gave the ring – a gift to him from the guys in his squad – to me. I put it on, vowing to live my life like he had. To serve, protect, and defend. And I had never taken it off since.

I finished another rotation of shifts. Eight-to-fours. Twelve-to-eights. Came home weary and depressed. Spent some afternoons, evenings, and days off sitting in the café. Shoney had taken to meeting me at the Beal after I finished work or a session at the gym. He never lacked for company and was rarely sitting on his own when I would arrive. Good-looking – in a dark, impish sort of way – Shoney was full of charm and his motorcycle was always good for a thrill for the college kids. But he rarely stayed away from my apartment for more than a day or night at a time. He always came back, crawling into my bed, even if only for an hour or two before I had to leave for work. As if to reassure himself that I was still there.

I was. Waiting. Just like him.

Chapter Two
<=>

Back on four-to-twelve.

Was it me, or were things just getting worse all the time? Domestic incidents seemed to be up. Street fights were so commonplace, we just cruised and found them. And Death? He was working overtime.

Just on shift, we got a call about a smell coming from an overrun pit of a vacant lot. Vacant doesn't mean empty, however. There was a small colony of squatters, making little suburbs out of their cardboard boxes and bits and pieces of whatever they could find to make shelters. Harmless for the most part. Old alchies and the mentally ill refuse of society. As long as they didn't make any trouble for the regular neighborhood residents, we let them be. Just like the old song.

But it wasn't the neighborhood people complaining. It was the squatters. Turned out the smell wasn't the usual unwashed bodies and old food and dog crap. It was coming from a small corner of the lot and a neatly rolled rug. Well, we knew what that meant . . . and so did most of the lot residents. They might have been crazy, but most of them were plenty smart. We didn't even open up the rug before we called it in to the station house.

There were two of them. One a girl about all of fifteen, I guessed. The other was an infant . . . maybe two or three days old. Identification wasn't a problem. Half the neighborhood knew who the girl was and had probably suspected what had happened to her for days.

We were directed to the apartment of the older sister, a small, worn-looking woman who might have been twenty-five but looked forty. Her already anxious face went bleak when she saw us at the door, and she took the news like a back slap to the face; her head jerked a little and her eyes closed. Didn't scream or cry, just slumped a bit against the door frame before she asked us in and told us what we needed to know. The story was an old one. Older man seduces and impregnates young girl. Girl gets demanding. Man kills girl and child.

It didn't take long to track him down. We picked up the boyfriend, Hildo, a small-time numbers runner with a snotty attitude and a record longer than Tremont Avenue. None too pleased at our interrupting his day, he didn't deny knowing the girl but was deeply indifferent to her fate. I suggested he accompany us to the station. He needed some firm persuading before he agreed, the result of which was I was called in to see the lieutenant for a very unpleasant interview of my own. Put on unpaid suspension for a week in addition to the other nonsense I'd have to put up with. No doubt Hildo's lawyer would be down to the precinct before I managed to change out of my uniform, and that scummy little creep would be back out on the street before I managed to get home. He'd be back in business, and I'd be sitting on my behind in my apartment, trying not to think about dead children and possible lawsuits.

It was barely 8:00 when I got home that night, totally beat in body and soul. I had been expecting Shoney to be out with one of his numerous admirers. Instead, he was waiting for me as I walked in, and his energy level was the exact opposite of mine. He was nearly bouncing off the walls.

"Hey! Connie, Connie," he called as he heard my key in the door. He embraced me enthusiastically, kissing both my cheeks, then once – just lightly – my mouth. His eyes seemed overly bright; he was clean, shaved, his hair carefully washed and shining. Both ears sported new earrings (maybe even a few more than when we'd met), and his bell was prominent. I eyed him, wondering if he had moved from drink to drugs.

"What's up with you?" I asked, when I could get a word in.

"Come on, come on. Get changed. We're going down to the café . . ."

I was dying for a drink – for many drinks – and for music, but An Beal Bocht didn't have music on Wednesdays. I was also stiff and tired. Hildo wasn't the only one who was roughed up in the struggle. I had planned on a hot bath with a tumbler of scotch and some really plaintive music on the CD player. "God, Shoney, I don't know . . . I'm beat. I don't think I even have enough energy to be depressed, never mind go out. "

Shoney was so charged up that I could hear faint little silver murmurings from his bell earring. "Come on, Con. It'll be worth your while . . . I promise."

I looked past him to my bed and my neat, tidy bedroom. Then back to him. His huge black eyes reflected my dull, washed-out face. I relented. "All right; just let me get showered and changed and I'll be with you."

"That's grand, Connie!" He followed me into the bathroom. Turning on the shower, I gently pushed him outside. He'd been getting a bit friskier lately – cuddling a lot closer when he came into my bed and other little things, as if sensing my growing loneliness. But he moved away amiably enough.

Showering, I looked out the bathroom window, open a bit to keep the steam down, and could just see the rising full moon. The sight of it brought a wave of longing over me and the first bit of a poem entered my head.

> The Moon took form
> and came upon me
> Calling to my sleeping joy.

Terrible, of course. I'd have to remember it for later.

Shoney continued chattering away while I dressed. He'd been working through my books at random and often talked about them with great enthusiasm. He seemed to have a particular weakness for mysteries and for historical epics. He took the mysteries very seriously, discussing their finer points at length. And he laughed hysterically at the histories, some of which were considered the finest of their genre. What he found so funny in them he could never really explain. "Ah . . . it's just the way of it, like," he'd guffaw when I pressed him. But the mysteries were "Great stuff!"

Even as we headed for the café on his newly washed motor-cycle, he kept up a line of talk.

I guess I had expected it to be a quiet night at the Beal – Wednesdays usually were – but it was lively enough. There was a pleasant CD of some recent Klezmer/Celtic fusion band playing not too loudly. Dermot was behind the counter washing pint glasses, and Brenda was busy with the food. The Poet and his contingent were all there; he even seemed to have taken on an apprentice of some kind. More than a few students. One of the girls buttonholed Shoney the moment he walked in the door, and one of the boys from the college came up to him, but after a warm greeting to each, he gently evaded their attentions.

Giving a high sign to Brenda, we steered toward a clear table. Dermot brought two of the usual, and I instructed him to keep them coming. After a sharp look at me, he just nodded. A few minutes later, he sent over a bowl of thin vegetable soup and a plate of sandwiches on brown bread. I hadn't realized I was so hungry until I started to eat, then I nearly wolfed them down.

I pushed the plate toward Shoney and he picked up a half sandwich, but his restlessness made his appetite nowhere near a match for mine. He got up and down frequently, talking to this one and that one, then back to the table again to sit.

"What's up with you?" I asked wearily after his fifth foray. "If you want to go off with one of these kids, don't mind me."

"*Arrah*, maybe later, maybe later . . ." He grinned. "Just feeling the juices. Feelin' the flow. Moonlight and magic, don't you think?"

I had no clue what he was on about, but his mention of moonlight reminded me of the first line of my poem. I rummaged around for a piece of paper and finally begged one off the Poet. He gave it to me and then, without being asked, he handed me a pen as well.

I was about six excruciating lines into it when John breezed in the door with his accordion and a young woman I'd seen around once or twice. She waved a vague greeting to the room and kept on moving.

John came over to me. "What's goin' on?" He greeted me as he straddled the chair Shoney had left vacant for the *n*th time.

We chatted a bit, watching the girl set up the music stands and check mics. I nudged John curiously. Wednesdays were not entertainment nights. It was usually a more contemplative sort of evening; the poets came to write, people to philosophize on life with their chums, creative people to hold little meetings.

"Oh, Caitlin there, she's got a bit of a set piece wants trying out. She has me working on it with her. She figures tonight's a good night because of the full moon. She likes working things out by the phases of the moon. New stuff on a new moon or a full moon. A bit mad, you know." He winked good-naturedly. "But mad with talent too. So we asked Dermot could we come up on a quiet night and try it on a bit, and you know him. A regular patron of the arts. He's always on for things like that. We'll have things going on in a minute or two." Standing up, he clasped hands with Shoney, who was on his latest visit to the chair. John moved off to help Caitlin with the set-up and Dermot brought me over my third drink.

After a few minutes, I really started to get involved in the poem again. I was getting down into the core of what the poem was trying to become. I wrote and crossed out and wrote again; the pen leaked a bit.

John started playing some gentle reels and Kerry slides. A few minutes later, the girl joined him. I hadn't made note of the instrument she'd carried in but now I saw it was a lap harp. She and John swung into a group of familiar tunes: "The Belfast Hornpipe," "The Black Silk Slip," "The Sweets of May," "The King Over the Water." The set was lively and up to John's usual standards of excellence. Then they paused, and the girl started to play a solo on her harp. It didn't sound like much at first. It started low, and I couldn't make out any theme to it, just a soft, almost out-of-reach tune. Gradually though, it became the sound of a low breeze, a light wind across a field, moving through flowers and corn. I'd never heard anything like it and neither had the others in the café. John's accordion came in, adding the sound of yellow flowers dancing, cornhusks rustling. The wind blew across a little river, tickled the sides of the hills.

It was wonderful and different. Wild and sweet. And yet . . . unfinished in some way. The wind became a breeze again, moved back into its source, and faded away. The harp dwindled to only a lingering vibration before the girl stilled the strings with both hands. All was quiet.

For a moment, the customers were as still as her hands. Then there was enthusiastic applause and cries of "Good on ya, Caitlin!" and even "Brava" from one of the college kids. Caitlin just bent her head for a moment, and John saluted the crowd before they took a break.

Dermot passed around the basket. "For the *myoo-zi-chuns!*" his lyrical Dublin phrase called around the room and the bills flew in. I took the first bill that came to my hand and tossed it in without a look.

Shoney had stayed glued to his seat the entire time the piece was playing, his long, nervous fingers holding my wrist. He released it now with a tap and stood up to look out the window. Everyone had gone back to the activities that had absorbed them before Caitlin's performance. John and Caitlin moved over to the front corner to confer with one of the other musicians I'd seen playing fiddle on *seisún* nights.

I felt an odd, tingling lift to my mood and had a moment of brief, interior silence before Brenda brought my next pint. The music had distracted me, and the poem had slowed me down. I looked down at the last line I'd written . . . and then looked up through the window.

They were there.

⟨⇒⟩

Motorcycles lined up. They jumped off and surrounded Shoney, exchanging hugs and kisses all around. He could hardly be seen for the tangle of leather-clad bodies embracing him. But I could see the cloud of moon-pale hair that meant Neve was there. That wretch Shoney hadn't even hinted this was the reason he'd insisted on coming to An Beal Bocht.

I was rooted to my spot, ink-stained fingers worrying the paper I'd been writing on. And through the window, Neve's eyes met mine over Shoney's shoulder.

The whole group came through the door of the café, bringing a scent of leather and spring into the smoky room. And then it was my turn to be surrounded and embraced. They were hugging me, clapping my shoulders, ruffling my hair, crying my name and Shoney's name, and murmuring words I didn't catch, but which conveyed far more emotion and gratitude than I thought giving the kid a place to sleep warranted. Soon enough, though, they all passed around me like water around a stone and, as they trickled away, left me facing only Neve.

I stood like the stone I was, just looking at her. She was lovelier than I dreamed or remembered. Delicate yet striking features, high cheekbones, the willowy body encased in black jeans, a red silk shirt, and a black leather jacket. The cloud of pale hair, festooned with its ribbons and beads of glass and stone. She slowly, deliberately, came and took my face between her hands. Her thin, strong fingers holding me still, Neve stared into my eyes until I could see my own face reflected back at me.

"Oh my heart's treasure," she murmured.

"Neve . . . I missed . . . I wanted to. . ." She stopped my stumbling words with her mouth. Not normally given to public displays of affection, I wouldn't have broken away from her for all the world.

When I could breathe again, we joined the rest of her crowd at their table in the corner already loaded with drinks and food. Neve sat on one side of me, her slender length pressed comfortably against my thighs, hips, and shoulders. Shoney sat on the other side, passing me drinks and nudging me with good humor. The sounds of bells and laughter filled the café, and John and Caitlin were coaxed to play another set. Neve's gang cheered them on and a few pulled out penny whistles and bones to join in, making a cheerful pick-up band.

I sat in their midst feeling something closer to contentment than I'd felt in years. I didn't even want to rush Neve back to my apartment. But I did wonder what I was going to do with Shoney when we did go, as I knew we would. I supposed he could go back to sleeping on the couch. At that point, he caught my eye and, giving a wink, reached into his pocket, took the spare set of keys, and tossed them to me. "Here you go, then! With my thanks." He grinned widely. "I won't be needing them again, for I'll be off with this mad crew this time for sure!"

Neve squeezed my hand, then whispered in my ear, "Let us go, my heart." And, with only the sketchiest of goodbyes, we left the rest of the group and took the motorcycle back to my apartment.

Things went even more passionately than our first time together. The intensity of it was such that I did weep afterward, cradled in Neve's arms, clinging to her as she murmured to me. I was terrified to fall asleep for fear she'd be gone again when I woke. But hard as I fought sleep, emotional, physical, and spiritual exhaustion overcame me and I went down into oblivion between one heartbeat and the next.

<=>

I woke into a cold, gray, drizzling daybreak, and beside me lay Neve. She was so still, quiet, and pale that she seemed something from my dreams of her. Then she cried out and thrashed like someone in the grip of a nightmare. I stretched out a hand to stroke her face and called her name. Inhaling sharply, she opened her eyes, looking fearful and confused before she focused on my face. After a moment, Neve smiled and stretched, lifting her arms high above her head. "Good morning, *mó stór*," she whispered, lowering her arms around my neck to pull me to her for a long, tender, and very real kiss.

"Are you all right, Neve?" I asked. "You seemed to be having a bad dream."

She was quiet for a moment, hugging me to her. "It's nothing for you to think on, my heart," she sighed, her eyes dark. "Not yet, as it is." Then she moved slightly and looked at me again. "Now, Connie, I must ask you something and you must answer."

"You can ask me anything, Neve."

"Be honest now, my treasure." With her fingers, she combed my hair from my eyes.

"I will, Neve." My heart beat slightly faster.

"Have you anything to eat in this flat of yours? For it's truly famished I am!"

I was blank for a moment until I caught her eye and saw the laughter there. I captured her hands in mine and when we had finished wrestling – and then finished loving again – we were both ravenously hungry.

We raided the refrigerator and gorged ourselves on orange juice and cream cheese and day-old bagels we toasted in the oven, cookies, and strong tea, and wine. We talked easily and laughed often, our conversations wide-ranging and heartfelt. We were never out of each other's reach for more than a few necessary moments and would immediately resume touching and kissing, as if for reassurance. In the late afternoon, we showered and I lent Neve one of my over-sized T-shirts for sitting around in. We cuddled up on the couch under a worn comforter while we watched *Casa-*

blanca on my DVD player because when I mentioned it as one of my favorite movies, Neve said she'd never seen it. She cried at the end, and I comforted her and we made love again. It rained all day and when night fell we ordered in, eating our food from the cartons.

Toward midnight, the rain cleared up and the wind blew hard, scudding the clouds across the silver face of the moon. Neve and I lay on my bed, limbs entwined, me playing with her hair, she twisting my ring, both of us illuminated by moonlight and temporarily sated with each other. Our breaths matched rhythms and I felt tears welling up in my eyes again. Neve stirred a bit, only to embrace me more tightly and rub her face near my ear as she whispered into it, "I have to thank you, my heart."

"Thank me?" I raised my head in surprise. "For what?"

"For looking after my brother."

Shoney was her brother? He had never once mentioned that. "It was no trouble," I assured Neve. "I enjoyed having him here." I was surprised to find it was true. I might even miss having the bugger around. "It was . . . good, you know, having someone to look after. Though he didn't need me much."

Neve hugged my neck and snuggled in closer. "It's a gift of greatness, is true hospitality. That which opens the door with no thought of reward."

I shrugged, embarrassed. A few moments later, Neve dropped off to sleep and, after watching her for a while, I rose from the bed, pulling on my jogging pants and a T-shirt. I rummaged around on the floor until I found my discarded jeans and the folded piece of paper I had put in my pocket before leaving the café. Sitting by the window, I smoothed the paper out and found a pen in the end table drawer. There was just enough moonlight to make it possible to read the poem I had started.

Thinking for only a few moments, I finished it all in a rush.

The Moon took form
and descended upon me
Calling to my sleeping joy

At her beckoning
I rose and cried
Embrace me with your grace

She became a glowing beam
and swallowed me
Until I became her inner dark

And from her womb
I was born anew
Thrust out into my own life

Covered with the skin of love
I made of my heart
an offering

She took it
kissed it
and returned it

You, my Moon
My lover
My mother

Have made me
Graced me
Released me

Whole and illuminated
I burst from within
my battered shell

Oh, let me surrender
to your pallid light
and become You.

I read it over one more time. Well, it was no *worse* than my usual efforts at any rate. Laying it down on the end table, I crawled back into bed beside Neve, wrapping myself around her fragrant warmth. My face buried in its favorite spot between her neck and shoulder, I fell into sleep.

<=>

I felt the empty space in the bed when I woke in the moments just before dawn, and knew that she was leaving. I turned over and saw her, dressed in her jeans and T-shirt, sitting cross-legged on the floor. She was reading my scribbled mess of a poem. Finishing it, she folded it up and put it in her pocket, then came back into the bed without a word. She took my face in her hands, in that way of hers that made me tremble, and stared into my eyes. Hers were so dark, I still could not determine their color, and my face – pale and stricken – was reflected in them. She pressed her face to my cheek, inhaling deeply.

"I shall hold you in my heart, my treasure, until I see you again. You are all-in-all to me. There is but a trial or two left. I swear that to you."

My heart sank and lifted at the same moment. I knew there was no holding her here. And I knew that she'd be back. How I would go on until then was up to me, I supposed.

<=>

I was summoned to the precinct for another interview with reference to the Hildo matter. This one involved the captain, the union guys, and Hildo's lawyer. There's no point in going into unpleasant details. Suffice it to say that the result of expressing my side of the story – and my opinion of Hildo, his lawyer, and my superior officers – was that I was further suspended for a month without pay and then would be off the streets to work a desk job for another sixty days.

I knew I'd been stupid even as the words left my mouth, knew what the result of my behavior would be. Suspension was getting off easy, and I knew that too. The only thing that saved me from harsher discipline was a string of commendations I'd somehow managed to acquire over the years. But it still seemed like Purgatory to me. I was a cop. Without that, I didn't know what the hell I was going to do with myself. Brood, I supposed. Think – and drink – way too much.

Spring was a long time coming; Easter was just around the corner but the weather was still cool and damp. I huddled into my jacket as I made my way to An Beal Bocht. The days had gone as slowly as I'd feared and I did, indeed, spend far too many hours in the café, just trying to kill time and fight loneliness. There's only so much gloomy poetry anyone can write, and the house was too quiet with Shoney gone and no sign of Neve showing up.

In an attempt to fight off the effects of spending so much time drinking and listening to music at the Beal, I'd upped my visits to the gym to three times a week, letting Cal beat the depression out of me in a good workout and taking the roughest massages the place had to offer. I tried to keep up my exercise routine at home, but instead I'd wind up drinking, watching old movies on television, or listening to some of my more melancholic music. I sometimes thought it was a good thing I'd handed in my service weapon when I was suspended and that I was not one of those cops who collected guns.

I tried to comfort myself that Neve would be back. That my suspension would end. That life – such as it was – would go on. Actually, that wasn't much of a comfort. What was I looking forward to? When the suspension ended and I was back on the streets again, the higher-ups would always be watching me. My every arrest would be questioned, every scuffle with a suspect would be examined under a microscope. Could I spend another fifteen years on the job with someone breathing down my neck all the time? It depended on how much I allowed the job to define my life.

As for Neve, what was my future there? An unknown quantity of time in which Neve would show up, then leave again? How often would she fill me up with something beyond description and then leave me to deflate like an old wineskin? As long as I let her, I realized without bitterness. After all, being filled up and then emptied was better than being empty all the time.

◄⇒►

It was a quiet night at the Beal. I looked around for Dermot, but he wasn't there. It was Brenda behind the counter, pulling pints, phone tucked between shoulder and ear, heavily involved in conversation and looking worried. She glanced over, caught my eye, and gestured for me to hold on for a moment longer, so I found myself a seat. Brenda pulled another pint, before hanging up the phone a few minutes later.

"Sorry, Connie," she said as she came over to the table with my drink. "A friend's in a bit of trouble and we were trying to figure something out."

I assured her waiting had been no problem and asked if there was anything I could do. Brenda shook her head, but promised to let me know. She went off to make me a sandwich.

On impulse before coming in, I had nipped into the little candy store next to the café and bought myself a notebook and a box of pens. Now, I opened it, stared at the white blank page, with its neat blue lines, and sighed. I fiddled with the ring on my finger as I tried to formulate some cohesive thoughts. I had no real plan for what I was going to write down; I just needed something to do. I had some kind of vague notion of getting a computer-literate friend to do a desktop publication of my poems as gifts for friends. Well, for Neve, really. But maybe I'd write some other things down as well.

A couple of hours passed pleasantly enough. Brenda came by with my next few drinks, not even pausing to talk a little. The place had filled up until it was busy but not crazed, and I noticed that Bronagh had come in as well to lend a hand with the serving. Things seemed normal enough, but even a suspended cop can't help being a cop, and after a while I couldn't help observing that Brenda seemed more and more distracted. Her eyes kept flicking to the doorway, and a few times she went out onto the sidewalk to peer up the block. Finally, on her next go-round past my table, I stopped her to ask what the problem was.

"My friend, Alvah; she should have been here ages ago. I'm a bit worried about her."

Turned out that Alvah had been the friend on the phone. And another of those old stories. Abusive boyfriend, planned escape – and now the girl was a no-show. Brenda wanted to go look for her at the boyfriend's apartment, not far from the Beal. Swallowing down the last of my drink, I closed my notebook and offered to go with her.

"Will ya, Connie? Sure, that'd be a great help!"

Bronagh was willing enough to stay and look after the café, so I grabbed my jacket and Brenda got hers, and we walked the few blocks to find her friend. I laid down the ground rules. We go over, find out what the friend wants to do, then take her out with us if she wants to go. Since I was on suspension, I had no official standing to arrest anyone. I was just there to lend moral support and a bit of backup in case things got ugly. Brenda nodded to everything I said.

The apartment was a couple of flights up in a fairly well kept building. Brenda knocked on a door that looked like all the others on the floor and called out to her friend. After a few moments, the door opened a bit, and Brenda spoke softly to the girl who was standing shadowed in the dark hallway of the apartment. I got a chill when I saw her.

One of Neve's tribe; no doubt about that. What was with these people? Why were they always getting lost? And why couldn't it be Neve who got left behind?

The boyfriend was out and Alvah let us in. She led us down the dim hallway to the living room. I don't know what I had expected, but the place was decent. Tidy, if not immaculate, and tolerably well-furnished. Nothing appeared broken or damaged. Until the girl turned to face us.

The dark purple bruise on her cheek was all the more startling because her skin was so fair. Red-headed fair to match the cascade of red curls. There were livid finger marks on her delicate chin, and she moved with the stiffness that spoke of battered ribs at the least.

She was a pretty little thing, with the wide cheekbones and huge dark eyes that characterized all of Neve's group. And she was tiny. Alvah barely came up to my collarbone, and she had a doll-like roundness to her limbs that added to her helpless appearance. I remembered her, because I'd had my suspicions that she wasn't old enough to drink, and when I'd mentioned it to Neve, she'd burst out laughing and assured me that the girl was "of more than sufficient years to be drinking herself silly, if she wished." The last time I'd seen Alvah, she'd been grinning and playing spoons with a keen enthusiasm at the café.

But she wasn't so lively now while we got the story from her. The girl had wanted to leave, had tried to, but the boyfriend had come in and heard her on the phone with Brenda. He'd hit her around until she was sick, then he took her motorcycle keys and left.

I felt a cold, hard fury starting in the pit of my stomach. What kind of animal could use brute force on a delicate little thing like this? But then again, I'd seen parents beat a child who couldn't yet crawl, never mind stand, and who certainly couldn't defend itself against someone ten times its size. I was amazed by my own capacity to still be shocked by human behavior.

Now all Alvah wanted to do was get her few things and go. She turned her big, dark eyes on me. Brenda was the one she had called, and Brenda was the one hugging her shoulders, but it was to me she looked as she said, "I need to be going from this place now." Her voice was trembling, but firmer than I'd thought it would be.

"Do you want to go to the police station and fill out a complaint against this guy?" I asked. "Do you need a doctor?"

Alvah shook her head. "I just want to be out of here. But I don't know where to go until I can join up with the others."

"On the next full moon, I suppose," I muttered wryly, and she nodded solemnly.

Brenda offered her place, but I knew she shared her apartment with three other people and what the girl needed now was peace and quiet and a place where the boyfriend might not think to look for her.

"She'll come home with me." It was a statement, not a question. There was something about Neve's friends that just made me blurt things out. "Where're your things?" She went into the bedroom to get them. It was just a small leather knapsack and her motorcycle jacket that looked as if it would weigh her down. But now that she'd made up her mind and had a place to go, she seemed to be moving a little better.

I was helping her into the jacket when I noticed the blood trail on her neck. I gently pushed back her hair and saw where the little silver bell had been ripped from her ear lobe. The *bastard*. Alvah's eyes filled with tears and, as with Neve and Shoney, I could see my face – angry and set – reflected in them. The cold hard fury in the pit of my stomach turned to fire. And the boyfriend picked that moment to come home.

⟨⇒⟩

He hung in the doorway for a moment, taking in the situation: the three of us, Alvah in her jacket and with her bag. Not a bad-looking guy. Hair a light sandy-brown, blue eyes and a spattering of freckles. He wasn't much taller than me, and was sturdily built with the kind of muscles that come from working construction or sheetrock crews.

"What the hell is going on here?" Narrowing his eyes, he frowned at me first. He wasn't very drunk, but he was at the wary and suspicious stage. His glance cut over to Alvah and Brenda, then back to me. Sizing us up, no doubt.

"Alvah's leaving now," I said. "We'll just take the keys to her motorcycle." I held out my hand.

"What if I don't give them to you? Maybe I don't want her to go." He was fairly calm and not directly menacing, but I noticed him shift his weight. I didn't move from the position I had assumed the moment he came in.

Alvah spoke up then. "You'd best let us by, Paul," she said quietly. "It's going I am, and you shouldn't try to stop me."

Paul's look skimmed between Alvah and me. He dismissed me because of my size, which was a mistake. But his bigger mistake was taking his eyes off me to glare at Alvah, because I took that moment to shift my weight as well, making it seem casual, as if my legs were tired from standing.

"Who's going to protect you?" Paul sneered in her face. "This lot?" He shrugged his shoulders, hunching down a bit. A forward momentum type. "You're not going anywhere unless I say so."

Alvah looked at him with an odd kind of pity in her eyes. "Ah, don't, Paul," she sighed. "Let it go, for your own sake."

As was typical with this type, a soft answer did not turn away wrath, but seemed to enrage him all the more. Paul made a lunge for Alvah and never expected what came next.

I had positioned myself in the narrow hallway, braced lightly against the wall. As he went forward, I brought my leg up with sharp force, my knee catching him directly in the solar plexus. He doubled over, and I brought my locked hands down between his shoulder blades. Stronger than I'd thought, he was barely down before he was struggling up, still reaching for Alvah. I shot my foot up under his chin and followed that with a straight-arm punch to the side of his thick head, my heavy ring scratching his temple.

I told Brenda and Alvah to move out. But as Alvah stepped by me, Paul reared up again and head-butted me, catching me painfully in the hip. Even off-balance as he was, it had enough force to knock me into the wall and he followed it up – still on his knees – with a wild but effective punch. I slid down, back to the wall, letting him think he had me and then got my knee under his chin and gave him a good, hard shove, then a kick to his rib cage.

Gasping, he rolled over on his stomach but didn't try to move in on me again. Instead, he grabbed Alvah's ankle and yanked her off her feet. She went down like a rag doll, bumping her head on the doorframe. Paul's back was to me and his legs were churning as he pushed himself up on her, punching her. She was struggling to get away. Brenda was bouncing around in the hallway, trying to do something, but she couldn't get in past Alvah, and there was no way for her to hit Paul without hitting the girl as well. The amazing thing was that there was no screaming or shouting from any of us.

I managed to get to my feet behind Paul, but I knew trying to lift him off Alvah would be useless. Down on the floor like that, a person taller and heavier than me was impossible to shift. So instead, as he drew back to hit Alvah in her most delicate spot, I overcame any lingering reluctance to actually do the guy damage and hauled off and kicked him straight between the legs.

Now, this doesn't always work. In a real rage, you wouldn't believe how much pain the human body can take. I've seen grown men get kicked hard in the testicles and still keep coming. The pain sets in later, of course. But there was no problem here. Because it had been cold the last few weeks, I was still wearing my heavy boots. I also got lucky in that his legs were wide enough apart as he fought to hold Alvah down that his balls made a good target. The kick hit home first time. It might have been even more effective if he hadn't been wearing jeans, but you can't have everything.

Paul screamed then. A high-pitched, sickening shriek. And he let Alvah go. Brenda immediately grabbed Alvah by the jacket and hauled her out into the building hallway past Paul, all curled up on the floor. Alvah straightened her jacket and then leaned over Paul.

This was a scary moment for me. I've seen women – some beaten so badly they had broken bones – still feel sorry for the guy who had smashed them around. I figured if Alvah was that type, I would just leave her here in disgust. But she just stared at Paul for a long moment, then said in a voice of ice, "I was almost sorry for you that you had to be the one for this. But it had to be someone and you'd had it coming for a bit, I believed. Now, I hope you're crippled in your manhood and that you never pass on a single bit of your vicious line, you miserable piece of *chach*!" And then she spat on him.

I reached down and searched his pockets, turning out everything looking for the keys to Alvah's motorcycle. They fell out, as did his pocketknife, a few dollars and coins, a rolled joint . . . and a little silver bell earring. This completely undid me. There was a white noise roaring in my head.

I took up Paul's pocketknife and then jerked his head back. Brenda made a strangled sound, but Alvah said nothing, the dark pools of her eyes reflecting the scene. As if from another place, I could see myself in them: on my knees, straddling Paul's shoulders, my face a mask of white.

"You bastard," I hissed in his ear. "I could cut your throat for you . . ."

"For God's sake," he managed to croak out, "For God's sake . . ."

He kept his knife sharp, I'll say that for him. Before I could lose my nerve, or he could move, I pulled out his ear lobe and sliced a bit of it off, taking his own little stud earring with it. I don't think he realized what had happened at first, until I threw the knife and his piece of ear down in front of him.

"There: that's something for the ladies to ask about."

Alvah and Brenda were staring at me, and I pushed them toward the staircase. We had been remarkably lucky in that no neighbors were sticking their heads out to see what was happening. Slamming the apartment door behind me, I gestured for Alvah and Brenda to run down the stairs. I didn't think Paul would get up and follow us, but I wanted as much of a head start as possible.

<=>

Out on the street, I had to figure out how to get Alvah back to my place and her bike away from here. It turned out (I wasn't surprised) that Brenda could ride a bike and had a place to keep it stored out of sight for a few days. And – another bit of luck – I had no sooner handed her the keys when a cab pulled up at the corner to let someone out. I thrust Alvah into the back seat and jumped in after her, telling the driver to go. I made sure we were more than halfway down the next block before I gave him my address.

I had a moment then to take a good look at Alvah. She was sitting very still, staring at me. Shell-shocked, I thought, and I didn't blame her. I had never been in such a vicious fight, or done such a bloody deed in all my life. Even my scuffles on the force, such as the one with Hildo, had never descended to what would have to be called the personal. I was feeling sick and sweaty by the time the driver pulled up in front of my building. I paid him – more than I should have – and led Alvah upstairs.

The first thing I did was pour us both a drink. Alvah downed my best scotch like it was water and then held out her glass for more. I poured us both another few fingers' worth, and we sipped it in a more controlled fashion.

When my shakes had finally subsided a bit, I had a minute to think of what to do for Alvah. Something comforting. So, I went in and ran her a bath. I made it as nice as I could for her. Her body had started to stiffen, making it difficult for her to undress, so I gave her a hand. Besides, I wanted to see if her bruises and injuries warranted a doctor's attention or if I really should call the cops. She was far more shy of my seeing what Paul had done to her than of my looking at her body. The marks seemed to be more surface and painful, than deep or serious, except for the lacerated earlobe. My best guess was that she'd heal up in a couple of days. At least, physically she would. How she'd be emotionally... well, that I couldn't say. The thing that was hardest was washing her hair, because her sore ribs made keeping her arms up painful. So I washed it for her. I was clumsy at it, because I had never had long hair, not even in my college days, and Alvah had a lot of it. We managed, though, and I even combed it out and braided it, so it wouldn't tangle when she slept.

I had some painkillers and muscle relaxers left over from an injury I'd had a few months ago. Alvah was so small I cut them both in half before giving them to her to take (with lots of water this time) and tucked her into my bed like a child. Then I went to take a long, hot shower.

I took the other half of both pills and made myself a bed on the couch, thinking I'd pass out from sheer exhaustion. But, no. My mind was keeping me awake.

One of the things worrying me was what Paul would do when he could finally pick himself up off the floor and stop his ear from bleeding. If he decided to swear out a complaint against me, my career – such as it was – would be over. I wouldn't be a cop anymore. And if I wasn't a cop, what the hell would I be? My wings had already been clipped by the suspension. And if I was being strictly honest with myself, it might have been the right thing.

I thought about my father. I studied his ring – symbol of his life's work – and felt no regrets at all for knocking Hildo around, or for beating the living daylights out of old Paul there. But I couldn't bear the thought that the rules and regulations were in their favor. Never mind that Hildo had probably (*probably*, hell – he *had*) killed two children. Or that Paul thought it was his right to beat a girl less than half his size and weight for whatever twisted reason he came up with (not to mention that he would have liked to do a number on me and Brenda, too). In spite of all that, I'd be legally – and to some extent, I admit, morally – in the wrong. If a person with authority – say, a gun and a badge – used it to execute their own code of law enforcement . . . Well, civilization wouldn't last very long, would it?

Lying alone on my couch in the dark, cold night, I broke out in a nauseous sweat as a realization hit me. I just might not be able to go back to the job. And what earthly use would I serve if I wasn't a cop?

This circular thinking was too much for me. I got up to get myself another drink. And that, mixed with the medication, finally knocked me into sleep.

<=>

The next day passed in a kind of depressed blur. I examined and reexamined my conscience a thousand times to see if I could regret what I'd done over the past few weeks, but I couldn't.

On the second day, I hauled myself up off the couch and went to clean up and face the world. I made a good job of it and, somewhere around the third washing of my hair, I resolved to just let whatever was going to happen happen. Lying around wouldn't change it.

I was starving by the time I finished dressing, and I realized I hadn't had a decent meal since that night at the Beal. Guilt assaulted me now. I had neglected poor Alvah. Hadn't even seen whether she needed so much as an aspirin. God knew what the poor thing had been eating.

But when I looked in the bedroom, she wasn't there. I found her in the kitchen, making a pot of tea, dressed in one of my old shirts. She seemed better, not moving as stiffly. She apologized for just helping herself around the house, but she hadn't wanted to disturb me. To my concerns about her eating, she smiled and said she'd made out; she didn't eat all that much and there was more than enough for her. Gesturing to her odd attire, she explained that she'd tried washing her clothes in the sink, but some of the bloodstains didn't come out, and the jeans still weren't dry.

I needed to go to the store for some supplies. I took her jeans with me and tossed them in a dryer at the corner laundry before going into the supermarket. I picked them up on on the way home. When I got home and we had eaten a more substantial meal than either of us had managed in the last twenty-four hours, I suggested going out, but she shook her head.

Alvah was a lot quieter than Shoney. Her presence in the house was soft and gentle. Like him, though, she spent a lot of time examining my books and movies, my CD collection. She didn't fixate on one type of thing, but liked to pick them up at random, try them out for a little while, then put them up again, sometimes not even bothering to finish a movie or book, or listen to a CD all the way through. Once I caught her laughing when she found some book on Celtic mythology I'd long forgotten I owned, and she'd been perfectly disgusted with my DVD edition of *Excalibur*.

Over the next days, the bruises on her face faded, and soon I noticed that her movements – again, unlike Shoney, who had been quick and restless – were graceful and fluid. But she was still very quiet and subdued. I found an old silver chain in the drawer where I kept the little bits of jewelry I still had – things that were gifts from my parents, mostly – and fixed up her little silver bell earring on it to hang around her neck. This brought real brightness to her face. She clapped her hands and exclaimed, "*Arrah*, Connie, you're a wonder!" as I slipped the chain over her head. She stood up on her tip-toes to put her arms around my neck. I hugged her gingerly and she kissed me lightly. Then again a little more pressingly.

I gently disentangled her and convinced her to go out. I'd been out to the gym for a workout and massage, but it had been four days and Alvah still had not left the apartment. She was living in my old shirts but none of my other clothes would fit her, so I finally talked her into a shopping expedition. It was already late in the afternoon, and in any event my residential area didn't have a line of clothing stores that would suit a pretty redhead who rode a motorcycle. So I decided on really making a trip and heading down to the East Village.

Alvah loved the subway ride and she really perked when we got off at Sheridan Square and walked to the East Village, looking around at the passing crowd. Not chatty, like Shoney, but very pleased and animated now, she pointed out things that caught her interest: an incense vendor, the fruits-and-vegetables array at a corner Korean grocery store. She stopped to examine some T-shirts displayed in a window with things on them that made me blush. One couple on St. Marks' Place – all spiked hair, tattered jeans, and studs with multiple earrings – made her laugh. "Sure they'd fit right in at home," she declared.

I offered to buy her clothes, but she seemed to have plenty of her own money on her and very definite ideas about what she wanted. One store we stopped in catered to a more Gothic crowd, and some of the clothes were very dramatic, even a little overpowering for Alvah, but she enjoyed looking. I was glancing around, just waiting for her, when I spotted a beautiful shirt. A soft, very pale champagne color – almost the exact shade of Neve's hair. The material was a lustrous raw silk with a row of tiny buttons and just a bit of lace at the collar and cuffs. The price tag made me blink, but only for a second. Then I bought it. After that, I went a little crazy and bought jewelry and scarves and hair clips and a brocade vest that I knew would look wonderful on Neve. In another store I got a distressed copper necklace with little flicks of amber stones and amber earrings.

Afterward, both of us loaded down with bags and boxes, Alvah and I had dinner at the Afghani restaurant, sitting at the outside tables in spite of the chill, just to watch the passing scene. Alvah seemed refreshed and more relaxed as the evening wore on, and I took her for an egg cream at the candy store on the corner of Second Avenue and St. Marks Place. I splurged on a cab ride home, flashing my badge when the cab driver whined about going all the way to the Bronx. Alvah dozed off during the trip, leaning against my shoulder, her thick red curls brushing fragrantly against my nose.

Home at last, Alvah went off for a bath while I made tea. Then, as an afterthought, I poured us both a couple of drinks. None of Neve's crowd was shy about their liking for alcohol, and that included Alvah. Fresh from her bath, she smelled of honeysuckle and was wearing something soft, loose, and flowing that she had bought that afternoon. We had a quiet, companionable evening, alternately sipping tea and whiskey, eating the little cakes I'd bought at the Ukranian bakery on Second Avenue and idly listening to my latest CD acquisition. Finally, I rose to take my shower, while she cleared away the tea things.

The room was dim when I came out of the bathroom in a T-shirt and shorts, toweling my hair dry. I was ready to collapse onto the sofa, but Alvah was still there. She was sitting on one end, sipping another whiskey. "Sure, Con," she said, her voice soft and rather hoarse, "you should take your own bed back. You're too long for this thing, entirely."

I poured myself another drink. Sitting down beside her, I could see she was crying. Just little silent tears flowing down her pretty face. I was trying to figure out what was wrong and what to say when she threw her arms around me. "Oh, Connie, I'm terrible afraid, so I am."

"Of what?" I patted her gently, rubbing her shoulder blades. "Of Paul? You don't have to be . . ."

"No! Well, not really; not anymore. Oh, Con, it was awful. Much worse than I thought it'd be when I first went in . . ."

I couldn't figure out what she was talking about, but she went on in a sort of breathless rush. "No, it's not Paul , it's . . . it's the fear that I'll never enjoy the touching again. The lovemaking will always be shadowed by . . ." She clung to me tighter and put her lips to my ear. "Oh, Connie, Connie, love me. That would heal all. Love me, *agrah*, just for tonight, do . . ."

I had become very aware of her in my arms. Of the feel of her soft little body and the fragrance of her hair. Of her lips on my face. I held her tightly for a moment, then put her aside a little, still hugging her shoulders. "That may not be such a good idea, Alvah. Not with me at any rate. You don't really want me."

"Why not? Why not?" Her huge reflective eyes were shining with tears. "You're so kind and so strong." I shook my head, but she just kept on. "Is it angry with me you are? For what you had to do to Paul? Ah, Con, that was a great thing! That was justice!"

I shushed her. No, no, I assured her, how could I be angry with her for that? No, Paul got what was coming to him, and not just for her, but for every woman he'd beaten before and to come.

"Is it, then, you don't find me desirable?"

"No! God, no, Alvah. You're a delicious little armful. Anyone would want you . . . It's just that I . . ."

"Just?" she prompted, studying my face.

"It's just . . . Neve . . ."

"Ah." Alvah turned away.

I stumbled on, "I think I'm . . . I don't know if I . . . I'm in love with her, I guess."

"I see. So that means there's no comfort or love in you for others?" Her voice sounded angry. "Where I come from such a love would mean nothing much. It's selfish. Do you think you'll have nothing left for Neve if you give some to me, who needs it?"

"No!" I was hot with embarrassment and awkwardness. "No . . . it's more like . . . Neve might think me faithless, or untrustworthy or something."

"You know nothing about Neve MacLear, then. Or about any of us."

She was right about that, I thought, as I got to my feet to get myself a drink and restart the CD of the moment. I looked out my window to the street, up over the rooftops to the cloudy sky. Twisting my ring over and over, as I asked the question over and over. *What did I know about any of them?* I knew only that I was drawn to Neve in a way I'd never felt with anyone else. In a way that frightened me, I wanted it so much. She made me feel – really feel things – in ways I had been losing for years. As if, burned down as I might be, Neve found it enough. And more than enough. And yet, Neve disappeared for a month at a time, and all I had to remember her by was someone left behind.

There was another puzzle to me. *Why* did they get left behind? They had transportation, they had money, they had social skills better than mine. Yet, each time, I was the one who found them and cared for them.

And what did Alvah mean that things with Paul were worse than she'd thought they would be? How could she have expected what Paul would inflict on her, unless she knew him from before? And knew what he was capable of? Yet, she displayed none of the classic behavior of a battered woman. She seemed perfectly convinced that a night of friendly lovemaking would bring the healing to a close. I wanted her to feel better. I felt responsible for her, now that it was me that "rescued" her and looked after her. And . . . Well, God knows I'm only human – to turn down a lovely offer like Alvah's was not easy.

Ah, but . . . Neve. She had left me last, promising to return . . . What did she do the rest of the month? Did she lie down with others and feel the same joy? Possibly. And yet . . . And yet, she had said I was "all-in-all" to her. And that there were just a few more "trials" to come. I poured just another light splash of the whiskey. What kinds of trials? Trials for what? It had been more than two weeks from Neve's departure to my rescue of Alvah. Had beating Paul been another test? Did I do too much or too little?

Shoney had also had made known his interest in sharing my bed in more ways than one. But charming as he was, I had put him off and he took it with good humor. And now here was Alvah, begging for touch, for comfort. The past few months had brought more interest in me sexually than in most of the past seven years put together. But which was the right way to answer?

Such a love wouldn't count for much where she'd come from, Alvah had said. Where *did* she come from? Where did any of them come from that they were so different, and where did they go? Besides to my apartment, that was.

I wanted to ask Alvah if her request had been a test, but that seemed an insult to add to her other injuries.

"I think it's time for bed," I said quietly, coming back to the couch.

"Ah, well, I'll sleep here." She shrugged and started to move away.

I caught her gently and pulled her into my lap. "There's no need for that," I kissed her. "There's plenty of room in my bed for both of us."

And there was.

⋖⇒⋗

I went back to my routine of going to the Beal after that. Now that I was aware of Neve's schedule, I kept an eye on the waxing moon. Alvah took to going with me to the café, but there was no one could have mistaken us for a couple. After that first, comforting night, there was no real flame of passion between us, and we were more like affectionate cousins than lovers. Now she was flitting around like Shoney had, flirting with this one and that one. I was glad for her and relieved for myself, though I had residual worries about how I would face Neve when she came again.

Poetry night rolled around and I read a selection of my poems, including the one that Neve had taken with her. Alvah was there, sitting with her new friends, cheering me on. She seemed quite taken with the Poet's apprentice – a soft, dark haired, dark-eyed boy of mixed racial heritage, who was pretty much besotted with Alvah in a frightened, respectful sort of way. My last selection was one I had been fighting with for a few days.

> Those deeds I've done, I've done by right
> Of will and fear of lonely, dark sorrow;
> Those dreams I've dreamed on cold dark nights
> Have lingered in the short bright morrow.
> My childhood tunes and happy careless songs
> Have given way to melodies of pain;
> And all the choruses sung long,
> Have emptied out and back again.
> I need my life to be full in measure

To know that deeds I've done in my days
Are not pointless emptying of treasure
But set paving stones for lost pilgrim ways.

Oh make my Fate neither Heaven nor Hell –
But to ring to the call of Justice's Bell.

(A *sonnet*, no less. What the hell could I have been think-ing? Some people make fools of themselves – some make *big* fools of themselves!)

When I finished, there was applause from all the other depressing poets, and I stepped down. Brenda and Dermot were both working that night, and when I sat at a corner table, Dermot brought me over my drink. "Jayz, Connie, a regular poet lawr-ee-ott, you're getting to be!" He set the pint down and clapped me on the shoulder. "That's on the house. Brenda told me what yas got up ta there earlier. Wish I'd been there – he wouldn't've got off so light, I can tell ya! Great stuff! T'anks for lookin' after the little one there." He gave me a wink. "I'm sayin' nuthin' mind you . . . but I t'ink you'll find that crew pretty grateful." With another slap to my shoulder, he moved away, leaving me more confused than ever.

⟺

The night of the next full moon rolled around and the weather had finally caught up to the season. The trees out-side the café were in full bloom, their little white flowers blowing everywhere. Instead of making me feel better, the burst of life just served to depress me further. There were several days to run on my suspension before I had to report to my desk job, and I still wasn't sure what I was going to do. Even though I hated the lowlifes and the sheer brutality of what I saw day after day, even though I felt strangled and suffocated by the rules and regulations, by the constant second-guessing, I needed to feel I was doing *something* – something worthwhile for the good people of this world. And if not as a cop, then where would I find meaningful work? Work I was suited for?

A private investigation agency? No. I couldn't see that for myself – prying into other people's dirty little secrets. Provide personal security for some fat cat? Some guy who got his money off the people I saw struggling every day working at minimum wage so his stock options would be secure? Forget that. Also forget about selling insurance or some other desk job. All my years on the job had burnt me down to one pure essential element: I needed to be of service. I needed to serve something or someone. To serve and protect. My life mission. My world statement.

Expecting – hoping – that this was the night I would see Neve again, I prepared carefully. Bought my first new clothes in ages – including new underwear – got a haircut. Alvah smiled when she saw me all ready to go to the Beal and gave me a friendly hug. She was starting to get wound up, too, happy to be seeing her crowd again.

And I had it in my mind that I wasn't going to be taking care of someone left behind this time. This time, I wanted *Neve* to stay. I wanted life to make some sense. And being with Neve made sense to me. If she could forgive me for "comforting" Alvah. I couldn't really say I was sorry – it really did seem to make Alvah feel cleansed and whole again. But, I also couldn't bear the thought that an act of true friendship (and, yes, a kind of love different from the love I had for Neve) would put a barrier between me and the woman I was thinking about loving for the rest of my life.

We arrived at the café and saw Alvah's motorcycle – washed and shiny – sitting outside. It was smallest machine I'd ever seen that could still be called a motorcycle, almost all red with black trim. Alvah ran her hand over it with a happy and proprietary air. Dermot and Brenda were inside, setting up before it got too busy. When Brenda saw us, she gave a high sign and tossed the keys over. I caught them and handed them to Alvah, who gave me another kiss and hug and wandered off to attach herself to the Poet's apprentice.

I got a table, hooking two chairs with my feet, where I could see the door and watch the musicians wandering around talking to this one and that one and organizing themselves in a way known only to them. It looked like the full contingent was there. A banjo player and fiddler who were regulars were already fixing microphones to stands, and a singer – whom I'd mentally dubbed "the Thrush" for his warbling, old-fashioned style – was discussing the finer points of some tune with a bodhran player I hadn't seen in months. John was there, of course. And Caitlin. I hadn't heard the talented harpist since her haunting performance the night of the last full moon. I wondered if her piece was finished yet.

Finally, they were done with setup and had settled down to play. Brenda, with a knowing laugh, ruffled my hair and delivered my drink and a sandwich. John, together with the fiddler and bodhran player, launched into a lively set of tunes: reels chasing each other 'round about and then melding into hornpipes, eventually slowing down to waltzes (I always liked the way John played them on his button box). Then the Thrush sang an old-fashioned song I hadn't heard since I was a kid: "The Rose of Tralee." The one that starts off, "The pale moon was rising . . .." I involuntarily glanced out the window. The moon was, indeed, rising. But there was no sign of Neve, or the others.

Then Caitlin started on her set piece. It had definitely matured in the past month. As before, it started soft and low, and I could see the beauty of the land as the wind moved across, feel the wildness of the sea – could hear the wind roar as it drove across ancient stones. When John came in with his accordion, flowers danced on breezes, heads nodding, little silver sounds coming from them. Then the fiddler joined in and rains came, sweeping down from the mountains, melding into the brooks that became streams that became rivers that rushed to embrace the sea. When the bodhran vibrated, I could see the mountains rising from the oceans caressed and buffeted by the wind to become boulders to become rocks to become pebbles to become sand to join once again to the sea.

The harp played on and on. Now the sun beat down and opened everything, and people rode in from the sea, migrating across the land and mountains, becoming a part of the trees and the rocks. Their lives rolled by, and they lived a lifetime and then two, then a hundred, then a thousand, with the sun moving on and making way for the sunset to spread a mantle of color across fields and mountains, only to dissolve into the blanket of blue night and silver moon reflecting on water, mountains, rocks, sea.

How could one express what you felt hearing music like that? I knew that to live in that place – to live with the *people* who lived in that place – that would be worth a life of service. That place would be worthy of devotion.

When Caitlin finished, there was a stunned silence for a long time. It had seemed as if the music would go on to the end of the world. Finally, Caitlin bent her head and raised her hands from the harp. The room erupted into applause and shouts. I could see Alvah weeping, and my own eyes were damp. The musicians had that exhausted, elated look of mystics after a vision. Caitlin still seemed to be vibrating slightly, like the strings of her harp. It is no wonder that genius seems to some to be a form of enchantment.

Alvah had made her way across the room to throw her arms around me in an emotional hug. She whispered in my ear, "They're coming, so." She must have felt the *zing* that hissed along my nerve endings, for she laughed and, putting her hands on my shoulders, turned me around.

And there was Neve, shining like the moon, surrounded by her "troops," as I'd come to think of them. My eyes met hers, reflecting back my image to me. I opened my hands, but otherwise didn't move.

Behind Neve, I heard the cries of happiness to see Alvah, and one of the bigger fellows swept her up into his arms. Alvah was passed from person to person with hugs and kisses. I saw Shoney lift her high and then toss her to the next person, all of them laughing and exclaiming over her. The last person to embrace her was Neve, who enfolded Alvah tightly and kissed her cheeks. I could see they were both crying as Neve held Alvah's face with her thin fingers and looked deeply into her eyes. "Is all well with you, *alanna?*" One of Neve's fingers must have brushed Alvah's ear, for she tilted the girl's head a bit and saw the tear in her ear, still red and livid against the white skin. Neve blanched. "Oh, my sister," she breathed. "What have we done to you?" The others gathered around to look, and a very angry sound went up from all of them.

"It was nothing, *a chara*, for me," Alvah assured them. She pulled Neve's head down and whispered to her. Neve's eyes came up to meet mine. "Indeed? With the pig's own knife?" She kissed Alvah's cheek again. "You're a brave one, and we're all proud of you. You've done well by us, and for your pain, we're sorry."

Alvah said. "It was nothing. It's done now." She reached over and took my hand. "Connie O'Sheen has avenged me! There was justice in the act and warning for the future! Connie." She turned back to me. "Please accept my thanks." And then – in the single most embarrassing moment of my life – Alvah kissed my father's ring and so did all the others. Each and every one – male, female, large, small – lifted my hand and kissed it. I begged them to stop and tried to pull away, but no one paid a bit of attention to my protests. I uncomfortably looked over at the rest of the café, still filled with people, but – except for Dermot, Brenda, John, and Caitlin – no one seemed to notice what was going on at all. It was almost as if we couldn't be seen or heard.

Last came Neve, who reached for my hand. I pulled it away and took her by the shoulders. "Don't . . ." I started to say, but she flung herself upon me and kissed me until I thought I'd faint. By the time we broke apart, the mood, spell, whatever, had broken and the Beal was its usual humming self. Dermot was passing around the collection basket, and money for the musicians was flying into it like green leaves in a breeze. Brenda was now busy over at the corner table with Neve's crew, taking drink and food orders. John was chatting with one of the girls, and Alvah had pulled in the Poet's apprentice to sit with her.

⟨⇒⟩

Later, after much drinking and singing and merriment, I rode back to my apartment on Neve's motorcycle, arms around her waist, face pressed to her shoulders. I could feel the wind whipping away the pain and loneliness of past weeks. I wanted nothing more – for that moment – than to stay this way, inhaling the moonlight scent of her.

When we got back to my apartment, Neve embraced me passionately. "Again, I must thank you for looking after one of my own." She kissed me over and over. "Alvah is precious to all of us."

And then I thought of Alvah and that one night. I thought of all the bags and boxes full of gifts I had so happily bought for Neve. I thought of how Neve looked lying in my bed, sitting at my table, laughing and singing at the café. Of how she would take my face between her hands and envelop me with her dark, bottomless eyes until I could see my soul reflected back from them.

Neve picked up on my mood. "What is it, my treasure?" she asked when her kisses brought only half-hearted responses from me.

I figured it was better to bite the bullet and get it done and over with, so I sat her down on the sofa then and told her all about what happened with Hildo and how I'd been suspended. About my emptiness without the work I'd done to blunt the sword inside me. Of how I'd thrown myself into going to rescue Alvah from Paul and how I'd felt about what he'd done and what I'd done to him. How all that came around again to the fears and doubts of going back to the job . . . about how I couldn't imagine who, or what, I was without some greater good to serve. And about Alvah.

I tried to find something that would explain how rescuing Alvah had given me feelings towards her that were protective – caring, yes – as if I were responsible for making her well. But how it was nothing like what I felt for Neve. I could feel all my doubts returning. Could she understand and forgive me? Could she accept what I was at the hard, unadorned, center of my soul?

Neve listened to me pour out everything without interrupting. When I finally wound down, she took my hand and said, "But, my heart, what else could you have done? You could have taken no other way and still be you."

"Oh, Neve . . . I'm so afraid I've failed you."

"Treasure of my heart," Neve pulled me close to her, "there has been nothing you've done that has failed me. You've done everything I've hoped for – and more. Far more." She stopped any questions or further protests from me. We made love with a depth of feeling that nearly blasted me with its strength and made Neve a part of me for always.

Later, when we got up for something to eat, I brought out the packages I'd been saving for her. Sitting cross-legged on the bed, sipping wine and eating cheese and crackers, I watched while Neve exclaimed over each item and praised its color and texture. She loved the jewelry, immediately putting on the necklace and earrings. She looked exquisite clad only in copper and amber as she flung herself back on the bed with me and covered me in kisses.

Propping herself up on her elbows, Neve ran her hand through my hair. "I like your hair like this," she said, smling.

"So straight and clean – like you." Her fingers traveled down to trace my brow and cheekbones, then across my chin and lips, then down my throat to caress my collarbones, until she nearly hypnotized me.

"Connie . . ."

"Uhmm?"

"Have you ever wondered where I come from and where I go?"

"I have. Of course I have."

"And do you remember when I told you there were just a few more trials to go through?" I nodded. "Well, my heart's center, you have passed your trials. Oh, Con, beyond anything we could have dreamt of. And I am so proud of you . . . to have chosen you."

I thought I must be asleep, I was so confused, still fighting with my own regrets and doubts. "What trials, Neve? When did I get tested and for what?"

"The trials for a champion are these: hospitality, courage, justice, and compassion. And you've shown all those traits in full measure. The first, hospitality, was when you took Shoney in, with no thought of return or reward, and looked after him with care." She held up a hand to keep me from interrupting. "The second, courage, came when you went to help Alvah – someone you didn't know – on only the word of a friend. The third, justice, was when you did *not* cut Paul's throat, but served him only what he deserved. The last, compassion, came on the night you comforted Alvah when she needed you."

"Oh, Neve, I was so afraid you'd think me . . . unfaithful."

"How unfaithful? Am I not your heart of hearts – as you are mine?"

Pulling the sheet around her, she rose from the bed like a column of light. Her hair stood out around her, the light from the window catching the ends and making them glow, the beads and ribbons twined through it like little lanterns.

"And now, I ask you, Connie O'Sheen – having passed the trials – are you willing to help my people in their time of need?" I sat up a bit to look at her in surprise. "Oh, Con . . . we're in terrible trouble. There's a darkness coming on us and we need help. So, at the favorable times we go out into the world – your world – in groups to look for you and others like you. Heroes. Defenders. Champions. We look for those who are discontented with their lot in life. Who yearn to serve something bigger. And I knew – the moment I saw you – you were a burning flame for service!"

I shrugged, embarrassed. "It's you I burn for, Neve."

"Ah, but dearest, you could not love me half so well, did you love not honor more." She grinned widely at my expression. "Did you think us only a bunch of ignorant gadabouts with no knowledge of literature, music, and art? We're civilized creatures, we are, with a wide range of interests in the modern world." Her expression sobered then. "Now, *astor*, my heart's treasure . . . will you – only if you *truly* desire it – will you be my champion? Will you give up your life here and come with me to fight for me and mine?"

Maybe I should have been angry that she hadn't asked me all this at our first meeting. Maybe it should have made me feel used that she had waited all this time, had put me through these months of longing – had not even asked if I wished to go through these "trials." But I wasn't angry. It didn't make me feel used. It made me feel . . . strong! Capable. *Worthy*. I had passed tests. I had proven I was someone who could give service, protection, and defense. To Neve. To her people. All the other questions could wait. All the other answers were irrelevant.

"Neve." I slid off the bed to kneel before her, took her hands in mine and held them so tightly I was afraid I'd hurt her, but also afraid to let go. "Neve, I have loved you from that first night in a way I have never loved anyone. If this is enchantment, so be it. If this is a dream, don't wake me. If it's a champion you want, choose me, Neve!"

"Ah, Con. What of your job here? I know what it means to you. What of that?"

"What of that?" I held her hands to my face. "It doesn't mean – it *cannot* mean – what it used to for me. I don't accomplish anything anymore, Neve. And I'm tired. Tired of fighting harsh shadows and losing. If there's anyone, or anything, that *needs* me for fighting, then take me and let me serve and protect you and yours always. I would die for you, Neve. I would die for your people. Never leave me. I don't think I could bear it again."

I know what you're thinking. And I absolutely agree. It sounds ridiculous. And terribly melodramatic. But it seemed to be the only way to express things that were true. Certainly, Neve was happy with my answer. And I was happy with Neve.

She took my face between her hands. "If that is what you truly want, *agrah*, then I do desire and plead with you to come with me and be my champion. Serve, protect, and defend me and mine."

"I will." It required no further words.

"Then there remains only one more question." I braced myself and Neve asked, "Connie, are you able to ride a motorcycle?"

I laughed and said that I could, though it had been a while. "It's like riding a horse," she assured me. "It all comes back to you."

<=>

A long and very pleasant time later, Neve snuggled up against me and sighed with contentment. "Oh, how I will be envied by all the others for my wise choice of champion."

"Why is that?" I asked.

"Because, my beloved, in addition to your other gifts you are a poet!" She laughed. "And warrior-poet is to be prized above all others." I protested that I wasn't much of a poet, but she kissed me and smiled again. "And you're a fabulous lover as well. Sure, everyone will be asking me to lend you out – but it will be a long time before I'll be doing that! I pledge my heart to you, Connie O'Sheen. And you must pledge yours to me."

"I did that the first time you kissed me, Neve," I replied and took off my ring – the one that had belonged to my father. The one with the stone as dark and reflective as Neve's eyes. The symbol of his life – and mine. I believe he would have understood and approved my choice. I slipped it on to Neve's finger – it was only a little loose – and closed her fist around it. Then she reached up and took off her little silver bell earring and extended it to me. And so we sealed our bargain.

<=>

And by now I guess you know what I wound up writing in that notebook I bought. I'm leaving it here on the little table in the foyer for someone to find – just in case anyone wonders what became of me. And if you're really all that curious, you'll go to An Beal Bocht and ask around. Dermot might give you some hints. Or Brenda could give you a wink. John and Caitlin may possibly play you a tune or two. They know more than they say.

And if you think you're of warrior stock – or if you're seeking for something or someone to fight for – come by on the night of a full moon and wait. We can always use more help.

Do me just one favor? Bring CDs and batteries with you.

I Fell Off My Name
By Micah Juliot
⟷

MICAH JULIOT is a Spanish teacher from west-central
Wisconsin. His appreciation for writing and languages
grew during high school and during his years in college,
where he studied English and Spanish at the University of
Wisconsin, La Crosse. He briefly lived in Spain in 2004, and
has returned twice since then. He began writing creatively
in college. He is inspired by many authors, including Wil-
liam Faulkner, Flannery O'Conner, and José Saramago. He
currently resides in Tomah, Wisconsin with his wonderful wife of three years and their three cats. Here's what he
wrote about "I Fell Off My Name":

> "I Fell Off My Name" is inspired by a real
> place and a real person. The second time I
> traveled to Barcelona, I stayed in Hostel
> Rembrandt for three nights. The hostel
> manager was a pleasant man who I imag-
> ined felt as trapped as Kamal, the character
> in this story. Of all three days I stayed there,
> there was not a day – or even a time of day
> – when "Kamal" was not present behind the
> counter of the hostel, working his tedious,
> endless job. During one of our many chats,
> he informed me that he rarely was given
> a day off, and that he was never capable
> of experiencing the city I'd come there to
> enjoy. He never spoke Spanish because his
> day was consumed by tourists from all over
> the globe. I imagine that he sits behind the

counter of the small, packed-together hostel
to this day.

<=>

My name is Kamal. I tell myself this because if I do not then
no one else will. If I have any surnames or further names
that my parents gave me on the day I was born, they have
become superfluous. They are like the faces on a photograph
taken a century ago. Through the ages they have faded with
time, lost their value through misuse and disuse, until one
day they simply became unrecognizable. I have no checks
to sign. I have no friends who may use my other names in
playful banter. No woman I know who gently whispers my
name, ensconced between a fortress of blankets late at night
while we gently feel each other's warmth. I have no mother
to lovingly coo my name over regular telephone conversations, or tell me how much I mean to her on my birthday. I
am. And that is all.

Hostel Rembrandt is where I work, but it is more than
a job. It is more than a career, even. It is the career which
has consumed me. It represents that which has drawn all
other events and moments in my life to fulmination. I am
the manager by title, but in truth this hostel is the manager
of my life. It is tells me where to go. It tells me how long to
sleep and when I may eat. It tells me what I am supposed to
say and when I am supposed to say it. It tells me how much
money I am worth and how often I am to be compensated.
It is like a colossal beast. I am aware of its presence. I can
feel its enormous penumbra fall over everything I do. I live
within its fervent evil. Yet the only proof of its existence is
the disembodied voice I hear over the telephone which con-
firms its will to me. My superior, equally unnamed, calls to
inform me when I have wronged the hostel, or whenever I
need to adjust my pattern of behavior. He also calls whenever my plaintive supplications are rejected. I have lost his

name as he has lost mine. Since my hiring three years ago I have seen the man but a handful of times. But I hear his voice almost constantly. This is where I sleep. Where I eat my food. Where I breathe. It may be where I die.

Today is a Friday. I know it is Friday, not because the day holds some special significance for me; nor is it because of the traditional relief from work which comes with the day. I know it is Friday because there is an influx of patrons at the Hostel Rembrandt. There are so many that pour in and out that sometimes they run together into one amalgamated being. Short people. Tall people. Smiling and angry. Hairless and pilose. And I am the one that sits behind the counter, telling them the price they pay for their slumber while the true master surrounds me.

It is six thirty in the morning and a man is checking out of the hostel. He stands in front of me. His eyes are hidden by swaths of hair as he rattles his fingers against the countertop. His earlobes have plugs in them and thin strips of skin are stretched inches beyond normalcy. A woven cap hides the rest of his hair and I ask him for his room keys. *That was great, man – thanks for everything. I'll totally come back here next time I'm in Barcelona.* I thank him in the usual fashion. It is comforting to have a complimentary guest to begin my day, but I am aware that such an event is rare, and that it is even rarer that such an occurrence is emblematic of the rest of my day. I smile, and as he leaves I request that he rate the hostel favorably on a popular travel website, cursing my own words under my breath for trying to further the existence of this foul beast. I know he will not do so at any rate. Any man who obviously ingests as much marijuana as he does would find it difficult to use a computer regularly, much less to do so for my or the hostel's benefit.

The door has not even closed behind the young man when it is thrust open again. In walks a couple, a man and a woman. Obviously British by their accent. I swear silently, *Damn.* The British are known, and rightfully so, as the worst travelers. The woman wears a pelisse and a large hat, while the man has a blue button-down shirt and glasses miniaturized almost beyond credulity. They step up to the counter. The woman looks about nervously at the confined and dingy state of the lobby. The man speaks first. *Is this Hostel Rembrandt?* I nod but say no words. *Because it took forever to find. You guys need clearer indication outside there – smashed between everything else. We wandered those streets for forty-five minutes longer than we needed to.* His chastising voice reflects off me. *How long will you be staying, sir?* He looks back confused. *What? What're you saying? Goddamnit they can't even find someone from Spain to run the bloody hostel. If I wanted to hear someone like you I'd fly to fucking India, am I right?* The woman wraps her arms about his and whispers in his ear. There is fear in her voice, and though I cannot make out the words I understand what she is telling him. The man responds to her. *No no no. Look, we made reservations here and this is where we'll stay for at least one godforsaken night; it will be okay. Okay?* Now he looks back at me and nods towards an open door to my left. *Is that one of the rooms?* Again I nod noiselessly. *What the hell kind of place is this? It's so fucking small I could barely stay there myself – and we're both supposed to stay in one of those rooms? God – those pictures on that website are pretty damned disingenuous, don't you think?* He's trying to intimidate me, trying to get me to lower the cost on the already bare-bones price, but I cannot. The hostel will not allow me and so I tell him the price and wait while he lividly tromps up and down the lobby. When finally he realizes there is no haggling, and that no amount of complaint will magically improve the rooms or accommodations, which are equally as bare-boned, he furiously pays for two nights and whisks his woman, who shivers with terror next to him, to a nearby room.

I open a nearby drawer. There are stacks of papers. Pens scattered randomly as though a bomb had exploded. One piece of paper stands out. *Call me*, is all it says. *Call me*, with a series of numbers after the mandate. They are written, seemingly unrelated, but together they make a complete entity. Like pieces to a puzzle that separate are meaningless, in sequential order they derive purpose. I do not know the name behind the numbers and they do not know mine, but their presence is a comfort. Their preceding words are a warm reminder of a happier moment.

Now two women walk through the front entrance. Their tentacular arms spread out wildly, shifting at any given moment. They are like a living portrait. It is quite apparent by their general demeanor and comportment that they are both quite drunk, even at this point in the morning. They are laughing heinously, and the noxious scent of alcohol and cigarette smoke steams from their every pore. They approach the desk and giggle uncontrollably. One of them, a blond woman with pasty white skin and hair that is wavy enough to not be straight, but does not quite bend enough to curl, addresses me while the other, a darker-skinned and darker-haired girl, hangs upon her arm and twirls the blond woman's hair. She begins to stumble through words, slurring out in French that they are in need of a room for a day or two. I confirm back to her in French the availability of our rooms, doing so in as few words as needed, and I attempt to attain the woman's identification while remaining professional. The darker woman begins slowly kissing the other woman's shoulder. Grasping her tank top she begins to pull it down, nearly exposing the other woman's breast. She does not seem to notice. She smiles and wrinkles her nose playfully at the other woman, while I attempt to ring her credit card through the hostel's ancient machine. I turn back to see the second woman gyrating against the other's side, rhythmically touching her everywhere. The blond woman closes her eyes and bites her lip. I sigh peevishly as they continue with their pseudo-coital actions. Finally she takes notice of me long enough to take her card back and snatch away the key, barely taking the time to hear me shout *Room number seven*, as their moans already permeate the hallways. There was a time when moments like those would have been excitement enough to keep me grinning for at least a few hours. Now they slide by as if they never were. They are so common.

Another couple arrives. Ostensibly American, they are unassuming, smiling and seemingly satisfied within each other's grasp. This, perhaps, is the more rare sight than the other. To see people arguing or drunk, to see them lustful or devious, belligerent or depressed, these are all much more common than to see the contentedness that now stares into my eyes and asks for a room for a night. It is almost laudable. And yet I feel the bitter sting of envy pierce my soul. They are rather indiscernible people in terms of their physical presence. Neither above average in height or weight. Their clothes are baggy and worn. Their backpacks are only shades of gray and brown, avoiding any more lurid hues. There is nothing about them that shouts luxury, yet I would give anything to step into their lives and feel what they feel. The man speaks Spanish with me briefly. *¿Cuánto cuesta el cuarto?* he warbles with a thick accent, but grammatically perfect. I am taken aback, but I respond in Spanish as well, and eventually, after a few paused exchanges, we determine prices and where they will be lodging. It is amazing, because no one speaks Spanish to me. I am surrounded by the irony of living in Spain and yet never using the national language. I am at least conversational in six languages, from Hindi to English and German, but rarely have I been able to use the language embraced by the culture within which I find myself immersed. It is like living trapped on an island while still being capable of seeing the mainland and its entire normalcy. The man provides one last warm smile – *Gracias* – before grasping his backpack and making his way down the hallway, his partner silent, but pleasantly so, behind him.

Again I open the drawer nearby and stare at the slip of paper. *Call me.* I hear the words and see them repeated in my head like a song that has but one simple lyric. I want to pick up the phone in the lobby. I want to dial the sequential numbers and hear the electronic hum against my ear as the device attempts to connect me with a familiar voice on the other end. *Call me.* I can see the gentle outline of her face superimposed upon the wall opposite. She had a name, but she did not write it down. Laura, maybe. Or Lori. At any rate, for a while I assumed it was because I was unsure of her name that I did not call her, but now I know differently. It is because I am captured. It is because Hostel Rembrandt will not allow it.

It may have been a month ago. Probably not longer, but it feels as though I met her long ago. She stayed in this rat hole for the better part of a week. She was like a florid angel. When she walked by my desk there was a moment when the air cooled slightly, amidst the humidity and mad heat of the Spanish summer. Her hair was fiery and curled along her skin crisply, instead of sticking wetly to her frame, as though her head was itself a living, moving wildfire, constantly consuming but never extinguished. Her smile was excruciating in its amiability. *You're still here?* she would ask me almost every morning. I could not withhold a grin. *Always.* She laughed, not mockingly, but appreciatively. I knew I loved her. On her third night in the hostel I presented her with a free bottle of wine. *What is this for, Kamal?* My flesh prickled whenever she used my name *Well, for drinking of course!* Then, as she gave me a look of exasperation, I continued, *You see, I had a bottle here, but I have no reason or chance to drink it; I think a beautiful woman like you could find much better use for it.* Her dark eyes blinked at me slowly. Her mocha skin made her ethnicity indefinable. And I loved it.

Over the course of those five days or so she became my reason for being. She was the spot of light in my mind that sheared off the dark madness all around me. Whenever I felt I might not take it anymore, whenever I felt that the heat combined with my lack of sleep and the blathering patrons would drive a final frisson of death into my mortal being, she would walk past the desk, give me a sideways glance, and giggle happily. She would talk to me periodically. Once she asked, *Where would you recommend eating tonight?* Professionally, I would take out a map of the mighty city of Barcelona, pointing out restaurants here and there. *Paella is exquisite here. I love the tapas at this café.* Suddenly she thrust her hand upon my elbow and looked into my eyes. *Would you like to join me, dearest Kamal?* My throat constricted with excitement. I knew the answer was yes, but that damnable hostel, which kept its eyes upon me in all directions, forced me into an involuntary negation. *No; I cannot.* She was truly disappointed. *Why can't you ever leave here? Isn't there someone else to take a shift at the desk?* I shook my head, equally sad. *There is not. I cannot leave here.* There was confusion in her eyes. *Don't you get days off? When do you have time for yourself?* My throat was now constricted upon itself. I could feel its sticky membranes rubbing against each other, trying to form words but failing to do so. *What are you, tied to that chair? Is there some curse upon you which will not allow you to cross the threshold of this building?* Her words were so near to truth that I could not bear it. Tears welled in my eyes and I only shook my head, turning away. Finally I managed a brief response. *There is no one else here to work the desk. I have not had a day off work since last year.* She looked at the ground, frustrated. *Well, okay then. If you change your mind, here's my number. Call me. I'm moving in with a friend of mine today. She's just arriving in Spain. I'll be in Barcelona for a few months for my internship, though.* She wrote the command *Call me* as if to reiterate her sincerity, and her phone number. It was the final night of her stay. I have not seen her since. And I have forgotten her name.

The afternoon sheds itself slowly. I feel each minute like a weight upon my skin. It is as though I am trapped within a slough. I leave briefly to get some food from a nearby market. It is my only respite and it can be but for thirty minutes. An apple, two tangerines, and a loaf of bread. This is what I will eat this evening. I am not allowed to enjoy a glass of wine with the travelers in the hostel. I cannot afford an extravagant meal. Rather, I cannot afford to spend the time it would take to eat an extravagant meal.

The night is filled with many of the same trivialities that I find myself mired down with during the day. The Englishman raves about the constricted space in the rooms in addition to the shared bathroom down the hall. *You're telling me I don't get to take a bloody shit without the rest of the hostel hearing about it then, are you?* I shrug my shoulders. Responding would only cause more harm than good. *I'll probably fall in that shower of yours, crack my head open, and lie bleeding for hours – it's like showering in a damned coffin.* The mental image he provides is actually quite enjoyable, but I refrain from showing any amusement.

After the Englishman finally returns reluctantly to his quarters, I walk up and down the hallways. It is nearing eleven o'clock, and while that is a relatively early hour by Spanish standards, almost none of the travelers are from anywhere near Spain, and consequently are mostly confined to their rooms. Some have left to go out drinking. I can see them imbibing on the inebriations of life. I feel some envy, but I have long since accepted that that part of my life is dead.

The first door on the right is open. The two Americans who had come in last today sit on their respective beds. The man has a map of Barcelona out and a pencil locked in his jaw, as though keeping it tightly there will somehow improve his thought process. The woman on the other bed speaks up. *We need to see Sagrada Familia and the Picasso museum tomorrow*, and he nods his head in agreement, while two fingers on his right hand scour the map in search of the best route.

The next room contains the French travelers, the two women. Their door is closed; however, the actions taking place within are unmistakable. At first I think that one of them is crying. Then I think it might have been laughter.

Quickly I realize they are neither weeping nor giggling – their sounds are rhythmic, primal. They are repetitive and atavistic. Their calls rise higher and higher and louder and louder every second, and I fear the intensity of their love-making will tear the hinges off the door and reveal me standing outside in the hallway.

I reach the end of the hall. The last door, also on the right, is ajar. I look inside. Another couple, who had checked into the hostel two days ago, a man and a woman, are inside. They are both naked. She sits atop him and moves slowly. Unlike the two women down the hall, they are completely silent but for the groaning bed beneath them that complains with every movement. I can see her supple back. The indents where her bare shoulder blades are visible. Her figure is like that of a goddess, and it rises like a boat out of the ocean with each thrust. It is a beautiful sight. But I do not watch. Instead I silently close their door. I can feel the hostel calling me back to reality. Its will, like spiders' legs, gently closes about me and leads me back towards my room. I feel pulled down into my twin-sized bed. I yawn instinctually, knowing that sleep is nearing; and then I fall asleep.

<=>

My name is Kamal, I tell myself as I gain consciousness. It is the first thing I say to myself out loud every day. Partly to confirm that I am still here, to reveal my own existence, if to no one else then to myself, and partly because I wish there would be an echoing cry. That there would be a reciprocal voice next to mine telling me something soft like, *I know your name is Kamal*, or some such response. My solitude is quickly confirmed and I prepare for another day.

It is six o'clock. This day, a Saturday, is much less active than the former. All my residents have either decided to sleep late, or have already motivated themselves to get out of bed and leave to see the sights and sounds that Barcelona has to offer. At any rate, there is no one checking into the hostel, and certainly no one has decided to check out. I log on to the hostel email and find nothing but advertisements and spam, trying to trap me into this offer or that. I check the hostel calendar and realize that none of the guests are scheduled to leave today. It is a rare occurrence that I find myself with nothing to do and nothing to anticipate. It makes me uncomfortable that, even when I am without a task to perform, I am disallowed from enjoying the moment. I have no friends to call. There are no films I can watch. I cannot access frivolous websites without receiving admonishing phone calls from my superior. The hostel knows all that I do. And so I sit with my hands on the desk and stare silently for what seems an eternity.

I open the drawer next to me and stare at the paper for a few minutes. *Call me.* I want to, and my hand reaches instinctively for the receiver on my right, but I know I will not. One of the guests stumbles out of his room, interrupting my thoughts. He is clothed in a football jersey, and this reminds me that there is an important match on television tonight between Barcelona and Madrid. It is one of the few pleasures I can indulge in because it does not take away from my ability to perform my duties, and I do not need to leave my work to watch the game. There is a television in the lobby, however unreliable and low quality it may be.

Morning slides into afternoon, inexplicably and insipidly. Guests walk in and out of their rooms, ignoring me as though I were a ghost. Finally I decide that I am allowed to slip from the hostel for a trip to the market, and I leave the steaming building, stepping into the scorching Spanish sun. I remember loving Barcelona so much when I arrived in the city. Its splendor and its grandeur were all too much for me to soak in. Now I feel that I was deceived somehow. In the face of its beauty I was blinded to the ugly truth that was now all too evident, hidden behind layers of mosaic structures and the façade of culture: the truth that I was invisible in a town such as this. That no matter how hard I tried I could never make myself known. I walk through the Boquería, Barcelona's largest marketplace, glancing at the fruit stands, shelves filled with candy, and wholesale pigs behind glass displays, as though they might run away if they weren't prevented from doing so. I can smell the seafood at the other end of the market. I love seafood here in Spain, but it saddens me that I have no time to prepare a dish which includes it. I settle on a sandwich that has a few scraps of chorizo and shrimp laid within it, and a slice of melon. Then I return to the Hostel Rembrandt.

In the afternoon I anxiously await the coming football match. I visualize the players stroking the ball down the field almost lovingly in their approach to the opposing goal. Each goal itself seems as though she is a woman in need of seduction. They must dance about, pass the ball, kick precisely yet forcefully, all to achieve the seemingly unachievable. Guests walk in and out and I address them with a half-heartedness associated with my dream-like state. Those that check in and out of the hostel are of little importance to me at the moment. Finally the moment arrives when the game is about to begin. One of the cleaning assistants on duty stops by the desk. *Turning on the match?* I nod and make my way to the lobby. Because it is so close to my desk, I can still see if I am needed by any current or future patrons.

As I turn the television on it occurs to me what might happen. Nothing. A black aperture stares back at me and I see my own reflection. Perhaps I have not turned it on. Perhaps I imagined doing so. I flick the switch off, then back into the on position. I hear an electronic whir. I touch the cable running from behind the set towards a nearby wall. The screen comes to life. It is white. I cycle through the channels, desperately, but find nothing. Behind me, at the front desk, I hear the voice of the British tourist. *A little help over here?* I ignore him. I slip through different inputs, adjusting wires and slapping the side of the infernal box. Nothing changes.

Hijo de puta, son of a bitch, I swear in two languages, but it makes no difference. The other worker who had volunteered to watch the match with me has lost interest. *See you tomorrow,* he says and closes the lobby door behind him, undoubtedly going to watch the match at a nearby café. And yet I remain. I am punching the television now. Hitting its sides with all my might. I hear the tourist still waiting for attention at the desk. *Am I invisible over here or what?* My eyes shed tears. It seems so trivial. But it is not. It is one more symbol of the control I have lost. The control I may never have again. One of the patrons, one of the French girls in a nearby room, opens the door and curses me in French, hostile towards the noise I have caused. There is an icepack on her face and she looks as though she is recovering from a heavy night of drinking. She probably is. I don't care. I ignore her furor and continue to pound on the television. *Please.* Now I am not begging it to show me the match. I am begging it to take me wherever it has gone. Wherever its images have gone that used to flash across the screen, wherever the pixilation has bled to, I want to be taken there. Yet I remain.

Behind me the British tourist pounds his fist on the desk. *Goddamnit, would you leave that thing alone long enough to help me out over here?* I turn around. His face is red and his hands are balled up into fists. *All I want is some directions to the damned post office. You think you can handle that or do you want me to write it in another fucking language for you?* I step towards him. Hatred is boiling inside me. I can hear nothing but the empty static of the television set behind me. Somewhere there is joy. Somewhere there are comrades drinking and watching television. Somewhere there are men and women making love; there are people living and there are people dying. I experience none of those things. I reach the furious Brit and place my hand up near his face, shaking. *What the hell?* he cries out as I slam my fist down next to his. *¿Qué puta quieres idiota?* I scream. He is taken aback. *¿Quieres que te pegue en la boca?* He grabs for the door handle to his room behind him, unsuccessfully. *What? Speak English, you bloody wanker!* I continue my tirade in Spanish. *¿Por qué no te callas? ¿Por qué no hablas Español en España eh? ¡Cabeza de piedras!* I have not spoken Spanish so much in months, and it feels good, like water rolling down my throat, as the words come off my tongue. Tears of fear well up in his sockets. *Jesus Christ, have you totally lost your mind?* I am still near his face but I do not touch him. *¡Lárgate! ¡Vete ya cabrón!* He finally retreats to his room and slams the door. *Come on, honey – the clerk has totally lost his goddamned mind – we're getting out of here right now.* I punch the wall next to his room and leave an indentation of my fist, breaching the skin of the hostel. The reverberations echo in the hallway.

An hour later I am sitting at the desk, once more alone. The British couple left five minutes after my outburst, screaming obscenities, simultaneously fearful and vulgar, in my direction as they closed the door to the lobby behind them. Behind me the imprint of my hand stands out in the wall like a bruise on a person's face. The broken television and the heat have combined with my spirits with entropic results. I cannot even lift a finger. A man comes in and asks for a room and I ignore him. I will not even look him in the eye when he waves his hand in front of my face.

I know what needs to be done. I know what I must do now. I have pierced my bonds, and I must cut them off, before I am consumed by the wrathful flames of the ignominious building. I pick up the phone and dial a number. My fingers are shaking with each numeral, but they gain confidence with each subsequent number. On the other end, a man picks up the phone. *Hello?* I respond. My words are as terse as they are precise. *I am quitting. Today.* There is a pause. A sharp, sucking inhalation. *Do you have any idea what you're doing? I'll have you thrown out on the street tonight! I've done everything for you!* I respond to the hostel owner, *I understand that. I am afraid that I cannot perform my duties any longer.* This time there is no pause. *You're a dead man! You think you can just find another job? Not after this! I know people. You screw me over like this, you won't be able to even get an interview this half of Barcelona! Where are you going to live, huh? You're nothing! I gave you this damned job. You think you can just back out like this?* He is trying to bait me into staying. But I know the truth. The truth is that while living here I have not lived at all. *Goodbye.* I hang up the phone.

There are but two tasks yet to perform. I return to my quarters. Before I am thrown out I must gather my things, and so I do. My clothes all fit within an old grocery bag I find beneath my bed. I place two books and a notebook into a knapsack, as well as a handful of accoutrements. All my possessions fit easily within the two sacks. Anything left I do not truly need. When I return to the lobby there is an irregular stillness. As though the hostel is waiting, crouching, hiding so that it might better see what I will do next.

I imagine many things that I might do to this infernal place. I see myself setting the walls on fire. Burning it from the inside out. I see myself defecating on the carpet. Kicking in a few doors. Stealing what little change we have behind the desk. Perhaps I could throw the damnable television, which in my hour of desperation failed even to provide moderate amusement, out of a nearby window. I could do all these things, but instead I sit down one last time behind the desk, feeling the familiarity of the chair cushion my frame. I open the desk. *Call me.* The note reaches out to me. I pick up the slip of paper while I pick up the phone. It all has a taste of finality. I dial each number as it is written. I feel as though I am unlocking a secret code. A secret code, and on the other end there is the hope for happiness. I can hear someone rushing up the stairs of the hostel. The footsteps creak as the building bemoans my actions. It is finished now. I have dialed each number, and I place the receiver to my ear. I can almost see her glistening skin as the electronic connection is made and I hear a ring on the phone. Her elbows as they leaned up against the desk, her smiling towards me as

I performed my mindless duties. I imagine the way she will smile as we sit down at a café together for the first time and enjoy a glass of wine. *See, don't you wish you'd done this with me earlier?* she will say. The phone continues to ring. I am suddenly terrified that she will not answer, but as I am about to lose all hope, I hear a distant click, and then a pause. *Hello? Lara speaking.* I breathe a sigh of relief. I can feel the hostel's blistering anger amalgamating with the Spanish summer heat. Where it has brought me death, I shall create a new life. *Hello, my name is Kamal.*

Hazel
By Ashley Baldwin
<⇒>

ASHLEY BALDWIN lives in Phoenix, Arizona with her husband and their three daughters. She hopes to move to Southern California at some point, or at least somewhere near an ocean, preferably where the temperature is always seventy-five degrees. Ashley has her BA in Sociology from Arizona State and is currently finishing her first novel. Here's what she wrote about "Hazel":

> My heart's compass seems to invariably point West: toward the Pacific Ocean, to the Ferris wheel on the Santa Monica Pier, to other places I have fallen in love with over the years. I wrote "Hazel" after taking four road trips to Los Angeles in the span of nine months. Three of those four times I went to see my favorite bands perform. My love for the city, my obsession with music – live music, especially – helped inspire me to write "Hazel."

<⇒>

My father sat on an old milk crate writing on a sheet of paper with a sharpie. A woman leaned over his shoulder, laughing. He said something I couldn't hear, then wrapped his fingers around a glass and finished whatever was in it. The woman grazed his fingers when she took the glass. She walked past me, her heels clanking against the sidewalk.

His eyes followed her and, because of this, he saw me. He narrowed his eyes, and in the dark night, barely lit by a small street lamp in the parking lot, I wasn't sure if he recognized me.

"Sorry, hon, I'm not talking to any fans until after the show, but maybe if you're lucky, I'll let you buy me a bourbon." His voice was exactly as I remembered. Soft, husky, scratchy, as if he smoked too many cigarettes. He turned back to his work, and I stepped toward him, walking to the only spot on the patio where the light hit.

"Dad, it's me," I said. My voice shook as I spoke. My stomach churned. The whiskey I had consumed was burning a hole in the pit of my stomach. It was surreal to be standing in front of my father. It broke my heart, but it also gave me hope.

He looked up, narrowing his eyes again. The sharpie fell from his hand. The clink was loud in my ears, as if he had dropped something much heavier. My father stood quickly, putting his hands on my shoulders. His fingers were callused from decades of guitar playing. His hair had started to turn gray at the temples. He looked the same as I remembered him, only older. "Hazel Lynn."

I nodded. My mouth went dry. I licked my lips, stared at cracks in the sidewalk. I looked up at him again and realized the people who told me I looked like my mom were crazy. I had my father's eyes. His cheekbones. His coloring. I looked just like him.

"What are you doing here?" My father removed his hands from my shoulders, stepped back, and looked at me. The woman reappeared with another drink, but he dismissed her with a wave. I watched her walk away, and turned back to my father, who had a cigarette poking from his mouth. "I . . . do you care if I smoke?"

"No," I said. I took a few steps back. The more distance between us the better. The night felt cold, thick with possibility, but also heavy with past betrayals. I thought of the things

I had pushed away as a preteen, how I had forced myself to let go of my father for the sake of my mom's feelings and my own. She had told me what he did – how he broke her heart, how he told her that he didn't want this life, that the road was the only place for him. The pain felt raw all of a sudden, new, as if the betrayal, the abandonment just happened. I remembered the tears my mom cried on the drive to Arizona, how I vowed to forget him because it was the only way not to hurt. But I hadn't forgotten him. Not really.

"How's Sally?" My father coughed. He took a drag from the cigarette, blowing the smoke toward the starless sky. He focused his eyes on me for a second, and I was shaken. "What are you doing here?" he asked once more, coughing again. I stared at him. I didn't know if he was asking in the existential sense, or if he meant in LA, or at his show.

I considered the question.

I hadn't planned on moving back to Los Angeles. There were too many things, memories that I couldn't force myself to forget: Ferris wheel rides in Santa Monica, Shirley Temples at my dad's rock 'n' roll shows in Hollywood, me on his shoulders walking through Chinatown, silly surf lessons in Malibu. My father had been my hero growing up, but my mom had been my anchor. The day we packed up and left, my mom sat me down and gave it to me straight: "He told me he didn't want to be a family anymore. He said he was better off on the road." She looked me straight in the eye. That night when we drove through the sandy deserts, I truly did believe we were better off. If he didn't want to be a family, then I didn't want him to be in our family either.

Back then I learned the truth about heroes: More often than not, they end up disappointing us, shattering our dreams, and leaving us to pick up the pieces.

I was twenty-three when my best friend Roxy suggested we move to LA.

"We need to move before we end up a part of the scenery, shriveled up from the heat; before we turn to dust. We need an adventure!" she had exclaimed, throwing her arms in the air. We were in my bedroom at home. She was spinning in circles. Roxy always had a flair for the dramatic. But I was starting to feel that maybe she was right, and that a change, a move, was just what we needed.

It wasn't surprising that my mom felt that moving was the last thing I needed.

"Hazel, I'm not so sure about this," she had said with a long, drawn-out sigh. She was overseas with her boyfriend Thad, and her voice kept going in and out, muffled over the transatlantic phone lines. "Stay in Arizona. Get a job with your degree. Stay with me." It didn't matter that she'd been spending a lot of time globetrotting with Thad. She wanted me to stay.

"I hate Arizona," I'd said. I was already packing my stuff while I was on the phone. I felt guilty, too, as if I was betraying her. But the need to do this was pulling me with such force that I couldn't ignore it.

"But LA?" she asked. "Are you going for your dad? Are you going to find him?"

"No." My answer came automatically, a reflex. But when we hung up five minutes later, I realized I wasn't sure what I would do, and that I had probably just lied to my mom.

Of course my father was in the back of my mind the whole time Roxy and I planned our move. Was he still in LA? It was possible he had moved. If he hadn't, was there any way I would run into him? If I ran into him, would he recognize me, or had I already become a distant, fuzzy memory, muted from too many drinks and drugs over the last decade?

Our friend Ryan was letting us stay at his studio apartment in Brentwood until we had our feet under us. Roxy and I had a grand plan: we would get jobs with our degrees, make thousands of dollars a month, and be able to afford our own two-bedroom apartment somewhere in LA by the end of the year. It was October.

I spent a lot of my free time hanging out at Dick's, a dive bar a few miles from UCLA where Roxy worked. At Dick's there were two ratty pool tables, but I liked the dart board best. I'd find someone to play darts with, giggling girlishly, always pulling my dress down. It wasn't a pride thing or a slutty thing, but I liked the free drinks that came with the coyness, the way men would look at me in surprise when I actually – shockingly – turned out to be a good player and beat them. I liked it when they called me beautiful.

I never found myself particularly beautiful. People told me I looked like my mother when she was younger, and my mother was gorgeous, but I never saw it. My mother was half-Brazilian and looked it – curvy body, curly brown hair, beautiful facial features. I felt so much plainer than her, so much simpler, as if the Brazilian blood and features skipped over me completely. The only things I liked were my hazel eyes. And, as it turned out, my hazel eyes were what inspired my dad's number one hit, "Hazel Lynn."

The boys I dated in high school would always sing me the first line, as if quoting my dad was a turn on: "Hazel Lynn, her name the same as the color of her eyes . . ." Even after eleven years, I still heard that song everywhere: shopping malls, movie theaters, at concerts when bands were setting up. It even played at my senior prom. I locked myself in the girls' bathroom and didn't come out until the plucking of guitar strings left the hotel ballroom and was replaced with a Justin Timberlake song.

"Hazel! You need to look at the bulletin board." Roxy was pouring drinks for drunk college guys, and I had a whiskey sour that a handsome med student had bought me before throwing up all over the floor. So far, it had been an eventful Thursday night.

I hopped off my stool, carefully stepping over the place that had just been mopped and the other sticky spots on the ground. The bulletin board was nailed up in the hall on the way to the bathrooms, a place for show flyers and lost-dog posts. I saw it immediately – a pink flyer with bold faced writing: Max Jackson LIVE at Silverlake Lounge, October 29, 2013. Below was a black-and-white picture of my dad, Xeroxed and copied to the point of total blurriness. My heart started to race. Nervous energy surged through my body. Was it adrenaline? Dread?

When the hallway was clear, and I was sure I was alone, I lifted my fingers, touched the hot-pink flyer gingerly, and then, in one swift motion, ripped it off the board. The show flyer was a surprise, and my hands were shaking as I stared at it. I always knew seeing my dad was a possibility, but for some reason I hadn't expected it to be in paper form on the bulletin board of the bar Roxy worked at.

"Silverlake is a ways from here, isn't it?" I sat back down at the bar and looked at my best friend.

Her kohl-rimmed blue eyes met mine. "It's not too far away."

I sighed. "Gas is expensive, Rox. I mean, we barely have money to eat. And Silverlake is probably a forty-mile roundtrip from the apartment." I ran my finger across the bar where a crack was beginning to form.

Roxy leaned on her arms, her eye contact unwavering. "Forty-mile roundtrip to see your dad, Haze. It's worth it."

"Is it?" I looked at the flyer. I picked it up, studied it, stared at my father, unrecognizable in photocopied form. "He left us." The hurt flooded back quickly, a tsunami of pain crashing me back into the past. Watching Los Angeles disappear as my mom drove on the I-10 heading east, swearing we were done with this place. And then there was a shift in emotions: I mean, this had to be a sign, didn't it?

Roxy let out a breath. She bent down, grabbed a wet cloth from behind the bar, and wiped down the counter. She scrubbed at a coke stain, then stopped and met my eyes again. "It's been over a decade, Hazel. Maybe you should give him a chance to explain." There was a beat. Roxy brushed her bangs out of her face with a free hand. "That song is actually kind of sad . . ."

"I try to avoid that song. Or any of his songs for that matter." I looked at the flyer one more time, then shoved it into my purse. I stared at the ice melting in my glass. I did anything to keep from looking at Roxy, because I knew she would convince me to go. In my heart of hearts, I had a secret that I had never told anyone, not my mother, not Roxy. I listened to "Hazel Lynn" sometimes. Usually when I felt overwhelmed or emotional or I wanted to cry. My father's voice was the only thing that could comfort me.

"Give him a chance." She tapped on the bar, and I looked back up at her. "Maybe he'll surprise you."

My brain had already started to spin circles. The Dad-related indifference I had been holding onto was starting to dissipate. I had hope, damn it. I had hope. "What if he doesn't surprise me? What if he hurts me?" My voice sounded small and childish.

Roxy looked me straight in the eye.

"You're a grown-ass woman, now, Hazel Jackson. It's time to take chances."

<=>

That night when we got home I closed myself outside on the patio and listened to the song I had spent the last decade listening to in secret. I put my earbuds in, took a deep breath, and pressed play.

"Hazel Lynn, her name the same color as her eyes
I miss her every day. I see her in the sunrise,
I won't leave you. It was you who left me . . ."

<=>

I spent the next two weeks siphoning wi-fi from Ryan's neighbor, searching for secrets about Max Jackson on the internet. There was nothing overly scandalous – no dead strippers, broken syringes; no exposés about my dad being a womanizer, no secret families. The more I searched I found other things: paparazzi captured photos of my dad leaving rehab in 2004; articles about charity work in New Orleans in 2008. What was going on here? Was this really the guy who insisted that he didn't have a place in his life for a family? Was this the man that had broken my mother's heart? The man in the photographs, on the computer, seemed like a stranger. He was no longer the famous guitarist of Double Squared. From what I could see, the only thing that had stayed the same was his hair.

"I wish I could go with you," Roxy told me the night of the show. She was getting ready for work, and I was searching the closet for something perfect to wear. Nothing shouted at me: there were no I'm-seeing-my-dad-for-the-first-time-in-a-decade! dresses, so I settled on a pair of jeans and a black tank top.

"It's okay," I said, looking at Roxy as she pulled her hair up in a ponytail.

"You nervous?" She sat on the edge of the bed and waited for an answer.

I was nervous. I felt I was going to be sick. My mind was racing so much that I couldn't think straight. I was dizzy, excited, and scared. What if he disappointed me? What if everything my mom said was true, and he just ended up being a total jackass?

"Nah, I'm fine. It's no big deal." I sounded nonchalant, but I wasn't. I was eleven again. Full of hope. Scared. Happy. Optimistic. But part of me was certain I would end up brokenhearted.

I drove to the Silverlake Lounge, taking the 405-North, then merging onto the 101, getting off at Silverlake Boulevard. I arrived way too early; the night sky had barely started to turn dark. I parked in a tiny parking lot built on an awkward slope, and I sat there for a long time, battling my nausea and nerves until I saw people shuffle into the small dive bar.

The bar/venue itself was rectangular on the inside with a tiny stage in the corner. The floors were sticky and slick, and it smelled like bourbon, stale cigarette smoke, and a mixture of perfumes. The smell took me back, made me remember the times I had gone to my dad's shows as a kid. That smell, the smell of stale cigarettes and sticky sweet bourbon, was impossible to shake. There was something comforting about it as a kid, standing close to my mom, waiting for my dad's band to go onstage. The smell was a constant, something to be counted on.

The bar was already filling up with women, wearing perfume so strong I had to hold my breath when they walked past me and way too much makeup. I took in my surroundings. I was sure this was not unlike some of the venues I had been to as a kid, but I couldn't conjure any of them up in my memory. I could remember the feeling, the anticipation, and I felt it now, just waiting.

Conversations between women that were too young or too old for my dad filled the room.

"I wonder if he has a girlfriend. Remember a few years ago when we saw him in Austin? Best sex of my life."

I cringed. A knot formed in my stomach, and the dread I'd been trying to push away came creeping back. My father, the sex symbol. It was nauseating and heartbreaking. Maybe I had made the wrong assumption before: maybe he was exactly the person my mom made him out to be.

"There he is!" another voice said. "Back there. By the bathrooms. Should we . . . ?"

The two women disappeared in the direction of the bathroom, backs straight with determination. I tried not to think about what the women expected to happen when they followed a musician into a bathroom. I turned toward the bar. I had fifty dollars to my name, but I needed a drink.

"Whiskey sour?" I said to the balding man behind the bar.

"Four dollars."

I gave him the money. I threw the drink back. It tasted more whiskey than sour. I hoped the whiskey would give me some kind of courage and make me feel less out of place. Miracle whiskey and liquid courage.

The two women walked back from the bathroom looking disappointed. One of them was flipping her hair back, trying to appear as though she hadn't just offered herself up on a silver platter to my dad. The other was staring at the ground. I watched them and wondered, *Aren't you a little too old for this?* But, then again, maybe there isn't an age limit for throwing yourself at a rock star. And with that thought, I felt the courage hit, and I shuffled toward the back myself.

I could have found my father in a compromising position, with other women, or doing drugs, or worse. Instead, I found him in the dark of the night, alone. Well, more or less.

"How's your mother?" My father tried again, looking at me oddly.

I suddenly couldn't talk. There were so many things I wanted to say, but the words wouldn't form. I couldn't say anything. I cleared my throat. I looked up at the sky. "Mom is fine. She's traveling. Look, Dad, when we left, she told me that you said you didn't want to be in our lives anymore. That you had left us, not the other way around." I thought about the song.

My father was rubbing his neck furiously. His cigarette was almost down to the butt, still ashing orange. "I told her that, yes. But there's more –"

"You didn't want to be a part of my life, did you? You wanted your groupies. Your alcohol. Your road life. You couldn't be held down by a family."

"Hazel . . ." He shook his head at me. "That's not true."

"Max. It's almost show time." A man in a leather jacket appeared then disappeared.

My father, Max Jackson, looked at me helplessly. "I didn't feel like I could be a good dad to you at the time. And yes, I said that I didn't want to be a part of your life, but I was protecting you –"

"That's such a load of bullshit!" I yelled. "Protecting me? You were protecting you." Hot tears stung my eyelids, but I wouldn't cry. Damn it, I would not cry.

"Your mother wasn't innocent in all of this either, Hazel! She had sex with Roger Lee. She was in the wrong, too. It wasn't just me." He looked at me. He kept my gaze, as if he was trying to get through to me, make his case for the past decade in a small space of time. "Look, we were young. The two of us. I was twenty-three when you were born," he said. He looked at the open door of the bar, and then back at me. "I need to finish my set list, and then I have a show to play. I'm sorry. If you stay, we can talk more after the show."

His eyes met mine and, in the dimly lit courtyard, I knew this wouldn't end the way I wanted it to. I wouldn't have the relationship I had with my father when I was ten years old. We wouldn't leave drinking Shirley Temples, driving to the beach and watching sunsets. There wouldn't be Ferris wheel rides and surf lessons. That was a lifetime ago.

I knew I should go, but I stayed. I turned and went inside, not saying another word to my father. Most of me wanted to leave Silverlake, to never set foot in this place again. I would have been happy if it had been wiped off the map altogether. But I stayed.

I lucked into a stool by the bar. It was a good spot. This way I was on the edge. It felt safe on the edge. Less claustrophobic. Less likely to get hurt.

At 9:30, my father walked onto the tiny stage with his vintage Gibson. Beside him, a sign lit up the wall. It said "Salvation." He sat on a stool, settled his guitar onto his lap, and started to play. I watched him from the outskirts. My heart was racing, stuck somewhere in my throat. Watching him play was amazing, just like I remembered it as a kid.

The lights dimmed, and more people walked in. Everyone was silent. The only thing that mattered was my father on the tiny stage.

"This one's an oldie but a goodie," he said, grinning into the microphone. He cleared his throat and started to play a familiar song. The strumming of chords, strings pulling. "You could say that I'll be gone in the morning. That much might be true . . ."

My mind wandered. I thought of my mother, of how she had told me that my father didn't want us anymore. When I was older, she told me about the girls. He kept a list in his acoustic guitar case, under the velvet inside, with all their names. He even wrote a song for one. Her name was Candy. The song, my mother said, was about a prostitute who chewed Bubblicious. I never listened to it.

My father had said my mother wasn't innocent, and maybe that was true. But I took her side years ago, and even now as I watched my father onstage, I knew I couldn't forgive him. He could have been there for me, but he wanted to tour the country, have sex with strange women, and play music every night instead.

He could have been a rock star and a father. There was a time when he was. Mom and I were on the tour bus, driving city to city with him. I fell asleep to the sound of the wheels as they hit potholes on the highway. I was six again, soaring down interstates, sitting between my father and mother on a tiny couch in the corner of the bus. I was seven, eight, nine, watching my dad onstage in different cities. He called me his Hazel Lynn. I looked up to him then.

The overwhelming desire to flee hit me just as my father was finishing his first song. I carefully got off the stool, brushed past sweaty bodies – men yelling like frat boys, women swooning like teens. I made it to the door and stopped. I could still see my father on the stage, the "Salvation" sign shining above him.

"This next song is for my daughter, Hazel, who is actually here in the audience right now. Hazel? Where are you, honey?" my dad asked, searching the dark room. My breath caught in my throat. "Well . . . Anyway, this is a song I wrote for her. It's called 'Hazel Lynn.'"

I almost stayed. He was playing the song. My song. My song.

It was possible my dad would make it up to me, that he would put the pieces together, that we would go to the beach, watch the sun rise together. It was possible he was still the man who had been my hero as a child. But I realized that I was putting a lot of hope into a man who had broken my mom's heart and mine, who had chosen the road life over his family.

The funny thing was that he could have fixed it, had he tried. If he had apologized. If he had explained himself instead of brushing me off and finishing his set list. If he hadn't, once again, chosen his music over me – it might have changed things.

And I could have stayed.

But I didn't.

The Undying Passion
Vivian Too Yee
⟨⇒⟩

VIVIAN TOO YEE is a freelance writer. She recently discovered her love for writing short fiction stories and has been actively writing and submitting her works to various writing contests. In 2013, she placed first runner-up in her college's annual writing event, AJC Poetry Fest 2013, under the short story category. Also in 2013, she was awarded first runner-up in Singapore's annual nationwide writing contest organised by A*STAR, the IHPC's Science Chronicles 2012 Contest. Variety is what excites her about writing – she is never satisfied with a certain genre or style of writing and is always eager to take up a new challenge to write something she has never tried writing before. Here's what she wrote about "The Undying Passion":

> We all have this one thing that we are willing to die for. It could be our religion, our family, friends, loved ones, or even our favorite cat. It doesn't matter. This is a fundamental sentiment so empowering and destructive, so great and terrible. I was keen to explore this mystical characteristic of human nature, and the core inspiration for my story was one of the people who inspire me most: Dr. Alexandre Chao. Dr. Chao was a vascular surgeon at the Singapore General Hospital (SGH), and was only 37 years old when he succumbed to the SARS virus during the 2003 epidemic. He voluntarily cut short his leave in the United States to join his colleagues in the fight against

SARS, and even when he contracted the virus while trying to save numerous other victims he did not regret his decision. Dr. Chao's courage and intense love for his occupation moved me. For quite a long time I was motivated to write a heartwarming story about someone who was not afraid to give his life for something he was passionate for. When I was sitting in front of the glow of the laptop screen, wondering how I should write it, an image popped into my head: a place of serenity, with sweet foamy waves crashing against the rocky shore. And that, ladies and gentlemen, was developed to become "The Undying Passion."

<=>

Teardrops clung like dewdrops to her eyelashes. She was tired of crying, tired of feeling that heavy weight pressed against her chest every time she breathed. If she could, she would stop breathing, stop feeling. Maybe then her eyes would stop that infernal, perpetual rain.

Surely, if one wished to die, falling from a great height would be the grandest send-off?

She did not know. But to a broken soul, feeling the rush of the gentle wind seemed like the last attempt to grasp hold of reality.

The fall from grace. How ironic.

She walked slowly, putting one foot in front of the other. Half a meter from the edge, she closed her eyes submissively and walked on. In three steps, two, then one, she did not stop. Extremely relaxed, the ends of her lips curled in a weary smile.

Her feet left the edge of the precipice.

◄⇒►

"Ha! *And* as usual, *our* Lydia is set to beat all of you!"

"Stop that, Sue, you're embarrassing me." I blushed.

A string of delighted laughter escaped Sue's mouth when she saw the annoyed faces of the other members.

"What did I say wrong? You have already perfected the somersault, the pike position, and the rip entry." She laughed again and shoved me hard on the back. "Now go and show them what you're capable of."

I walked steadily to the tower. The coach was already at its base, holding a black clipboard, whistle at the ready. His wizened and tanned face was emotionless as always, but I could have sworn I saw confidence in his eyes when I headed towards the tower.

Calmly, I ascended it. I didn't stop at the one-meter springboard. I didn't even stop at the three-meter spring-board. By the time I stopped climbing I was at the ten-meter platform, looking down at the little shrunken figures of my coach, Sue, and the rest of the divers. The air felt the best up here. Nowhere else did I feel so alive and refreshed.

Diving was part of my life, part of my every breath. Whenever I closed my eyes I could almost feel the rush of the wind on my face, the exhilarating adrenaline pumping through my blood as I fell towards the depths of water. I loved diving more than anything in my life, more than even myself. I could train day and night, climbing and falling more than a hundred times on some days, and I was never tired of it. This was my passion – it was what I lived for, and with every dive it took me to greater heights.

I had promised myself that my next goal would be the Olympics next year. Our coach had already been selecting athletes to represent our school, and it had to be the crème de la crème who upheld its name and prestige at the inter-national games. For the chance to leave a mark of glory in Olympic diving history and to realize my dream, I had worked doubly hard to perfect the few hardest maneuvers and familiarize myself with the ten-meter dive, the longest dive of all.

Here I was, ten meters above ground, ready to prove to the coach that I would be the right choice. Looking down, I was surprised that the water looked so blue and inviting today. I gave a thumbs-up to the coach, then grinned in Sue's direction. She waved back enthusiastically.

The coach blew his whistle. I stretched my arms to the sky and smiled confidently. Feeling sudden strength flow into my legs, I sprang from the diving board.

Up I went, and for a moment I was stationary at the highest point of my spring; then I was rushing towards the water. Wind rippled past my face, and my ears hummed softly. I wrapped my arms around my body to perform a seven-hundred-and-twenty-degree, mid-air twist.

That was when I felt it. A sharp pain in my chest, as if my lungs were constricting. I could not breathe. My eyes blurred and my head pounded. My eyes rolled into their sockets as I gasped in vain for air. The pain in my chest was excruciating. I could not control my body anymore. My arms flailed like a rag doll's as I fell through the air. Someone somewhere was screaming a horrifying scream, but I could barely hear it. Down I went, further and further from the diving board until, with a sudden freezing coldness, I hit the water and light was no more.

◄═►

"Oh god, oh god, oh god, thank *goodness* you have come to, Lydia," Sue rattled off between sobs. "Oh god, oh god, oh god . . ." And she started to cry all over again.

The first thing I noticed when I opened my eyes, even before I heard Sue's voice, was how bright the room was. I was in a place so white, and everything around me was so clean, that light reflected off every gleaming surface. Then I

realized I was in a hospital ward. Though I had been uncon-
scious, I remembered every detail of the incident before I
fainted.

There was a knock on the door, and it slid open smoothly.
The coach came in, followed closely by some other students,
all wearing grim faces. The scene was almost comical; for all
they knew I might have been well enough to get up right
away and go back to diving school.

When the doctor came in, I sat up and was so eager to
hear him say I could be discharged.

Except that was not what he had come to say.

I listened to what he was saying, in his seemingly far-
away voice.

For a moment I thought he was joking. I laughed, told
the others to pull off their melancholy faces, and waited for
someone to scream "April Fools" in delight.

No one did.

<⇒>

It was the dead of the night. Sue and the others had been
avoiding me since yesterday at the ward, so I sat alone at
the poolside, a pathetic wreck of an athlete. My eyes were
swollen from crying, my heart was aching, and my mind
was unclear. The words of the doctor still reverberated in my
head, like a mad halo I couldn't get rid of. He had told me
that the series of convulsions and spasms I had experienced
was barotrauma. According to him, this normally happened
to deep-sea divers during their ascent or descent, but due
to the weakness of my lungs caused by over-exertion, any
sudden change in altitude, even if it was only a short distance, would trigger a pressure difference that deformed the
tissues in my lungs permanently . . .

Meaning, I was never to dive again.

And in that one moment, my whole world had crashed.

<⇒>

I blinked into the blinding sunset and took a deep breath.

Although the coach had wanted me to rest for a few days more before moving about, I had convinced him that I was all right and that I wanted to enjoy the breeze of the sea for a while.

Sitting in silence, I let the salt-and-pepper wind brush against my cheeks. It was a soft, silky kind of touch, not as harsh as the feeling when I dived.

Something warm stirred in my heart. Up here, high on the rocky cliff by the raging sea, I felt once again the same delight as when I was on the springboards and diving boards for the first time back in diving school. I felt the same enthusiasm and love for diving as when I first attended diving lessons. A wave of nostalgia swept over me, and I was suddenly overcome by the urge to cry.

Beneath me, the sea water looked so different from the pool back at school. It was a deeper blue, darker and more mysterious, more massive and majestic. It teased me to jump into its swirling currents.

It beckoned to me, calling out to me in soft, glittery voices.

I was ready to make one last dive.

Everyone Hates the Grays
By Chad Stambaugh
⟨⇒⟩

CHAD STAMBAUGH is a retired U.S. Marine. Chad is the Co-Founder of 11th Hour Paranormal Research Society. He's currently working on a Bachelor's in English Literature. His never-ending pursuit of education has led him to also pursue becoming a Demonologist to help those in need of help understanding the realm of the paranormal. Chad lives in Fresno, CA, with his wife Crissy. He has three children and three grandchildren. Here's what he wrote about "Everyone Hates the Grays":

> This short story started out as a school project: to write about racial prejudice that still unfortunately exists in the world today. Instead of having society set up the way it is today, I put a twist to it, so that the Germans and the Axis powers had won World War II instead of the allies. This gave me an avenue to show racism in a new but critical way.

⟨⇒⟩

Look, my life didn't change the day I met Randy; it's not quite that dramatic. My politics and my religious views are the same today as they were yesterday. Honestly, I have to say if I were faced with the same situation again, I probably would not have done the same thing. I'm not one of those politically correct bleeding hearts who have their token Gray friends, and pretend they are the same as everyone else. My sister Amanda and my brother Gunter are positive I was just feeling guilty. You see, when I was younger I went to school with a "Gray" and spent a good portion of my day tormenting him. I never thought about that until yesterday, so I couldn't have felt guilt about some f*ing Gray whose name I don't even remember. Furthermore, for all I know the guy wasn't even a Gray at all. They're normal when they're younger. You know, they all have blue eyes until they're about fourteen or so. We just call people Gray because it's the worst thing a person can be, and if you really want to cut someone down, that's what you call them. Everyone does it. I felt no guilt.

I was working the third shift at the hospital that night. I was outside smoking because we don't get much business in here this late, and blowing up rubber gloves is only fun if you have helium. Helium is always fun. The ambulance drove up, and the police piled out first, with the EMTs wheeling Randy on a bed behind them, strapped in and sedated. They're always sedated when they come here.

Randy was different from the other Grays they bring in. First off, he looked like everybody else. Although he was wearing sunglasses in the middle of the night, they didn't seem odd on him. It almost seemed a bit cool. He was tall, and handsome, not that I noticed. He wore clothes that I probably would wear during my off hours, and when he yelled at them to let him go, he didn't have that Gray lisp they all seem to have. The cops asked me where to take him, so I put out my cigarette and gestured for them to follow.

They don't seek out the Grays anymore. I mean, this is the Fourth Reich, after all. In fact, if the Grays keep to themselves, and don't attract attention, no one would ever think of making them undergo the treatment. Obviously Randy didn't lie low. Most likely he was caught driving. Driving has been a hot issue lately. The Grays say they should be given government licenses to drive. I'm not sure where I stand on this issue, but I'm not sure you can say you have the right to do something when you've never had the right to do it in the first place. I mean, Grays have never been allowed to drive. They mostly have poor vision and don't see things the way we do. They're weak and don't react quickly enough. Religious scholars say they see with the eyes of Satan, and the more they see, the more evil has a chance to spread. I'm not sure I buy that, but I certainly respect their right to believe it.

When I glanced at his arrest record I found out I was correct. He was caught driving . . . at night, and for the fifth time. One hundred years ago any Gray breaking the law would have been shot on the spot, but we live in more humane times. Dyeing the eyes blue or brown is the standard treatment for gray eyes these days. It does cause blindness in almost every case, but it's better than having those gray eyes staring at you all the time. That's just creepy. And, truth be told, it's better for them not to be different. No one likes the Grays.

In my own defense, I was bored, and he was carrying a pack; a good pack, not this government crap you get issued every week. He offered me one, and who was I to turn it down? I usually wouldn't share a smoke with a Gray, but it was Christmas Eve, and I was Jonesing big time for one. At first I was nervous, but I was curious to see what a Gray looked like up close. Even under sedation he didn't make it easy. His gaze would fixate on things other than my eyes, and unless I looked down and around, I wouldn't have seen that his eyes were gray and not blue. It made perfect sense to me that he would have gone this long without being discovered. He was an expert at deception. A liar by birth, no doubt.

The fact that he never looked directly at me, and his lids were always covering his eyes, gave the impression that he was standoffish, or rude. I realized, however, that he was doing this even under sedation, so it was probably a trait he developed as a kid, to appear more like everyone else.

The smoke made his eyes less detectable. I asked him how he learned to do that, and he just looked at me. He looked straight at me, not over to the left or right, but right into my eyes. I had never seen gray eyes look straight at me before. It was an eerie feeling, but also one that didn't scare me, for some reason. It was creepy though.

I asked him casually why he wasn't with his family this Christmas Eve, and he said he had no family. After he told his parents that his eyes were turning from blue to gray, they never treated him the same again. He said holidays got harder and harder for him because no one would ever look at him. They figured that if they pretended his gray eyes didn't exist, everything was fine. I asked him if he could blame them, and he said nothing. I asked him if he had anyone else to spend the holidays with, and he said that he did not.

It was illegal for the Grays to be with anyone but other Grays, and he found that most Grays hated themselves . . . thus other Grays. It was a vicious circle, but one that made maintaining relationships haphazard. That made sense to me. He asked if he could put his sunglasses back on, and I said sure. I could see his eyes open wider under the shade, and it occurred to me that perhaps his eyes were more sensitive to light than my own. And he wasn't really hiding his eyes from me, but rather from the light.

I told him he must be relieved that now that his eyes would be dyed he could go home, and his family would finally look him in those eyes.

"What's the difference?" he said. He told me that the reality of being a Gray is that no one truly looks past it. No one will ever see anything but the gray. His life would always be about that. If I dyed his eyes blue tonight, he'd be blind, and his life would never change. He still would never see anyone looking into his eyes, and his whole life would still be about being Gray. The only thing that would change was what other people saw, not what he was.

In our society we ruled out genetic disorders as excuses for defects a long time ago. The official word from the government was that although gray eyes were a deviation from our superior genetic makeup, they were merely a shade of blue. Gray-eyed people are like this because they never developed the ability to play sports, which stimulates the eyes muscles and causes the blue pigment to dominate the gray. They also very rarely look up, thus not enabling the sunlight to penetrate their irises. I believe that. I really do.

I let Randy go that night, not because the spirit of Christmas moved, but because I needed to. I didn't feel guilty, like my brother and sister said. I didn't let him go because I thought he'd go out into the night and find someone to look into his eyes, because he wouldn't have. I let him go because I did look into his eyes. I took a good long look and I saw him. So few people are honest with themselves, and the Grays are truthful because Gray is their truth. They wear their entire existence in the color of their eyes. It determines everything they do and say. It determines who they are and what they become. Every aspect of their lives will come down to the gray. And when I looked into his eyes, I saw my fears, and I saw a reflection of who I was. I can't explain it, but even while I was seeing all that, I was only seeing gray; maybe when you're gray that's all there is.

I didn't do Randy any favors anyways. He will be caught again and eventually his eyes will be dyed. I did nothing but give him more time to spend looking at a world that doesn't want to look back at him. Who'd want that? He shouldn't have chosen to be that way.

Kindness is a Four-Letter Word
By Charis Reich
⟷

CHARIS REICH is a 24-year-old Bachelor of Theology graduate. She lives in Red Deer, AB, Canada and works for a local event center while at the same time getting her writing career off the ground. Ever since she could put words together she has been writing and creating stories, and at a young age decided that choosing just one career was too difficult, settling on writing because, in a sense, it was an opportunity to experience all of them. Her particular favorite area of creativity is spoken word (also known as "slam") poetry. Here's what she wrote about "Kindness is a Four-Letter Word":

> I have spent the last few years volunteering at various homeless shelters and soup kitchens and have experienced some of the kindest people in some of the most heartbreaking situations. Not enough of them get their story told, and in this world of technology and self-focused responsibility they are often treated with disrespect, or overlooked entirely. Though Melanie is a completely fictional character, her relationship with those who pass her by on the street embodies the daily experience of so many actual people. My grandpa, who passed away a few years ago, was also an accidental inspiration for this piece. I included some of my favorite anecdotes about him and hope that through this story he will be remembered as one of the kindest, most loving, spunky people

you could ever meet. After all, life is more about those you meet than the things you accomplish, and not enough of us seem to grasp that concept. I am constantly amazed that something as small as going out of your way and saying "hello" to someone can have a life-changing effect. "Kindness is a Four-Letter Word" demonstrates how sharing genuine love with someone else – anyone else – will ultimately change your life, and it gives an example of the beauty that comes from even the most unlikely of friendships. May you find unlikely friendships along your own life's journey.

They call me the collector. I collect thoughts and experiences. I collect the memories of others that were never my own. I have enough memory fragments to piece together a hundred lives, but none of them quite fit me. At one point, I may have been a father, I may have fought in a war, I may have traveled to the moon. I don't remember. I remember a thousand other things that may or may not have happened, but I don't identify myself with any of them. Rather, I almost experience them passively, as if I witness each one taking place in front of me. Out the window and across the field, I see a battle taking place. Men, nothing but helmets and fear huddled in trenches, barbed wire and a rain storm surrounding them, explosions like drums coming in from above. Have I seen this before? Was I there? Can I fit into the scene playing out in front of me somehow? The trouble is, at the end of it all, I don't even remember who I am.

"What do you think he's staring at?" one attending nurse, Linda, asked the other.

"You've got me," Sam replied, peering out the window at the sunny evening outside. There was nothing but clear skies and green, lush, rolling fields expanding into the distance. No remnant of any battlefield that captured Gerard's imagination was visible to the two nurses. He continued his internal dialogue, not realizing they were there.

"Well, let's get him to bed. Mr. Smallinder? Gerry? Are you ready for bed?"

Gerard, who had been expressionless and lost in his own thoughts, suddenly returned to reality. His dull eyes brightened momentarily at the recognition of company – such a sparse treat these days – until the word "bed" sank in. Reluctantly nodding, he stood up to get ready. Both nurses offered their help, a habit from working with so many physically and mentally deteriorating patients, but he shrugged them off, capably walking to the bathroom.

He carried himself strongly, standing upright, with no hunch to give away his seventy-two years of life experience, his tree-like legs not showing even the slightest tremor of weakness. Every day he would go outside and walk the perimeter, fence to fence, corner to corner, and often engage in intense, though somewhat scattered, conversations with himself – or, rather, those that occupied his head. Once a month, when each of the patients was given a treat from the nurses, he would sit by the biggest tree in the small back yard and eat Skittles, his favorite candy. Life always made more sense when he was eating Skittles. Sometimes he would try to offer them to Reginald, the squirrel that lived in the tree, but after accepting them once, Reginald knew better now, and would only look on in skepticism from a distance.

After dinner in the dining room, he would wander back to his room and sit in his chair, lost in thought for hours, reliving events that he may or may not have experienced himself. Some were memories pulled from the news, or events he had heard about from others, and some were works of complete fiction – movies he had seen and books he had read. One moment he would be defusing a bomb and the next the bomb would turn into a small child he was carrying in his arms. Tears would escape his eyes as he experienced (or relived) the beauty of that intimate moment, but before he knew it, he would be travelling the world in a hot air balloon, then landing on the moon – convinced of its reality, until a nurse brought him back to the present and helped him get ready for bed.

When he emerged from the bathroom, having changed out of his beige slacks and blue golf shirt into a dark grey pair of sweats and a faded, oversized Snoopy shirt, the nurses gave him his evening medication, and tucked him in for sleep. They always made sure he had a full glass of water and a fluffed pillow before gently closing the door as they left. Gerard had many fond memories of this place, of the nurses making sure he got a second bowl of pudding when it was offered for dessert, or keeping him company on days when it was too wet or cold for him to take his walk outside. When other guests had visitors, the nurses would do their best to include Gerry in group activities, in hopes of distracting him from his own lack of company.

Though most nurses would consider him crazy, suffering with Posttraumatic Stress Disorder, which was believed to have later caused his schizophrenia, Gerard was actually one of the nicest patients in the facility. He did not talk often (except in the yard, where he thought no one was around to hear him), most likely due to his inability to distinguish reality from a dream, but, when he did, he was always polite and well-mannered, making sure to give all his attention to those he was talking to. The nurses especially lit up when they saw him, going out of their way to say hi and ask him about his day. When he disappeared one day, the entire compound was concerned, confused, and terribly sad to lose such a bright addition to the facility.

It happened by accident, actually.

‹⇔›

Despite her colorful outfit, she seemed to blend in with her surroundings better than a ninja on a moonless night. Clothed in a purple corduroy skirt, with mismatched yellow-orange and blue-green patterned socks, she was noticeable from a mile away – if you were paying attention, anyway. Add the bright pink, polka-dotted shirt and orange safety vest, and your eyes would ache just to look at her; and yet it was as if she wasn't even there. Standing defiantly, and slightly comically, in slippers much too large for her seven-year-old feet, she attempted to interact with the oblivious crowd meandering up and down the main street by jingling a chipped green mug that contained a nickel, a quarter, and nothing else.

Even though she was small and had only a bleak existence, she had lofty, hope-filled dreams. One day, she hoped to live in a room the size of a castle, with a purple door, purple drapes, and purple bedspread, covered in beautiful purple flowers. That was her idea of heaven. Purple was her favorite color, and if she was going to have impossible dreams, she might as well like the colors in them. Dreaming like this was her only escape from the reality that life had been unkind to her. Her current situation was nothing to dream of. An old potato sack stuffed with shredded newspaper for insulation, and a crate to help shelter her from the wind and elements, in the back alley a couple blocks down, were as close to a bedroom as she could get. Sometimes she would find discarded flowers in the trash from the flower shop located on that block and would put them in her chipped mug and water and take care of them until they withered and died. The longest a flower had lasted was three days, but she didn't mind. There was always another one to love, another one to focus on and distract her from her current existence. These flowers were the only things she loved. They were her only company.

If the mismatched clothes and chipped mug weren't a sufficient clue, one look at her uncombed, ratty, strawberry-blond hair was enough to demonstrate that she had no home and no one to take care of her. And yet strangers continued to walk around her, so caught up in their own worlds that they didn't even have time to acknowledge her existence, except maybe to drop spare change in her cup and continue on their way. Caring about yourself in this world is hard enough, without having to care about someone else too. Especially someone who isn't your responsibility.

A graying woman in white gloves, a fur shawl, and a blue dress stopped for a moment to search her purse for a suitable coin. She barely glanced at the young girl before dropping the coin in the mug and walking away, smiling at herself for a job well done. She didn't even hear the young girl say "thank you" before her mind had wandered back to more important matters.

Clumsily, the young girl brushed a clump of hair from her face with her small fingers, then decided she might as well get comfortable. It was barely noon, and she had nothing but free time to enjoy the sunshine and watch people. Leaning against a warm brick wall, she sat on the grass and set her mug beside her. People-watching was her favorite – it was her opportunity to pay attention to those who paid so little attention to her.

A man walked by, engrossed in his phone conversation. She listened as he explained to his wife how, yet again, he would be home late tonight due to work, and "could she please keep some food warmed on the stove for him," before he walked completely out of earshot.

A real home . . . I wonder what it's like to have one of those? she pondered silently for a moment, before spotting another couple across the street, holding hands and talking. As they stepped into a coffee shop, the man held open the door in the most gentlemanly fashion, and the woman daintily planted a kiss on his lips. At that moment a group of teenagers walked directly in front of the little girl, and she didn't see the man stop for a moment and glance across the street before joining his wife inside. The teenagers were giggling about how smoothly they had skipped school without being caught, and discussing what movie they should go to. "Do you think we could get into an 18A movie?" one asked, followed by laughter from the others. "If we can skip school, we can do anything," responded another, and they continued down the street.

A man walking a dog passed the teenagers in the opposite direction, followed by a woman pushing a double stroller – twins. A few more walked by glued to their phones or other electronic devices.

Closing her eyes, the girl with the mismatched socks and clown slippers decided to simply listen to the commotion for a moment. There was something beautiful and sad about the noise of hustle and bustle. In some ways, it made her feel less alone in this scary, dark world. On the other hand, nobody could see her, so maybe she was even more alone than she thought.

Clink. Someone had dropped money in her mug. Assuming they had already continued walking past, she didn't bother to open her eyes. Besides, the sun felt warmer when her eyes were closed.

"Excuse me," came a male's voice, close to her. A pause, waiting for a response. The girl's ears perked up. *I wonder who he's talking to.*

"Excuse me, little girl," came the voice again, and she opened her eyes abruptly as a hand touched her shoulder, fear crossing her face as she took in the eyes staring back at her.

A couple in their thirties were crouched in front of her. The man held a crisply wrapped sandwich in his hand. Glancing at it, she saw a sticker on the front. She recognized the colors and funny symbols from the coffee shop across the street. Often she had watched people emerge from that place with white cups and lids, all with matching pictures and symbols. One time she found a discarded cup in the trash and spent an hour studying it, hoping the lines and marks that made up the different symbols would suddenly make sense to her. Eventually she gave up and threw it back in the trash.

She recognized the couple. They had walked into the coffee shop minutes before, holding hands and kissing. What were they doing here now?

"We're sorry," began the man. "We didn't mean to startle you. We just thought you might be hungry. What's your name?"

"Melanie," she whispered shyly, glancing at the sandwich again, tummy grumbling. It had been days since her last real meal – scraps from the garbage across the alley didn't count.

"Hi, Melanie. I'm Tony, and this is my wife, Claire. Would you like this sandwich? It has turkey, tomatoes, pickles, lettuce, and three different types of cheese." Tony and Claire eased onto the grass beside Melanie and handed her the sandwich.

Immediately Melanie began to unwrap it, inspecting it and smelling it. "What's the yellow stuff?" she asked, still skeptical of the smiling couple watching her intently.

"That's called mustard," Tony explained. "Some people don't like it because it's a bit tangy, but it's my favorite part of a sandwich." He winked at his wife, and they both smiled.

"That's true!" his wife piped up. "He puts it on everything."

Melanie watched Claire as she talked, fascinated by the honey-sweet sound of her voice. It was kind and genuine. *I bet she's a wonderful mother,* thought Melanie. *I wonder if my mother had a voice like that.*

"Honey," Claire continued, glancing at the watch on her dainty, slender wrist, "I'm sorry, but we have to go or we're going to be late."

"Oh. You're right. Our appointment." Tony turned to Melanie. "It was wonderful to meet you, Melanie. I hope we see you again. Enjoy your sandwich." He pulled a ten-dollar bill from his pocket, placing it in her cup alongside the coin he had given to instigate their meeting.

"Thank you." Melanie smiled and, for a moment, her whole face lit up, eyes sparkling. She watched as the couple continued on their way, hand in hand down the street, talking and laughing as they went. Once they were gone, she finished unwrapping the sandwich and sank her teeth into it, enjoying even the mustard she had been so unsure about. She decided she liked this kind man who had brought her food. If he liked mustard, then she would too.

<=>

Gerard wasn't intending to leave and he had nowhere to go. He liked everyone there and, most days, simply needed some fresh air to get away from the voices that were a part of him. Generally he and his voices got along well enough, but today they were arguing. The disagreement centered around the best way to defuse a bomb. He knew better than they did – from his own memory, or perhaps someone else's (he wasn't quite sure) – but they weren't backing down, convinced that simply plunging the entire device in water was better than cutting some measly red wire. *What if it's the wrong wire and causes the whole thing to blow up*, they argued with him.

He wandered outside, taking his well-worn path through the grass and following it mindlessly, caught up in the discussion going on inside his head. When he reached the new hole in the fence, he didn't even realize it was there. Walking right through it, he explained to himself why his idea was the better one. "I would know!" he announced confidently, even though there was no living soul to hear him. "I used to be in a bomb squad, back in the war." Did he? In all honesty, he had no idea if he did, but he hoped it would be enough to quiet them down for a moment.

To the west of the home there was nothing but a farmer's house and rolling fields. This was where Gerry's bedroom window faced, where he enjoyed watching the sun go down in the evenings, and where he sometimes projected battle scenes from deep inside his memory. To the north, however, where the fence had been cut open, nothing but a thin line of trees separated the patients at the home from the rest of the city of which they were a part.

Gerard had entered the city and wandered down three or four streets before realizing he didn't quite know where he was. Fear gripped him and his pulse quickened. Turning around, he realized he didn't recognize his surroundings at all. A young man walked past him and smiled in his direction. Unsure how to react, and not trusting his own instincts based on previous experiences, Gerry looked down and intently studied his feet until the young man was a safe distance away. After a moment ,he looked around again, hoping that something would look familiar. When it didn't, he sat down, overwhelmed by his own emotions.

After a moment, a sense of excitement ignited him. He was so sure that he would die in that home before getting the chance to have another real life experience, and now he had that chance. The fear dissipated as he looked around again, no longer viewing this street as an unknown territory, but instead seeing a new adventure waiting to happen. For a moment he wavered between emotions, fear and excitement fighting for precedence.

In the end, adventure won out, pushing fear to the back of his mind, but not so far that he didn't flinch the first couple of times a vehicle passed him. *Vehicles look much funnier than I remember them looking.* There was an odds and ends store here, a flower shop there, a music store around the corner. He had no money but that didn't matter. He could smell the city air, listen to the commotion, and watch the lives of others happening around him in real time. Reality was solidifying around him, no haze or quick change of events taking place to make him question it. He breathed in again, a rush of excitement filling his chest. All this noise and distraction also helped to silence the voices, and for the first time in years he felt as if he was entirely in his right mind. Memories and reality were beginning to separate, and details about his own life were beginning to surface.

A face came to mind. A beautiful woman. Dark hair, olive eyes, a smile so bright it would make the sun jealous. It took a moment to remember who she was: the love of his life. He took a deep breath, chest expanding, heart full of excitement overflowing into his lungs and throat. Another moment, another memory. She was no longer here. She had passed away many years ago. Having been the only one who visited him, the only one who had cared about him, she had taken all of that care with her when she died. His chest tightened and sadness gripped him. The real world wasn't the great place he remembered. His breathing quickened as he allowed fear to take over again for a moment. Maybe being out in the real world wasn't such a good idea.

"Hi there." A small, sweet voice pulled him out of his head and back into the present. Glancing around and seeing the dense traffic and extensive number of pedestrians, he deduced he must be downtown. The voice had come from a small girl who was watching him intently.

"Well, hello to you too," he responded as pleasantly as he could muster, as he glimpsed an army of German soldiers in the distance, marching to a consistent beat and disappearing behind a building. He looked away only to suddenly see the same beautiful woman from his memory moments before sitting on a bench, holding a young child. He blinked twice. She was no longer there, and he glanced back at the young girl in front of him, closing his eyes again for a moment to see if she would disappear too. Though he intended to keep walking, one look at her outfit stopped him in his tracks.

Chipped mug, purple corduroy skirt, slippers at least ten sizes too big, and a rats nest where her hair should be. She couldn't be more than seven or eight years old, and she lived on the streets? She begged for money, and all these people just walked right past as if she didn't exist? Things sure had changed since the last time he'd been out in the world. What was society coming to?

"What's your name?" Melanie asked, in the curious and confident manner that only seven-year-olds can master. She wasn't sure why she'd stopped him, but he had looked so sad that she couldn't help herself. There was something warm about him. Something that made her want to hug him or crawl into his lap and have him read her a bedtime story. She had a very keen sense about people.

"I'm Gerard, but I think most people call me Gerry." He awkwardly continued, "And what's your name?"

"Melanie," she said brightly. "Are you okay? You looked sad."

Truly, there is nothing more heartwarming than a child showing genuine concern for another human being, and Gerard's heart melted for this poor but delightful girl in front of him. "Well, you see, Melanie," – he crouched down so that he was eye level with her – "I lost someone very dear to me, and I was just thinking about how much I missed her."

"Oh. I understand. I lost someone too." A pause. "It's hard being lonely, isn't it?" she mused, sharing the wisdom and depth hiding behind her young age, and then added, "Would you like to sit with me a while?"

"Well . . ." He was caught off guard for a moment. "I would be absolutely delighted." After all, he had nowhere else to be, and this girl needed a friend. And, if he was going to be honest with himself, he needed a friend more – at least, one that existed entirely separate from himself and did not take up living space within his very full and crowded head.

Such an odd pair they were, a gray-haired old man and a bubbly, colorful, mismatched young girl. They began to ask each other questions, Melanie being sure to mention that her favorite color was purple, and Gerry sharing that his favorite food was Skittles.

"I've never had those before, but my favorite food is mustard." Melanie thought back to the sandwich from earlier, and the man who had demonstrated kindness to her. She still had half the sandwich, along with the ten-dollar bill, wrapped up and well hidden inside her potato sack bed. No human or rodent would take them from her.

"Mustard? That's an interesting choice," Gerry quipped, a smile deepening the wrinkles covering his face. This girl really was unique.

They continued their conversation for the rest of the afternoon, neither paying attention to the changing position of the sun, or the cool air that began to settle in. And, for the first time in a very long time, they both felt as if someone could truly see them.

<=>

The couple drove home from their appointment, still reeling from the day's news. They had decided to make a day of it, parking in the suburbs and wandering through some of the different trinket shops downtown before their meeting. They stopped at their favorite coffee shop and Tony, being the loving husband he was, decided they should buy a sandwich for the poor little girl in mismatched clothes.

"It's the least we can do," he convinced Claire, though she needed no convincing. His kindness to others was one of the reasons she had fallen in love with Tony in the first place. A little kindness could go a long way, and she had a huge heart for children. This made the day's news even more devastating.

Before the appointment, they had enjoyed a wonderful afternoon together, reminiscing about their teenage years, and the wonderful memories they had as a dating couple, and Tony finally getting the courage to pop the question. He had just turned twenty and was working with his dad's logging company. That was over fourteen years ago. It wasn't much, but it was enough money to support Claire as she went back to school. Her mother passed away five years into their marriage, and her father (if he was even still alive) was completely out of the picture, so in many ways Tony was the only family she had. And she had been so looking forward to starting their own family one day.

Only now, she no longer had anything to look forward to. The tests had come back conclusive that day. Claire was barren. Several other options were brought up to the couple, all of them excessively costly and time-consuming.

The drive home was quiet, Tony glancing at Claire and back at the road repeatedly. At one point he put his hand on her knee, rubbing it gently. Claire huffed in the passenger seat, heart heavy and head hot. Her gut was twisted in anguish, but no tears escaped her eyes. She didn't return Tony's concerned looks, but calmed down at his gentle touch on her knee. When they pulled into the driveway, Claire jumped out before the car came to a complete stop. She wanted to get away from this awful situation, wanted to go back to earlier today when everything was fine, when they were laughing and reminiscing and sharing life together. Once inside, she ran up the stairs, hoping that if she could go to bed she could wake up and find out that this was a horrible dream. She passed the baby's room, door open, fresh green paint on the walls, and nothing except a crib on the floor. *The power of positive thinking, right?* she thought bitterly, and turned to leave.

Tony stood behind her, taking everything in. They'd been so hopeful, and had so many conversations about what life would be like with kids. Claire recalled the excitement she'd felt when they finally found out she was pregnant, followed by the complete devastation and betrayal of miscarrying the child months later.

For a long time no words were said as they held each other's gaze. Then Tony silently pulled Claire in, wrapping his arms around her and resting his chin on her head. She knew she was in a safe place and, for the first time since hearing the news, she finally let the tears go, sobbing loudly onto Tony's shoulder as he held her close and kissed her forehead. Her screams pierced his heart, and he silently cried with her as they mourned the loss of a child they would never have.

"I love you," he whispered after she had calmed down. "And we will make it through this."

"It's not fair," she responded angrily, pulling her head away from Tony and looking up at him. "There are girls like Melanie, abandoned in the streets, living a pathetic excuse for a life because of choices her parents made, parents that didn't deserve to have children in the first place, and you and I, the most deserving parents I know, can't have a child. How does that happen?" A pause. "What kind of person allows their child to live that kind of life?"

"I don't know, love."

Claire stayed in bed for the next three days, and Tony called in sick for both of them at work so that she didn't have to be alone. She barely ate or slept, and their bedroom was quickly covered in tissues and tissue boxes. Tony, not knowing what else to do, sat and held her, making meals and taking care of her when she needed it. Neither spoke much, silence filling their house as they cried. As much as Tony wanted to be there for his wife, he needed to grieve as well, so for a few days they shut themselves off from the world in order to deal with their own pain together. From here on it would just be the two of them, and they were thankful they had each other.

<=>

Melanie was standing on the street, eyes fixed on two individuals a couple of blocks down. Her mother had said she would be right back, and had told Melanie to stay put as she went to talk to some strange man. He looked as if he hadn't showered in days, a grease shine reflecting off his hair and forehead as he glanced around nervously. His left eye twitched periodically, and his hands fidgeted with a small elastic band while the two talked. Even though it was far away, Melanie could still see the exchange that took place. Money into his hands, a clear glass bottle of some kind along with a needle into hers. Medicine, maybe? Was she sick? It reminded Melanie of the needle a doctor had used on her once a couple of years ago when she was sick.

A loud bang from behind startled her, and she frantically turned, alone and terrified. No one else registered the same fear or reaction, and she heard a voice say "just a car backfiring," as a couple wandered past. Looking back to where her mom had been moments before, she saw only empty space. No greasy man, no mom, no medicine.

"Mommy!" she yelled. "Mommy, wait for me!" Tears blurred her vision as she ran toward where her mom had been. Nobody was there. All she saw were legs surrounding her, attached to bodies, cold and unemotional. "Mommy!" Melanie screamed again as she sat on the curb, hoping someone would hear her.

"Mommy!" Jerking awake, Melanie sat up, and looked across the alley at Gerry. He had been watching her thrash about, heard her calling for her mother, and was about to go over to her when she woke herself up. He crossed the alleyway to sit beside her, and leaned his back against the brick wall.

After their delightful conversation that afternoon, and discovering that Gerry had nowhere to sleep that evening, Melanie had offered him some prime real estate in her back alley, saying he could stay there as long as he liked. She appreciated the company, so when she woke up from her nightmare and saw him there, her heart began to steady. Gerry, recognizing the tension and fear that a bad dream could cause, gently placed his arm around her, pulling her close. She was safe now. When her heart had slowed completely and her tense muscles began to relax, she told him what happened. As Gerry listened he thought about his past, how life had brought him to his current position. In an effort to distract Melanie from her own horrific experiences, he began to share his own story.

"When we were first married, before we had our daughter, my wife would take the neighborhood kids to the mall after school. Many of them had parents who worked all the time, and she didn't like that so many were home alone at such young ages. There were maybe six or seven that would go with her on a regular basis. Sometimes I liked to embarrass her. She would be wandering around the mall with these kids, and I would walk up behind her, start dragging my leg, and speak out of only the left side of my mouth.

"'Hey, lady!' I would shout, 'Are all these kids yours?'

"And she wouldn't know how to respond. She hated when I did that, but I would laugh and laugh about it – about being the crazy man who would harass her and her kids. Eventually she laughed about it too, but in the moment she was too embarrassed.

"Then I actually started to go crazy. Post-traumatic Stress Disorder, they call it. By the time we had our own child, my mental stability was starting to deteriorate. She couldn't trust me to be alone with the child because of my unpredictability, and that made me angry.

"We started fighting more, and I think, deep down, she was really scared of me. Scared that I would fly off the handle. I was taking medication, but it wasn't doing its job. By the time our daughter was sixteen, I was prone to angry fits. Constant frustration, built up for the last twenty years, had taken its toll. During one of those fits I hit my daughter, and that was the last time I saw her. It was soon after that incident that I was admitted into a home for my safety and the safety of others. My wife would visit me, but my daughter never did. She never forgave me. A few years later, my wife passed on. Car accident. Then no one came to visit me anymore . . ." He trailed off, wiping a tear from his eye.

After a moment, he snapped back into the present. "But! I learned something while I was there. I learned that the only way to deal with pain is to find something to laugh about!"

He continued, "I remember this one time, when my wife and I were first dating. I was at work, just about to take a break for lunch. My wife brought a picnic basket, suggesting we walk to the park together and enjoy the lovely weather outside. As we were walking, she says to me, 'Honey, is there a specific reason you're wearing two different shoes?'

"I looked down at my feet and couldn't help but laugh. Who walks out of their house wearing two different shoes without noticing it? One was a light brown and the other black. You would have to be blind not to notice the difference. But do you want to know the funniest part? One had laces, and the other was slip-on. How had I not noticed that I'd only tied up one shoe when I left for work? They were completely different styles, and I hadn't noticed all day! We had a good laugh about that for a long time." He chuckled again, reliving the memory, when life was still sweet and simple.

Melanie giggled, imagining the moment with him. Her laughter was light, a welcome distraction from the fear that had consumed her minutes before. She laughed in spite of herself, a bubbly, uncontrollable giggle that rose up from her gut. A sense of peace and calm washed over her as she studied her new companion. She'd never had someone to look out for her before – at the age of seven she had been on her own entirely. A gift, that's what he was, and she suddenly felt safe. She recalled the many nights waking up to a bad dream and hiding in the dark until the sun came up, too scared of what the alley may hold to even make her way to the safety of the main street. Now, safety was here, in this man who silently held her close. Breathing in, she reveled in this new experience, hoping that if she held her breath long enough, it would never go away.

"Gerry," she said, after a long, thoughtful pause, "do you want to be my papa?"

Tears in his eyes, Gerard studied the disheveled little girl who had just opened her heart to him. Her eyes seemed to get bigger as she stared at him, hopeful and terrified of his answer. What if he didn't want her, just like her mom hadn't wanted her? He was the only person she had opened her heart to in a long time, he realized, as he said, "Melanie, I would *love* to be your papa."

It was the start of a friendship, as they settled down and fell back to sleep, tucked in behind a garbage bin, a patched and tattered quilt covering Melanie and an old potato sack on top of Gerard. His feet and legs stuck out the bottom, the cool air of the evening penetrating his socks and shoes, but it didn't matter, because for the first time in a really long time, he was part of a family.

<=>

If he hadn't decided to pick up flowers for Claire on his way home from work, he probably wouldn't have seen her again, but even though neither expected it, they would become fast friends before long.

"Hi, Mr. Mustard!" Melanie had forgotten his name, but remembered his favorite food.

She was dressed in the same spunky clothing, hair clumsily blowing in the breeze. Her eyes were somehow more full of life than the last time he'd seen her. With a smile, she transformed the entire street into something beautiful.

"Hello there, Princess Melanie," Tony responded lightly.

"Where are you going?" she queried, putting emphasis on the *you* the way a mother might when making sure her child wasn't up to something suspicious.

"Well, I was just about to pick up some flowers for my wife." And then, as if struck with a great idea: "Would you like to tag along? It's just down the street."

Pausing to think about it for a second, Melanie nodded and turned to an older gentleman sitting against a wall, handing him her chipped mug. He was muttering quietly to himself, half in this world and half in another. Squatting in front of him and peering into his face, Melanie explained, "Gerry, I'll be right back, okay?" Hearing his name seemed to shake the man out of his stupor, and a smile came to his face as his eyes registered Melanie's.

"You stay safe now, you hear?" he responded gruffly as he peered up at the strange, well-dressed man taking his only friend away. He seemed friendly enough, but looks could be deceiving. *What does he want with my Melanie?*

Their eyes locked for a moment, Tony's widening in surprise at the realization that Melanie was not alone out here, then narrowing as he studied the dirty clothes and messy gray hair of the old man.

As they wandered to the flower shop, Tony asked Melanie about her friend. "That's my papa. Okay, he's not really my papa. He just kind of showed up the other day, and he seemed really lost. We became friends and I found out that he had no idea where his home was anymore. He's so kind, but also sad. I think he has a lot of regrets. He's my papa now," she explained in a disjointed manner.

As they entered the shop she stopped, mouth agape, staring at all the different colors and types of flowers surrounding her.

"What's your favorite kind of flower, Melanie?" Tony asked, realizing he wasn't going to get any more information about the strange old man. *She's not your child. You don't know anything about her. Maybe she doesn't need saving,* he had to remind himself as they browsed the shop.

"All of them!" she exclaimed, taking in the store. Her eyes swallowed flower after flower as she attempted to convert every colorful piece of nature into a concrete image in her mind. If she had her way, all these flowers would be included on the walls of the castle-sized purple room in her dreams. She had stopped breathing, so focused was she on the rainbow of colors surrounding her. Finally, her eyes rested on a bouquet of crocuses, and she released the air that had been tightening her chest for the last half-minute. Each flower was shaped like a wine glass, dark purple at the tip of each petal, lightening slightly closer to the centre, and ending in a sturdy, dark green stem. A bright yellow centre stood up defiantly in the middle of each family of petals, tall and straight for all to see. She had never seen anything quite like them, and began to study the petals intently.

"That one. That one's my favorite," she decided finally, not taking her eyes off it for a second.

Tony, enjoying Melanie's first experience in a flower shop, went to the counter. "Can I have a dozen red roses, and that bouquet of crocuses?"

As they left the store he handed her the flowers she had picked. Pulling her aside, he crouched down to her eye level. "These flowers are very precious and need to be taken care of. Can you do that for me?" She nodded. "Good. Did you know that you're as precious as this flower? I need you to do something for me."

Melanie was beaming. She'd taken care of dying flowers for a day or two in the past, but never had she been given the opportunity to take care of healthy ones that were her very own! She stared intently back at Tony, waiting for him to continue.

"I need you to take care of yourself. The streets are really dangerous, and you are a special girl. I don't want you to get hurt. Okay? Can you do that for me?"

"Okay. I'll do my best. Thank you for the flowers, Mr. Mustard!" As bright as a light bulb, Melanie was glowing the entire way back, excited to share her new gift with Papa.

Gerry watched them come up the sidewalk, grinning at each other and talking as they walked. That grin, it seemed so familiar to him, and there was something about the sparkle in Tony's eyes that brought on a sense of déjà vu. Then again, some days everyone seemed familiar to Gerry. He dismissed the thought and smiled at Melanie as she bounded up to him excitedly, talking non-stop about her beautiful flowers, showing him and calling them her crickets. Before Tony continued on his way he corrected her. "They're actually called crocuses."

"Oh, right! Crocuses," she directed to Gerry, then turned back to Tony. "Thank you so much, Mr. Mustard."

"You can call me Tony, Melanie. And you're so welcome. Don't forget what I said, okay?" He began to make his way down the street.

"I won't," she called after him, watching as he turned the corner, bouquet of roses firmly clutched in his left hand.

Tony. I'm sure that name is familiar. But why? Gerry politely smiled, nodding at appropriate times as Melanie continued to gush about her beautiful new flowers. The way she was raving, one might think she had never been given a real gift before.

Tony continued on his way, musing about the simplicity of going out of one's way to show kindness to someone. *I guess you never know how much of a difference it might make.*

⬍

Over the past few weeks, the two had become such close friends that Gerard couldn't imagine himself without Melanie anymore. Between the few dollars she would make in her little mug and the amount of uneaten food that people would throw out, they were eating just enough to survive. When one of them woke from a bad dream, the other would be there to offer comfort or a laugh. Gerard's voices had almost entirely gone away, Melanie was such a soothing, peaceful presence for him; and no longer being confined to the four walls of his old home also helped. He no longer needed the voices to keep him company. He had family.

Gerard tried to remember back to the days of the home, when he would spend most of his time wandering and muttering incoherently to himself, then sit by a window, take some medication, and go to bed. His routine was his life, nothing but a boring, lonely existence. It wasn't that the home was such a bad place, just very routine. And routine can become boring and hopeless, if one is stuck in the rut for too long. Actually, the only thing he missed was the monthly gift of Skittles he would receive from the nurses. Now that he thought about it, he could really go for some Skittles right now.

"Whatcha thinkin' about?" Melanie asked, interrupting his thoughts and bounding up to him in the back alley. She was excited to tell him about her larger-than-usual financial haul of the day.

"Oh, nothing much, just Skittles." He smiled. He couldn't help but smile around this bundle of energy and joy that wouldn't let the world get her down.

Melanie looked puzzled for a moment before remembering. "Oh yeah! Those candy things, right?" A pause as she glanced into her mug. "Well, Papa, I think you're going to like my news. For some reason, people are generous today, and if they're as good as you say they are, I'd love to try some Skittles."

Walking down the street, they seemed an odd pair. Because of his current sleeping arrangement, Gerry was stiffer than before, and was starting to develop a limp in his left leg. *Now that I think of it, I miss my bed too.* He was also still dressed in the plain beige slacks, blue golf shirt, and brown sports jacket he had on when he left the home, though they were significantly dirtier and more wrinkled now.

They'd gone to the gas station a few days earlier, Gerry taking his time in the single bathroom to wash his hair with hand soap. He also removed most of his clothes, attempting to wash his torso, legs, and feet with sink water. It was the closest he could get to a real shower. After emerging, Melanie took her turn, clumsily attempting to do the same thing, though missing several areas of dirt, and ignoring her hair altogether. When she thought she was done and presented herself to Gerry, he walked her back to the bathroom and helped wash her hair before they returned to their home on the street. Since then, much of the dirt had returned, and it would soon be time for another sink bath.

They embarked on their adventure, back to the gas station. Melanie held his hand the whole way, almost letting go twice when she got too excited and forgot that he wasn't as young and energetic as she was. Altogether, they had acquired just over twelve dollars. They had enough money to buy two over-priced and dried-out packaged sandwiches, with just enough left for a dessert treat. Compared to how they had been eating, this was going to be a feast!

They were perusing the candy bars when the two young men in oversized hoodies came in. Melanie didn't notice, and Gerry chose to pay little attention to them, instead focusing on describing the different types of chocolate bars to her. Having never had any of them before, she didn't even know where to start.

"This one is tiny individual squares attached together. Each one is covered in chocolate and filled with a sweet caramel inside. And that one has nuts and caramel and chocolate all mixed in together." As Melanie asked about different chocolate bars, he continued, "This one over here has a long, cookie-like inside with chocolate on the outside, and it breaks into four different pieces. And this one . . ." He continued for a while as Melanie absorbed the information and the options in front of her. This may be her only chance to experience something as sweet as this, and she didn't want to be disappointed with her choice.

Eventually she settled on a bag of chocolate-covered peanuts. They weren't quite a chocolate bar, but she figured they were just as good. If she was careful with them, they could last a lot longer than a chocolate bar ever could. She wanted to make sure she enjoyed them forever.

Arms full of merchandise, they made their way to the counter. Melanie was struggling to hold her sandwich, chocolate, and about twelve mustard packets she intended to take home with her in her small hands. Dropping two packets, she crouched down to pick them up, causing her to drop a third one. Setting everything down, she took a moment to readjust so that she could hold everything in her hands before standing back up.

Gerard, however, had stopped entirely, drinking in the gun, the hooded boys, and the terrified young female cashier behind the counter. The momentary pause was noticed by the young man with the gun, and he turned toward the old man and young girl. Gerry pushed Melanie out of the line of fire before she had a chance to realize what was happening. "Stay down. Hide." Her precarious pile of mustard packets flew everywhere.

Too many events occurred at once not to cause some chaos. First, the cashier took the distraction by the old man as an opportunity to press the silent alarm, not realizing that the other hooded figure was still keeping an eye on her. He extended his arm to grab his friend and alert him. At the same time, Melanie rolled into a magazine rack, having lost her balance when pushed by Gerry, causing not only her packets of mustard to fly everywhere, but also the rack full of magazines, making a loud crash when it hit the floor. The young hood with the gun flinched at the exact moment his friend grabbed his arm to warn him of the alarm. It was too much commotion for the young man and, as he flinched, his finger jerked back, a loud bang echoing throughout the small gas station.

<=>

"I've been painting." Claire still hadn't gone back to work. She wasn't ready to face her coworkers, and was distracting herself by finding projects to do at home. Painting was her newest distraction.

"Painting what?" Tony asked, positioning his phone between his ear and shoulder as he dug into his pocket for keys.

"The . . . room." *The baby's room.* "We still had some primer left over, and I found some purple paint stashed away in the garage. I don't remember where it came from, but I figure it's as good a color as any."

Tony listened to his wife's voice, noting how hollow it sounded, and not just because of the tinny cellular device relaying it to him. He was glad she was up and about, though – he hated going to work and leaving her there to lie in bed all day. "That sounds great, honey. I can't wait to see it when I get home."

"Tony," Claire interrupted abruptly, changing topics completely. "I've been thinking a lot about my dad. I think . . . I think it's time to get in contact with him again. I've had a lot of time to think . . . And I think it's time I forgive him. He's the only family I have left, apart from you. And maybe the only family I ever will have."

"Are you sure? I mean, that's a big step." Tony's concern was evident.

A pregnant pause. "Yes. I'm sure. I'll tell you more when you get home."

"Okay." He wasn't sure what else to say, so he added, "I love you. I'm just walking to the car now."

"I love you too."

The difficulty with working in a downtown office was that parking was often a struggle, and Tony had learned to leave his car around the corner from a gas station a few blocks down. As inconvenient as it was to walk the extra few blocks every day, it was still easier than finding a closer parking spot. He noticed Melanie and her elderly friend – *Papa Gerry, was it?* – staring longingly at a row of chocolate bars inside the gas station as he walked past. Melanie was positively glowing with all the options, and he smiled, remembering the flower shop incident the week before. *What a precious, precious girl.*

Tony was almost at his car when the gunshot went off. It sounded as though it came from the direction of the gas station, where an innocent girl may have been caught in the crosshairs. He took off towards the building, calling the police on the way. As soon as he entered the store, a frazzled, emotional Melanie ran up to him, refusing to leave his side. She had some blood on her hands, but it didn't look as if she was hurt. *Thank God.*

The boys had taken off on foot immediately after the shot was fired. On their way out, they'd stopped just long enough to stuff their pockets with as much loot as they could carry. Frozen in place, the cashier stood behind the counter, staring vacantly into the distance, a phone held loosely in her hand. Gerry was on the floor. He had managed to drag himself to the counter to lean against it. Bloody red hands covering his stomach, eyes wide and face ashen, he was in desperate need of medical attention. A red bull's eye expanded around his fingers as his jacket continued to soak up the blood oozing from the bullet wound.

Unzipping Gerry's jacket and lifting his shirt, Tony did his best to get a good look at the extent of the damage. Melanie cowered behind him, silent tears trailing down her cheeks, unable to witness her new best friend in such a traumatic state. He applied as much pressure as he could, and the paramedics and police were there within minutes, ready to take over. As the paramedics lifted Gerry onto the stretcher, his jacket shifted and a piece of paper drifted to the ground. It was a picture of a young girl, no more than fifteen. Tony reached down and picked up the picture, intending to return it, but pausing to take a second glance when he realized the girl in the picture was quite familiar to him. He studied it for a moment longer, beginning to connect some dots. Looking at Gerry, who was now being carried out to the ambulance, Tony began, "Is this . . . ?"

"Yes," Gerry answered as Tony trailed off. "That's my daughter." Then, after a moment, he added, "Claire," before the ambulance doors closed behind him.

⬅⇒➤

When they got to the hospital, Gerry was awake again, hooked up to a dozen machines, waiting to be taken into surgery. Tony had brought Melanie with him, not feeling right about leaving her by herself after such a traumatic experience. *The streets won't miss her anyway.* They couldn't go without his wife, though, so he had called Claire.

"Hello? Tony? Where have you been? You were supposed to be home over an hour ago!"

"Claire! I think I found your father."

"What do you mean? He's not lost. He's living in a home, remember?"

"Well, actually he's not anymore." A pause. "He's hurt though. I'm coming home to take you to the hospital to see him."

Claire phoned the home that her mom had visited so many times before passing away. After getting the runaround from one of the nurses on reception who couldn't give information out to anyone but family, Claire explained her situation, sharing as many personal details as she could remember about her mother and father. Finally, she was transferred to one of the head nurses. "I'm sorry about all the delays, miss. Your mother requested not to have you on your father's emergency contact list, so when he went missing we had no one to contact since your mother has passed away."

She ended the call just in time for Tony to arrive home. Claire hadn't changed out of her painting clothes, and paint flecks decorated her hair and skin. Tony rushed her out the door, explaining everything as thoroughly as he could. Spotting a very traumatized and teary-eyed Melanie in the back seat, Claire sat beside her and comforted her. She held Melanie close as the young girl wept openly on her shoulder.

Melanie was scared to be on her own again. The last time she'd experienced anything close to gunfire, she had lost her mom, and now she was losing her new papa, the only person who'd come close to being family since. She clung to Claire, unwilling to loosen her grip.

When they made it to Gerry's room, Melanie was the first to go in, running up to the bed, shouting "Papa!" and giving him the tightest hug she could. Thankfully, she was a small, feeble child, and couldn't squeeze hard enough to cause anymore discomfort to Gerry's already damaged body. His face lit up when he saw her, moisture filling his eyes as he looked at this puffy-eyed little girl.

"I'm so sorry, Melanie. I'm sorry you had to experience all of that and we didn't even get to enjoy our dinner. What an awful thing for you to experience."

"Oh, Papa!" she exclaimed, her eyes misting up. "I thought you were gone. I thought I would be all alone on the street again. I need you, Papa. I need you." Snot and tears soaked her shirtsleeves from wiping her face. Gerry hadn't felt needed by anyone in a very long time.

Outside the room, Tony was helping Claire mentally prepare for a reunion with her father. Their last encounter had not ended well. Gerry had slapped Claire across the face and she had left the room crying, refusing to see him after that. It was not the first time things had been violent between them. He had been unpredictable and angry often, and that moment was the end for Claire, who could not handle the stress of having an unpredictable, dangerous father. Remembering that moment still brought tears to her eyes and tightness to her stomach. She was incredibly unsure about meeting him again.

He didn't know she was out there, but she could hear Melanie telling him stories and him responding with laughter and love. She remembered when she was a child and would laugh that way with him. He would prop her up on his knee and tell her all sorts of stories, some true, some not. When he talked about an octopus's tentacles, he would tickle her, and would vibrate his knee for her when talking about a cowboy riding through a forest. Those were the good times, before his episodes started. Before he became an unsafe place for a small child. She smiled for a moment. They had been such a close family, and as she recalled the deterioration that followed, her smile faded.

"I'm not ready for this, Tony." Her heart was beating fast and her eyes were fighting back tears.

"I know, love. I know." He pulled her close. "I don't mean to add pressure, but this may be your last chance."

Tony and Claire made their way into Gerry's hospital room, Tony first, Claire peeking out from behind him. When Gerry spotted her, his eyes widened in surprise, then tears filled them as he watched her intently, no longer paying any attention to the animated child beside him. He didn't know what to expect from this beautiful little girl of his, who had now turned into a beautiful, paint-flecked woman. He realized why he recognized Tony. When the two had gotten married, Gerry's wife had gone to the wedding, bringing back pictures to look at afterwards. Claire had deemed it best to not invite him. His unpredictability and anger could have ruined a happy, love-filled day.

After a long silence, Gerry managed to find his voice. "Claire . . ." He searched her face. All he could see was sadness as her puffy red eyes misted over again.

She didn't know what to say, frozen to the spot and staring at the feeble man she'd been so afraid of. He looked different now, aged by life experience as much as time passing, pale due to loss of blood, and no longer exuding the demeanor of power and control she remembered him fighting for so often. Life had worn him out since her mom had passed away, and she knew he wasn't the same man who had hurt her all those years ago.

"Hi, Dad . . ." she faltered, her voice catching, and a fresh wave of tears filled her eyes.

Dad. She called me "Dad." Gerry's eyes were overcome with moisture also when he heard the sweet voice he never thought he would hear again.

Tony, sensing their need for privacy, walked over and grabbed Melanie's hand, pulling her out of the room and suggesting they go on an exploring adventure in the hospital.

"Dad," Claire began again, biting her lip anxiously.

"Claire," Gerry started at the same moment. There was a pause as both waited for the other to continue. After a moment, Gerry broke the silence. "Claire, I love you. You are the most precious daughter a father could ask for, and I have spent so much time regretting my past actions. I am sorry. I'm sorry I took my anger out on you so often, and caused such an unhealthy home environment for you. I'm sorry –" his voice cracked, and he cleared his throat before continuing. "I'm sorry for the fear I caused you, and for not telling you more how much I loved you and how proud of you I was. I know this doesn't undo the years of damage I caused, but I do hope that one day you can forgive this old, mentally sick man."

"Oh, Dad," she whispered, voice cracking and tears flowing freely. She moved forward and sat on his bed. Looking into his eyes, she answered, "I forgive you," and instinctively grabbed his hand. No words were spoken as they looked at each other, held hands, and cried.

They sat that way for a while, until Gerry broke the silence. "I love you, my little girl."

"I love you too, Dad." Claire leaned in and gave him a hug, kissing him on his cheek before pulling away again. Both felt lighter, no longer holding on to the regret and bitterness that had defined each for so long. Gerry began to share some of the experiences he'd had with Melanie over the past few weeks, what a delight she was, and how much she reminded him of Claire at a young age; and Claire told Gerry that she couldn't have kids, tears leaking from her eyes again for a moment.

After a few minutes Tony and Melanie returned, Melanie triumphantly holding a bag of Skittles in her hand. "Look what we found, Papa!" The bag was opened already, and as she spoke, Melanie's tongue flashed a blue-greenish color. "They're just as good as you said they were! Do you want some?"

As Gerry was about to respond, a nurse walked in to take him down for surgery. The bullet had penetrated both his stomach and liver. His insides were mangled, and though he was putting on a brave face, he was in excruciating pain, medication only numbing it slightly. All three took a moment with Gerry to give him a hug and some encouragement. Claire kissed him on the forehead and whispered, "I love you, Dad," her tears spilling onto his face.

Melanie slipped a Skittle into his hand "just in case you get hungry in there," and added, "I love you, Papa. Thanks for taking such good care of me."

Tony added, "It was nice to meet you," to his goodbye, shaking Gerry's hand awkwardly.

"You take good care of my girls until I get better, okay? They are so precious and need to be treated that way."

"I will. I promise." Tony put one arm around Claire and the other around Melanie, pulling them close as Gerry was wheeled away for surgery.

<=>

I, the thought collector, have collected many thoughts, sharing them as I go. I have managed to give a young girl hope, bring laughter, and restore a relationship I never thought would be restored. My collection is complete, for now . . . Gerry's internal dialogue continued as he breathed into the mask, drifting off into a blissful sleep. For the first time in years he had no dreams, no regrets. No voices were fighting for his attention, no other visions filling his memory. He was at peace – completely content as he fell asleep for the last time.

The World Was an Island
By Abigail Anderson
⟨⇒⟩

ABIGAIL ANDERSON is a sophomore at Danville High School in Kentucky, where she is an A+ student. She wrote her first story in third grade and has always enjoyed writing. She will attend the creative writing summer program at Brown University in June 2015 and hopes it will give her a glimpse of what intensive writing is like. She enjoys reading, competing in her high school speech tournaments, and playing with her dog Allie. Here's what she wrote about "The World Was an Island":

> Before I wrote this story, I was in a creative slump. I could only see what everyone else was writing about, and it seemed like all the good ideas were taken. Stories on love or family or other ideas were swirling in my mind, and I couldn't seem to grasp my own. I cannot remember the exact day, but all of a sudden, I thought, "What about a story that has none of usual factors?" There is no beautiful romance, no death-defying action, no suave hero, nothing of the sort. I wanted it to be different from what people normally read; I wanted to shake things up a bit, and I hope this story does the job.

<=>

Day 5,843

It is the anniversary of the day I was born. That's what my lifegiver says.

She says it like any other thing.

I see how it is because nothing changes this day. The sea still moves. The light still shines. The sand beneath my small feet is still hot, burning against my skin. I don't move my feet, though. The burning is welcome.

It doesn't bother me. It never did.

I view the sea, taking it in as I do every morning. It stretches far and wide, but my lifegiver told me that this is all there is. It is only us, and we are all that's here. I feel lucky that we were chosen, that we are all that's in this span of sea and land. She says it's only this circle of land, and as far as my eye can see of water.

I sigh, the sight as beautiful as ever.

I hear the distant chimes, and I know my lifegiver is calling for me. I take one last glance at the water, sparkling under the light, but before I can run back to my lifegiver, something moves in the sky. I look up, shielding my eyes from the light. A bird swoops down, and I am scared. But it only lands softly in front of me with a piece of fabric tied to its back.

I move slowly to the object because I fear the bird. It just stares at me, so I unwrap. I then run back because the bird is too close to the sea. The sea is dangerous; my lifegiver says it can sweep you away, forever floating into an uncertain fate.

I avoid the poisonous waters.

At that moment, I hear the chimes a second time. I can't let them ring a third; then I deserve a punishment. I set down the fabric with my fingertips and tell the bird to stay. It just cocks its head. I turn and run.

The sand turns to a dirt trail, and the trees enclose me. The fruit droops down from the branches, and animals scurry out of the way. I pass the great rock wall where I keep track of the days. Little tick marks. I already put one down for today.

When I finally get to the clearing, I am only a bit out of breath. My lifegiver stands on the porch of our hut by the chimes, smiling. She holds out her hands to me, and I only walk up to her, careful not to touch her. I may not initiate physical contact. I learned that the hard way in my younger days.

She leads me into the hut to the straw table. On it are two plates, one with bananas and berries and the other with a rabbit, skinned and cooked. It smells delicious and I waste no time consuming it. She doesn't touch her food.

I pick up my cup, which is the shell of a coconut with a makeshift lid of bamboo. A straw pokes through, and I wrap my mouth around it and suck. It tastes bitter and gross as it slides down my throat. My stomach tightens as it enters my system, but I also feel better. Calmer. Lifegiver never lets me get through my meal without it. She sits and stares at me with a smile on her face.

When I am finished, I take up my plate and cup and set them on the counter; we have nothing to wash them with. She gets up too, and speaks to me for the second time that day.

"Did you like your meal?"

I respond simply.

"Yes."

Her smile melts away. She moves up to me and hits me hard across the face. I don't wince or move. I just take it because this happens at least once a day. Her fingernails cut into my cheek. I am now bleeding.

She says, "Do not respond without 'Lifegiver.'"

"I am sorry, Lifegiver."

She envelops me in a hug, and I quickly accept it. She whispers in my ear.

"You know that I care for you."

I say what is okay. "Yes, Lifegiver."

She releases me and tells me to get moving. I leave the hut, and I hear her bang around behind me. It is Lifegiver's alone time. I will be back soon.

I head back to the shore where the fabric is. I study it closely. It's blank, but then I realize it is folded. I open it, confused.

Hello. Just write your name, where you are, and give it to the pigeon; he knows where to find me.

I sit and stare at the fabric. Who wrote this? There is only Lifegiver and the animals on the island.

The pigeon (I suppose this is the pigeon) steps closer to me. I set down the fabric and run to my wall.

Where I keep the days marked.

I consider going to my lifegiver, but I don't. This is a secret.

My lifegiver says she has none.

I now have one.

Oh, my lifegiver. Of course! I have no secret. This is just a funny joke.

I pick up the charcoal and run back, relieved to see that the pigeon and fabric are still there. I consider how to start and finally settle on this.

I am Saoirse. I am on my circle of land surrounded by the poison-ous waters.

I step toward the bird cautiously. It waits. I bend down and take the string, tying the fabric back onto the bird. As soon as I finish, I jump back. It takes off, soaring over the waters.

I sit on the sand until the chimes ring for night sleep. I head back to the hut.

My lifegiver says, "End of day."

"End of day."

We share our secret together.

And I fall asleep on the ground, dreaming of wings over the sea.

⟺

Day 5,844

When I wake, it is early. My lifegiver is out gathering food for our meal.

Gathering. How clever.

I remember the pigeon.

I run out and mark my wall.

I head back to the shore, and there is the pigeon. I untie the fabric and take it in my hands.

Hello, Saoirse. Thank you. What do you mean by "circle of land"? Do you live on an island?

Once more, I am confused. Is what I am on called an island? I turn around as if the answer will present itself.

My lifegiver is so clever.

I had brought my charcoal with me and etch my words.

I suppose it is an island. But sea is the only other thing. You're very clever, Lifegiver.

Satisfied, I tie the fabric on the pigeon. It sails away.

The day goes as usual.

I eat.

I drink.

I get hurt.

I get hugged.

I give alone time.

I go back.

I sleep.

I dream.

I wait.

⟵=⟶

Day 5,845

I mark.

The pigeon is waiting.

I take the fabric.

Lifegiver? There is more besides the island you're on. Tell me; what do you drink?

A drink. I drink my drink and that is it.

This is not funny anymore.

There is no world.

There is only us.

This is not funny anymore, Lifegiver. Please do not muddle my mind with this trick. There is only us on our circle of land. You give me that vile drink, the one where I feel calm. That's it.

The pigeon leaves.

I feel nothing.

⟵=⟶

Day 5,846

Another tick.

Do not drink that drink anymore. Find a way to get around it. There is more. It extends beyond your sea. And I am in it.

But Lifegiver is here.

How can this be?

I don't believe it, and I don't trust you.

It leaves.

I head to the hut.

"Lifegiver, why are you tricking me?"

She turns, confused.

"What?"

"Why are you sending me the messages on the fabric, Lifegiver?"

She demands I go get the fabric.

I say I cannot.

She pushes me down. She kicks me until my stomach feels missing and I bleed all over. She says that the fabric must be my imagination. There is nothing else besides us now.

"Is there a world, Lifegiver?"

She punches me. It hurts worse than usual. My nose bleeds. I don't stanch the flow. I deserve the pain for such a question.

"Sit."

I sit.

She tells me a story.

There once was a woman. She lived in the world. It was big. There were so many other beings. They were all nasty and they judged her. They judged her because her mind was better than theirs. It saw the world clearly.

She got on this big boat to get away from the beings. Just for a little while.

On the boat, a man talked to her. He didn't judge her. He told her she was beautiful, which is pleasing to look at.

She thought he was nice.

He led her to his room, and he tried to hurt her. She tried to leave, but she couldn't. He hurt her bad. He did bad stuff to her.

The boat sank a day later because of "mechanical failures." The woman was the only survivor.

She washed up on a deserted circle of land.

She believed she had been saved.

She began a new life.

The man had given her the seed of a different new life. She cultivated it.

It was me.

My lifegiver ceases talking, and I just stare.

"Thank you for the story, Lifegiver."

"The world is gone now. It ended on that boat."

I nod.

Did it?

"The people who were in the world were bad. Do not go see the bottle again. I forbid it."

I nod again, but I have this strange feeling in my gut. It's new.

It's different.

It's electrifying.

⬅⇒➤

Day 5,847

Another tick.

It feels laborious.

Lifegiver told me to stay in the hut while she went out, but as soon as she left, I snuck to the shore. I don't know why I did it. I felt compelled, moved towards the fabric and the mysterious writer.

It was as though it was calling to me.

Please do it, but still act as though you are drinking it. I am not your enemy. I am your friend. Believe it.

I think.

What is a friend?

Lifegiver said that the people were bad, but that is past tense.

I am present.

And so is my writer.

Friend.

It sounds good.

But do I believe?

I will trust you because you say you are a friend. I do not know what it means, but I like its sound. I am on this island. This is all I know.

This joke is very long.

I am not sure this is a joke anymore.

<=>

Day 5,848

Another one.

Lifegiver gives me the drink, and she stares at me as usual.

She's squinting at me and not smiling.

Does she know I escaped yesterday?

Do I drink?

What do I do?

I look at the window behind her and yell, "Lifegiver, there is a bird on the window!"

She gets up and goes to the window; she doesn't like birds and their freedom of flight.

There is a hole in the boards beneath my chair; I dump the drink in it, sad to see it go.

Lifegiver comes back and hits me for there not being any bird.

I give her the empty cup.

She smiles, and her eyes are once again open wide.

"You drank that fast."

"Yes, Lifegiver."

And she turns away.

I sigh.

<=>

Day 5,849

One.

I get rid of the drink once more.

I am proud of you. I will help you. You will not be in pain much longer.

Pain?

This morning was the first morning when I did not wake up with a calming sensation.

I feel anxious.

On edge.

Cut off.

Not calm.

My throat feels dry, and I cannot make it moist anymore.

The island is very clear now.

And I do not like it.

What have you done to me? Why is my island so strange? What is happening?

The light is warm, but I shiver.

⬌

Day 5,850

A small line carved in hard stone is a powerful thing.

I am letting you see clearly. I am helping you. Drink the liquid. There will be more when I see you.

My vision is most certainly clear. I see the package that came with the note. It is a little glass bowl hanging by rope that the bird carried. It is a clear liquid, so clear and pure. I take a tentative sip and almost drop it. How amazing it is! The slightest drop soothes my throat, and I do not hesitate to gulp down the rest.

I close my eyes and appreciate the feeling it gives me.

The colors are less vivid, the light is less glaring, Life-giver is seemingly scarier, and I am more nervous.

I can hardly talk, but it is not because of my throat.

I'm not sure why.

I'm not sure all that is here is normal.

When you see me?

So far, my friend has not lied to me.

And I do not believe he will.

Lifegiver asks me why I cannot speak well.

I say I am sick.
It is not a lie.
I am sick.
But of what?
That is what consumes me.

⟵⇒⟶

Day 5,851

So many marks.
Do you know how to build a boat?
Like the one Lifegiver was on?
I drink the clear liquid as I answer.
No.
I heard my lifegiver moan in her sleep. She said the word "alone."
I never ask what it means.
But I think I feel it.

⟵⇒⟶

Day 5,852

These marks seem overbearing.
Here is how you build a boat.
Sip.
The mysterious person wrote how to build a boat.
So that is what I do. The knowledge just came to me, caressing my brain and enveloping me. I work expertly and quickly, not knowing how I build the boat when I do not know what a boat is.
I finish.
It is a wooden square with a wooden pole sticking from it. I used the thick leaves on the island as a "sail."
What do I do now?

Drink.
What do I do?
The island seems smaller every day.
It feels as if the water is getting closer.

<=>

Day 5,853

The marks are dark and numerous.
Put it on the water. The water is not poisonous. I promise. Put it on the water and leave your land.
And go where?
If you are not my lifegiver, then who are you?
I do not drink the clear liquid.
The waters still don't touch me.

<=>

Day 5,854

Tick.
Time grows near, and my body is being turned inside out once more.
All you need to know is that I am saving you. Do you trust me?
Saving?
I thought I was safe.
I do.
But maybe I am not.

<=>

Day 5,855

The marks count my days.
Then sail.

It is a strange word.
I have never had to use it.
But I can guess what it means.
Sail away from the land.
Like the pigeon.
This boat is my wings.
And I will be gone.
Away from the island.
Away from the world.
No. Not the world.
I will. I will set to sea for your land. Look for me. Promise?
Unknown territory may not always be bad.
Sometimes, the bad is right under you.

<=>

Day 5,856

The last tick.
I successfully acted like usual.
I said goodbye for the last time.
I see that she is not okay in the head.
And I am sorry.
She did keep a secret.
I did as well, Lifegiver.
I promise. Do not worry, brave one; the water will carry you right
to me. I will see you on the other side.
The other side.
A rush courses through me.
I think it is excitement.
Lifegiver occasionally feels a burst of excitement.
It's one of her many moods.
I touch the water with my foot, and it feels . . . nice. Cool.
Different.
The water was never poisoned.
The land was.

I do not believe it is her fault.

I get on my boat with the pigeon.

I hear the chimes ring for the first time.

I push off.

It is scary at first, but it becomes natural.

I hear the chimes a second time.

The sea. It is so great.

It is so beautiful.

This is the world.

I am headed to the other side.

The chimes ring a third time, and I do not worry.

This is no longer my world.

I don't know where I am going, but I know that I will get there.

And the island fades to a dot behind me as I journey to a new life.

As I journey to a greater beyond.

I smile.

My world was an island.

Only now do I realize that it is not.

There is more to this life than me.

There is more.

I was okay with not believing it because it was bliss.

But now that the truth is here, I am even more okay.

I may have belonged to Lifegiver once, but I do no longer.

And I look ahead to my endless, open sea.

⟨⇔⟩

I lose count of time, but all of a sudden I think I do not need it.

There is a brilliant light, far brighter than the sun.

I hear something, something lovely and tinkling that can only have one name: laughter.

And I see pure white, clean and wholesome.

The white blocks out all but one thing.

A figure.

A black, shadowy figure.

I am scared at first, but I soon realize I need not be.

This is my mysterious person.

My savior.

The blackness is only because of the white light, and I'm sure that if I saw my hero without the light, he would exude his own light, one that is selfless, helpful, and kind.

There is a strange pull in the left side of my chest. I grab it and wince, thinking I am sick.

A voice comes, powerful and eternal. I cannot help but listen.

It is the figure.

"That is your heart, child. Listen to it, and let it be your guide."

I look down, and I feel something.

Thump-thump-thump.

It is my heart.

And I only now notice its beautiful beat.

I take the figure's advice and let it be my guide.

Your heart should never rule your head.

I do not know where that strange thought came from.

My head whispers to me to go back to the island.

To leave the man.

The light.

The greater beyond.

But I do not listen to it, because sometimes your head is wrong.

And I feel with all my soul and power and even my mind that this is one of those times.

I stretch out my hand, wanting to feel the palm of the one who gave me new life.

My heart starts to speed up, and it beats with ferocity; beats so fast and hard that I have trouble breathing.

My face is wet, and my eyes are sweating. It confuses me.

Then, a surge rips through my heart. I clutch it, thinking that it is the end, that the man brought me here to die and rot in the waters and that it was all a lie lie lie.

But it isn't.

The surge is a tidal wave of emotion. I feel pain in my body, guilt from leaving Lifegiver, sadness from abandoning the island, and . . . something else.

A word comes to my mind, just one more word. It gives me the hope to press on. It gives me the courage to continue. It gives me strength to reach for what's ahead.

Love.

In my existence, I have never thought that word. I didn't know that word existed. It was strange hearing it, not having known it before, but I know it now. The man has brought it out in me.

He has brought out love.

And I am so . . . happy.

Another strange word and emotion.

I ask one final question before my greater beyond comes closer. The question is brought on from my newfound love, and I can hear the fragility and weakness of my voice.

I have always been tough.

But love does some amazing things.

"My lifegiver . . . will you save her, too? Please?"

I then regret my question.

I expect him to hit me. I expect abuse, hateful words, stinging me and knocking me down until I feel like nothing.

I expect a stupid question like mine to be put back in its proper place.

I expect him to change his mind and send me back, back to the island of loneliness and fear and captivity.

I do not expect what actually happens.

The man smiles, and it is not one of mockery. It is of kindness, understanding, and most of all, love.

We only just met and he loves me.

My eyes sweat again.

No, not sweat.

Tears.

I am crying.

These emotions run through me forcefully. And I get the strangest thought that without all of what I am feeling, I wouldn't even be human.

Was I human back on the island?

I do not know nor care. What is in the past has already gone, and all I will do now is look forward at what's to come.

With my whole human heart.

He answers with a timeless and comforting voice. Patient. Strong.

"You do not have to fear. Your lifegiver will be safe. I will get her, and you will never fear again."

I now fear nothing because this man has saved me. He brought me out of the dark and into the light. He is my now and forever.

And I can't wait for what lies before me.

And as he reaches to me, I know in that moment that I am

truly
absolutely
finally
free

Pieces of Art
By Kimberly Bunker
⟨⇒⟩

KIMBERLY BUNKER graduated from the University of Notre Dame with a B.A. in Music and St. Joseph's College with an MFA in Creative Writing. Her stories have appeared in *Glimmer Train*, *PANK Magazine*, the *Used Furniture Review*, and other magazines. When she's not working on her novel, she is practicing aerial silks or perfecting a new vegan recipe. Here's what she wrote about "Pieces of Art":

> Senior year of college, I took a class in charcoal, and I loved it. I was good at it, or at least good at replicating existing images. I couldn't imagine a new image and draw it, but I could copy a picture pretty accurately. Then I started to get lazy – I remember I was drawing from a photo of a mountain and, instead of giving sufficient time to a section of grass in one corner, I scraped over the whole square with the side of the chalk, thinking that would do it. It didn't. It looked terrible, and I tried to salvage it with more broad strokes and erasing, but eventually I resigned myself to the fact that I had to draw each blade of grass individually.

> That was one of "those" moments. When I went outside next and saw each blade of grass – which wasn't even that much on a city street – I was struck. What if even God didn't gloss over details? Had he created every blade of grass separately? What would that mean?

The idea hung around unattended for a while. I knew I wanted to use it somehow in a short story, but I was intimidated; I didn't know what to do with it. I think that's when ideas percolate, though. Stories tend to strike at the right moment. One day, I read "Darker Shadows" by Austin Ratner, and I loved how he treated the phenomenon of shadows getting darker – he just put it in the first sentence. That took away some of the fear. So I sat down to write, and "Pieces of Art" – an early version, anyway – wrote itself.

I.

One morning, Rae Ann van der Belt woke on her living room couch, bleary-eyed and disoriented, from a dream in which God was not a priest but an artist.

At first she didn't move; her face remained smushed into the crevice where the throw pillow met the cushion, one arm buried in that crevice and the other hanging limp over the couch's edge. If she moved, she feared, the fragile dream-wisps she still retained would slip through her mind, like water through a sieve, and be gone.

This is what she dreamt: she was walking through a market with her son Gregory, and he wanted to see the model trains. It was a hot day on a dusty street. A faceless crowd surrounded them on all sides, so they couldn't move much faster than a shuffle. Somehow, amidst all this, it was clear, it was in the fabric of the dreamscape, though not in a way she could put her finger on, that God was an artist, and that her understanding of him as something akin to a priest, displeased and frowning down from the sky, was all wrong.

Gregory was too small to see anything but people's legs, so she held his hand and walked behind him. As they approached the model-train maker's booth, the crowd parted, and she saw all the detail, the colors, the care and planning the train maker had put into each piece, and she was overwhelmed with awe.

The trains were at eye level for Gregory, so he could only see those on the table's edge, closest to him. He picked out the one he wanted, a blue caboose with silver trim. Fifteen dollars, said the vendor, and that was when she realized she had no money. She stood behind her son, checking her pockets for cash, feeling frantic because she knew she had none. She kept trying to tell the vendor that they would go get money and come back. It was imperative, the way dream-missions often are, that he understand that she would come back. But he was a vendor, and she didn't have any money, so he didn't believe her.

<⇒>

II.

The television was still blaring from last night. Rae Ann felt shaken and not at all rested. Why had she dreamt she had a son named Gregory?

Jeremy was standing over her in school clothes, brown hair flopping over his face and shirt untucked, backpack hanging open behind him like a gaping mouth. She rubbed her eyes. "It will rain," said the television.

"Ma," he said. The tip of his guitar case loomed over the back of the couch, obscuring her view of him. "Ma. I missed the bus. I need a ride to school."

She stood and rubbed her eyes, letting her surroundings fall into place: coffee table, time for school, sun streaming in horizontally, possibly a Thursday. Her lower back was already sore from the way the cushions sagged in the middle, and the muscles in her neck felt petrified. She was embarrassed that Jeremy had caught her sleeping on the couch, where it was more obvious that she hadn't risen to see him off than if she'd stayed in her room.

"Do you have lunch?" she said, extracting her jacket from the hall closet.

"Yeah."

He followed her outside, leaning sideways to offset the guitar, and they walked single file down the street to the car. In the driver's seat, Rae Ann turned the key in the ignition and groped around at her feet for her sunglasses for a full minute before giving up. Jeremy leaned his forehead against the window, his guitar propped against his knees. The sun glared harshly off the steering wheel and dashboard. She drove.

"Jeremy," she said, once they were on the road, "do you think – what do you think about the world? In general? Do you think it's a good place?"

"I don't know," he said defensively. "It's okay, I guess. Why?"

She considered telling him about the dream. "No reason." She glanced at the visor's mirror above her and was accosted by the sight of last night's makeup and her frighteningly pale skin. She looked sickly, as if her skin was made of uncured clay. She flipped up the visor. "What do you have today?"

"Music."

She nodded, wondering if she should have known that. "I'm really proud of you for spending so much time in the band room," she said. "I can pick you up late if you want to stay after school today."

Jeremy continued to stare out the window. "K," he said.

"And please go to math class before you get in trouble. I'm going out tonight, so I'll make some dinner for you early, okay? How's five o'clock."

"Out? Where?"

"With Pete. Movie."

"Ugh. *Mom.*"

"Not talking about this now. Goodbye. Be good." She put the car in park as he slammed the door and joined the stream of kids making their way into the middle school. Another sunny day.

Rae Ann leaned against the steering wheel and watched him, almost indistinguishable from the other students, except for the guitar case, until he disappeared through the doors. It was too much effort to keep track of all her responsibilities, let alone Jeremy's. For the second time today she did not feel ready to move from where she was.

What to make of such a dream?

<=>

III.

Indeed, what to make?

"Pete," she said to Pete that night. She'd managed to coerce her hair into something she'd once read was a *chignon,* and was feeling much sexier than this morning, having showered and applied new makeup. "What do you think of this: God is an artist, not a priest. We're not meant to divide things up into good and bad, and then argue about it. We're meant to see beauty, and make things beautiful."

Pete looked up from his mussels. They were at a fancy restaurant with white linen table cloths and dim lighting. Pete was a public defender who sang in a choir on Sundays, went to morning AA meetings, and biked to work when weather permitted.

Rae Ann played with the napkin in her lap and tried to ignore Gregory, the little boy from her dream, who had been lingering just behind her thoughts all day. The level of detail in her memory of him alarmed her: there were times this afternoon when she could picture him more clearly than she could picture Jeremy. He had a large round head and solemn eyes, and when she looked down at him from behind, there was a hairless white spot at the center of his whorl of hair, as boys with that haircut often have.

"In other words, you want to do things that make you happy, and disregard right and wrong," said Pete, pushing his glasses up his nose. He had a red linen napkin hanging in a diamond shape from his collar, and stringy gray hair to match his stringy gray voice. There were deep lines in his cheeks and neck, and he had a faded quality, which Rae Ann thought made him look as though he had stepped out of a Polaroid. "Right?"

Two things in particular were bizarre about her memory of Gregory: first, that he was so vivid and detailed and, second, the act of looking down, in a dream, at all.

"No, not really," said Rae Ann, stirring her bisque. It was much too hot in here for the heavy purple sweater she was wearing. The post-shower freshness she'd reveled in all the way here had melted into a damp coat of sweat as soon as she'd arrived. She could also feel her hair threatening to slip out of its bun, and knew it must look nothing like it had in the mirror when she'd left, because now she could see blurry wisps of blond in her periphery. "No. I'm thinking about . . . what if the parameters of life aren't about what we shouldn't do, but the possibilities of what we can do, which might be limitless, even though we treat them like limits?"

"I'm not following," said Pete.

"I mean, rules are so sterile. They're so black and white. They don't allow for personal expression. What if art were the new morality? Where what's celebrated isn't blind obedience, but thinking of new things? Imagination? After all, someone had to imagine us once, right?"

Pete chewed thoughtfully and stared at the floor next to the table. This was their second date.

"People say we're made in God's image. Well, God isn't held to morality, right? He kills people all the time, and gets angry, and manipulates and lies, if we're talking about the Bible or the Quran. But he always *creates*. I'm saying, maybe creativity is more important to whatever's responsible than morality."

Pete continued to chew the same bite through all of this, and then swallowed heartily. He was nodding, but not because he agreed. "Have you been reading about this somewhere?"

"No, it's just an idea," she said.

Pete spoke slowly and it made her uncomfortable; it made her talk to cover the silence. She thought maybe Jeremy was right about him, and decided she would split the tab and then call it off after dessert. The thought of Jeremy sent a pang through her heart when she remembered finding his lunchbox on the kitchen counter after dropping him off. For some reason, imagining him at school without a lunch made her profoundly sad. "I had a dream last night. I was with my son Gregory, and we were at a market. And the whole time, it was – it was obvious, it was so clear, that God is an artist, not a priest, the way I think a lot of people think of him. Or her." He chewed and nodded. She said, "The term 'God' being used loosely."

"You have a son named Gregory?"

Impatiently she said, "Yes. He's with his father."

"And you have the other one here with you?"

"Yes, all the time. The one you met," she said, since she'd never see him again. "I only see the little one on holidays. He has a different father." That would end things once and for all, she thought.

"How old is he?"

"Four and a half." Why am I saying all this? She noticed her newly poured Shiraz and took a gulp. "Anyway, my dream. I just think it's an interesting theory."

In his silence she had time to feel mildly distressed. Where did all that come from? Yes, she had a son in the dream, and he was very realistic, disquietingly so, but that didn't mean she had to pretend he existed for the sake of conversation. What if Pete finds out? How would he find out? What kind of person makes these things up?

And then: Well, it was imaginative, at least. Why did I add the bit about holidays?

Still nodding, Pete said, "I see. I do think it's a positive thing to stop seeing your higher power as judgmental and corrupt. If you identify with artists, then maybe it would be beneficial for you to relate your higher power to one. But I don't think that erases our moral responsibility."

She took another sip and nodded. "No," she said.

"I think anything that makes you truly connect with your higher power is a positive thing," he continued. "Although it can be hard not to rationalize things you enjoy. That is, convince yourself that those things are right, morally speaking."

She watched his eyes. He was gazing at the candle flickering between them. His face looked thin, gaunt almost, and there was something sad about the way he ate each piece with such care, and now laid his silverware carefully athwart on the plate and looked up at her. He wasn't trying to make her uncomfortable, and he hadn't judged her about Gregory. She noticed wrinkles around his eyes she hadn't seen before. He had a good point. And maybe it was nice that he didn't fill every second with chatter.

She pondered another moment in silence before returning to her soup. "Just something I was thinking about," she said. "Anyway. Do you still want to see a movie?"

<=>

IV.

Rae Ann had never been the religious type, mostly because of the giant priest thing, but her dream got her thinking. In retrospect, she had never really articulated her idea about this cosmic priest, which now seemed silly and vague, but it had been a pervading notion, one that persisted without much variation all her life. She had always assumed that the object of pious people's worship was a narrow-minded God who made up things like sex just to torment people, and was outdated, and didn't like anything except church music, and damned people to hell for doing things they didn't think were wrong, and didn't understand social norms, and was only concerned with boundaries and sycophants. But if what she dreamt was true, and instead God was the ultimate artist, then things made sense: because the only thing anyone really knew about any higher power at all, whether it was Jehovah or Allah or a life force, was that it had created something. Therefore, she reasoned, the only truly divine characteristic we know of isn't goodness, but creativity.

She imagined how frustrating it would be for a great artist to be standing overhead, looking down and hearing everything it made complain that it was so draconian and prude, when it only wanted to hear new music composed, and intellectual bar conversations, and for people to bond with each other and chase after their dreams. Or how frustrating it would be to be so brilliant that you invented sea horses and logic and atheism itself, while down here some tiny indignant person insists that you are too facile to exist. She pulled her comforter up over her shoulders and pretended to sleep.

V.

So were the religious types preaching on street corners, and all those devout church people wielding their silent judgment against her, with her single motherhood and pointless lies and sleep-in Sundays, this judgmental bunch which somehow extended to include those parents who packed

their kids' lunches for them and went everywhere in cou-
ples, even though Jeremy went to a public school – were they
wrong to focus on morality, even nominally? Was there some
connection between packing a kid's lunch and his going to
math class? Was every religion wrong, with its invectives to
be good and fair and merciful?

Probably not, she supposed, because good is good, but
there must be more to it than that. What if by being good
we're allowing our inner creativity to thrive, and allowing
others to pursue theirs? What if being good isn't good in
itself, but because it's conducive to maximizing beauty?

Yes, thought Rae Ann, staring up at the paint swirls on
the ceiling, maybe morality is the means and art is the end;
we need to be good to each other, to take care of each other,
because only in a fair world where everyone is loved and has
enough to eat can we all be free to create.

Why did I pretend I have a son named Gregory? she
worried.

She'd changed her mind: she liked Pete and wanted
to see him again. She liked how he listened to her dream
theory and allowed there to be silence in the conversation,
and he didn't agree or disagree too quickly, and he didn't
apologize for his beliefs or say things he didn't mean. He
was thoughtful. His fadedness, his unassuming qualities
which at first made him dull, now made him seem gentle.
He'd even acted impressed, earlier that night, when she told
him she'd brought Jeremy's lunch to school for him, and he
didn't seem to think it was particularly sad or her fault that
he'd forgotten his lunch in the first place. But now she could
never be close to him, because she'd told him she had a son
named Gregory, and then elaborated on it to the point of no
return. Why did she do that?

She lay awake in her bluely dark bedroom, the sheets
a tangled mess around her feet, watching headlights pan
across her walls. She'd fallen asleep a few hours ago but awo-
ken to the horrible recollection of having told such a gratu-

itous lie. After dinner Pete had taken her to the indie the-atre to see the new Woody Allen movie, innocently thinking she was the proud mother of two, and then they'd strolled around downtown talking, and then she'd said she had to go home because she needed to be at the hospital in the morn-ing. Which was now in an hour and a half. Now he could never trust her, and understandably. She couldn't just say it had slipped out, or that she was kidding, or in any way excuse such a thing. She rolled over and thought she heard a guitar playing down the hall.

Also, Gregory was not fading the way dream figments were supposed to. She remembered how he held her hand and she led him from behind, so she could look down and see the hairless spot on his big round head. She couldn't imagine any real child at that age walking so calmly through a crowd, in front of the parent. When she stood next to him at the train vendor his eyes were dark and serious, and he didn't speak; he just pointed at the train he wanted, and waited, and during her frantic search for money he made no sound. He was docile and obedient and overall quite unlike how Jeremy had been as a four-year-old. Jeremy also had brown hair that recently had exploded into a thick, shaggy-dog look, and his eyes were light brown and almost translucent, like honey, and sometimes when she saw them she forgot to look away. As a four-year-old, and still now seven years later, Jeremy was reserved and unresponsive; he could appear docile on occasion, but behind his eyes there was none of Gregory's composure. His had something more like rebellion, a distrustfulness that made Rae Ann nervous. When she tried to talk to him, his face went blank, as if he were putting up a wall; and, now that she thought about it, what scared her was that the wall might be just the begin-ning, and that his distrust was directed at her.

The clock read four thirty. Her bed felt hard and too high off the ground, and she had trouble thinking of herself as in bed, as opposed to on it. She wondered if that was what kept her up at night and, feeling defeated, took a pillow and sheet and went down to the living room.

⬅⇒➤

VI.

Rae Ann was an RN at Memorial Hospital on the south side of town. Today she had the day shift in post-op. She spent her lunch break in the cafeteria with a clipboard and a Styrofoam cup of coffee in front of her, hoping Jeremy had caught the bus and gone to math class, and wondering why he didn't like Pete. He'd only met him for two minutes last week. She considered how to rescind the Gregory thing. The more she thought about last night, the more she liked Pete and thought he'd be good for her. The cafeteria was almost empty. She doodled aimlessly on her yellow pad and thought about the model trains at the dream-market again.

Something else she'd taken from her date with Pete was that he'd implied that she could relate to artists better than any other profession, even though he knew she was a nurse. This was flattering, and she added it to the things she liked about him, but wondered whether it was just another, less overt level of deceit she was subjecting him to, letting him believe she was artistic.

She brushed a stray fuzz of hair behind her ear and it fell out right away. The trains gave her an idea. Maybe she could be artistic, she thought. Without a clear plan or plot she began to write:

Once there was a boy who wanted to be a train conductor, but he couldn't because he had a horrible eye condition which affected his vision badly. He read books and studied trains and did everything he could, but when he was a teenager, he couldn't even get a driver's license because his perspective was so bad.

His eye condition, however, made him a great painter, because what looked normal to him looked three-dimensional to other peo-

ple. He didn't know it was anything special, but he painted as if his life depended on it, because it took his mind off not being able to follow his true calling. And he made so many paintings of all different kinds of trains, and they all looked three-dimensional in a way that nobody else in his art classes could pull off, and word got around and he became famous for painting these beautiful trains.

Eventually he made enough money to have corrective eye surgery. And when he finally had normal vision, he never looked at his paintings again, because he became a train conductor right away. And he never looked back, so he never saw what his paintings looked like with normal eyes.

She had to stop writing when her lunch break was over and she was needed in post-op, where a man would be coming out of surgery with plates in his shins.

Feeling rather accomplished, she packed up her things, tucked the paper into her pocket, and went upstairs to tend to her patients.

⬌

VII.

That night Rae Ann asked her extant son Jeremy if he had done his math homework. There had already been two calls home from his teacher this week.

"Nope," he said, his shaggy head bent low over an electric guitar. He sat on his bed facing her, but for all she could see of his face from her stance in the doorway, he might as well have had his back to her. She thought she heard a tenuous "Sweet Child o' Mine" riff in the cloud of sound emanating from his amp.

"Honey," she said, "it's really important to do well in school. It will keep your options open when you're older. I'll help you with it if you want."

He ignored her plea. "Are you going out with *Pete* tonight?"

She frowned. "It's ten o'clock. I would've gone by now." She leaned against the doorframe and scowled into her tea-cup. "What is it you don't like about him, anyway?"

He continued to pluck laboriously. "I don't know."

She wished she knew what to say to him to make him put his guitar down for a moment.

"You sound good."

Grunt. More wrong notes.

"Is it hard?"

"Yeah."

"You know, Pete sings. I think he likes Guns & Roses, too. Maybe you two have something in common."

"Uh huh."

"And he rides a motorcycle."

The music stopped for a millisecond and then continued.

She dragged her tea bag around the cup by its string and watched it create a tiny whirlpool in the middle. "Did you get the sandwich I left for you this morning? On the counter?"

"Yeah."

"Was it enough?"

He said something inaudible.

"Was it?"

"I said yeah."

What would an artist do, to help her connect with her son?

"Okay, well, please do your homework. If you need me I'll be in my room. I'm working on a story I'm writing."

"K." Unimpressed. Damn.

Rae Ann sighed and retreated to the couch, where the TV was still on from dinner. It was a reality show about other people's silly lives. She sat down and stared at it blankly, feeling her inability to connect with Jeremy more sharply than usual. What could she say to him that wouldn't bore or annoy him? Anything she said came off as too par-ent-like. Not that she had anything especially wise or mean-ingful to say, even if he would hear her. Parents are so often the last people a kid will listen to, she thought, yet they're the ones who want that kid's attention the most. What did other parents talk about to their children? How could she convince him to go to math class when she herself had never been good at math, and also skipped it occasionally, and still had turned out fine?

Her cell phone vibrated on the coffee table and woke her out of a trance. The reality show had gone to a split-screen of credits and previews for next week. The phone informed her of a text message from Pete. She was cheered also to find there was a missed call from him from that afternoon.

If god is an artist, said the text message, *does that make us pieces of its art?*

Meet me for tea/coffee at 8 tom. night? said another, which came as she was deciding what to say to the first.

Maybe it does, she answered, *and I would love to.*

<=>

VIII.

The next night she rushed through the front door after work, sweaty and late. Upstairs, she hurried to change in time to meet Pete, regretting that she didn't have time to shower, though the thought that he would notice or care seemed so unlikely it was almost silly. She spritzed on perfume.

When she left, Jeremy was sitting at the kitchen table, surrounded by books and paper and mechanical pencils, and it was only in the car that it registered he was doing his math.

<=>

IX.

Pete's mug of tea sat untouched on the miniscule table between them. He'd ordered a scone but it hadn't come yet.

Rae Ann stirred a spoon around her mug, listening to the clacking sound it made, trying to restrain an urgent, coursing anxiety that was building up inside her.

"I've been thinking quite a bit about what you proposed the other night," Pete was in the middle of saying. The clacking made her more anxious, but she kept doing it. All she could think about was whether Jeremy had looked disappointed, maybe even vulnerable, when she'd announced she'd be back later, or whether she was imagining it.

Pete continued, "I've been wondering . . . what would it, what would it mean to believe that? How would it change how you behave?"

Rae Ann looked up. A sense of déjà vu distracted her from hearing his question fully. To her left the rest of the café was warm and pink and smelled like coffee, and to her right, through the window, it was so black and rainy that she could see only blurry circles of white and red instead of cars. Pete's gaze was fixed on his tea in concentration.

"I, um," she said, then paused. "I don't know."

Pete nodded, patient, his hands clasped around one knee. He wore a maroon sweater vest and slacks, and next to his chair was his motorcycle helmet. It was round, black, and conspicuously dry.

"Why do you ask?" she said. Her voice sounded tinny and annoying in her ears, especially compared to his, which was soft around the edges, like worn flannel.

He exhaled. "I'm curious," he said. "I think it would be a life-changing belief, to admit something like that, for someone who believed it fully."

Rae Ann nodded also, vainly willing his flannel-like qualities to soothe her nerves instead of make her even more impatient. Hers was the kind of anxiety that eclipsed any other line of thought. "I . . . I think . . . yeah."

Her whole leg was shaking under the table. The raindrops made ovals on the window that slid down the glass in fat rivulets. It was getting louder. She'd left him with dinner in the microwave and a half-hearted promise for something better tomorrow, and he'd grunted in return, from the kitchen table where he sat with a textbook and calculator laid out in front of him. She kept picturing herself planting a kiss on his shaggy head as she breezed past him, half an hour ago, but she hadn't. Why hadn't she?

"Pete," she said. The idea flitted through her head to mention Gregory's nonexistence, but it disappeared as quickly as it came. "I'm so sorry. Please don't take this the wrong way. I'm not feeling well. I should probably go lie down."

Pete looked disappointed, and as concerned as any caring person would, or one who didn't expect to be lied to about pointless things. But she did feel unwell; her stomach churned with the uncertainty that she'd made the wrong decision in coming here, in leaving Jeremy on a night he might not have wanted to be left. She pictured herself from the outside: a woman barely holding it together, thinking that having food in the house and keeping bills paid counted as parenting, that showing up for work every day was tantamount to a successful career, and expecting her son to only see her good side – that she wanted to be a good mother – and to reward her for the attempt without any practical evidence of it. Of course he wouldn't talk to her, she thought, when she barely talked to him except to demand new answers to questions she'd asked a thousand times already. Why was all this hitting her now? she wondered, as Pete went to cancel his scone order, which seemed both pathetic and valiant, in that it was something she would never have thought to do. She felt calmer knowing she'd be leaving in a minute, as if she'd managed to reverse a mistake before it was too late. It wasn't even nine yet; maybe Jeremy would still be in the kitchen.

Pete gave her a cheek-kiss and wished her a safe drive home and respite from her ailment. Indeed, she got home safely, found Jeremy on the couch watching TV with his homework still spread out on the table, and it was within minutes of walking in the door, dripping wet but overcome with relief to be there, that she received a phone call inform-ing her that Pete had been in a motorcycle accident on his way home.

<=>

X.

She sat in the waiting room, feeling strange to be on the receiving side of treatment, even vicariously. He was in sur-gery. She felt desperate; she felt on the verge of losing some-thing precious. She could explain away the Gregory thing somehow, and Jeremy would grow to like him, and they could spend their Saturdays together, the three of them, having musical reveries and cooking dinner and playing cards instead of watching TV. Thank goodness someone had seen something and stopped to help, or else he'd still be lying on the highway's shoulder with cars spraying past in the relentless downpour. Apparently an SUV had cut in front of him and driven him off the road. Thank goodness also that that someone had checked his phone and called the last person he'd called. It struck her like a raw, sharp blade in her chest that she didn't know Pete well enough to have been notified any other way, and that it was only by chance that she was here now. She was also struck by the futile irony of sitting here waiting, a trained nurse employed at this very hospital for over a decade, unable to do a thing about it. She thought maybe she was wrong about the God thing and this was a sick punishment from the narrow-minded deity whose image she'd rejected. She sent a broken scraggle of thought up to the ceiling and hoped whatever heard it would understand.

Jeremy sat in the chair connected to hers, slumped and staring at the floor. He'd come without being asked, following her to the car exactly the way he had the morning before. She was filled with gratitude for his company, but now worried that he regretted coming. She started digging through her purse, her hand trembling as she rummaged through receipts and change and old gum, looking for something to offer him. Beneath everything, she found a crumpled sheet of yellow paper, the story she'd written just that afternoon, though it looked ragged and smudged enough to have been there for weeks.

She read it over and decided it wasn't finished. With an unsteady hand she rewrote the ending:

One day, on his day off, the boy-turned-conductor was walking through a seaside village where he had come by train, and he wandered into an art gallery. Hanging on the wall were pictures of trains that reminded him of something familiar. And they all had a shimmery quality as if they were real.

"Who painted these?" he asked curiously.

The kind-hearted shop owner told him the story of the train lover with the eye affliction.

"If the poor kid hadn't had the eye affliction," the shop owner said, "we wouldn't have these beautiful paintings."

The train conductor was shocked. "I painted these," he said to himself, and recalled all the time he'd spent making them. He had forgotten how he'd spent those two decades of his life, now that he'd spent three doing nothing but conducting trains. He realized he'd had a whole life before his conducting days that he never would have had, had the eye condition not prevented him from conducting in the first place.

"I'd like to buy one, sir," he said, but he didn't have enough money.

"Jeremy," she said when she was finished, "what do you think of this?" and she handed it to him.

Jeremy yawned and read it. "It's good, Ma," he said. "It's sad, though. Why didn't he have enough money? Did train conducting not pay enough, so he wished he hadn't stopped painting?"

Rae Ann stared at the yellow paper in his hand, then looked up at him, his shy, honey-brown eyes peeking out from under his shag of hair, and she wanted to cry; she had such a smart, caring boy, coming all the way to the hospital with her for this man he didn't like, and telling her her story was good, even though it probably wasn't, and even asking a genuine question about it. She felt tears in her eyes and wondered again, with a sickened heart, why had she made up Gregory? And this time she wondered, was Jeremy not enough?

"I don't know, honey," she said. "I didn't think about that." And seeing her tears he looked away; then he took her hand in his and laid his head on her shoulder.

Gabriel
By Lenisa Kelly
⬌

Lenisa Kelly is a Panamanian-American writer with a Bachelors degree from Texas Women's University in General Studies with a focus on English and Criminal Justice living in Houston, TX. She's a contributing fashion writer for Everythinggirlslove.com and has had short stories published in *The Inkling*, a Lonestar College writing journal. Here's what she wrote about "Gabriel":

> The story "Gabriel" came about from my fascination with the idea of angels, demons, and all things apocalyptic. I wanted to explore the idea of looking at religious literature through a new-adult fiction lens. It is the first chapter in a developing complete novel.

⬌

"The rain woke me. Each drop pummeled me like a tiny, unsympathetic fist. Breathing stung. Swallowing was impossible. I could sense my feet and my hips, but they felt independent of each other. I knew my legs were broken. My left eye was already swelling, though my blurred vision had less to do with the swelling and more to do with the six shots of bourbon and the three scotch and sodas I'd had before getting in my car. The smells of rain, gasoline, and shit washed over me. Evacuation of the bowels accompanied the blood loss. They were dead, broken and battered. I saw an arm close by a melted tire. It was charred slightly, with a gold butterfly bracelet around the wrist. I threw up. It's funny. I served two tours in North Korea, killed ten in an attack on the hospital I was stationed at, yet the sight of a child's severed arm and the smell of her burning flesh brought up my dinner. I think about them every day. I think about what they did at school, where they were coming from. I think about what she was like. I think . . . I think she could have been the daughter I gave birth to; that one day the same thing could happen to her and there would be nothing I could do about it. Today is the anniversary of that day. It's been one year since I killed a mother and her two children, a boy and a girl, and it's been one year since my last drink. My name is Celeste, and I'm an alcoholic."

"Hi, Celeste," say the fifteen or so other alcoholics and sponsors sitting in the room, watching me from below this stage and podium.

I descend the stairs towards the back of the room. From the corner of my eye I spot a man staring at me. His eyes are green, his face alluring. I make eye contact. There is something so familiar about his eyes, comforting, like a cup of warm tea. The slamming of the door at the back of the auditorium breaks my attention, but only briefly. When I turn back, the man is gone, and I feel the same emptiness as when I left home for my second tour.

I listen to four more of my peers tell their stories of hitting rock bottom and conclude my night with the dry, coaster-like cookies, and the watered down red punch that tastes nothing like fruit, provided on the refreshment table. My one-year sobriety chip is bronze like an award, but although they want to make it seem like an achievement, it's a reminder of what I have made of my life, a spiral of sorrow and survivor's guilt.

The bus ride home is uneventful, save that a homeless man pisses himself on the second row of benches and is kicked off by the driver. The streets of New Orleans are still crowded at seven o'clock at night, though not nearly as much as normal. It's Monday night, and the Saints are playing at home against New England. Every television will be tuned to the game, a much needed distraction from the ongoing war with North Korea, China, and Afghanistan, and the names of the soldiers killed in combat scrolling down the screen on the all-day news channels.

Football season is my favorite time of year. Because his only child was a girl, my father would dress me in a Bears jersey two sizes too big for me and put my hair in a messy attempt at braids, with orange and blue bows to accent every Chicago Bears game. The world was at peace then; well, peaceful compared to now.

War has taken over the hearts of people who were once happy to relinquish their civil liberties for the security of the suburbs and reality television. Chemical and biological warfare restrictions have long been abolished, with the first influenza bombs that went off simultaneously in Boston and Houston in twenty-thirty.

Luxuries like watching a football game and drinking a beer come few and far between. Football is the only sport Americans now participate in. With the cessation of immigration also came the demise of soccer, basketball, baseball, and every other world sport. It is truly a game of the people now, a glimmer of hope in an otherwise depressingly hopeless world.

My shift at the hospital starts at six in the morning, so watching the game is out. I haven't watched a game since the accident; somehow, watching football without a beer just doesn't seem right, like eating a cupcake with no icing on it. I've always been partial to the thick, sugary icing.

I turn on the news and grab a bottle of ginger ale from the refrigerator. The reading out of the daily death toll of American soldiers fills my one-bedroom apartment, bouncing off the dark-wood floors and the low-set ceiling. My stomach rumbles, but the shot of the body bags returning to base quickly silences it.

As I listen to the names a few stand out. Walter McAdams; we were in basics together. We called him Reckless. I guess we should have seen this coming. Anthony Scoviano, the Italian Stallion. He was part of our Medevac team a few years before my discharge. He was sweet, good looking, one of five children, and the only boy. A lump in my throat makes me cough. I don't know why I watch this shit.

I turn off the television, shower, and ready myself for bed. I set my alarm for four. I need to get in a run before my shift. I've replaced one addiction with another; sweat for alcohol. My bed swallows me in its soft sheets and memory foam, quelling the anxiety that slowly builds during the course of the day. My eyes grow heavy and sleep stealthily moves in.

His lips taste like fresh peaches. His skin is soft cotton. His embrace sends bolts of lightning up my spine and out to my fingers and toes. His breath grazes my neck beneath my right ear. His shoulder-length hair brushes my cheeks. I spread my fingers through it, kneading it like dough. I find his lips again and pull them toward me softly with my teeth.

He forces my legs open and I willingly wrap them around his hips. Our breathing synchronizes; our chests heave and press together. His strong hands lift me, easing his entrance within me. I quiver as each stroke inside me sends a shock through every nerve ending in my body. I'm alive; before the tours, before the drinking, before the funerals and the sadness. The numbness I use to shield me from the sorrow is gone. I feel everything.

We inhale. Together, we explode. My body drinks him, ending my long thirst. His eyes blaze, two rich emerald gems. His chest rises. His back arches. His neck rises to the heavens. White light blasts from his open mouth. A pair of wings, feathers like fresh spun silk, spread to each end of the room. My heart skips. I'm scared, I'm fascinated, and I'm hungry for more. His arms wrap around me as the beam of light fades. His wings follow suit, igniting every skin cell they touch. I sink into him, wrapped in soft feathers, warm skin, and a feeling of bliss.

"Wake up," his deeply velvet voice whispers. "Celeste."

My eyes shoot open, bullets from a hair trigger. My chest heaves. My nostrils flare as I try to regain a foothold in reality. It's three thirty. I wipe the sweat from my brow and flop back onto my pillow. The ceiling fan hurts my eyes in the blue glow of my cable box. I exhale heavily after a deep yawn. I guess I have more time to run.

As I walk to the bathroom I feel the residual moisture of my excitement between my thighs. Embarrassment washes over me, as does a smile. I recall the dream as I wash off and put on sweats. His eyes. Those eyes; so familiar, so comforting.

The faster I run, the better I feel. The adrenaline is calming. It's always been that way. The military seemed like a natural choice; I'm best under pressure. By four forty-five I'm bored with running and get ready for work. My scrubs are red today, embroidered with my last name, Augustine, in white. A gift from my mom and dad before her breast cancer, and his heart attack two months after it took her. I miss them.

I catch the five-twenty bus that lets me off in front of the hospital. Only one other person rides, apart from the driver: a girl in her mid twenties, probably a nurse's aide. Judging from the puppies on her scrubs, she probably works in the pediatric wing. God bless her.

I have just enough time to stop in the café for a coffee and to say hi to Dolores. She's sixty-eight, a born and raised Creole, and she's as pleasant to talk to as the sweet-potato pies she brings during Christmas. She doesn't know about the accident; no one does, except the people in HR and my former boss. Because of my service, and a good military lawyer, I received a sentence of time served, mandatory AA meetings, antidepressants, antipsychotics, community service, and weekly visits with a therapist. Dolores likes me because her son was killed in the war two years ago. I get the pies he can't enjoy, and she gets to see an empty dish and imagine it was her son eating from it.

"You two would have been a lovely couple," she always says. "I wish you two had met."

I thank Dolores for the coffee and the smile as I check out, though she never lets me pay for the cup. I shove three dollars into her tip jar next to the register and wave goodbye. I know I don't deserve her kindness, the pies, the coffee, or the freedom to enjoy any of it, but I'm grateful and burdened by all of them.

I check in at the nurse's lounge and exchange reports with the night shift nurse, Samantha. A single mother of one, whose middle-aged mother watches her son overnight while she works, tells me about the events of the night. Nothing beyone the usual trauma: three gunshot wounds, a stabbing victim, and a couple of car accidents. The stabbing victim was pronounced dead about twenty minutes ago. After rounds, that's my first stop for the night.

His name is Timothy. He's an organ donor. Thirty-two and in fairly healthy condition, his cell phone has a picture of him and someone I assume is his girlfriend – no ring impressions on their fingers – as the wallpaper. They look happy. I call the ICE number on the phone and inform her that he's been involved in a stabbing. Her name is Katherine, and I wait to tell her he's gone until she gets here. Her knees buckle and some aids help her to her seat. This part of the job never gets any easier.

A few hours into my shift, a new batch of emergencies comes in. A couple of burn victims from an electrical fire in Metairie, three college guys from a bar brawl on Bourbon and – the one that catches my attention most – an infant going into anaphylactic shock from exposure to peanuts.

A push of epinephrine stabilizes her, though the allergy isn't what unnerves me. As an intern and two nurses wheel her away, I get the report from the EMTs that brought her in.

"Eighteen-month-old Caucasian female with severe peanut allergy found a couple of Peanut M&Ms between the couch cushions and ingested them. She had two seizures back to back in the ambulance," says the female EMT. Her partner introduces me to the child's frantic parents. I reassure them we are doing everything we can and move to assess her.

My feet stop in mid-stride as I see a pair of green eyes watching me from the hall leading to the emergency bay. Without realizing it, I'm running towards them; those piercing green eyes that seem so familiar, so comforting. The warm, humid air hits me as the doors slide open and the sunlight's heat crashes against the cold, conditioned air of the hospital.

People walk about the emergency room parking lot, but I recognize no one. The eyes are gone, and the quiver of excitement dissipates.

I am haunted by them. I see them everywhere. I see him everywhere, ever since I was little, and even more since the accident. I saw him over me, attending to my wounds. I thought he was my EMT, but when I asked, no one knew who I was talking about. And now I dream about him. I long for him; a stranger with green eyes.

The rest of the night is quiet. The anaphylactic child wakes up crying, a sound more welcome than deathly silence. Timothy, the organ donor, is our only fatality tonight, though he will give life to someone else. That's the way it is. Life goes on.

Report takes longer than I anticipate, and I miss my usual bus by five minutes. I walk two blocks to Tulane and South Prieur to catch the bus there. The next bus should be by in about ten minutes, but rain clouds are rolling in. I wait alone, hoping I can get home before the first drops fall. I have no umbrella and my hair is already puffy from the humidity. I'm not going to spend my three days off detangling and resetting my curly hair.

The people driving along Tulane after 6 p.m. have no patience. The long work day, the traffic, and the general gloom that looms over us on a daily basis find release on their commute home in the comfort of their cars. Horns honk as lights change from red to green. Brakes squeal as yellow turns to red. The occasional curse from an open window, by someone who's had enough, infiltrates the usual traffic sound. A shouting match ignites between an elderly man in a truck and a teenage boy in a Mercedes Benz. Their hands wave malevolently at each other through their back and front windows and I can't help chuckling to myself. Even in the midst of war, people still cannot be cordial to one another. This is our world.

"Celeste." I hear a whisper behind me. The rhythm of my heart changes. I turn to find the eyes I ran out of the hospital searching for; the eyes that seem to follow me wherever I go, that invade my restless sleep, and my listless wakefulness.

I stumble backwards, taken off guard at his closeness. I'm a soldier, trained to be aware of my surroundings, yet I didn't hear or see him. I lose my footing on the edge of the cement and trip into the street, into the oncoming traffic of impatient people on Tulane. My palms scrape the pavement, and I wince at the squeal of breaks and the honk of a semi's horn as it barrels down on me, trying to catch the stale green light.

I try to complete the gasp that is yanked from my lungs, but his hands wrapping around me, pulling me into his chest, interrupt it. A blast of wind punches my face as together we soar into the air out of the semi's path.

His eyes pierce mine, as every instance of seeing them rushes into my mind. A whooshing sound draws my eyes towards the massive brown wings flapping behind him, keeping us in the air. I want to say something, but my voice is stolen from me, like the gravity that secures me to the ground, and my grip on reality. I have to be dreaming. This can't be real.

"What are you?" I manage as he tightens his grip around my waist.

His voice is melodic, like your favorite song lulling you to sleep. "I am Gabriel."

Virginia is a Different Country
By Max Everhart
⟨⇒⟩

MAX EVERHART has a master's degree in creative writing
from the University of Alabama, Birmingham. His short
stories have been published in *CutBank*, *Elysian Fields Quar-
terly*, *Slow Trains Journal*, and *Juked*. His short story, "The Man
Who Wore No Pants," was selected by Michael Knight for
Best of the Net 2010 and was nominated for the Pushcart
Prize and Dzanc Books' Best of the Web anthology. *Go Go
Gato* is his first novel, and the first book in the Eli Sharpe
Mystery series. *Split to Splinters* (Eli Sharpe #2) has just been
published. Here's what he wrote about "Virginia is a Differ-
ent Country":

> The germ of "Virginia is a Different Coun-
> try" sprouted nearly ten years ago when I
> was writing my Master's thesis and dating
> my then girlfriend now wife. After living
> together for more than a year or so, I started
> to think about marrying her, but I knew
> she wasn't so keen, and I wasn't so sure
> how I felt about the possibility of being in
> love and not ever getting married. Anyway,
> that's where the conflict between the pro-
> tagonist's parents came from. The rest was
> inspired by a childhood obsession of mine
> to do something "worthwhile" by the time I
> was thirty-five, which is why I had the pro-
> tagonist's mother join the Army Reserves.
> Too, I'd just read and thoroughly enjoyed
> Benjamin Percy's excellent short story col-
> lection *Refresh, Refresh*, the title story of

which concerns a group of teenaged boys whose fathers get called up to active duty. (Alas, my story ended up being very different than Percy's). From there, I sprinkled in some other personal obsessions (golf, characters named after states, &c.) and after repeated revisions, "Virginia is a Different Country" became what you now see in print. I hope you like it, as it took me quite a while to write . . . and even longer to get published.

<=>

Two things happened on June 4, 1990: I turned twelve years old, and Mom enlisted in the Army Reserves. She came home from work that night with Chinese takeout, plopped the greasy bag on the kitchen counter, and ordered Dad and me to sit down. After we joined hands around the breakfast table, Mom prayed for our health and happiness and that the divorce lawyer she worked for actually used the breath mints she'd put on his desk.

"Happy Birthday, Simon." She let go of Dad's hand first then mine. She stared at me with those green eyes. "It was now or never, doodlebug. You can't be over thirty-five or Uncle Sam won't take you."

I watched Mom pour soy sauce all over her plate, my fists clenched. She combed through mounds of rice and vegetables with a pair of bamboo chopsticks. When she found just the right piece of broccoli, she chewed and swallowed the stalk and began telling me about all the cool video games she'd bought for my birthday.

She said, "I've got first dibs on the one where the fat guy with the mustache rescues the woman he loves."

"Enough." I poked at a pimple on my chin, glared across the table at Dad. "Mom's gone G.I. Jane and you're just gonna sit there?"

Dad's face was red and peeling from working at Muddy Creek Golf Course all day without a hat on. He smiled in my direction, and his teeth looked extra white, his hair blacker than ink.

"I've asked your Mom to marry me thirty-six times," he said, "and I still haven't heard the word 'yes.' I'm through trying to predict her behavior."

"Amen." Mom blew a kiss that Dad caught and stuffed in the pocket of his purple-and-yellow Hawaiian shirt. "And by the way, dear, it's thirty-seven times."

I slammed my hand down on the table, rattling drinks and plates.

"Somebody better start talking," I said.

Dad put one hand on his chest like he had heartburn, the other on Mom's shoulder. "We bought you those detective novels you wanted," he said.

"And I picked up a German chocolate cake from the grocery store," Mom said. She dumped a heap of noodles and tofu chunks that looked like little blocks of puke on my plate.

I shoved all the vegetables and non-meat aside. Mom's hair was bright red and curly that month.

"Mom, why couldn't you have got a part-time job at Walmart instead?"

"Because," she said, "you can't learn anything about yourself stocking shelves in the Women's Wear Department. The army is a place to challenge your –"

Dad scooted his chair away from the table, scratching the hardwood floor with a *fruummppp*. His flip-flops flip-flopped toward the refrigerator, where he filled up his mug with homebrewed beer the color of chocolate orange juice. Sitting back at the table, he folded a napkin and placed it in his lap.

"Please," he said. "A new subject."

"After the six weeks of Basic Training, I'll only be gone one weekend a month. And I'll get another paycheck – a paycheck, a gun, and boots."

Mom rambled on about all the new experiences the army had to offer – shooting rifles, running ten miles a day, attaining an official rank. Dad shoved *lo mein* noodles around his plate.

"Jesus, Virginia, you sound like the commercials." Dad undid the top button on his shirt. Curly black hairs sprouted from his chest. "Somebody talk about the weather."

Mom said, "I have to report for duty soon. Just imagine all the fun things you guys can do when I'm gone."

Dad downed half his beer in one gulp and said, "I read in the *Winston-Salem Journal* about a ninety-year-old lady who passed out from heat exhaustion yesterday. They had to take her to Baptist Hospital for IV fluids and lime green Jell-O."

I flicked a piece of tofu off my plate.

"Mom, soldiers can't be vegetarians."

"Oh? The brochure didn't mention anything about meat-eating as part of the training."

I smelled Mom's perfume, the fruity conditioner she used that was definitely not tested on laboratory animals. "And soldiers don't wear makeup either."

I leaned back in my chair and folded my arms the way the homicide detectives on TV did when questioning a suspect. "I'll bet you a week's allowance that you've never even held a real gun before, have you?"

Dad said something about the heat-exhausted old lady having two rabbits and a turtle.

"Seriously, Mom. Can you run a mile in under six minutes? Do a hundred push-ups without passing out? Sleep in a barracks filled with men?" Before she could answer any of my questions, a fork crashed on my plate, the sound of metal on metal jarring my brain.

Dad said, "Finish your dinner. Those presents won't open themselves."

<=>

Over the next two weeks, Dad spent most of his free time on the back porch watching the purple flashes of the Bug Zapper. I sat with him for the first couple of nights, brought him sweet tea and Moon Pies, but the only thing he wanted to talk about was the short, happy lives of bugs.

"Your mother is her own woman," he'd say, whenever I commanded him to come inside and watch the Braves game with me.

Meanwhile, Mom had set up camp on the living room couch with coffee and a stack of Hemingway novels. Between chapters, she wiped lipstick off the rim of her mug and made notes on a yellow legal pad. Every hour or so, I'd refill her cup, stirring in half-and-half, two packets of Equal, and a dash of salt.

<=>

At dawn on the day Mom was scheduled to report for Basic Training, she popped her head inside my bedroom door.

"I'm going now," she whispered. "Are you awake?"

I pretended to sleep – one eye peeking, one arm dangling off the side of the bed. I pulled the covers up to my neck. I smelled her fruity conditioner. I listened to her pants swoosh as she stepped into my room and dropped something on the pillow beside me.

"My only son." She hovered over me for a second or two, breathing. I felt her eyes moving across the side of my face. "Be good," she said.

I opened my eyes after I heard the front door shut, and rolled over to see what she'd left on my pillowcase.

"An ink pen?" I chucked it against a poster of Michael Jordan dunking a basketball. I cursed myself for thinking I could change her mind by flossing my teeth and washing dishes and taking the trash out without being told. I cursed Dad for volunteering to drive her to the Army Reserve Center in Winston-Salem.

<=>

Later that day, after the sun disappeared behind a big, blue-black curtain, Dad rolled the grill into the backyard, unfolded two lounge chairs, and popped open the Igloo cooler. We each chose a chair and sat down. Dad tossed a can of Coke in my lap, cracked a Budweiser.

"We're bachelors for a while," he said. "Here's to it."

Dad chugged the beer in seconds flat, grabbed another from the cooler. I gave my soda a good shake and sat it on the ground beside his chair. My stomach was in knots. You could have fried an egg on my forehead it was so hot out.

"What kind of mother joins the army on her son's birthday?" I asked. "What kind of mother leaves her son a pen before she goes away to Basic Training?"

Dad drank part of the beer and said it wasn't as good as the stuff he made, not by a long shot. He handed the half-empty can to me. "You want to finish it?" he asked.

The can was so cold it burned my hand.

"She might get homesick while she's gone," Dad said, the patio lights shining on one side of his face. "You should write her a letter. Let her know how you're doing."

My stomach churned and bubbled like I'd eaten too many Now-N-Laters and drank too much Mountain Dew. Across the street, Tanner Bowles – the biggest bully at Old Richmond Middle School – and a couple of his buddies were popping off fireworks in a field filled with oak stumps and chiggers and poison ivy. The sky lit up red, white, and blue. All three wanted, "More, more, more." I walked to the edge of the patio for a closer look at the show, the churning, bubbling feeling in my gut getting worse.

"I'm worried about Mom." I listened to the boom-boom-boom of M-80s. "Maybe a doctor can put those suction cups on her head, hook her up to a machine that beeps, and figure out what's wrong with her. If our insurance won't cover those tests, you don't have to pay me an allowance anymore."

"Help me cook, son."

I felt a big, warm hand on my shoulder. I brushed it off.

"All right, but I'm not writing Mom any letters."

We both stood over the grill, beers in hand. Dad squirted lighter fluid on the charcoal. The flames shot up high, and he dropped two rib-eyes on the fire, blood dripping off the meat. I sniffed at my beer again. I tried it and wished I hadn't.

"You don't have to drink it." He took off his t-shirt and slung it over his shoulder. "I was trying to cheer you up. Cheer us both up."

Tanner lit a round of cherry bombs and tossed one into our next door neighbor's magnolia tree. I stepped away from the grill's heat, peeled off my t-shirt.

"Tell me what's wrong with her," I said, holding the beer can with both hands, daring myself to drink it fast. "Does it have something to do with why she won't marry you?"

Dad poked the steaks, beads of sweat trickling down his hairy chest and stomach.

He said, "Remember last summer when Mom's boss flew the three of us to Hawaii for vacation?"

The memory of it hit me fast – the clear blue water, the soft sandy beaches, the resort's ten-page menu filled with pictures of multi-colored fish. I didn't sleep at night because I was sure one of the island's many volcanoes would erupt, and I might miss it.

"Yeah, I remember. Hawaii might as well have been another country compared to Tobaccoville."

Dad laughed, and I watched the skin around his eyes crinkle.

"Virginia – I mean, your mother – is the same way. Like a different country. Beautiful and fun – but a little scary."

"I'm not scared of Mom."

Dad kissed my forehead and his whiskers scratched my cheek. He asked how I liked my steak cooked. I swallowed some beer without puking.

"You should be mad she joined the army," I said. "I am."

The bully shot a bottle rocket that skidded across the road and fizzled out between Mom's tomato plants. Dad yelled for everyone to be careful, and I took another man-size drink of beer, felt the alcohol in my blood, in my head and legs.

"The kids at school said Mom's a bitch for not marrying you – that you can't control your woman. Is that true?"

Dad grabbed my wrist and pulled me in close enough to feel the hairs on his arms tickling my skin. The fireworks stopped. Gray smoke lingered in the air.

"Don't ever use that word again," he said, and went back to poking the meat.

<=>

With Mom away at Basic Training, Dad and I settled into a routine. During the day, I went with him to work – a par-3 golf course with big brown patches in the fairways and sand traps filled with crushed beer cans. The hours were long. The clubhouse had a tin roof, no air conditioning or cable TV, and I spent my time cracking my knuckles, chugging Yahoo, reading Raymond Chandler novels, and using my ink pen to write nasty letters to Mom that I never sent. Sometimes, I helped Dad mow the greens or weed-eat the rough, but it was tough pretending not to notice the sad look in his eyes and the whiskey on his breath.

At night, I cooked dinner for us both – Oodles of Noodles or frozen pizzas topped with cheddar cheese, Goldfish crackers. While I was in the kitchen, Dad drank Evan Williams straight from a pint bottle, took to watching CNN Headline News instead of Sportscenter.

While Mom was gone, we stopped playing Chinese checkers. We stopped answering the telephone when it rang. We stopped going to bed at a decent hour.

I remember one night I walked into the living room and found Dad on the couch wearing nothing but his underwear and a pair of argyle socks.

"My boy," he said and pulled me onto the couch, sloshing liquor on my shorts. "Here's how Mom and I met. UNC-Asheville. Psychology 101. The asshole in charge, pardon my French, sprung a test on us, and I tried to cheat off your mom's paper, which is something you're too smart to ever do. Right? Anyway, the professor flunked me. Your mother, Virginia Clementine, offered to be my tutor. Relative happiness ever since."

He kept me up until dawn that night, filling my head with stories of Mom hiking up Cold Mountain in the middle of December and dropping out a month before graduation to follow the Grateful Dead around. I crawled into bed after he finally passed out, frightened by something in his voice.

<=>

Mom came home from Basic Training on a Sunday near the end of July, 1990. She walked into the living room wearing Wranglers and flip-flops. She was smiling – smiling and limping and smelling like a mixture of rifle grease and soap. From across the room, I watched her study Dad's whiskers. She ducked away from his lips, kissed his hand instead.

"You stink," she said, turning her nose up in the air. "This house stinks."

She smiled wider and crunched potato chip crumbs on the floor as she limped towards me. I put my hand on the brick fireplace and looked around. There were Slim Jim wrappers on the couch, drink rings on the coffee table. Trash bags lined the walls. Brown water leaked from the ceiling. Mom stopped to admire the pyramid of Budweiser cans blocking the TV, and I chewed my fingernails, braced myself for the hug.

"I missed you," she said. I closed my eyes and sank into her arms, her smell. I ground my teeth and fought, but just as the warm, safe feeling began to flow from her to me, Dad pulled her off me.

"Go run your mom a hot bath," he said, his fingers greasy on my arm. "And don't ask her a bunch of questions."

"A family of talkers," I said and ran upstairs to do as I was told.

Mom locked the bathroom door behind her, turned on the water. I listened to her whistling and humming from the hallway.

What the hell are you so happy about, I wanted to ask.

Downstairs, Dad sat on the couch watching the evening news, rubbing Aloe Vera on his face. I sat down on the arm farthest from him. He patted the empty seat beside him and pointed at the TV screen.

"Gas prices are skyrocketing," he said. "We're gonna be at war soon."

"I've never even heard of Kuwait," I said. "Where is it?"

"Look it up." Dad pointed to a stack of Encyclopedia Britannicas collecting dust by the fireplace. "Now keep quiet. I want to hear this."

We watched a thirty-second bit about men in desert camouflage and dented helmets. These men had dark skin and black eyes. They spoke gibberish. A woman's voice interpreted what they said into English. Yes, they were Iraqi soldiers. Yes, they praised Allah. And yes, Kuwait rightfully belonged to them. Saddam Hussein, their hero, said so.

After the news anchor called for another commercial, I felt Dad's hairy arm bristling the back of my neck. I asked him why we had to watch the news all the time, why we cared what was going on way over there. Mom limped down the stairs in a short pink bathrobe.

"Because we're Americans," she said and plopped down on the La-Z-Boy, her hair wrapped in a towel the shape of a beehive. "It's our job to protect those who can't protect themselves."

I stared at her. She looked different. Her hair was no longer bright red and curly. It was brown and short and spiky in the middle. Her legs, which dangled over the side of the chair, were hard, covered in purple bruises and red cuts.

"The army is for freedom everywhere, for all people," Mom said.

"You sound like the commercials," I said. Dad poked me in the ribcage.

"Private Benjamin." Dad waved Mom over to the couch. "Please sit with the family." He pulled us both towards him and turned up the TV. President Bush, silver-haired and talking like a cowboy, sat behind a desk. He demanded action. I listened to him use words like "aggression" and "fear" and "liberty." I smelled Mom's fruity shampoo, Dad's underarm stink. I curled my toes and wished Mom had never put on those stupid black combat boots.

By the end of the president's speech, Mom's hands were gripping the edge of the coffee table. She was leaning forward like a pit bull ready to attack, legs flexed.

"He's right," she said. "Something must be done."

I turned to Dad, asked him if he was ready to call the doctor and schedule those suction cup tests yet. He told me to go outside and play.

I shut the front door behind me, stomped my feet in place for a ten-count, and pressed my ear against the door.

"I'm serious," Dad yelled. I ran down the gravel road until my heart pounded in my ears.

<=>

The next day, I began investigating my mother, Virginia Clementine – the way the detectives in my gumshoe novels did.

After my parent's secret talk, Mom promised to spend more time with the family. Because she started coming home every day from work at two instead of five or six, I had plenty of time to shadow her movements. Everything I learned I wrote down in a black notebook I kept hidden in my pillowcase – along with a few issues of *Playboy* and half a pack of Camel Lights I'd stolen from Dad.

I listened to the tone of Mom's voice when she spoke on the phone, when she told Dad she loved him. I checked out books on decoding handwriting samples and personality types from the library. I read and re-read Mom's "Things to Do" lists. I paid attention to things I never noticed before, like the way she walked, sat, ate, slept, sang, prayed, and drove.

I learned a lot about how Mom refused to parallel-park and how her cursive writing slanted a little bit to the left; but I didn't have a clue why she'd joined the army or why she wouldn't marry Dad.

So I started going through her personal stuff when she wasn't around. I read mail and looked through dresser drawers and checked pants pockets. I poked around closets.

Then I got over my fear of the basement.

Down there, among Dad's bowling trophies and my Sherlock Holmes novels, I found a clue: a box labeled PERSONAL, PRIVATE. The box had a flip top and handles on the side, but I tore into it with my pocket knife, my stomach bubbling and rumbling as I worked. Inside, I found a musty-smelling photo album stuffed with birth certificates and four-leaf clovers and report cards. I found pictures of my grandparents, two strangers Mom never spoke about. I found love letters from old boyfriends. I found poems about trees and wind and love. I found a cartoon drawing of a girl on a unicorn.

As a detective, I read the love letters first. I read and thought and tried to understand the meaning in every word, the feeling between the lines. "Love is an ocean," I read out loud.

I studied every photograph of Mom, from baby to girl to grown. I looked into her green eyes and saw her swinging on swings and riding ponies and wearing a cap and gown at high school graduation. I saw her kissing boys on the cheek, smiling back at her mother and father across a Thanksgiving feast that would have made the first pilgrims proud. I found one picture of her with Dad. They were lying on a beach with white sand. They were holding umbrella drinks. They were snuggled up together beneath a palm tree. I was sure they were happy.

By the time I turned to the end of the photo album, I'd come to a conclusion: Mom seemed normal.

Later that same night, after I'd spent a couple of hours writing about Mom's photo album in my black notebook, I opted for direct confrontation.

Mom was in the bathroom putting green gunk on her face when I walked in without knocking.

"I went through your photo album today," I said, checking out the dark circles under my eyes in the mirror.

She smoothed more green gel into her cheeks. Her eyes were a lighter shade of green than the gunk on her face.

"Nobody likes a snoop," she said.

"You know what I think? I think you were adopted. I think your real parents are probably looking for you."

She smiled at her own reflection. Her eyes twinkled.

"If only I had an imagination like yours."

The bathroom smelled like pine and mint. I popped my knuckles.

"Okay. You're not adopted. But is something wrong with you?" I cracked my thumb, pointer finger then the pinky. "If there is, don't you think you should tell me about it?"

I heard Dad in the living room coughing cigarette smoke. CNN blasted out the latest news on the Middle East. He'd been sitting there for hours, drinking whiskey with Coke, his collared shirt stained with fast-food grease. Every once in a while, he'd curse the president's name and check baseball scores on ESPN.

Mom tightened her pink robe, turned, and put her hand on my cheek. Her palms felt rough on my skin. My stomach rumbled and groaned.

"Sometimes," Mom said, looking like a green monster with green cat eyes, "I need to try things. Things you may never understand. Things I don't fully understand. Things that have nothing to do with you – or your father – or the love I have for our family. Do you understand?"

I gave my knuckles another crack. I heard the TV make a Special Announcement. The news anchor finished, Dad slammed the front door, and I backed away from Mom.

"I don't understand," I said. "I wish I did, but I don't."

Mom turned on the faucet and began washing the green gunk off her face. A lump formed in my throat.

"What I do understand is that we're not a real family." I put my hand on the doorknob and turned. "I do understand that."

<=>

According to the last entry in my black notebook, dated August 21, 1990, Mom was impossible and I'd had enough playing detective. And my Plan B of being good – washing Dad's truck, keeping the grass cut, and not squirming in my seat during Sunday church – wasn't working out. Plus, the war talk was getting louder. Every night Mom, Dad, and I watched the oil fields burn. We watched the crazy guy with the mustache talk gibberish. We listened to President Bush make threats. The news anchors even said he might call up the Army Reserves. That meant Mom. That, I decided, could not happen.

On the night of August 21, Mom and Dad came to my bedroom to talk. I remember Mom stood by my bed holding a glass of wine the color of blood. I remember Dad was holding a rolled-up copy of *Time*. When Mom bent down to kiss my forehead, I turned my head and blurted out, "It's time for you to quit the army and marry Dad."

Dad smacked his thigh with the rolled-up magazine, grunted, and stomped out the door.

Mom pushed a clump of brown hair behind her ear. I thought about the black notebook and all the time I'd wasted trying to figure out why she wouldn't marry my dad, why she joined the Army Reserves on my twelfth birthday. I could feel another pimple on my forehead – deep below the skin, painful like a bruise.

Mom said, "You still don't get it, do you?"

"No." I wanted to take a needle to the pulsating zit on my face. "You talked, but didn't say anything." I sat up in bed, hugged my knees to my chest. "Here, I'll say it for you: Simon, we are not a real family."

Mom sipped her blood wine.

"I love you," she said. She moved closer, her warm breath tickling my nose.

"Get out of my room. Please."

<⇒>

I awoke sweaty and exhausted the next morning. I heard coffee beans grinding and Dad's voice vibrating the walls. Invisible hands gripped my stomach and squeezed. I'd never heard Dad yell at Mom. "Men never yell or curse at a lady," Dad told me more than once. "Even when they deserve it."

I tip-toed to the door and pressed my ear against Jose Canseco's chest to listen.

"You're not going," Dad said.

"We've been called up to active duty. I have to go."

Mom's voice sounded calm.

"Virginia, you don't get it. This isn't popping off guns at the range. This is real."

"I know what it means."

I heard dishes break. I slipped into the hallway, sat down at the top of the stairs where I could see the action. Dad wore a shirt with a collar and black golf shoes. Mom wore tan camouflage, a matching hat pulled down low.

"If you don't get out of this," Dad said. He held the gravy boat over his head, then gently set it on the counter by the sink. "You have to get out of this."

Everything went quiet. Even the bacon stopped frying. After what seemed like an hour, Dad crunched his golf spikes across the floor and wrapped his arms around her waist. He said her name over and over again. "Virginia. Virginia. Virginia."

As Dad stooped way down and laid his head on her shoulder, Mom wiped her nose on her sleeve, rearranged her spiky brown hair. I crawled down seven steps, my heart pounding in my ear.

"I don't want to get out of it," Mom said. "I can't get out of it."

Near the bottom of the staircase, I leaned against the banister. My parents were just a few feet away. I could smell the polish on Mom's boots, Dad's aftershave, and the bacon sizzling in the pan. Dad took his head off Mom's shoulder, and it was like watching TV. Except I couldn't change the channel. Or make the people on screen do the right thing. I could only look on – helpless, alone, my stomach tied up in knots.

Dad said, "Yes you can get out of this. Tell them you're pregnant and crazy. Show them your flat feet. Tell them you have a venereal disease. Tell them you're staying here. I'll put my clubs back in the garage and we'll drive down to the courthouse and get married – like we should have a long time ago." With one deep knee bend, Dad grabbed Mom by the waist and lifted her off the ground. She dangled an inch off the kitchen floor. "We'll take the kid to La Paz for vacation. Stuff him full of *chalupas* and Jarritos soda pop."

My heart wouldn't quit. I thought Dad was going to win. I was rooting for him. He set her down and kissed the back of her neck. Mom shoved the bacon around the frying pan with a spatula, leaned back into his arms. I'd heard many versions of this proposal – minus the yelling.

Mom pushed away from him, pulled her cap down lower.

"Do you know what it does to me?" she said. "You not understanding the things I have to do?"

Dad broke more dishes. I watched. My feet were blocks of cement. My arms wouldn't let go of the banister.

<=>

There were no hugs or kisses before Mom left, just a bright yellow taxi crunching gravel and churning up dust as it eased down the street. Dad and I watched from the front porch. The driver turned left onto the highway. I slapped myself in the face a few times extra hard. I didn't cry.

"That's that," he said after his cigarette burned out and he threw it on the lawn.

Dad went inside and came back out with a pint of whiskey in his hand. He sat down beside me on the porch, offered me a sip. I smelled the bottle cap, shook my head. I asked what would happen next. Overhead, the sky was blue.

"Will they send Mom to Kuwait?"

Dad's throat moved when he swallowed. His eyes were the same color as the liquor he drank.

"Is Mom a good shot?"

One of our neighbors drove by and honked, but Dad didn't wave. "Did she say she'll marry you when she gets back?"

"Who the hell knows?" Dad scratched at his chin whiskers. "Stop asking me questions I don't know the answer to."

A spasm rolled through my gut. I jumped off the porch, ran to the bushes, and puked. I started crying. I curled my toes and waited for Dad to come and comfort me. When he finally did, his breath made me gag some more.

"You let this happen." I kicked him as hard as I could in the shins. "If I had a knife right now, I'd stab you."

I stood up and punched Dad in the kidney, in the chest. He didn't move. He didn't block me. He just stood there, one hand holding his stinking bottle of booze. "Let it go," I heard him say over and over again. "Let it go."

<⇒>

Later, a red BMW pulled into our driveway. The driver, a blond woman with dark eyebrows, honked twice. Dad and I were back on the porch, watching heat trails rise off the half-gravel, half-concrete road we lived on. His whiskey bottle – like my aching stomach – was almost empty.

"Go inside." He staggered to his feet, hiking up his khaki shorts. "I'll be right there."

I watched him wobble down the front steps, bottle in hand. I cracked my knuckles.

"Who the hell is that?" I asked.

Dad turned, told me to go inside. His voice was cold. I pulled hard at the sleeve of my t-shirt and the fabric ripped. "Tell me who that is," I said.

Dad took a step towards me, stumbled, then took a step back. The blond lady honked again, and Dad threw one of his flip-flops at the car.

"Son." Dad dropped the empty bottle on the ground, wiped sweat off his flaky forehead. "Virginia – your mother – is not my wife. Now go inside."

I slammed the front door shut behind me. As I waited for Dad, both hands pressed against the door, I counted to one hundred, two hundred, five hundred, one thousand, but something had changed. My heart wouldn't pound. My blood refused to boil. I kept counting, wondering where that hot, bubbling feeling in my gut had disappeared to.

When I heard the car squeal out of the driveway, I sank to my knees and started counting out loud.

"One thousand one, one thousand two, one thousand three..."

The Banshee Ciana
By Katherine Wielechowski
⟺

KATHERINE WIELECHOWSKI is a Nebraska native who currently lives and works in Kearney, NE. She started writing seriously while attending the University of South Dakota, where she double majored in English and History. Her self-diagnosed ADD is blamed for her inability to stick to one genre, and she has dabbled in historical romance, fantasy, action, dystopian fiction, and nonfiction. While Katherine is attempting to publish her first novel by traditional means, her novella series, *1-800-Henchmen,* is available for download. She is surrounded by friends and family who act as cheerleaders and are constantly giving her welcomed advice and inspiration for her stories. Here's what she wrote about "The Banshee Ciana":

> Inspiration for "The Banshee Ciana" came from a fantasy novel I was writing. Ciana is one of the main characters, and the story follows her travels with her best friend, who is an assassin. I touched on her origin story a little in the novel, and she was such a fun character to write that I wanted to give her a rich backstory to tell how she became a Banshee. I thought that it would slow down the timing of the novel's plot to include it, so I decided to write it as a short story instead. I have always been interested in Celtic mythology and much of it involves the Banshee, so I wanted to put my own spin on it with Ciana. I also pulled a little inspiration from the Valkyrie of Norse mythology by

using her bravery in battle as a reason for
the gods to reward her.

◄═►

"Run, Ciana! Run to your father!" The seeress pushed the
young woman out of the hut, urging her to hurry.

"Grandmother! What did you see?" Ciana clung to the
door post, resisting the old woman's hands on her back.

"Death! Your father, the men must leave their camp!"

"Gods!" Ciana breathed as she lost her grip on the wood
and was propelled down the path by her grandmother.

"RUN!"

The one word brought Ciana to herself and she ran,
faster than she thought possible. Her skirts tugged at her
legs and she stopped briefly to tear the material on the sides
so she could stretch out her stride. Her breath whistled in
her throat and her lungs burned from the effort, but her
grandmother's warning quickened her feet.

The sun just was beginning to set behind her when she
finally reached her father's camp. She was stopped by the
sentries, but they let her pass when they saw it was their
chief's daughter. She ran through the rows of tents, keeping
her father's standard in sight, high above the tents, where
she knew his pavilion would be. When she finally reached
it, she did not slow down. She ran through the flaps, startling the men inside.

"Father!" She gasped air into her abused lungs.

"Ciana! What are you doing here? It's not safe. You
should be at home!" Midir strode angrily across the tent
and grabbed his daughter's shoulders as her legs gave out.
"Water!" he yelled at his servant as he carried Ciana to a
stool in the corner. He knelt in front of her as the servant
brought a cup. He helped her drink and brushed the dark
hair from her face.

"Ciana, why are you here?" he asked gently.

"Grandmother saw –" She gasped, trying to catch her breath. "Death here. You need to leave!"

Midir put his hand over his daughter's fingers where they clutched his arm. "The Illiuts have retreated. We are victorious and will leave in the morning."

"No, Father! You must leave now! Grandmother –"

"Blathnat's visions are not always right, Ciana," Midir scolded kindly, and pressed a gentle kiss to his daughter's forehead.

Ciana stared at her father, the man she looked so much like, from the black hair to the unremarkable brown eyes. They were both tall and slim with sharp features. He looked tired and was covered in dirt and speckled with blood. She did not think any of it was his but could not be sure when she noticed the bandages on his leg and around his upper arm. He still wore his leather and plate armor and tall leather boots, but he had removed his sword belt and helmet. She glanced around the tent and saw his three commanders in similar condition.

"Please, Father?" Ciana begged quietly, a tear slipping down her cheek. She suddenly felt five years old again, asking her father to watch her practice, rather than the twenty-five-year-old woman who was to be named her father's successor and first woman chief of the Corsair Tribe.

He wiped the tear way with a knuckle, the gentlest he had been in years. "We can't, Ciana. There are too many men to move this late, not to mention the injured . . ." Midir stood and spoke with the servant who stood outside the door. When he was done, he addressed his daughter from across the tent. "Ciana, Angus will set up a tent for you and take you home in the morning."

"But –"

"We stay, Ciana," Midir cut her off, all gentleness gone and replaced by the steel and fire of the chief.

Ciana's temper flared in her chest and fire flashed in her eyes. She jumped to her feet, spine straight and eyes locked on her father. "Ennis, Gaeth, Murchadhm, will you give me a moment with the chief?"

The men looked between their chief and his daughter for a long moment, unsure what to do. Midir, with his eyes on his daughter, nodded slightly, excusing them.

As soon as the tent flap fell back into place, Ciana crossed the tent in three long strides and stopped just short of her father.

"Blathnat sent me to warn you that if you stay here, you will die. She is more often right than wrong. Why do you stay?" Ciana gritted out from behind clenched teeth.

"I've told you, daughter. It is not possible to move the men."

"Then you've condemned them to die!" Ciana screeched.

Midir slapped Ciana's cheek lightly, enough to sting but not enough to hurt. "Watch your tongue! I am chief and I decide what to do with my army! This position is defendable. I will not risk the lives of the injured by moving them for no reason!"

"So you will let them all die because you are too stubborn to listen to Blathnet!"

"ENOUGH!" Midir roared, grabbing Ciana by the shoulders and shaking her roughly. "I –"

"MIDIR!" A shout came from outside of the tent. "The Illiuts return!"

Father and daughter turned as one toward the tent flaps as sounds of fighting and horses screaming filtered through the thick canvas.

"Hide." Midir released Ciana and quickly buckled on his sword.

"Father –"

"HIDE!" he yelled as he ran for the door.

Ciana stood in the center of her father's tent, unsure what to do as the sounds of fighting grew closer. A scream escaped her throat as a passing horse tangled in the tent's ropes and ripped a whole panel from the side of the tent, exposing her to the fighting outside.

"Princess!" Gaeth, followed closely by Angus, rushed inside the tent and surrounded Ciana. "You must run, get to safety!"

"Angus!" Ciana screamed as an Illiut warrior rushed them and raised his sword to kill the servant. A clang rang out as the sword was stopped by Midir's blade.

"Get my daughter out of here!" Midir quickly killed the man and the two who had followed him into the tent as Gaeth stood at his side and Angus tried to pull Ciana to safety.

She turned back once, just in time to see an Illiut push his sword through her father's chest. She screamed, a blood-curdling sound that made all men within earshot stop and turn. She pushed past Angus, pulled her father's sword from his limp grip as he fell and pushed it through the Illiut warrior's chest in one smooth move. The man gasped in surprise, sprinkling Ciana's face with his blood as he exhaled. She pulled the sword from his dying body and removed the head from the next man. Gaeth and Angus moved to her sides and protected her as she killed two more men in her grief-induced rage. The three were quickly overwhelmed and Ciana was cut down soon after Angus and Gaeth fell.

As Ciana fell, she looked to her father's still form, his eyes open and unseeing. She felt tears trail down her cheeks. "I'm sorry, *seanmhathair*. I failed." She whispered an apology to her grandmother with her last breath.

<=>

"Wake child." A voice that was somehow deep and wispy at the same time came through the darkness.

Ciana slowly opened her eyes and blinked in the bright light. Five people stood around the stone altar on which she lay. She remembered the battle and gasped back the tears brought by her father's death. Pain exploded from her side.

"I died," she whispered to the figures. She heard a girlish giggle and turned to the sound. The figures were becoming clearer and revealed three men and two women. All looked young, yet ancient, with their long hair, flowing robes, and fathomless eyes.

"You did," the giggling woman, who wore dark, red-colored robes, said kindly.

"You don't have to stay that way," the man in the midnight blue robes said.

"You were courageous in battle," the man in the brown robes whispered.

"You brought honor to yourself and your house," the other woman, who wore emerald green, continued.

"You are here to make a decision," the man in white explained.

Ciana realized that the man in white's voice was the first she had heard. "What decision?"

"Will you become *bean chaointe*?" the man in white asked.

"A Banshee?" Ciana tried to sit up, but could not move. "You want me to become a Banshee?"

"Yes," the man in blue answered.

"You can avenge your family," the woman in green whispered.

"And kill your enemies," the man in brown muttered.

"And help others do the same," the man in white finished.

The woman in red sobered. "'Tis forever, child. You scream for those about to die and help the justly vengeful find solace."

"I'll live forever?" Ciana asked slowly. "Nothing will kill me?"

"The end will come when you tire and let go. You will live as long as you let yourself," the man in blue explained.

"Vengeance," Ciana whispered, seeing her father's death again in her mind. "I accept."

Ciana saw the man in white smile before the five placed hands on her. Then the light grew blinding and she closed her eyes.

Ciana sat up with a gasp. She was back on the floor of her father's tent, a few feet from his still form. The battle still raged around them. She felt herself changing. She stood. Suddenly, she was floating off the ground, her battered dress was replaced by flowing green fabric, and the hair that blew around her was white-green in the light coming from her skin. She threw back her head and screamed the scream of the Banshee.

Every man on the battlefield heard and was afraid.

She screamed again and the Illiuts pressed their hands to their ears to block out the sound and the pain.

Silence fell on the battlefield as Ciana's toes touched the ground. She was back in her dress and her skin was the right color, but her hair was white. She also had two long knives on her belt, a quiver across her back, and a bow in her hand. She dropped the bow and pulled the knives from their sheaths. She turned to the nearest Illiut warrior with a cold smile.

"The Banshee screamed for you." She decapitated him in one clean swing before moving to the next. She fought her way across the battlefield, leaving no Illiut alive behind her. Her tribesmen gathered around her, fighting with her, taking courage from her strength, believing that nothing could stop them with her at their center.

As suddenly as the fighting had started, it was over. Her tribe, the Corsairs, broke through the Illiut line and found themselves staring at a field, empty except for the dead and dying. They had fought so hard for so long that it took them a moment to realize what they were seeing.

Ciana raised her bloodied knife over her head. "VIC-TORY!"

Her tribesmen yelled in celebration, raising their swords and bows. Ciana laughed, happy to see so many had survived. She turned to congratulate the man to her left when an arrow struck her just above her heart. The force drove her to the ground.

"Mercenaries!" somebody shouted, and the exhausted Corsairs prepared for battle again.

"They killed Ciana!" a man near her yelled when he saw her drop. Her name became a rallying cry as they pulled strength from her death. Vengeance would feed their tired souls and give them victory yet again.

Ciana opened her eyes to see the Corsair warriors running toward the line of mercenaries that marched across the battlefield. She rolled to her back and grimaced as fire flowed from her wound across her torso. She gently touched the shaft that protruded from her chest and hissed at the pain. She slowly sat up and reached over her shoulder to see if the tip had come through the back.

"Finally, something good," she muttered as she felt the iron arrowhead. Ciana pulled her dagger from her boot and awkwardly sawed away at the wooden shaft between the arrow and her shoulder.

"This is an interesting find on a battlefield." A gravelly voice rose from behind. She stilled as a chill rolled over her. "'Tisn't every day I find a comely woman so scantily clad outside of a tavern."

Ciana was suddenly very aware of her ruined dress, which had only gotten worse as she had fought. The skirt was reduced to dirty strips, her right sleeve was completely gone, there was a hole in the side where she had been stabbed, and somehow the bodice had been ripped low enough that only her corset kept her chest covered. She surreptitiously took hold of one of her knives with one hand, holding her bodice closed as she slowly rose to her feet, trying not to jostle the arrow. She held the knife tight against her side, trying to conceal it in her tattered skirt. She turned and found the most revolting man she had ever seen leering at her.

His hair was thinning on top but what he did have hung in dirty, greasy clumps around his dirty face, while his dangerous smile revealed a mouth full of rotten stumps where teeth should have been. He was dressed in leather and hides, both so dirty and bloody that she could not tell what their original color had been. He held a large, rusty sword in his right hand and a huge wooden club in his left.

"Don't come any closer." Ciana heard her voice catch and cursed herself for being scared. Was she not Banshee, who screamed death and were immortal? Why should she fear this man?

The man laughed and took a step closer, unafraid at her warning. "I just want to help you."

Ciana shuddered at his tone, which was anything but sympathetic. She took an unwilling step back. "I said stop, troll!"

"Now, how did you know who my father was?" He laughed and moved closer.

Ciana cursed silently. Trolls were strong and surprisingly fast for their size, and he did not look as if he was joking about his lineage. She took another step back and held more tightly to her knife. She would only have a moment of surprise and she did not want to waste it.

"Come now." The half-troll laughed again and suddenly reached out and grabbed Ciana's left elbow. He pulled her close. She lost her hold on her bodice, but she did not notice as pain from her wound flashed through her.

He roughly grabbed the arrow shaft, snapped it off and tossed it aside before grabbing the arrowhead and yanking it from her shoulder. Ciana screamed at the pain and nearly fainted.

"Now that's done, we can have a little fun." He laughed as he pulled her closer.

Ciana tried to pull away so she would have enough room to use her knife, but she was no match for his strength. She felt a scream in the back of her throat. The Banshee took her.

The half-troll's eyes grew round as he released her and backed away. He raised his hands to block her scream from his ears, but they fell limply to his sides as a sword point parted his leather chest plate.

"Didn't like him anyway," a tall man said from behind the half-troll as he pushed him off his sword.

Ciana's attacker fell forward and landed on his face. She stared at him with her mouth open, not sure what had just happened. She looked up at the man who had stabbed her attacker in the back, hoping for answers. She was expecting to see one of her tribesmen but she found a dark-haired man, dressed all in black, cleaning his sword with a bit of cloth. He wiped the last of the green-tinged blood from the steel and tossed it on the half-troll's body.

"You all right?" he asked as he sheathed his sword and tucked both his hands in the back of his belt. He nodded at her shoulder but made no move toward her.

Ciana nodded dumbly.

"You just had an arrow ripped from your shoulder. I doubt that," he said with a slight smile. "May I?"

Ciana frowned but felt herself nod. The stranger did not move.

"Do you mind lowering that? I don't plan on getting impaled today." He looked pointedly at the naked blade she held in front of her.

"Oh." She slowly sheathed it and bent to tuck it into her boot. She also picked up her other knife from the ground and sheathed it as she stood up. The stranger had not moved and she appreciated his caution.

"Ready?"

Ciana nodded and he slowly walked toward her, holding his hands out slightly so she could see them. When he reached her, she could finally see him clearly. He had darker skin, suggesting he was from the north. He looked just a few years older than her, but his eyes were ancient. Her eyes lingered on the three long scars that ran down the left side of his face and disappeared into his tunic.

He gently pulled the cloth away from her shoulder so he could see the wound. Ciana looked straight ahead, unwilling to see the damage the arrow had caused.

"Huh," he said softly.

"What?"

"It was this shoulder, wasn't it?" he asked, confused. He looked over her other shoulder, hoping to see an arrow hole there.

"What? Of course!" Ciana finally looked down, only to find the skin unbroken on her shoulder. There was no blood, no scar. It wasn't even red. The only indicators that there had been an arrow through her shoulder were the matching holes in her dress.

"Were you the one who screamed for our friend?" He nodded his head toward the body at their feet.

"I . . . I think so," Ciana mumbled, finally realizing what her deal with the five gods really meant.

"Banshee?" The stranger stared at her in amazement, searching her eyes for the answer.

"Yes," she whispered, stunned at what had happened.

"Are you a Corsair?"

"Yes. Daughter to the murdered chief. The chief in my own right now, I suppose," Ciana replied, wondering for the first time how her choice would affect her future with her tribe.

The man chuckled darkly. "I wouldn't set my foot solidly on that path if I were you. I saw you fight the Illiuts. You are very good with those knives. And being immortal? You would be a good person to have at my back." He held out his hand for her to take. "Baylin. If you need a traveling partner, find me."

Baylin released her hand and Ciana watched him walk away, finally realizing he was one of the mercenaries the Illiuts had hired. He did not rejoin the fighting as she expected. He walked away from the battle and disappeared into the darkness.

Ciana shook herself, preparing to return to the fight, when she staggered on her first step. She felt faint and dropped to her knees on the bloody field.

"You left so quickly that we did not have time to give this to you." The woman in red and the woman in green appeared in front of Ciana. One held a wooden bowl, the other a silver flask.

The woman in red giggled as she reached out to touch Ciana's hair gently. "You are tired. You will need this." She handed Ciana the flask. "'Tis carask milk. The drink of the immortals. You cannot drink mortal drink for it will make you ill. This will sustain you." She giggled once more before stepping back.

The woman in green stepped forward and touched Ciana on the shoulder. She then handed Ciana the wooden bowl. "'Tis mollet grain. The food of the immortals. You cannot eat mortal food for it will make you ill. This will sustain you." She touched Ciana's shoulder once more and stepped back.

"You can mix them together to create a porridge. The mollet can also be made into cakes, or eaten dry," the woman in red added as the two women faded.

"The flask and bowl will never be empty. You must not tell anyone this or allow a mortal to eat it," the woman in green ordered.

"Go blessed," the women said together as they disappeared completely from Ciana's sight.

Ciana looked at the flask and bowl in her hands. She sniffed the carask milk and wrinkled her nose. It was tart and pungent yet had a hint of honey and berries. She sipped it and was surprised at how delicious it was. She scooped a few of the dry mollet grains out of the bowl and crunched on them. They were rather bland, but a strong wheat flavor slowly developed as she chewed. Ciana sipped on the flask, ate more mollet and felt the strength return to her limbs. She pulled a leather pouch from a dead Illiut, stowing her flask and bowl in it before swinging it over her head to hang across her body. She picked up a discarded bow and pulled an arrow from her quiver.

"Get off my land!" she growled as she started for the fighting. Suddenly the Banshee took her again. She threw back her head and screamed. As her feet touched the ground once more, she started running. "GET OFF MY LAND!" she yelled, loosing an arrow that embedded itself in a mercenary's forehead. She kept loosing arrows on the run until she reached the front. She tossed the bow and pulled her knives from their sheaths. She slashed the first man she came to across his stomach and slit the second's throat. She worked her way through their ranks, sensing more than seeing her tribesmen rally around her again to follow in her wake. Finally, the Corsairs had done enough damage that the mercenaries sounded the retreat.

"Let them go!" Ciana yelled. She turned when she heard her order echoed from her left. Standing in the middle of his own pile of bodies, surrounded by their tribesmen, Ciana found her brother. He was just a year younger than her, but at times she felt ages older than him. He was a head taller than her, but they had been practically mirror images. Both took after their father, but Ciana's jaw and nose had been softened into beauty where Finn and their father's features were strong and sharp. She sheathed her swords as she ran to him. "Finn!"

He turned just in time to catch her as she threw herself into his arms. "Ciana, thank the gods you are safe! What in Faavian's Hells are you doing here?"

"*Seanmhathair* sent me. She saw death here." Ciana's voice caught as the tears found her. "Father's dead, Finn."

He kissed her hair and squeezed her closer. "I know. We found his body in the tent right before the mercenaries attacked." He set her at arm's length, holding her by her shoulders. "What did you do to your hair? And your dress! Ciana, how long have you been here?" He pulled off his surcoat and dropped it over her head to cover her destroyed dress, helping her adjust her quiver below the fabric.

"I arrived shortly before the Illiuts attacked a second time. I was trying to talk father into moving the men away from the camp. He died keeping me safe."

Finn wiped the tears from her cheeks, leaving trails of dirt and gore behind. "Did you fight?"

Ciana stood up taller. "Of course. Until one of them cut me down." Finn's eyes followed her hand where she touched her side. The bloody hole in her dress marked where her mortal wound had been.

Finn quickly crouched down to examine his sister's side but shook his head with a sigh when he could not find anything. "Ciana, there's nothing there. Your side is fine," he gently scolded, assuming the battle had addled his sister's brain. He noticed a piece of rope at his feet and picked it up before standing. He wrapped it around Ciana's waist to keep the surcoat in place.

"I died, Finn. The gods sent me back. I am Banshee."

Finn gasped, knowing no one would lie about such a thing. He finally took in his sister's appearance. He rubbed a lock of her white hair between his fingers, hoping the color would wipe off. The weapons she wore no Corsair or Illiut had forged. He finally met her fathomless eyes. She looked like his sister but felt different somehow.

"It was you who screamed," he whispered, searching her eyes, hoping it wasn't true but knowing it was.

"Yes."

"We must talk to the elders." Finn grabbed her hand and began pulling her along behind him.

Ciana planted her feet and jerked him to a stop. "Finn, first we take care of our injured and dead. 'Tis what father taught us."

"They are being seen to. We must talk to the elders." He yelled orders at one of the remaining commanders as he pulled Ciana toward the corralled horses.

Ciana tried not to be mad at him for assuming control when she was their father's successor. She told herself that with the confusion of the battle, few would know that Midir was dead and that she was their new chief. The men were simply following the chief's son's orders. Ciana's long stride kept pace with Finn's and soon they were both mounted and racing for Gulver's Blush, the lone town in the Corsair's territory, used as a trading post and home of the elders and others who chose not to ride with the herds. It was also the home of Blathnat, and was where Ciana had been when her grandmother sent her to the battlefield less than twelve hours earlier.

"We'll gather them in the hall," Finn called to her over the sound of their horses' hooves.

Ciana shook her head. "No. *Seanmhathair* needs to know what is happening. We will gather at her cabin."

Finn bared his teeth in frustration. "Ciana, we are meeting with the elders! Blathnat isn't one!"

"You know better! She knows more about this tribe than those doddering old men! She must be there!" Ciana growled.

Finn finally gave in just as they reached the edge of town. They pulled their horses back hard, dropping them to a walk. Finn pointed at a boy as they passed him. "Luc, gather the elders and have them meet us at Blathnat's! We have word of the battle!"

Ciana's jaw dropped as she watched the boy bow to Finn and run off without question. "Finn, I am chief now, not you!"

"Our father just died and you want to argue about this?" Finn stopped in front of their grandmother's house and jumped off his horse, frustration pouring off him in waves.

Ciana dismounted right behind him and the siblings tied the horses to the fence in front of the cabin. "Now is the time to get it sorted, Finn! I am chief and have been since the moment father died. If you don't respect that, the others won't either!"

Finn roughly grabbed Ciana's arm as she walked past him and pulled her around to face him. "Then act like the chief and the others will have no choice," he growled. He jerked away from her and marched down the path to Blathnat's door.

Ciana snarled at his back but followed him. As Finn reached for the door, Blathnat threw it open.

"Finn!" The tiny woman pulled him into her arms, glad he survived the battle. Tears streamed down her face as she finally released him. "Ciana!" Blathnat shoved passed her grandson and pulled her granddaughter into a tight hug.

"Father is dead," Ciana whispered, her voice catching on the unshed tears.

"I know, lass," Blathnat whispered back. She kept hold of Ciana's shoulders, forcing the younger woman to stoop down so she was eye level with her grandmother. "What happened? No, shush." Blathnat studied Ciana, her eyes delving deep, her magic seeing what the normal eye could not. She took in the white hair, the different eyes, the aura around Ciana that was much changed from that of her granddaughter. Blathnat touched Ciana's cheek. "Banshee," she whispered as new tears trailed down her cheeks. "Come!"

Blathnat roughly pulled her grandchildren into her cabin and forced them into chairs at her table. Finn stopped her pacing with a hand to her arm "*Seanmhathair*, the –"

"Hush, Finn. Speak, Ciana," she ordered. Ciana nodded and quickly explained everything that had happened that night to the last two family members she had left. Finn listened, his eyes wide with surprise. Blathnat held Ciana's hand, a mixture of pride and reverence on her face.

When Ciana finished her tale, Blathnat reached out and gently touched her cheek. "My granddaughter. A Banshee."

"She's dead, Blathnat. Why do you act this way?" Finn lashed out, missing his beloved sister even though she sat next to him at the table. He knew things would never be the same between them.

"She is Banshee, Finn! You should be proud of her! The gods honored her bravery on the battlefield! Never has a woman of this family proven herself such!" Blathnat scolded Finn while praising Ciana.

Ciana's heart broke when she heard her brother say that she was dead. She technically wasn't alive as she had been, but she still breathed and felt as she did before. With every passing minute she realized more of what she had given up for her chance for revenge against the Illiuts.

"I can never be chief, can I?" Ciana asked quietly, studying her hands where they lay on the table. Blathnat's voice trailed off and Finn stared at his sister. After a long silence, Ciana looked up at them. Her voice was emotionless when she spoke again. "The elders would never allow it. I am Banshee and immortal. It took father nearly two years to convince them that I was his successor when I was human. They would more likely allow a troll be the chief than me now. At least trolls die."

"Ciana . . ." Finn reached over and put a hand over hers.

She looked up at her grandmother, who was staring at something no one else could see. Finally her eyes cleared and she looked at her granddaughter sadly. "No, Ciana. You cannot be chief."

Ciana nodded slowly before resting her head on her crossed arms and sobbing for all that she had lost. Finn slid his chair closer to her and wrapped his arms around her. Blathnat stood and put a hand on each of their shoulders.

"My grandchildren have lost so much in so few years," she whispered, a tear rolling down her cheek.

A loud knock on the door rousted them. "The elders! They have come," Finn exclaimed, finally remembering that he had invited them.

Ciana slowly stood and wiped the tears from her face. "I'm leaving."

"Ciana, no!" Finn jumped to his feet and wrapped her in another hug.

She let him hold her for a long second before gently unwrapping his arms from around her. "Finn, I can't stay here. The tribe won't be itself with me in it. They will always wonder if I will try to wrest the power from you. You will wonder that, too."

"I would never!" Finn exclaimed.

Ciana smiled and rose up on her toes to kiss his cheek. "I will always love you, little brother. Long after you are gone, I will love you."

"Please don't, Ciana." Finn's voice caught on his own unshed tears.

She squeezed his hand before turning to their grandmother. "*Seanmhathair*, thank you," Ciana said simply, before pressing a kiss to Blathnat's weathered cheek.

"You make me proud, lass." Blathnat squeezed Ciana's upper arm.

Ciana opened the door to a surprised elder with his hand raised to knock again. She silently pushed passed him and walked down the path back to her horse. She paused, then turned suddenly, pulling a small pouch of coins from her belt. She tossed the pouch to Finn where he stood in the yard watching her. "Pay Tearn back for the horse."

Finn nodded, knowing that Tearn would never take the money. The man had loved Ciana since they were children and would be heartbroken when he found out that she was gone. Finn watched Ciana mount and turn her horse for the west. "Promise me, Ciana! You will come back!" he shouted after her.

She turned in the saddle, a bright smile on her face that did not quite reach the fathomless eyes. "Nothing could stop me!" she promised her brother. She felt his eyes on her back until she left the village and set heels to her horse. She had a mercenary to find.

Protection
By Brenna Conley
⟷

BRENNA CONLEY is a business copywriter with an honors degree in creative writing. Her writing is inspired by her hunger for travel, her obsession with detail, and her childhood love of mythology. Her lyric essays, poems, and short stories have been featured in *Ramifications* and *The Lindenwood Review*. In 2011, Brenna received the American Poets Academy Award; in 2012, she received the Hammond Poetry Award, and in 2013, her novella was short-listed for the Paris Literary Prize. She is currently planning a backpacking trip through Glacier National Park with her boyfriend, and working on her first children's book. Here's what she wrote about "Protection":

> The story of Demeter, Aides, and Kore has always been one of my favorites. It is a classic myth of power and betrayal – but despite most people's familiarity with the story, it is largely unexplored. It is a pure, bright continent. So, rather than feeling boxed in by its familiarity, I felt liberated. No one knows these characters, at least not intimately, and no one knows what they are truly capable of. I asked myself questions: What sort of relationship would develop between two women who had very little interaction with the surrounding world? What would be important to them? How would they perceive love? How would they create meaning in their lives? I started to build a world that was beautiful and harmless – a simple Eden

that couldn't satisfy the human longing for destruction. And then I dropped them into it, and I let them live. I let them etch out their own details and flaws. It turns out that the real story isn't what I was told as a child. There's so much more color and venom and sadness to these characters – and there always has been.

<=>

Kore

We saw two gold-jaw serpents circling one another in the creek bed, and Mother said it was a sign that the sky was breaking soon. We hurried to bury the seeds deep, deep enough that the sky wouldn't wash them to the sea. Mother's hands turned the dirt over and over in her rhythm, gentle and constant, displacing the wet silt below, spilling its syrup across the cracked surface. I shifted my weight where I crouched so that my figure mirrored hers; the lengths of our arms were pressed together and our pinkies rubbed warmly, a way of reminding her that I needed her as much as the earth did, that I ached for her in a way that the blind worms and the skeleton trees could never understand. I ached for her through the entire line of my being, beginning at my pale temples and coursing down my sides, into my ankle bones – for the taste of honey that hung from her, for the spots of silver on her dark arms, for the deep creases that gathered beside her eyes when she laughed. For the sound of her feet smacking the wet ground when it rained.

It poured on us then, the golden, churning sky, streaming down our bare backs into the shells of our palms. We flung water at each other shrieking, my mother laughing hysterically, head thrown back into the storm. I loved looking at her like that. She was glowing and fearless. I watched the rain pool in her laughing mouth and I thought, I will be like this someday. I will find a rhythm that the earth will follow. I will swallow the sky and become a deafening eruption.

⇐⇒

Demeter

I lied to Kore about the serpents because I wasn't ready for her to know yet about how one enters another, sometimes without permission. There were so many things I would have protected her from if I had had the choice. Those days seemed unending, when we knelt beside each other in the field and I taught her to read the grains of earth on her fingertips, to trace their origins and their bitter minerals, deciding where to plant the weaker crops, the sickly toma-toes. I felt my hands grow warm in the body of earth. I felt it push eagerly against me, straining with heat to create, to explode, to blossom into a million olive branches.

I was so big and clumsy next to Kore's delicate figure. I was overwhelmed with envy for her youth and her ability to bloom, the white bulb of her hips, pink buds of her breasts still slick with rain. There was something sensual in her arm pressed against mine, and it filled me with a greater heat still that throbbed through me and made my brown thighs sweat. I dreamed of her growing up, of the first time she would ever make love to a man, as I made love to her father, and she would know the ache of creation. I dreamed of her father, a fisherman I swept from his boat and carried into the cradle of a eucalyptus tree, whose broad back covered me as we moaned together in the soft dust. I dreamed of the salt that painted his lips, of the light in his gold beard, of the sadness and surprise in his face when I left him just as sud-denly, weeping, to return to my garden. My belly had grown full then and I waited, chewing basil leaves and twisting the flower stalks until they snapped in my hands. As I thought, it began to rain, and Kore gazed up at me, tilting her head at my silence. I threw back my head and laughed into the downpour. It was a sort of game I played, pretending that I was protecting her because she was a child, but my skin burned where my arm brushed against hers, streaked with mud, because she was mine alone.

⟵⇒⟶

Kore

We slept in the burrow, to hide from the villagers that sometimes wandered into our garden at night. We used to sleep each night among the roots of the orchard, but the villagers took to rubbing their hands across Mother's face as she slept, hoping her magic would heal them or that they would become immortal. They sucked on her fingertips and broke tiny golden strands from her head. She would wake up startled, the brush of fingers sweeping like spiders down her cheeks, her lips, her neck. They worshipped her feverishly for abundant harvests, begging for her hands to awaken the earth. She asked them not to return but they did not listen. Along the road leading from our garden to the village they built shrines to her, painting her face on woven corn husks with dye and mud, scattering the ground with wild poppies and violets. They were so infatuated with her that we grew afraid for our safety, and we dug the burrow together one morning in the softness of the dew.

We moved the dirt like bundles of cloth in our arms, lifting and dropping with such effort that the muscles bulged in our necks. The burrow was deep, lined with goose feathers and ferns, and we slept curled in its belly like infants in the womb. We would drape the opening with a woven net, covered in damp brush and moss. We pulled it across the opening from below, veiling ourselves completely in darkness. Not even the moon could reach us.

In the mornings we visited the village; we were much braver in the daylight than in the dark. We walked through the rows of a field, noting how carefully this man had planted his rows, or how this woman had laid her seeds too shallow. We dug our fingers into their earth – our earth – and felt the wetness, the firmness. Did the field need more water or more light? Were the trees keeping the wheat in shadow? The wheat needs full sunlight to yield the best harvest, Mother told me. We reported these details to the villagers, but their eagerness in our presence distracted them. Their eyes fell on the hammered amulet that hung from a leather cord around Mother's neck, an emblem of fertility, on the shining cloud of her hair, the dirt beneath her fingernails, the strange silver marks on her arms and chest. They watched me walk in a careful line beside her, trying to match her rapid pace with shorter, quicker steps. They watched our mouths move but did not hear our words. We were frustrated with them, but we loved them as one loves stupid children and we revisited the fields to tend them ourselves.

The villagers sat huddled in the Assembly beneath the sinking orange blossoms, discussing new details they had noticed. Mother could hear them from very far away, and we laughed together as she retold the things they said. Today, she'd whisper, they observed that your eyes have green lights in them like the sea. I often felt guilty knowing the things they said together in privacy, the things they confided. We were not of the village and I felt as though I was witnessing something strangely intimate that I had no right to see, that I ought never see. We always walked back to our garden in silence, shifting our eyes away from the makeshift shrines that scattered the roadside. We were alone in our heads then, remembering the villagers' eagerness and humility.

⟨⇒⟩

Demeter

My brothers and sisters never understood why the earth appealed to me so much. They preferred the cleanness of the sky, especially when it hangs with moisture before a storm. They did not crave the smell of dirt or the bitter juice of a leaf, split along its spine. They did not share my joy in the colors of the trees, one shifting so graciously into another, easily missed by the villagers, whose necks are curved downward, towards the plotted soil. I tried to explain these things to them when I was first born, but I quickly learned that gods are born with their opinions, and trying to change our minds is like trying to teach a mountain to grow down into the earth instead of upwards. I left them when I was still new and made my home here. We became friends, the earth and I, and the villagers learned to trust me tentatively and then to worship. The earth doubled in richness where my feet and hands brushed its crust, and those who saw this with their own eyes whispered of it to one another.

I built the garden in circular tiers, growing ever smaller as they reached higher so that the rain formed a sort of moat where it spilled and gathered around the bottom. The lowest tier was planted with vegetables – carrots, celery, rhubarb, butter squash, potato, radish, and arugula. In the next tier I planted ground fruits – pumpkin, melon, raspberries, and wild strawberries. Next were the herbs, poking their spindly heads from the dirt – thyme, basil, sweet rosemary, sage, cilantro, and parsley. On the top tier grew a profusion of roses, irises, violets, and crocuses, stitched together with thick briars. When Kore and I built the burrow through the top tier, we had to dig out some of our garden to make space for the hole, and we were hidden even more carefully then, in the chaos of plant life. We did not want to dig into the bottom tier because the runoff would have pooled into our burrow and drowned us as we slept, so we accepted that our hideout was finished, and we danced in celebration, our heavy heels pounding the dirt until it was hard.

Around the mound of tiers, I planted an orchard that would look from above like ripples, extending from the center of some skipping stone that had disturbed the earth's surface. The species were planted in concentric circles – orange trees closest to the heart, then apple trees, fat figs, olives, and the furthest circle was the eucalyptus trees, whose fingers extended to meet one another and close the circle. The fruit grew so thickly and ripened so quickly that entire branches snapped from their trunks, and apples lay rotting in the dirt, invaded by eyeless worms, weighting the air with sweet fumes that made our heads ache.

I sometimes hovered high above the garden to see the perfect symmetry of the place I had created. I would trace the circles from the sky with my finger, arm outstretched, squinting one eye, so pleased that I would sing. My voice was low and hoarse, and fell in uneven chords to the earth around me. The birds took to mimicking me in shrill harmony, forcing themselves upon the peace of the morning. One day I began to forget that a silence ever existed.

<=>

Kore

I always became very excited when I realized that Mother was planning another celebration, because she spent many days and nights making preparations, and because on celebration days I got to play with the children from the village, who I did not see very often because I was usually busy helping Mother, or learning from how she dealt with the villagers when we went into town. I asked her one day what we were celebrating. She said that we were celebrating my beauty and my youth, and that very soon my bleeding would begin, and I would become a woman, and I would learn the graceful language of bodies. I argued that we ought to have a feast for her too, because I felt selfish only having one for myself. She countered that she didn't want one, for she was neither young nor beautiful, as I was, and she was always the same, which was a truth not worth celebrating. She pursed

her lips and wound her fingers together, her knuckles cracking loudly, and the air boiled around us. I collapsed onto
the ground beside her, laying my head in her soft lap, her
crossed ankles carving into the dirt. She rubbed her hand
across my back and up to the line of my cheek, murmuring
how lucky I was to be so pretty and so bright, forever changing, letting the world course through me, heating my blood.
She wiped a bead of sweat from my temple. My body stirred
under the warmth of her breath, and I gazed into her face
from beneath heavy eyelids.

I didn't believe her. I knew that she had to feel sorry
for me, my finite body and soul, constantly wilting until
one day my skin would be as dried as an apple left too long
in the heat, and my teeth would rot and crumble into the
bread I chew. I had seen old women in the village and their
bodies disgusted me, their sunken eyes and tanned breasts
drooping to their stomachs. They could not kneel to touch
the earth, or splash in the creek or sprint through the fields,
looking for lizards. Mother revered them, in a certain way,
her eyes strong and her chin firm as she greeted them, clasping their hands in her own, sometimes kissing the tops of
their heads. But she did not understand how terrified I was
to touch them. I turned my face away when they came near;
I held my breath for fear that I would smell them, and that
the smell would creep inside me and burrow into my organs,
slowly corroding me until I was as shrunken and hunched
as they were.

Mother could not be expected to understand. She would
always appear youthful – a gorgeous, sun-drenched vital-
ity – and if she had not been Mother, who loved me so well
and gave me more than I deserved, I was afraid I would have
hated her for it. She had told me the story whenever I asked
– of the fisherman, my father, how she had seduced him in
the tangle of roots, the sticky heat, then realized he was also
the lover of her jealous sister and felt fear for the first time,
not able to bear the thought of his punishment if they were

discovered; and so she had fled, left him where he was sleeping, gently uncurling his brown fingers from her wrist. She remembered him still exactly as she had left him – his chest rising and falling, his naked body glowing with dust and golden hair. And then, how she had felt me growing inside her and had known that I was a part of him, this beautiful man, known that like him I would live, I would really live, and she had cried, her tears washing down her stomach and her thighs, flooding the dirt where hundreds of insects had gathered at her feet.

The week of the party, Mother's hands worked magic on the land, brightening and burnishing the petals until they glowed metallically, dusting the pollen from the leaves and spreading new soil across the pruned garden tiers. She would cross bright ribbons through the trees, green and blue, and tie from branches the most delicately carved wooden creatures: doves, swans, deer, foxes, elk, centaur, and boar, all hung from gossamer thread that was nearly invisible, except when it caught the sunlight. She'd invite the village children, the old widows she favored, whose hands she clasped, the rough men who stared at her when their wives weren't looking, her brothers and sisters, and we'd sprawl across the grassy orchard, feasting on the things she had made. This was one of the only times when the gods agreed to sit with us, to talk with us so freely, and to laugh and drink and dance in the company of mortals. Mother had roasted potatoes, drizzling them with duck fat, spices and honey, and stuffing them with boiled grapes and crumbling cheeses, and she had gathered many different types of fruits, cutting them into small pieces. She had simmered olives with lamb, in a sauce of oranges, apples, and sugar, and crusted with crushed pecans, and placed the meats and fruits in copper bowls that shone. It was all so beautiful, and smelled so rich and sweet, I felt as though I'd stepped into a dream from which I never wanted to wake.

✦

The children always played together, leaping in and out of great rolling hoops and hollering as we threw great clumps of dirt at one another, staying a safe distance from the elders, who ate slowly, chewing each mouthful more times than I could count.

But this celebration was different, for Mother had said I was almost a woman, and that I was beautiful, and I felt as though she had confided a great secret to me. I did not want to disappoint her with my behavior. I lay awake at night imagining the things we would eat, and the fun Mother and I would have, reclining in the grass and talking to each other intimately, watched by everyone. I would ask Mother to make a new gown for me, dark green like the deathless trees, with sleeves long and flowing like giant bells. I would rub black kohl on my eyelids to look mysterious, as Mother sometimes did, and smile sweetly at the men, and maybe I would be kissed hard on the mouth, and it would taste like strawberries and make my ribs shake. Mother would watch me then, my back pressed against a tree, and she would know that I was a woman.

✦

Demeter

I awoke one morning to realize Kore's celebration was three moons away. I scrubbed my cheeks with water and began organizing the tasks to be completed: arranging and tending to the garden, preparing the food, decorating the fields, making us each new gowns. We were usually naked together in the fields, and wore our brown sheaths to the village, but this was a special celebration and I knew she would want something eye-catching that showed off her small breasts and her supple waist. She must be so proud, I thought, to have that feeling of newness about her, clinging to her skin. I tried to imagine the joy of passing from girlhood into womanhood, but I could not, and so I contented myself by thinking of her finally being a woman, which was something I could understand. She would be my closest companion and I would teach her how a woman ought to act, and I would teach her the appetites of the body, and she would obey me.

I did not start the cleaning yet, for with moons to pass before the celebration, any strong wind or rain would undo all my work. Instead I began to plan the dress, traveling to the village to look at their cloths and threads. An old woman, gnarled like an oak, greeted me in the shop, bowing low with her arms and fingers extended towards me. I asked to see the cloths she had – a linen the color of too-ripe plums, a buttery yellow wool. I finally decided on a silk from the East, as soft as water and iridescent like fish scales; dark green that shone black in the candle light. I gathered the bundle into my arms, enough to make a shawl as well, and picked red-gold threads, the color of my hair, and a matching red-gold cloth to sew the girdle for her waist.

I would braid her hair, in the way she liked, woven with tiny white flowers, and she would be more beautiful than any living creature, in the sky or on the earth. I felt, in the pit of my stomach, a tiny seed swelling, the head of a green shoot unwinding, but I pushed it deeper, burying it, the ugly thing I would not recognize.

<=>

Kore

Mother always insisted on braiding my hair tightly, so tightly that my temples ached, winding it in a circlet around my head. She would weave flowers into my hair, sometimes pulling so hard that I'd yell for her to stop and then run off a short distance and hide in the shade. She was so patient with me, making a show of folding the flowers into the woolen pouch tied to a string around her waist, waiting for me to return. I always would, running back to settle myself on the grass at her knees, tilting my head back so her deft fingers could run across the smooth braid again, tucking in the loose strands.

When she had finished, she'd say, Stand back so I can tell you how pretty you are. I'd back away from her, twirling slowly, and end in a deep, mocking curtsy. But her eyes never laughed. She always looked curious in those moments, as though her eyes were not her own, or her smile had been put on a little crooked. Maybe she forgot then, to tell me how pretty I was, or maybe she'd just changed her mind.

One day, the heat was so oppressive that my entire body shone, my cheeks burned, streams of sweat ran down the bow of my ribs and gathered in the dark triangle of new hairs between my thighs. Mother sat behind me as always, my back against her shins, her fingers winding along the perfect braid of damp curls. When the inspection reached my temples, her restless fingertips paused. Her touch ran lightly down my cheeks, the line of my jaw and my neck, the muscles tensing and releasing in spasms so fiercely that I ached. Her fingertips found my collarbone, drops clinging to the sharp crest, and suddenly her hands dropped, reaching from behind to cup my small wet breasts, to squeeze them urgently, so hard it hurt, her hands hot and quivering. I held my breath, my blood surging, as her fingertips circled the hard buds of my nipples. She leaned forward and pressed the heat between her legs against my spine and murmured, My Kore, you are a woman now.

⟨⇒⟩

Demeter

When my brother Aides and I were newly made, we used to play a game called Want. We started by listing the smallest things – plum cake or a silver comb or a black and white dog, but then we would begin to list, getting louder and louder, the things we could never have. We were a lot like children then, although we looked the same as we do today. I told him I wanted to grow old with someone, to feel the exquisite wear of mortality on the body, to watch the way wrinkles climbed across our tan cheeks and laugh lines formed beside our eyes, as though to match each other. I wanted to wash beside an old man in the creek, my shrunken body shivering beside him in the cold water, the sun lighting up his silver hairs. I wanted to die in those same arms, curled against each other as we fell asleep, pleased with all we had done and seen.

Aides laughed at me and said, I want you as you are, to have forever without ever growing old, to grab you by the waist right now and drag you to my desert below the ground. You could make everything bloom for me.

As we talked, our fingers moved in and out of one another's, tangling together and apart, tracing knuckles, like rows of walnuts, the sloping lines of our palms. I thought it wasn't fair how he had been forced to live in the world below, exiled, while the rest of us moved wherever we wished. Spit flew from his lips when he spoke again, violently, repelling my sympathy to force his words inside of me, to puncture the softness of my body. He said, Sister, I want you in a terrible way, not a noble one, in a way that lets me know that we are no better than human. My face grew hot, and I laughed, leaning to rest my lips against the strong line of his tensed jaw. I closed my eyes. Brother, I growled, that's why you stay below the ground, where no one can see you or hear you speak. I knew it was the cruelest thing to say, that he had seen in me a startling lightness and beauty that he wanted for his own, but my purpose was in the tides and harvests of my earth and I would never desert them, not even for my dark wolf brother.

When Kore was born, he came with all my brothers and sisters to look at her tiny face and precious limbs, and to laugh at me for taking a human lover, as we are so apt to do. Even though it was evening, and the sun had set, his face glowed over the bundle of silk and the face, as pink as the tip of a rosebud, and when he turned to me his eyes were wild like a lion's. Sister, he said, I want.

<=>

Kore

I lay beneath the goat's knobby legs, staring up at her stomach. I had to knead the gassy spots sometimes to keep her from crumpling in pain. My fingers wound around in smaller and smaller circles, massaging the knots. Mother said that if I sang to her softly, tenderly, as if she were my baby, that it would help the pain to subside, but Mother is superstitious about plants and wild animals and sometimes I thought she just liked to hear me sing, tenderly. Maybe she liked to imagine that she was the baby and I was Mother, with the world in my palm.

I thought about the ginger root she would grind, smearing it across my shoulder blades before bedtime, so that I would never grow wings. She had been told by a man traveling from the coast that I would fly away from her one day, and so she straddled my back and rubbed the ginger root hard to the bone, until I screamed, to be sure there were no tiny growths there, no deformations beneath the skin. I knew this was her way of showing her devotion to me, to our togetherness, but sometimes I resented her for it, for the pain, and for the scratches and welts that ran the width of my shoulders.

Once she had ripped a crown from my head made of cypress twigs, which I had made while I was exploring the mountains. I had noticed the resilience of the branch's spine, and its firm, rich green needles, and had been excited to impress her with my ingenuity. She laid the circlet on her hands between us and said, Cypress is for death and for mourning. Cypress is the tree of despair. She let it fall into the dust and took my face between her hands. You are none of these things, she said. I saw that her eyes were red and I looked away, wondering if the words were for me or for herself.

I finished resting and reached up again to the belly of the kid, but he was not above me anymore and my eyes were flooded with light. Then a man stood above me, his feet spread apart, hands on his slender hips, his face shadowed from the sun behind him. I wondered at his tangled black hair, his deep red robe, and realized that this was Aides, the god of the world below ours, and I lay there looking up at him, sprawled like a pile of dust, meaningless in form. I had heard stories of the great wolf god from the village women since I was very small, as small as they had been when they had heard the stories they told me. If Mother was around, she would always cup her hands to my ears when they spoke of Aides, or would sing loudly into the sky, until her voice was rough, until she had drowned the women's words in song, and the story had escaped my ears.

When I was younger, I often gazed at myself in the ponds scattered around the rims of the village, where the irrigation water had drained. The surface was covered with the bodies of hundreds of mosquitoes, so the reflection was difficult to make out clearly, but I was never very happy with what I could see, studying for hours the indistinct face that I was to wear for my entire life. My hair was darker than Mother's, and always hung damply about my ears, sticking to the back of my neck in the heat, escaping the ribbons that wound it up into a knot; and my eyes seemed small and squinty, like a pair of blue clay beads hiding beneath my eyebrows. I blinked them, crossed them and pushed against them with my fingertips, seeing what I could make of them. I didn't often think of myself in individual terms: I belonged to Demeter, and was a sister to the earth, friend to the villagers. Thinking of the self was much less comfortable. I had a strange, senseless fear that if I thought too hard about Kore, or stared at her face for too long, she would disappear like a wraith of mist, and I would realize I had never existed as anything outside of those whom I loved.

My eyes moved across Aides as he stooped to gaze into my face. Instead of feeling fear, I was astonished that he could see me at all, and I wondered if he found me tolerable, or if he would laugh at me. His eyes seemed to go through mine, to a point that met in the strands of my thoughts, and I felt very small and translucent.

I tried to become aware of my own thoughts, to see them as he might see them, and guess how he would judge me accordingly. There was a thought, a memory of Mother's resplendent smile, her teeth stained red with juice, and her tongue so velvety and pink. Another of a boy I played with when I was much younger, making up naughty poems about the fat village women, about their breasts that drooped like melons onto their round bellies, and their backsides, probably covered with long dark hairs. There were even more ridiculous thoughts – a self-consciousness of the blush that stole across my cheeks, or of my budding breasts. A half-hope that his wild eyes were lingering over every part of me. There was the thought of the wild goats, and my hope that Mother would stew one for my birthday the next week. They were strange, the thoughts that drifted in and out of my awareness at any given moment, like honey bees moving soundlessly in and out of a hive. It made me wonder, then, what madness meant and if it was like hearing all those thoughts at once, trapping all the bees inside the hive, being the darkness filled with a sudden, angry buzzing.

Aides swooped me up suddenly in his warm darkness. I felt surrounded by heat, by feathers, strands of hair, breath. Then, one by one all my strands of thought were consumed by astonishment, by the brilliance of motion. I dipped into black.

As we moved – we didn't fall, it was much more as if the field was yawning, swallowing us whole, sweeping us down the blood that coursed through the earth – I began to really feel the form of his arms around me. They cradled my neck, my shoulders, the backs of my knees. His skin was warm to the touch. His presence gave the darkness substance, like the red glow that illuminates a charred ember. He was at once the most distinct form of beauty I had ever known and its complete deformation. I pressed my blue eyes into his swelling shadow to hide from the wind that scoured us, that left us clean and starved.

<=>

It was strange that I never felt fear during our descent, and I could not explain it except that it did not occur to me to be afraid. Never had I moved through the layers of dirt with such freedom, and it did not seem to me that any god who was so free, who so neglected the physical laws governing how beings ought to move through surrounding space, could be anything but magnificent.

I fell asleep then, slowly slipping from the furious wind. When I awoke, I was lying beneath the spindled arms of a cypress tree. There was no time of day, only a heaviness that one usually associates with twilight, but the sky was white and cloudless and the branches hung in such stillness that I was afraid to breathe. I thought I could knock a hole in the papery sky the size of my fist and tear away its pieces until I had made a hole big enough to climb through, that I could burrow a wormhole through whatever was beyond the sky, and make my way back to the world above. But even as this thought reached me it passed and I lay unmoving, mesmerized by the colorless bark above me, splitting open and sewing itself shut again. The burning curiosity had not left me,but had become a dull ache that soaked through my body, and it begged me to ask where I had been taken and where the warm arms had gone that had taken me there.

I lay still for so long that my shoulder blades became restless against the solid ground and I sat up slowly, as though waking from a sleep too deep for dreaming. I had not yet stood when the great cypress began to speak to me, or I imagined it speaking to me, a voice of shredded wood and moss, very difficult to understand; and his wretched mouth formed from the husk, which distorted itself into a crude opening, and gave off the smell of rotted meat. He welcomed me to the home of Aides, the god of the unliving, and directed me towards the place where all my questions would be addressed.

But I felt uncertain about the direction of anything, and so I supposed that the cypress had stood silently, sinuous and ambivalent, as most trees stand, so I turned my back to the trunk and peered in every direction. A bleached desert stretched forever around me, interrupted only by the violent slash of a river near the horizon. I decided to move towards the line of the river, wading eagerly away from the strange and twisted cypress, my feet dragging to make an unearthly set of prints behind me in the dust. I pretended then, to make myself brave, that I was a beast that crawled on its hands and feet, and that my mouth was dripping with foam. I pretended that I was terrifying to see, and that my wild scream could make even the harpies shudder and fly back to their dark nests.

It struck me how frightened I should be; that I, a young woman very much alive, should be wandering the sacred and terrible world of souls who had expired, ruled by a king who the village women claimed was more wild beast than man, who was rumored to take girls as lovers and then devour their corpses, except for their carefully peeled skin, which he spread like a canopy above his enormous, dark bed. I'd heard the villagers say that the sheets of his bed were drenched with the dripping blood, and that was why the silk was stained forever red, but Mother had warned me not to believe the tales the old wives whispered, and I tried to forget them now.

My soles groped the cracked earth for the brush of something soft, wet, living, a blooming weed or a blood-glutted beetle, but found nothing. They cracked and bled from the hard scrape of the land, and I laughed to think that my trail had become even more menacing. My eyes continued to search – for movement, for color. I thought how Mother would have cringed to see such a place, an earth without its emotions – of blossoming shrubs and dewy grasses, and grapes that burst on the tongue. She would have leapt across the scar of the land and where her feet fell, life would tumble, drenched in indigo, scarlet, gold. I thought she probably could have created an oasis for us, where we could soak in clear pools of water, and she would scrub the dried blood from my heels, and feed me my fill of honeyed fruits, letting me lick their sugar from her fingertips. She would hate to see me here, wandering alone through this despondent place, at times slipping in the wetness of my own blood, my lips breaking open into layers from the heat and my thirst.

I imagined her again, this time in a rage to finding me missing, digging her fingers into her eyes until they bled, screaming into the deepest wells, searching for me. I didn't want to imagine these things but at the same time they comforted me – she would not forget her Kore. She would find me. I remembered her fearlessness, her bold figure kneeling next to mine in the garden, her broad back shining and wet. I remembered the strokes of her trembling fingertips, and the warmth of her body pressed against my back as she murmured to me. I felt the familiar surge of blood and I cried then, like a child wailing into the thick air, until my noises were no longer human. The desert air dried out my lungs and I began to cough, falling to my knees in exhaustion.

After sleeping again, I walked on through the unchanging day. My stomach hummed angrily. My arms swung limply by my sides. I finally stumbled across a flock of harpies, crouching in a circle on the packed earth, peering up at me with their black, lidless eyes. The harpies, with the faces of women and the bodies of birds, were born of Aides, who had disguised himself as a bird to seduce one of Aphrodite's doves. Their eyes were black and cold, but I had sympathy for them, because everyone talked of their ugliness, their terrible birthright. The flock leapt to their feet, suspicious of my attention. Their cheeks were sunken, showing the bizarre curvature of their skulls, the skin stretched thin and red across the bone, and their wings were molting, the blue-black feathers landing in clumps around them. I should not have stared, for they are proud, as any creature that is part woman, and I forced myself to avert my eyes and continue wandering, in case they were deciding whether or not to tear me apart with their talons, and grind my muscles in their cracked teeth.

The river appeared no nearer, and I began to wonder if it was only an exquisite mirage, dangled before the eyes of a delirious woman, nearing death. The muscles in my throat tugged with the terrible tightness that comes before crying, but I refused to cry because I imagined my abductor watching me as I stumbled across his desert, hidden close by with some spell of invisibility. I wondered again what he thought of me and why he had brought me here.

⟨⇒⟩

Demeter

I had not known which day my brother was coming for her; I knew only that he was coming. I had seen him in my dreams, his shadow to my light, a complete otherness that looked so sweet and wild in my sleep. I imagined him touching me, his fingernails digging into my skin, hurting me, his hot tongue on the curves of my body, my arms bent behind me, face down in the dirt. I dreamed of him possessing me in ways that I had wanted to possess Kore, of submitting to him as she had submitted to me. He had taken her from me just as we were learning to belong to one another, just as she had become mine – but still I dreamed of him and my body went rigid – my wolf brother, the one who had taken everything from me, the one I hated.

I pretended to search for her, in the tree boughs and the river beds, creating a cloud of dust in my desperate wake, but I knew where she had gone, as it had been arranged. I played the game for my villagers, who needed to know the rules of how a person grieves, how a mother ought to respond to the loss of her only child.

I wandered among them, threatening the gentle people who had always loved the light of my face, my gentle voice. I had thought I would have to work hard to make it dramatic, to make for them a show of my misery, but it poured out of me as easily as breathing. I felt it entirely, and I allowed it to swallow me. This is, I think, what I had wanted.

⟵⇒⟶

Kore

I finally reached the river, hurrying so eagerly across the last stretch that I twisted my ankle sharply and had to drag myself the remaining distance. The river was empty of water and it did not gush or bubble like the river that Mother and I bathed in, or ripple brightly under the light, or cast up my reflection when I peered into it. In the river's trench I saw thousands of threads of mist twisting and writhing upon themselves like phantom snakes, each one curling and disappearing, and emerging as another thread, barely distinct from the one before. The threads together formed the rippling, frantic muscles of a human limb, if the skin were peeled back to expose the machinery. I hated the thing without knowing why, without wanting to understand its purpose or its grotesque elegance, and a shudder grew inside me stronger even than the ache, the burning of my body. I closed my eyes and imagined water, the cold green glass of the surface, the dark shapes of bodies moving together in slow motion, stroking each other with urgent hands, outlined in afternoon sun, as seen squinting up from a river bottom.

Though my eyes were closed, I suddenly felt Aides there, beside me, and my nose filled with the smell of hot metal, of dried dates, and sweat. Though I did not open my eyes to look at him, I could see his face as though my eyes were open. You dislike it, he said. I could see the sad way his mouth smiled, almost like a question, as he watched my face, the soft brown fringe of his beard and the strong angle of his jaw. Kore, he whispered, don't be sad. And I opened my eyes in surprise. I wanted to look at him with the boldness of a woman, to convince him, as I had convinced Mother, that I was not a little girl, not the weak Kore who needed words of comfort when she saw wolf eyes in the orchard one night, when she curled up tightly into a ball, so deep inside herself that she wouldn't come out for days. I wanted to say to him, I am not afraid, in a voice that was loud, and firm, and did not shake. But when I opened my eyes there was no one there, only the hushed stirring of the river. Watch, he said, though he was nowhere, and I remembered again the feeling of being watched as I wandered the desert. Watch, he cried, so loudly that pebbles scattered across the desert, disappearing into its cracks. The cry was so eager that my thoughts melted and I turned to watch the river.

I did not expect a cord of mist to rise, singularly, as though being peeled from the others, its other end winding and snaking out from the whole until the length of it was suspended in the air, entirely alone. As it hung, barely visible against the blank sky, the cord began thickening and contorting, rolling and stretching, all the time rising higher and higher above the desert. I heard laughter rumbling around me, from deep in the dust and the thick of the sky. It did not sound cruel, but rather like the laughter of a child who is so proud of what he has done, who is so completely happy that he becomes, for one moment, a spark of light. And for one moment there was a spark, cracking across the air like pure heat – and at this exact moment, the shifting mist flung itself into hundreds of shards that caught the light. With a sigh that rushed into the center of me, the shards merged and the thread plummeted into the river bed, concealing itself among the thousands of others.

I knelt beside the strange river, which I had hated with every piece of my heart because it was something I could not understand yet, and I became so overwhelmed with jealousy and awe that I wished to be a part of the river itself, just to explode so violently, to sigh with such exhaustion. Never had I felt such intense pleasure, such ecstasy, as I had been shown in that one moment, and I realized that this need was the center of my ache, which had filled me when I was so near to Mother.

<=>

Demeter

I had never felt pain before. I had never looked at the earth and found something lacking. I dipped my fingers into the new soil and felt only cold. I felt only the angry grit of it against my skin, and I snatched my hand away and smeared it across my stomach. Baby girl, baby girl, come back to me, I screamed into my fists, and the words tasted rich, like bloody venison. I rubbed the earth along the length of my body. I threw myself against the ground and I thought, If I don't break, the earth will, and I will find her below the garden. She'll love me still and I will kiss her on the lips. But the ground did not break and I did not break, because I was unbreakable, because I was unyielding – a mossy, faceless carving that watched the world spin, and the moon dip in and out of consciousness, and lovers fall upon each other like dogs, grow old, melt into dust.

I ran through the garden, scratching my arms with rose thorns, scratching my cheeks and my eyes. I tore everything: the orchids, the blackberries, and the twisting vines, destroying everything I had planted. In the culmination of that pure, wonderful sadness, fury welled up in my breast, and I began to spit on the faces of the trees, and I made them naked, bereft for the first time of their green mantles. I stripped the fields, stomping the grain to dust and emptying the earth. I let her children die, and her children's children. They would share my grief.

I looked coldly on the families that lay prostrate, praying to me in their humble fields, their bloated children chanting my name into the dirt. I walked through a field where one infant boy was being eaten by his family – their hands soaked in warm blood, wrist-deep in his split abdomen. They looked up at me wildly as I passed, reaching out to me, falling sideways onto the ground so their hands left deep red smears across the scorched corn husks. They screamed words at me that I did not understand, shreds of skin hanging from their lips. I decided there was nothing fascinating in this grief, nothing to comfort me in its monstrous frenzy, and so I left the earth.

<=>

I was no longer angry, sitting alone in the distant, glittering sky. My fury had faded away to something gentler and I was left exhausted, filled with the memory of a clear face, pink fingertips, a woman, wild strawberries, the sound of laughter.

I leaned over the earth and, for the first time, I let myself weep. I shook violently, and where my tears fell through the cold they froze into soft white snow that covered the earth. I remembered her high-pitched squeals when I had first shown her the mother fox and her cubs hidden in the undergrowth. I remembered how her hips had swung as she danced across the grass, swaying with the wheat, her hands circling in the air like birds. I had teased her then, and told her she had better stay on the ground and not go away and leave old Mother all alone. I remembered her laughing as she said, Mother, you're not old! You're lovely! But she had never promised not to fly away, or sink below the ground.

I remembered everything so vividly, the details I had neglected to be thankful for, the messy way her hair stuck up in the morning, twisted with brittle leaves. I buried my face in my hands and the stars looked away from me, ashamed to see me so fragile. The snow fell for months as I hid among the stars, drawing up every memory from the well of my mind – even the memories that made me hate myself for not noticing how perfectly she had loved me, for not noticing more carefully if she had freckles or if I was remembering wrongly. I drew up the memories of our arguments to torture myself, to draw out the winter. I was terrified I would forget the pieces of her, and how would I find her again if I did not remember her face? Or her voice? How long does it take to forget a person?

<=>

Kore

I began to ask him many questions. I was still brimming with curiosity though the ache had died to a quiet presence that rested in the hollow of my chest. He told me about the river of mist, that it was woven of souls who had passed, and that what I had seen was his greatest pleasure, his only source of joy in this place, but also a forbidden, sacred thing. If his brothers and sisters knew the game he played, his immortality would be stripped from him and he would be flung into the river to join the winding souls. I begged him every day to tell me about the sacred thing and finally I persuaded him. He said, Sometimes as I watch souls that pass into the river, I notice one that is brighter than the others, and this means it is lingering in life, that it has a craving for one more minute of life on earth – to change something, or see someone – it is always different. I can give them that moment, he said, his voice surrounding me in the desert. He laughed then and said, It is strange that in one moment, I see a soul live more than it has lived in an entire lifetime. Something changes when everything is taken away.

It struck me then how many beautiful moments on earth had been mine, and how many I had allowed to slip past me. I imagined how the earth had flourished since I had been gone, painted even more colorful and ornate by Mother's careful hands, and I imagined the burn of sunlight across my cheeks. I asked Aides when I could see my home again. I said, Your desert is all shadows of dust. I am beginning to forget what the color red was like. When I said it aloud, I realized it was true, and the corners of my mouth tightened.

<⇒>

I did not wish to leave him, for he spoke to me with more passion than I had ever found on the earth above. I had not yet seen him since he carried me below ground. He kept a distance and I knew him only as a rumbling voice that made my body tense with heat, and a consuming fear. I had not known that I wanted to touch him, with my fingers and my lips, as Mother had touched me that day.

We talked often, I nudging my words into the air, always surprised by the thunder that met them. The things I said seemed to surprise him, sometimes making him laugh; but sometimes we would argue, our tempers bearing against each other like gales of wind. He did not understand my fascination with immortality, my aversion to aging. He hated the shrillness of bird song; I rebelled against his desert's constant silence. Where is the rustling of the leaves? I would ask him. Where is the braying of donkeys, and the howling of mad dogs? And the creaking of tall grasses? I demanded these things of him angrily, saying that he must change his world or I would go. I would climb back to the world above and leave him alone. But he only laughed again, his voice settling into gentleness when I shouted these things. He knew I was powerless to leave him, that I was as rooted as the cypress tree, looking always to the heavy sky.

Aides told me I would see Mother soon. He said that I would be ready soon and that Mother was still preparing a place for me. I didn't understand then, because I remembered the carpets of flowers and strong, supple oaks that filled my home and I wondered what more she could be doing. I asked, What is taking so long? But he told me to wait and so I waited, just as I had watched when he had commanded it of me.

<=>

Demeter

In the third month of my refuge I was visited by Aides. I saw him standing in the cluster of stars and I thought, not for the first time, This is what love looks like. I felt a stab of envy thinking of his dark eyes following Kore's slender shoulders as she walked, that even in her infancy he had worshipped her beauty. I turned to him, measuring my words, reclining and stretching my body against the deep sky, looking at him as I had when he told me he wanted me in a terrible way. He said, You should return to earth soon. No one deserves the kind of deaths that your people are suffering. I tilted my

head back to bare my neck, and looked up at him indiffer-
ently, my face shining and scratched, my hair matted with
leaves and dirt. He looked away and said quietly, Kore wants
to see you. She's missing the earth, the sunlight, and I'd like
her to visit soon, if you'd like. I wondered what he had told
her, how much of it had been the truth. I nodded, and said,
Of course. Send my love. He left then, disappearing with the
snow and rushing back underground to Kore, to his beloved
one.

I became sick then in the folds of my robe, which I
stepped out of and threw into the black sky. I closed my
eyes and willed myself back to earth, back to the twisted
patterns of bodies and trees that I had left stretching across
its surface. They would destroy me for what I had done
to them. They would boil me and eat me, as they ate their
babies. There was something oddly appealing in it – the idea
of teeth tearing into flesh, teeth sinking into the sinews
of muscle, lips moving thirstily in the pools of hot blood.
What is it like to be hungry, to be starving? And how beautiful would it be to give in to that hunger, and to eat?

<⇒>

I opened my eyes and stepped into my garden. The snow
had covered the many torn flowers and leaves and blanketed
the naked trees. Maybe they will forgive me, I thought. Kore
was coming. I had to make things beautiful again, in the way
she liked – where everything is touched with a yellow light
and the flowers reach higher than her knees. I said aloud,
I will make things just as you like them, Kore. And you, at
least, will love me still. Nothing will have changed.

I spread new soil on the tiers, dug rich and wet from the
river bed. I knew it was less forgiving to the plant roots and
might choke them, but the sleekness of its surface was much
finer looking, almost like an animal's wet pelt. I hung colorful ribbons around the trees as I had on special days when

Kore was a girl. The long yellow and violet tails of the bows danced happily in the wind, and I wondered if it looked too childish for a woman. I ran the circle of the orchard, ripping down the ribbons as I passed. I would try again, this time stringing the layers of branches with lace as delicate as sea foam, gold thread, and tall white candles. Beside the stream, I found clumps of lavender that I picked and tied in bundles, binding them to the tall trunks. We would sit in the moonlight and drink wine together, until our teeth were stained and we collapsed against each other in the roots. I smiled. It was our own magic garden.

<=>

Kore

As we grew to know each other better, he began to leave many small gifts by the river for me so that, as I wandered alongside it, I would find them half buried in the sand and would dig them up on my hands and knees, like an animal uncovering its old treasures. Once he gave me a golden apple, and he said it was for the most beautiful woman in the world. He said that no one could take it from me. His voice had rippled across the unbroken white sky, and for a moment I was terrified that his jealous sister would hear, the one that Mother had told me about, and that she would seek me even here to punish me. I am not proud, I whispered into the air, I am not proud. I thought I heard an eruption of laughter, darting between the ground and the air like lightning, and I imagined his face, the burning eyes squinted with mirth, his lips parted to reveal the gleam of sharp teeth.

Another day – or night; there was no difference – I found a very small box, the size of my thumb. I did not see it, but stepped on it, and heard such a loud cracking noise that I let out a scream, much like an old woman would scream at having stepped on a mouse, and blushed deeply with shame.

When I opened the box, I found a glass ball the size of a pea. Holding the glass up next to my eye, I could see an entire world of tiny people; but in this world, the ground was hard and there were no trees or flowers. Instead, there were tall houses made out of stone and ice. I asked him what world this was, and he said it was the world above, but in a different time. I had carefully inspected the miniature world, waiting for something to grow, bent over it so that I could see it more clearly in the coolness of my own shadow. Sometimes I sat like this for so long that my neck throbbed and the glass bead began to swim in front of my eyes. I felt sorry for whoever lived on the tiny world, because they lived above ground, where there should be sunlight and meadows full of flowers, but they didn't get to enjoy any of these things. And again I thought how upset Mother would be to see the blankness of these worlds, the tiny world in my palm and the desert where I sat. I imagined the pale hair floating around her ears, and the heady smell of olives on her breath. I wondered what Aides had meant when he said that I would be ready soon, and I wondered why it was not enough that I was a woman, and she was Mother, and we belonged near one another.

I had not felt hunger since the first day I wandered the desert for the first time, but Aides enjoyed surprising me and this surprise was no different. He had built a giant banquet table by the river bed, and had laid it with a rich feast – of lamb, salad, fresh bread, rosemary oil, grapes; and at the head of the table, where I seated myself, a split pomegranate. I felt very small at the giant table, like a child's doll, and my feet barely reached the earth in the enormous chair that he had built for me. I sat alone, staring at the food and at the wonder of it all, having forgotten what an important part of life on earth eating had been, and realizing, suddenly, how I had missed the flavor, the warmth, even the animal quality of chewing and swallowing, using teeth to rip meat from the bone. I remembered with a pang of regret that Aides had stolen me moons away from the celebration, and I had never gotten to taste the rich foods Mother had begun preparing.

I took the silver spoon almost angrily, digging it into the heart of the pomegranate and scooping out four wet seeds. I pulled them into my mouth and rolled them around with my tongue, surprised by the heat that came from them, an unnatural, delicious heat, richer than anything I had ever tasted. I couldn't help myself, letting out a moan and grabbing more ruby seeds with my fingers, not noticing how they seared my skin. I swallowed them and ate more. I crushed seeds between my teeth, the juice running down my throat and drying on my skin. Suddenly I felt Aides presence, a warmth in my belly, between my legs and in my earlobes, and I was filled with him, with his raw heat. I was writhing with the pain of it, tears streamed down my face, and I fell from the chair; but I did not want it to stop tearing through me, welling up again and again. As my body rose in desperate rhythm, my back arched almost to the point of breaking, I became, for one moment, a spark.

When it stopped he left my body and appeared beside me, just as I remembered him from the day we left earth together. He did not speak to me, but I knew that I was his, that I belonged to him now, and by eating his fruit I had given myself to him. It had not been a gift for me after all, but his gift, the one thing he wanted. I buried my head between my knees and began to laugh, harder and harder until I was crying again. I did not want to admit how angry I was at being taken without my permission.

I had not realized that one person could enter another with so much violence, and I felt betrayed by Mother, who had not warned me or protected me. When her fingers had trembled across my back, and I had felt her dark heat, I had been eager for the tenderness of new intimacy. I was betrayed by my body, sweating with the exertion of pleasure, my toes curled tightly, desiring so much more than tenderness. Are you happy? I asked myself. Is your curiosity satisfied? I laughed manically, spit flying from my mouth, eyes streaming, rocking back and forth on the ground. I waited for the hysteria to subside and for the heat to leave my body.

Finally I rose, no longer laughing, and asked, Well? Am I ready for Mother now?

<=>

Demeter

The day that Kore came back to the garden, I woke up before the sun. I washed myself, as we often did together in the old days, and I pulled on my robe. It was strange, being conscious of my nakedness, but she was a married woman now and I felt she finally saw the dirtiness that our bodies can carry and the way a woman's body betrays itself with a man. I was ashamed to show myself to her, ashamed that I had not protected her, and that we were now equals. She arrived suddenly, rushing up through the layers of earth just as she had rushed downward, and it was as though time had frozen and she was in the field again, tending the goat's pains. When I first saw her in the pink light of morning, she looked like my baby again. I ran towards her with my arms open, to kiss her fingertips as I always used to, but she looked up at me hesitantly from where she lay, not moving to kiss me or touch my wet face.

She had a small smile, one that frightened me because it looked like the smile one gives a stranger or an acquaintance. Not the smile of a daughter who has missed her mother. My face fell though I tried to recover the smile, and I began to plead with her, using memories to barter for love. I said, Do you remember how we used to lie in this field together, our hair tangled in the flowers, our fingers twined together? I said, Do you remember how I promised I'd plant lavender and wisteria in the garden? They are there! I planted a whole row of them for you, my darling! I felt my voice climbing in sadness as the space between us grew wider and I tried to reach her before it was too late, to reach her with those hon-est words that I threw out, almost screaming. Kore, I cried – and as her name fell from my tongue, I fell upon the ground beside her and buried my face in her hair, because I did not want her to watch me anymore with those curious blue eyes. I felt as though I was being opened up and she was examin-ing each of my organs. In her small, white hands, she held my hideous heart.

Mother, she said, Mother! Don't be upset. It's all right. She paused then, her face full of something I could not place. He is good to me, she said, and I am happy. But I miss the colors and the wind on my ears. I miss cold water. I miss movement. I miss being alive! Just, don't cry. Let's be pleasant together until I have to go away again, when Aides comes back for me, as he told me he would.

And when she finished saying these things, I realized that my Kore had become a graceful woman, as I had always hoped she would, and that she'd changed while she was away, and she'd continue to change as she learned new things. I realized, with such clarity that I lost my breath, that she was not my Kore anymore, not any more mine than I was still the one she loved.

⬛⬛

Kore

It was strange, seeing Mother again. She did not look as I remembered her. The silver spots, that I used to trace with my fingers, like tiny beautiful constellations, looked faded and gray. Her face was thinner, pulled tight at the cheeks and the corners of her mouth. She was trying to smile, her lips curving up, her teeth bared, but there was something all wrong in the quality of it, the music of her laugh. I was afraid for a moment that I had returned to the wrong earth, that this was only someone pretending to be Mother, and that she would snatch me away from my husband and hide me away in a cave, and feed me to hungry pigs. But I saw her face fall, I saw the water brimming in her eyes and I knew it was my same Mother. I knew that I could not trust myself to feel sorry for her, and so I didn't allow myself to feel anything at all.

I watched her stumble over sentimental words, stringing them together like the lace in the trees. I didn't know what to do with them, because she spoke them to someone I had been, and not who I was, so I let them hover in the air above us, lovely and insubstantial, thrown about in the wind.

We walked through the orchards, following the paths of honey bees. I wanted to roll in the dirt of our burrow, to rub the wet soil across my skin, but it looked so neatly raked that I didn't want to mess it up. I studied the tree bark, noticing how colorful it was, how it was crawling with ants and scorpions, so different from the cypress in the desert below the ground. Small pink blossoms unfurled from the tips of the branches, almost white in the center and darkening at the petals' edges. I studied the sky too, the colors that passed through one another in waves, the orange that spilled across the horizon and seeped into the dusk. The night was warm, and I remember wishing that I could have brought Aides there, to the dark rows of the forest, so he could stand beside me and look up at the stars.

Mother tried to talk sometimes as we walked, but I preferred our silence. I was not responsible for her anymore, just as I had learned that she felt no responsibility for me. I was angry and relieved that a part of me I had not known existed had been filled, and she had no part in it.

<=>

Demeter

The thought had come to me on a day when Kore could still fit curled inside my straw basket, her thumb inside her mouth, the sweet noise of sucking and wet breathing. I had noticed the beauty of the day, when the blooms were firm and the fruit was heavy in the trees, and the air was as light and dry as a piece of blue linen, stretched behind the sun. I had noticed my own hands, still as round and soft as my first day on earth, with firm, brown knuckles rising like chestnuts from the skin. It is all changeless, I thought, the sort of vague happiness that seeps through everything. We are sweeping lines, ambivalent gaiety, elegant gestures without purpose. I longed, suddenly, for some explosion of feeling, for a distinctive moment within the passing moments of the day – I longed for a sensation strong enough to awaken me. I felt as though I'd been slowly lulled to sleep in the constant current of sunlight and breezes, that I had been only half-awake for all my existence, but was only now realizing it, and it frightened me.

Even the face of my sleeping Kore could not bring me comfort, not her fat cheeks, wet with spit, or her thick legs pulled to the swell of her belly. There was love within my breast, I knew, but it was an easy love, among a collection of convictions that had not been worked for, that I hadn't had the chance to earn.

I had yelled to my brother for help. Even as I had realized the soft numbness was there it had begun to creep through me, planting itself in the beds of my veins, curdling my blood. Aides appeared, the first time he had appeared to me since Kore's birth, although the villagers told me they had seen him stealing quietly through the village as a wolf, watching me as I knelt to tend their fields. I told him my thought, as one confesses their deepest regret, hoping that he would astonish me, set my life back in motion. I waited for his breath on the curve of my neck, for the blush that would spread across my cheekbone. But when he spoke I was truly astonished, for he said to me the one thing I couldn't bear to hear. Sister, he said, give me your child and let yourself bleed – let this earth bleed – so that when you are near death, and she is returned to you, you will know what it means to triumph.

I pushed him away, my voice rising into a fury that threatened to break me open, and I remembered his eyes, the night that he had looked down into the face of my baby. My wolf brother, his lips already imagining the taste of her warm blood, of her soft lips. He had seen how lovely she would grow, and he wanted her so. He wanted her as the thing he could never have. I wanted to spit on him, to tell him that she was not his answer to our old game; I wanted to turn my Kore into a constellation, to scatter her across the heavens, where no one would ever hurt her, and I would be the only one to love her.

His eyes were serious and he said to me, Call for me when you understand, and he disappeared again beneath the ground. I had tried to forget what he had said and I had held my baby in the curve of my arm, singing her the songs I had heard in the trees and in the wind, coursing through the wheat. The sun rose and fell and I tried to forget, but my bones were stiff with boredom, with the need to feel, the need to earn my love for this place I called home, to earn my joy. I explored every corner of my mind, searching for a way that he was wrong, that this wasn't necessary. I asked myself if the whole earth, and the whole earth's purpose, was worth this cost.

I called Aides back in the middle of the night, my voice cracking and rising in pitch. When he arrived, I opened my arms. First to the earth, the dirt swept in circles around me, then to the stars that also moved in circles, almost imperceivable to the eye. Finally, I opened my arms to my brother, then to my love, Kore, and my eyes were wet but I did not cry. I opened my arms and I submitted, because I knew the earth better than any man, or any god, and I knew that it was crumbling. I had heard the moaning of great volcanoes, and the shifting of the ocean's floor. The world demanded emptiness, brokenness, despair in return for the fruit it bore. I submitted to her sacrifice, giving possession of a life that was not my own to give, and in the heat that surged from his hand to mine, I felt a longing and a loss. I fainted, welcomed by the ground. When I woke, he had disappeared and it seemed in my mind only a vivid dream.

Kore's footsteps startled me. We played together in the creek, pulling up our gowns to our knees and screaming at how deliciously cold the water was, splashing each other as we used to. I tugged her hair and whistled to her and she laughed politely, the laugh of a woman who doesn't know how to pretend to be a child. We crouched together in the new garden, and if she noticed she did not mention the pot-pourri of torn petals that mixed with the newly spread soil, the missing roses that I had torn in my grief. Maybe she did not notice at all, because often she looked around at the earth more than she looked at me, as though she could memorize the sky's colors as it changed and bring them underground with her. I couldn't help wondering what Aides had told her of my betrayal, because she avoided my eyes so purposefully, and I asked her what she was thinking.

She filled the air with her lilting laughter. Nothing, Mother! she said. Only, she added, you never told me it would hurt so much! I wasn't sure if she was talking about me or her husband, or what she meant, so I sat watching her. She said, It hurts so badly but it is so wonderful, being broken and filled in places that you didn't know existed! She paused and glanced at me, and I wondered if she saw the blush creeping across my face, and how my lips tightened with anger. She was being cruel, bringing up things she knew I longed for, things she was too young to understand. A smile flickered in her eyes and she pressed on. When his hands are on my breasts, he – I made an abrupt noise, like an animal, and slapped her across the cheek, to make her stop talking and hurting me, or to make her hurt too. She sat stunned, her hand on her hot cheek, blood filling the print of a long, thin hand.

We didn't move for a long time, sitting there in the tall wands of grass, staring at the lines of red ants that striped the dirt. Finally she stood, turning her back to me. She said, There now, Mother, I'll die someday and you will live forever and the whole earth will grow new again and you will forget all about me and nothing I have now will matter then, will it? It will all be the same and I'll be ashes on the sea somewhere. Does that make you glad? That I will be as alone someday as you are now? I looked at her with such pain on my face, as though she had driven a knife through me, and I felt within me a great breaking. But she couldn't see it. She couldn't see my heart breaking on my face because her back was turned to me. Kore walked away then, and I knew I would not see her again for a very long time.

That was the shortest summer the earth ever had, for when Kore left again I fell into such mourning that nothing could grow. The ground became hard and cold once more, and the days were black as nights when the candles burn out. Those were the longest days of my life, considering the weight of what I had done: my arrangement with my brother – an understanding that without old age, there is no real youth; without sorrow, joy is weakened. Aides and I had put our fingers on the dichotomy that creates beauty in the end, the riddle that twists the earth. I knew, above all else, that I was being punished for loving this world more than the one above, where my brothers and sisters celebrated the permanence of everything they treasured. But we had realized it and could not undo the thought – nothing is as loved as something missed.

⟨⇒⟩

Kore

After the first visit above ground, I had no desire to return, and I remained in the desert with Aides for a very long time. I began to really explore the desert with new vigor and thoroughness, and I found that, much like people, deserts become more beautiful and fascinating as you spend more time with them. The desert beneath the earth, if that is actually where it was located, was constantly changing. It seemed to change as often as it pleased. I would wake after sleeping – I never knew how long – sleeping was a habit I maintained from my life on earth that was no longer necessary to my physical wellbeing – and Aides and I would eat breakfast on the giant table by the river, or practice dances that we had seen the villagers trying, or make love. Sometimes we would make love during breakfast, or throw our energy into a tremendous fight, throwing food at one another and yelping as it splattered across our legs.

I learned to draw souls from the writhing mass of the river, as I had seen my husband draw them out on my first day in the desert, and I understood then why he loved it so much, and why he had laughed like a child. As I commanded the soul's threads out of the riverbed I could feel them whirring, reverberating in the air as quickly as humming bird wings, and this was their uncontrollable delight. The threads seemed, when woven so tightly together, to be indistinguishable, but they were very much distinct people, who dreamed of one unfinished moment of life. I never found a soul so content that it did not want another minute alive, that it only wanted to rest peacefully in the world below the ground, muted and blind.

<=>

The soul of one woman, a mother of three boys, hummed so violently as she rose from the stream that I cried. I asked Aides if I could watch as her soul visited the earth again for one minute, because I wanted to know the source of her joy; and he drew from his robe a sharp knife of onyx, so I could see in the blade where she flew. And as I watched, I began to cry again, this time more loudly, for she entered the home of her oldest son, who was now a very old man himself, and she landed, like a blanket of smoke on his shivering body, where he lay beneath a thin sheet. Although I could not hear a sound in the blackness of the blade, I knew she was whispering to him and giving him peace, for I saw his lips curve slightly up at the corners before his body went rigid and his hand, turning the page of a book, fell heavily upon his chest.

Another soul – this one of a greedy man who had beaten one of his slaves almost to death – almost did not have enough strength to separate from the great arm of the river. I urged him upwards, commanded him to rise every time he faltered, and then sent him off to the earth, watching him in the face of the knife. He spent precious seconds trying to decide where to go, for nowhere on earth welcomed him, and his soul grieved, shaking in the morning air above the woods. He finally moved to the house where he was once called Master and found the slave whom he had beaten, the face still striped with scars. The soul wreathed the brown head, cooling him in the boiling afternoon. Seconds later he disappeared, slipping back into the thrum of the river with a sigh of repletion.

⬅⇒➤

Demeter

Aides had been right when he told me it would be almost like dying.

Yet, after a year passed with no sign of Kore, I had learned to find a kind solace in the depth of winter. The ground, covered thickly with frozen rain and the plants that had shriveled in the pale frost, all seemed full of my grief. Rather than feeling that I was the cause of this long winter, I felt that we were in communion together, that we had drawn together in our enormous loneliness. The grief that filled me was one of gentle emptiness, not of bitterness, as it would have been if the earth around me had been green and fertile.

I woke early to walk barefoot in the banks of snow, enjoying the burning and then the deadening of sensation in my toes. I no longer wore my hair pulled up at the nape of my neck, as women do when they can be seen, but let it fall across my face in tangles, hiding my swollen eyes.

The villagers had grown tired of me and my constant sadness. I was no more fascinating to them now than the fields they watched sullenly, waiting for some sprout, some sign of life. The relics along the roadside had been desecrated long ago, without fear of punishment, for I had already deserted them and there was nothing left for me to destroy. They had twisted animal bones like knives into the effigies, and drawn terrible, monstrous faces, painting animal blood across the mouth. I cringed and looked quickly away, pained to see the evidence of such conditional love. I had never really fooled myself into believing they loved me as a self, only as I belonged to them, and they to me; but they were all I had left to care for, and I tried to think of ways to win back their affection.

<=>

Kore visited again after much time had passed, and there was a lightness between us that I had missed since she had been taken from me, although she still would not kiss my lips, a small punishment for my failure to protect her. I was not angry with her for this, just as I did not begrudge the villagers for how they resented me, but I watched her longingly, staring at the beautifully full curves of her body and the deepening red in her cheeks. She would come brightly back into my life and the earth would light up – the snow drifts melting into warm creeks, and the garden humming with thousands of insect wings, and the sun's tongue lapping the hills.

Once the villagers recognized the constant coming and going of things, the pattern in which our brightness and darkness fell, they no longer prayed to me for the abundance of their crops or that their roots would grow deep and firm. They learned when to plant one crop, and when to gather their harvest; they learned which vegetables would survive the frost and which needed the grace of summer. Their faces grew calloused from squinting into the sunlight, from recognizing this new hardness of the world, and their hands became as capable and deft as mine, in the body of the earth.

What if love without cost did not exist, and all love consisted only of rhythms and reasons bound up, not only in the whole of a person, but in the ways they pleased you, the things they did or did not deserve? I closed my eyes and imagined Kore, her face, still, in front of mine; her eyes as blue as if they'd swallowed the sky, her lips parted to speak, caught with a thread of spit. I imagined her in my brother's bed, the great red canopy that enfolded them, their bodies twisted in the silk. I imagined, tears welling beneath my eyelids, that she lay in the crook of his arm, and that they spoke of me mockingly, laughing at my tender aloneness, at my obsession. I imagined all of this in the darkness of my mind and I felt, within my breast, an overwhelming, unmoving and gratuitous love for her, as she was at that moment below the ground, as she had been the day she was taken, lying in the morning field and, one day, when she would be no more. I felt, for the first time since her birth, that tiny, malignant seed dissolve from my belly, and all that was left was clean rain.

I wondered then if anyone had felt as I felt at that exact moment.

I decided to leave the orchard and the village, and the garden where I had always lived, that was more a part of me than my arms, my brown legs. I had lost Kore already, unexpectedly, and I decided to free myself of the idea that any one thing on earth belonged to me, and to leave it all entirely, to go somewhere new, a village of strangers in a land where the leather land met seamlessly with the boiling sea. I knew the villagers had no need of me now that I was antiquity, a sacred if unclear memory in their oral histories, and I was not worried for them.

I left during the harvest, as the leaves began to drop, just after Kore left me to return to Aides. I had not told her I would be going, but I knew she would be able to find me whenever she needed me. She was no more tied to our garden than I was, and it was easy to move between the underworld and the one above, to the distinct point of any person or place that one wished, as long as one held the thought carefully enough.

This would be the first time I had changed since the day Kore first visited ten years ago and I had been ashamed of my nakedness, but this day I wished for namelessness, not for grace or beauty. I dropped into the stream, dipping completely below the water, scrubbing the skin on my face and neck until it was pink and raw. I used the pebbles to scrape the fine dirt from beneath my finger nails, and rubbed lavender oil into my cuticles and the roots of my hair. The cloth I chose was thin and gray, and spun so finely that even the northern wind would not slip through and chill me as I walked. I draped it over my head as an old woman might, to cover my bright knot of hair.

I set out in an unknown direction, on foot, for although it would be quicker to move through the air, I wanted to have a true adventure, as a mortal might, moving slowly from one village to the next until I found one that kept my attention. In the autumn mornings I would rise, constantly comforted by the singing of the larks, and I would make my way towards where the sun rose, squinting into the blinding arc of the sky. I walked throughout the day, stopping only to notice plants I had never seen before, or to stoop and splash creek water on my hot cheeks.

The first village I came to was much more sophisticated than the village near my garden, which I could not call my village any longer because I realized it did not belong to me, any more than I belonged to it. This village was home to many warriors, who knew much about lust and blood, and the cost of each. The homes were three or four times larger than the small, makeshift homes of my village, and their walls were scraped smooth and decorated with ornate mosaics of bright pottery shards, depicting my brothers and sisters feasting in the sky. In the courtyards of the houses were red grapes, hanging low on their vines, and sparkling fountains that rose high into points, as sharp as the tip of a spear.

The trees were now completely bare, and I wandered on through the winter, embracing the cold as I did during my days of grieving. It had been so long since I passed through the first village that I almost changed directions and moved towards a different point on the horizon. But as I rose the next morning, still covered in exhaustion, I saw a marvelous city that the night had kept hidden from me. The city was ruled by an old king and his modest wife, who were said to dote endlessly on their infant son, Demophon, and treat their citizens with a rare consideration of justice and respect. As I walked through the city, I saw many colorful flags strung from window to window, and red flowers, for luck, bunched in vases on the windowsills. I noticed that the streets were swept clean, and that the children laughed as they played together, and did not quarrel. I wanted to meet the king and his wife, and give them my blessings for the abundance of their city. The streets of the city wound upwards, spiraling to a large house on the summit of a hilltop, with large, open windows, and barking dogs racing about the labyrinth of the gardens.

I entered the courtyard of the home. No sooner had my head passed beneath the arc of lattice than I was greeted by many smiling servants, each clasping my hands and asking where I had come from, and if I needed to rest. One of my sisters might have found such familiarity almost impertinent among strangers, especially servants, but I was so grateful for such a welcome that I kissed each on the cheek, my eyes watering. A man with a burnished red beard and a large, onion-like nose emerged from the house and greeted me, placing a warm hand on my back and guiding me to a couch in the shade, near the glow of an opened window. I smelled the spice of dried meats, drawn out by the breeze.

He asked for my name and I gave it to him, knowing that it meant nothing in this foreign place, where the sea did not smell of salt and fish, but of damp wood and lotus. He called for his wife, saying that he wanted her to meet me, for he knew a face that he could trust, and I was more than welcome in his home. A slender woman peered from the doorway, leaning her weight against the wooden frame, and balancing a white-haired boy on the curve of her hip. I tried to measure her from the laugh lines beside her eyes, to see if she was an equal of this kind, burly king, but I found that her eyes were guarded, and her thin lips were pursed almost in worry. She was, if not open, at least a very gracious queen, who had learned from a young age the rules of subtlety and hospitality, and she lowered her boy to the ground to greet me, clasping my hands in her small, cold hands, and pressing her cheek against mine. We talked for a while about the city's structure, their recent decision against war, and the craftsmanship of the windows, as the young boy crawled about in the dirt, giggling as the dogs licked his face clean. I couldn't help remembering Kore when she was so small, and helplessly tottered around the circles of the orchard on her chubby feet. I would hold out my arms to her, only feet away, and she would cry, that I asked her to cross such a distance. How she would have cried if she had guessed that, one day, we would live in different worlds, and would only dream of playing together in the orchard.

The king called to his servants for wine, which they brought in heavy carved wooden gourds. We crossed arms and drank together, a toast, the dark wine staining our teeth and making our laughter loud as night veiled the city. In the morning, the dogs huddled in the shade to avoid the scorching dirt, and the king, the queen, and I agreed in bleary voices that I would become nurse to the baby boy, and live in the airy house with them, as a friend and companion. We glanced at each other with red-rimmed eyes, and began laughing again, until our throats were raw and our breathing ragged.

I never stopped thinking about my daughter and her husband, not even during the winter I worked in the king's home. I glutted myself on my own hope of her return, that she would come home early or that she would choose to be mine again; that she would lose interest in her life below the ground and barter with him for her freedom. I was sickened with my need for a companion and, although I knew the betrayal had been mine, I felt betrayed both by Kore and my brother, and did not know which was the greater of the two.

Demophon helped distract me from this strange amusement of turning the same thoughts over again and again in my head until they dizzied me. He was strong, for a baby, and full of mischief, beaming a toothless smile up at me as I cradled his naked head. I would carry him on my hip around the city, letting him breathe in the ocean and the market smells, and the smell of people, of sweat, and leather, and perfumes. When it rained, we would lie on our stomachs together on the woven rug, watching out the giant window, and making noises of surprise when we saw the silhouettes of birds.

I had not felt so close to any mortal person, besides Kore, as I did to this king and his timid wife. I felt as though, if I were able, I would take a meat knife and carve my heart out of my chest and present it to them, if it would in some way make their lives richer or easier.

One evening, lying with my chin pressed to the floor, I realized how I could serve this family with my enormous gratitude. I would immortalize their son, Demophon, while he was still a baby, while the ritual would still work. I had realized too late for Kore the tension that was born from our differences, one lover mortal and one eternal. But I would show him how to shove his hands into the earth, how to taste the minerals, just as I had taught Kore, and he would teach these secrets to all his people, and he would be by my side always, son and companion.

I had to bite my lips to keep from crying out with excitement that I would be Mother again, truly, and that this time my companion would not abandon me. He would belong to me as Kore once did, and we would love each other unfailingly. His father and mother would not regret that I gave him this gift, for he would serve them dutifully, even into their old age, cradling their bony shoulders in his strong arms. And then, when they died and we set their bodies afire in pine boats that rocked in the white foam, we would weep together on the shore, united by our grief. Where once I lay in grief alone, now my son would comfort me.

I performed the sacred rights each night, after the king and his wife were fast asleep, closing the door to my chamber tightly. With a wooden ladle, I poured a sweet ambrosia over Demophon's head, holding him against my breast, so that it dripped down his pale skin and made him shine in the firelight. I stepped to the hearth and lowered him into the fire, murmuring to him, and he was not afraid, nor did he cry. The sparks crackled and leapt around him, but did not leave a single mark on his body or make his skin warm. Eventually, I knew the fire would burn away his poisonous mortality, the endless counting of time that I once thought so precious, and would leave him glowing and divine; and so I worked silently each night over the body of Demophon, waiting for the day when he would be fastened to me, like young moss on the bough of an ancient tree.

<=>

Kore

I loved hearing news from Aides about the world above, because it led to moments of reflection that pivoted on life other than my own. I heard, waking from a long, restless sleep, the voice of my husband, whispering to me through the canopy and shaking me softly. He said, I've heard a rumor that's circled among the birds that your mother, the good Demeter, has taken on an infant apprentice, and that she has bathed him in fire each night, to make him her immortal companion. The birds saw her from the eaves, and heard her whisper to him, my Son, my Son, as she held him to her breast. Aides paused and watched my face, his hands still lingering on my shoulders.

There is no word for the sound that rose from my throat, or how hard I beat my cheeks then with my fists, until they were gray from the blood pooled beneath the skin. I fell to my knees in the desert, and I could not feel the heat or pressure of his arms around me, although I knew they were there. And then I heard him telling me I'd be all right, and I fainted.

I woke because my body was singing with pain, running into the joints of my neck and my bruised jaw. I hadn't realized how old my body had become, not nearing death, but stiffer and more fragile than I had been as a girl. I ached to move, my eyes burning with blood and my lips stinging, cracked and swollen and filled with dust. Aides held water to my lips in the cup of his hands, and it ran freezing down my neck and pooled in my lap. I felt ridiculous for my child-like violence in such a mature body, but the wound still pained me, and the fury had not subsided.

I had never given my husband an order, and we had lived so happily and simply together that there had been no need, but the fury that welled up in me required that he listen to me now and grant this one request. Aides – I spoke so softly I wasn't sure if I said the words, or if I only thought them, and he understood me well enough. I want you to take the child's life, I said. I didn't stutter or hesitate, as hushed as I spoke, even though a tremor ran through my chest, and I knew he would obey, for my love had a cost, as does all love.

He turned from me, his chin propped on both fists like a little boy, and he looked vulnerable to me, as he had never looked before. There is no transgression as terrible as ending an innocent life with no cause, and I knew that in asking it of him, I diminished an intimate respect between us that would never fully be restored. But Mother had known the loyalty I had for her, and my fear of aging; she had heard me cry in the dead of night, terrified of dying in my sleep, and she had left me mortal regardless. That she would immortalize a baby she did not know, a baby boy that was not her own, was the second betrayal, yet it felt even more terrible than the first. Aides finally nodded and rose, not turning back to me, even though I shook all over and called out after him, wanting him to forgive me, although I meant what I had said.

He avoided me after, though I was not sure for how long. Time fell and shifted together like sand. But the stillness howled around me and I slept. I slept without thinking and without dreaming, and when I woke I heard the baby had died, and I cried into my hands, rocking back and forth, curled like a seed against the hard earth.

<⇒>

Demeter

I should have known how to protect him, how to keep something like that from happening to my Demophon. I don't know how she knew, but the queen ran into my room one night to see me standing over the boy's body, his arms and legs waving in the shroud of fire, and she ran at me and hit me with her tiny, cold fists, and then tried desperately to reach into the fire, shrieking in terror at the monster that burned her son alive. And my concentration slipped. My thoughts slipped from the sacred words. They caught in my mouth, and in my terror I faltered. Demophon cried, his torso suddenly engulfed in flame, welts appearing darkly, blistering and bleeding, the skin boiling as we watched, the high pitched screams cracking in the deep red glow. By the time we plucked him from the fire, he was no longer recognizable as a baby boy.

I did not move, staring at the tiny, misshapen figure. I was not ready for more grief, or dazzling fury. I felt as though – since the day I made the pact with my dark brother, the day I betrayed my beautiful Kore – my grieving had been endless. Even her visits were tainted with the thought of the solitude I would endure when she left again, and because of this I had neglected to laugh at anything! I had not laughed, or even smiled in years! Suddenly, I was overwhelmed with exhaustion, and the desire to let go of everything, even myself, to shrug off this consciousness that felt so heavy.

I raised myself before the crumpled body of the queen, who sobbed soundlessly on the floor. I wanted to leave, to have no part in the grief that continued around me, but I was ashamed, for this was her time to grieve, as it had once been mine. I threw off my cloak, letting my face and hair shine, and my gold body light the shadows of the room. You do not know me, I said to her gently, as you thought we knew one another. I am not made of this earth as you are, and neither will I return to it. I told her of the plans I'd made for her son, that he would live forever as my apprentice, and I held her face in my hands, trying to seep from her skin the worst of the sadness; but she could not tear her eyes from his burnt body, his legs tucked strangely beneath him.

I left the city then, knowing I could never again be to that kind family what I had been. I found, after many years, that they had forgiven me, and built a temple for me, and that every harvest they hold a festival in my name, celebrating the abundance of the earth and grieving its cost.

⬦⇒⬥

Kore

I visited Mother again in the springtime, noticing the pains she took to make the garden as beautiful as it had been when

I was young. There were new plants now, ones I didn't recognize, sapphires and marigolds that caught my eye, and yet
still the same, twining roses, remarkably piled atop our little burrow. Mother escorted me along the river bed, helping
me down the slope and slipping off my leather sandals so I
could feel the cool water and the polished stones against my
toes. She asked me if I remembered it all well, and I told her
it felt familiar, that I knew I had been there before, maybe
in a dream. Her eyes were bright as she pressed my hand,
the skin puckering into ridges along the deep blue veins.
Mother, I said, and I heard the voice of an old woman come
from my throat, but I did not understand how it could be
me; and I told her I wanted to race with her and to lie in
the field, hand in hand, our hair tangled in the weeds. She
leaned to kiss me, her face so wet against mine, and then
pulled me gently to my feet, brushing the dirt from my heels
before she slipped my sandals back on. We moved, so slowly
it seemed, to the field bright with yellow flowers, growing
so high, almost past our knees! I caught her hand in mine
and we lowered ourselves into the grass, squinting up at the
sky that stretched forever around us in all directions, feeling
the sting of ant bites against the back of our necks.

We lay for a while like that, without talking or moving,
just staring up into the sky and wondering about all the
things we might have done differently, and how strangely
we loved one another. The gnats landed again and again
on our eyelids, and we moved restlessly in the damp heat,
brushing them away with the backs of our wrists. And when
we finally fell asleep, I left the earth for the last time, my
hand and Mother's falling quietly apart, making circles in
the dirt where they landed.

Just Watch
By Lia Nasselquist

LIA NASSELQUIST was born and raised in a small Canadian town about halfway up the border between Manitoba and Saskatchewan. She is 19 years old and has dreamed of becoming an author since her childhood. "Just Watch" is her first published piece of work. Here's what she wrote about it:

> When I was in grade 11, my English teacher gave the class a short story assignment. The only instruction she gave us was to use the theme "Childhood." The original version of "Just Watch" was really bland, and I wasn't pleased with it when I handed it in. My teacher gave it back to me and told me she knew I could do better and suggested changing the flashback scenes. I rewrote them several times until I felt like the story had more emotion and meaning. I ended up getting 100% on the finished assignment and it is now one of my favorite pieces I've written.

<=>

Have you ever taken the time to just watch people? You can learn countless things about others, without ever actually speaking to them. I watch people constantly. I've always done it, and I will continue to do it until the day I die.

I am not a stalker. I am not a pervert. I've been called these things, along with others, more than I care to remember. I just enjoy watching people. I'm not doing anything wrong. If I were a woman, people wouldn't be so suspicious of me. Men seem to have a bad reputation, thanks to so many stories about predators and weirdoes.

My name is not important. People rarely remember it anyway. I am twenty-three years old, but I look much older. My pale skin looks cold, and my gray eyes constantly appear sad or lost. They're dull and almost lifeless, bored with the world. I don't look in the mirror often, and I avoid catching glimpses of my reflection. I probably look as though I'm currently battling my way through cancer. I am completely bald, by choice. It's easier to look at myself less when I don't have hair to worry about.

Maybe people think I'm a creep because I like to watch children. It just takes me back, and reminds me of my childhood. Kids aren't judgmental; they don't care what other people look like, or worry. They make friends instantly, even though they probably won't remember each other's names by the time they go home. Kids seem to be fascinated constantly, by the smallest things and most random people. They're naïve and innocent – blind to and unafraid of the shadow of their futures. These kids don't realize that once they grow out of their own shoes and take on responsibility for their lives, it gets harder.

Sitting on a park bench, overlooking a small playground, I remember my own childhood; the freedom and happiness, contrasting with the hard times that seemed so earth-shattering at the time. I remember being dragged to school day after day, because I hated trying and thinking, and the way I slowly stopped caring. *Why did I do that?* I should've cared. If I had known back then that this would be where I'd end up, maybe I wouldn't have been that way. Now, here I am: no job, going nowhere in life.

I'm pulled from my daydreams back to present day by two small words:

"Hello, sir." It's a small girl, around four years old. Her long blonde hair is tied back neatly in two French braids.

Her blue eyes look up at me with curiosity while her small fingers tug on the bottom of her light pink dress.

"Hello," I say quietly, my voice cracking in the middle. I clear my throat and try a smile.

"Do you want to come play with us? We're building sandcastles," she says, pointing behind her. I follow the direction of her finger to a small group of kids, staring at us, waiting.

"I'd love to," I reply, rising from the bench. The girl turns and runs back to her friends, her braids trailing behind her. I follow and sit down slowly in the sand.

"Hi, Mister," waves a young boy with orange hair and overalls. "Which pail do you want?" He holds up some buckets for me to choose from. I shrug and take a large purple one from his small, freckled hands.

The four kids and I make castles for what seems a long time. It's so peaceful. There are no disagreements over anything, just blissful silence and fresh air. I find myself enjoying the time I'm spending with these children. I momentarily forget about my own life as an outcast. For a little while, I finally belong.

We hear someone yell from across the park. It makes me jump. I glance in the direction of the noise, and the children do the same. A short, slim woman with dark brown hair in a short ponytail is storming toward us. The little blonde girl stands up and runs to the woman, wrapping her arms around her and calling out, "Mommy!"

"Get away from these kids, you *creep!*" the woman yells at me, her eyes like daggers. I look down at the sandcastles and at the circle of kids around me. Their heads are tilted in confusion and their eyes are filled with silent questions. I stand up slowly and brush off my pants.

"Sorry, ma'am," I nod at the woman and walk away. She's clearly both fuming and terrified. As I look back over my shoulder, I see her crouching in front of the little blonde girl. The woman has her hands on the girl's shoulders and seems to be making sure she's okay. *Is this seriously happening? I wasn't doing anything wrong, was I?*

I shuffle along the sidewalk, around the corner and out of view of the playground. I find myself dropping down numbly on a bench. *Is this really what has become of me? I'm a monster. People are scared of me.* I feel neglected; hated. At this point, I would give anything to be a child again. I am all alone, yet surrounded by people milling around the streets. Nobody acknowledges my existence. Even when they do, it's because they are afraid of me, or they think I'm dangerous in some way.

Suddenly, I'm back in my five-year-old body again, staring up at my very first school teacher. She pats my pale hair and smiles down at me. I feel her hand gently nudge me against the small of my back. I walk slowly and silently to a small table of other students and sit down. I join them as they draw pictures of fish and puppies, and can't wipe the smile off my small face.

I'm briefly pulled back to reality by a dog brushing against my legs as it walks past with its owner. Then, almost instantly, I'm catapulted back into the past.

"Go to sleep," I'm telling myself. "Close your eyes. Sleep." Over and over I beg myself to slip into silence and slumber. I'm pleading with my body to give in, to block out the noise. I can hear my parents fighting downstairs, and wonder if my little sister hears it too. I hope she's sleeping. My hands pull the blankets above my head, sheltering me. I'm fourteen years old, but I've been through a lot. I shiver as the arguing gets louder and louder. I clench my jaw until my face trembles, and squeeze my eyes closed tightly.

"Sleep," I whisper. "Ignore them. Sleep." I hear a loud noise, then silence. I'm holding my breath, waiting for a sound. I hear nothing. No yelling, no footsteps, nothing. I don't dare move a muscle. And that's when I know. He hit her. My father, in his drunken stupor, hit my mother. I feel the hatred sweep over me, and silently beg my mother to do something. I strain my ears, listening for something, anything. It feels like ages.

"Get out," I hear her say. "Get out of my house. Get away from my children. Get out of my life. I never want to see you again." Her voice is hushed. She doesn't yell, but I can tell she is furious. I hear the slight catch in her sentences. She's crying.

"Really?" my father says, loud, drunk and angry. He swears at her. A long stream of nasty words. Then I hear uneven footsteps, a door slam, and then silence again. I wait. I stay completely still, breathless and quiet. I don't move for a long time, and eventually I drift into unconsciousness to the sound of my mother's sobs.

The sound of traffic brings me back to the present. I begin to realize why I've always liked watching kids play. It's simply because my own childhood was cut short. I was forced to grow up almost instantly, to become a father-figure for my sister. I miss every single thing about the way my life was before the day I grew up – all my friends, every little memory, even the scrapes on my knees. I understand that nothing can bring my childhood back; I can't travel through time. I need to move on with my life and stop living through the lives of other children.

I stand up from the bench and start walking. I don't know where I'm going yet – all I know is that I'm moving in the right direction: forward.

Phoenix Sun
By Stef Kramer

STEF KRAMER is a writer, blogger, and CFO for a bank. She lives on a farm near Earling, Iowa with her husband, two amusing children, and brilliant pets. After receiving her Bachelor's of Arts in English at the University of Iowa, she went on to obtain her MBA at Creighton University. She has been named Outstanding Woman Banker by Northwestern Financial Review and received other various leadership awards. In addition to being an Author's First contest winner, she has received an Honorable Mention in the Writer's Digest Annual Short Story Competition. Her blogs can be found at www.stefkramer.blogspot.com and www.stefkramernovels.blogspot.com. Here's what she wrote about "Phoenix Sun":

> "Phoenix Sun" originated from a Gotham Writing Workshop assignment in which I was tasked to write about something I would never do – such as leaving a functioning family with a husband and children. I am a dedicated mother and wife, but the role is more demanding than I ever would've imagined. Whenever we hear of a woman leaving her family, it seems she is more harshly judged than if a man leaves his family. Even in this age of enlightenment, women are still expected to marry and have children in addition to any career calling. I was inspired to explore the motivation and empathize for a person, a mother especially, needing to take leave of her loved ones.

◄=►

My sister's wondering how long I'll stay. She doesn't say it outright. Silence is her tongue.

"Wanna go for a swim?" I ask.

Hunched over the sink, she scrubs the last piece of nothing on the pan.

Finally she spits, "My shift starts in an hour."

Grabbing an organic cotton rag and homegrown lemon spray, I fall to task on the already spotless counters. "Betsy in 4C will join me." I wait for a reaction, to which I receive none. "Might as well enjoy this Phoenix sunshine."

Lola shrugs. She hasn't been pent up in Minnesota the last ten years. Snowstorms. Summers with bird-sized mosquitoes. Kids. Always needing me. Only me.

After moments splashing the dishwater, my sister asks. Again.

"Have you called him yet?"

"I told you. Left a message when I got here."

She slaps the dishrag in the sink. "Over three weeks ago." Fragile, pretty bubbles float around Lola's hair, seemingly suspended. I'd pop them if she weren't giving me such a pissy look.

"I'm tired of taking his calls."

Her gaze locks onto me. "It's been long enough, Olivia. Almost four weeks since you spoke to your husband. Or your kids. Don't you think they miss you?"

The words are meant to sting.

About the kids. None older than ten. How *do* I feel? Not hearing their voices? Not holding my fifteen-month-old, constantly calling out for her mommy? Not seeing my boy blink at me as he waits for his lunch to be made? Not chauffeuring my eldest from activity to activity to activity?

I'm convinced I'm still tired.

"They miss a maid wiping up their shit."

I watch my sister, who makes a presentation every time she meticulously puts away her Williams Sonoma dishware. I would try to help her, but she doesn't like how I organize stuff.

As I step into the bedroom, Fat Cat weaves between my ankles, mewing for me to pick her up. "Not in the mood for you," I say to the ball of fur intent on clinging to me.

Once I realize the cat has determined my immediate purpose, I plop on the feathery bed, holding her.

I keep thinking about this book about a pioneer woman who never wanted to get married or have kids. She wanted to be a rancher on her own. Everyone shunned her – wrote her off as a radical lunatic. I asked Lola the other day if Mom ever pressured her about having a family. She looked at me and said, "When did our parents ever care about anything other than parties on the lake?"

Mom started calling me after I got married. It was clear. Her goal was to become a nana. That's what she'd say. Nana. "When you gonna start filling up that fancy house so I can become a nana?" We never called our grandparents by that name. It was just talk anyway. My parents never came around much to see the kids. Too busy. With what, I don't know. Mom "liked" a lot of my family's Facebook pictures though.

Fat Cat nestles deeper into my chest and paws at me, as if I'm under-performing. "Not doing my job?" I say to my sister's pet. "Someone's always needing something from me." I scratch the cat's ears until she purrs like a quiet motor, making my eyes heavy.

"I don't need anything," says my sister in the doorway, wrestling with the pant leg of her scrubs. "Except maybe a little help around the condo. That'd be nice."

"What do you want me to do?" I sit up, shaking off the cat. "Tell me what to do."

"Just go for your swim with Betsy. Have a good time while I'm at work, Liv. Don't worry about a thing."

As she turns away, I squeeze my hands together. I've told her what happened. She knows every detail of the months and the days before I left. "Fuck you, Lola," I whisper to myself.

Outside the window lies a dormant pool, with empty Adirondack chairs awaiting company. It seems hardly anyone visits the pool, except the pool cleaner, me, and Betsy. Lola tells me it's too hot to swim, which sounds like something I'd tell my kids when I don't want to do something with them.

I change into my swimsuit – Lola's swimsuit, actually. I left mine in Minnesota.

When I leave the bedroom, Lola stops me in the hallway. Her eyes have grown softer, watery.

"Do you want to send for the kids?" she says. "I'll pay for the tickets."

We're face to face, inches from each other. She doesn't get it. I need time. Space. At least until the day quits replaying in my head.

Belle, my baby, plays in the corner of the living room while Harper does homework on the dining room table. Jack is supposed to be watching the baby. Cartoons clamor on the TV. I'm making snacks when I smell that rancid, familiar odor. I walk around the corner and see shit spattering the living room carpet. Jack looks at me, terrified. I don't say anything, until I'm muttering gibberish and stuffing sliced apples and peanut butter sandwiches down the garbage disposal. I find myself locked in the bathroom, stifling screams and pulling out my hair. When I come out, Harper has taken Belle to the other bathroom. Jack has a bucket of water and a sponge, trying to scrub the mess himself. I tell him to wash his hands and go to his room. I put the sponge to the carpet, then begin to cry. Leaving the supplies on the carpet, I pack a suitcase. Then I tell my kids I'm going on vacation as soon as Daddy comes home.

"If you want me to leave, just say so."

She drops her head, then brushes my cheek with a loose kiss before she bolts out the door.

I pick up Fat Cat and stroll around the quiet condo. Hardly anything is out of place. A speck of dust on her ebony bookshelf. Magazines fanned on the coffee table. The litter box could use a scooping. Then I notice my purse stuffed under the computer desk. I let down the heavy pet and pull out my phone.

Rolling it around my palms, I think about the day John bought me the iPhone. I couldn't have cared less about the thing. But I pretended to be excited. I didn't always pretend. Then I pretended all the time. I couldn't pretend anymore. I stare at the screen for a moment before powering it up. My stomach plunges with each message bubble. There are lots. I power it back off. I leave to get Betsy.

The yellow, partially deflated rafts keep us somewhat submerged in the water – a trick to keep from becoming a raisin in this Phoenix sun. In her polka-dotted bikini, orange-tinted Betsy paddles closer to me, despite our being being the only two in the pool. She chatters over the country music on her iPod. Topics such as celebrities eating their placenta hardly give me a chance to speak. I don't mind. I don't feel like talking.

"So, you ain't looking for a job by chance?" she asks. "Buzzie's looking for help right now. You know, the kind that don't screw around. I'm working way more than I want." Her hands swim around the water as if her fingers are bored. Now I have spots on my glasses. "We could really use the help, and Buzzie's a good boss. He don't let them assholes work you over."

A waitress job. My thoughts flee to John. What would he say about me waitressing at a bar? I'd be serving up shots while he's making mortgages.

"Think you'd like waiting on people?" Betsy asks with a raspy laugh. She laughs at the strangest moments.

"Me? Mind waiting on people?"

My memory spins back to the night when everything began to unravel. Really unravel. Six months ago. The night

John wouldn't get up to Belle. I was exhausted. Not just tired. Drained to a core I didn't know existed. The two oldest kids were just getting over the flu, and I had sanitized everything in the house. Everything. As much as I fought it, I felt symptoms coming on. When the screams came from the baby, I told John it was his turn to get up to her. I couldn't do it. He told me that wasn't the deal. I was the housewife. He was the breadwinner.

I exploded. In my exhaustion and feverish state, I lashed out at my husband – something I had never done. I screamed at him, telling him he was a terrible husband *and* father who'd rather read his 401k statement than attend his daughter's soccer game. I told him I hated him. Who could ever love such a selfish, arrogant banker? He didn't say one word while I ranted. Then he got up to check on the baby. As I watched him leave the bedroom, my other kids stood at the doorway, staring. It took me half an hour to get them back to bed because my boy insisted on reading a book: *Alexander and the Terrible, Horrible, No Good, Very Bad Day.*

I felt bad. Until the next morning – when John's parents showed up at our house.

His dad watched the kids while his mom took me to her doctor, who put me on Xanax and Prozac. I hate the idea of taking drugs. My mom has a cupboard full of prescription drugs. I don't feel a need to refill my prescriptions.

Sitting up on my deflated raft I ask, "When can I meet Buzzie?"

Five times. I change five times before settling on my sister's black tank dress, which fits me too tightly in the bust and butt. What do you wear to a bar interview anyway? I hadn't planned for this when I left. I study my figure in her full-length mirror, which rarely gets used since she works most of the time. I groan over my flabby back fat and visible muffin tops; impossible regions to manage since the birth of my third child.

I cautiously sit on the chair as if I'm gonna tear the dress, and wait. I'm ready early, so I rummage through my purse to find my phone. Biting my lip, I power it up to accept the text and voice mails coming in. In the meantime, I send a message to my sister.

With Bets tonight. Lov Liv

Then I hold my phone and glance at the bubbles of texts. The number of messages sent from John and the kids makes me uneasy – as if I've jumped into the deep end of the pool and can't quite get to the surface fast enough. I make a decision. I punch his number. I call John.

On the first ring he picks up. "Babe. You ready to come home?" I listen for my kids in the background, but it's quiet.

"How are the kids?"

"Fine. With Grandma Pat this morning. I'm at work."

"On Sunday?"

"Why haven't you answered any of my calls, Liv? You taking your meds? You gotta be taking those . . ."

I put the phone down, but he's still talking.

When I lift my cell back, I try to interrupt. "I'm not coming back."

He pauses for only a moment. "Liv. You haven't thought this through. We haven't even talked about seeing a marriage counselor. I've already found someone who can help you –"

"I'm looking for a job down here."

He pauses for as long as he can, which is hardly a few seconds. "You stupid bitch –"

I hang up. Immediately he calls me back. I know he thinks I'm hearing his special ring tone of Phillip Phillips singing *Home.* He did that when he bought it. I changed the ring tone on the plane ride to Phoenix.

I don't answer. Then he texts he's sorry. I throw my phone.

Crumpling on the floor, I wonder. Maybe I am a stupid bitch. For leaving my family, my kids. I pull out a photo of my children – two girls and one boy. Harper. Jack. Belle. All blond. I had blond hair once. I've had lots of colors. Harper's a mathematician, like her dad. Belle's gonna be a pill. I can tell. She'll have every boy loving and hating her. I miss the boy most. I know parents aren't supposed to say that. But how can you not favor a kid that hardly talks? Puzzles and Spongebob. I think he's a genius, but I'm not sure. Folding the photo, I drop my head and close my eyes. I imagine what they're doing right now.

What makes a person *want* to become a mom? It's the worst. It really is the worst.

I'm a better person for leaving them. They'll grow up smarter, with more resources, by staying with John. He'll treat them all right. And the girls will have each other. Just like Lola and me.

The doorbell rings while my phone continues to buzz and ping. I put the crinkled photo in my purse. Before I answer the door, I pick up the vibrating phone and toss it into my purse.

"Liv!" Betsy says in her upbeat way. "You look amazing. Practically transformed! Really want the job, huh?"

I test a smile, hoping to hide the fact I just tried to leave my husband. "I guess I do."

Majerle's Sports Grill welcomes us with its terra cotta facade and open air seating of iron-wrought table sets. I've never been there, but feel a sense of relief that Betsy isn't leading me to some dive bar. The propriety of the establishment also makes me more nervous.

As soon as we step through the heavy oak doors a blast of frigid air hits me, and I regret my choice of a tank dress as I begin to shiver. The air conditioning doesn't hide the dankness of the bar, or the stale beer smell seeping through my nostrils. My pupils adjust to the dark lighting as I scout the surroundings. The place is shaped like a galley. To my left is the counter, running almost the length of the place. High-back black leather booths claim the right side of Majerle's, while high-top tables are planted throughout the center, ending any notion of a dance floor. Large screens are scattered throughout – seemingly the main source of light. Baseball games play without the sound. I hear a Black Keys song. Even though the song's rhythm elicits an enthusiasm associated with a night out, I'm straddled with nerves. Possibly regret. The brightness on the outside of the building hasn't followed me inside.

"Where is everyone?" I ask.

"Getting ready to reopen in two hours." She points to double stainless steel doors toward the back. "In the kitchen, where all the magic happens." She winks at me.

Vibrations in my purse continue to tap at my waist.

"You need to take that before I get Buzzie?" Betsy asks.

Except for the past hour, my cell has been off for three weeks. I could've turned it off after I spoke with John, but I didn't.

"Nah." Shaking my head, I dig my hand in my purse and power it down. She wags off to the back room, hips in full swing. I take a seat at the bar. My dress hikes up to the upper part of my thigh, so I curl into myself in attempt to bring it to a more conservative length. I wonder if I look like a middle-aged tart, trying to reclaim something she might never have had.

I stare at the labels of the taps. Blue Moon. Shock Top. Samuel Adams. Fat Tire. Whatever happened to plain old Budweiser? Do I even know anything about anything anymore?

Betsy barges out. A brawny man crowned with wavy black hair idles his way over to me. I'm expecting him to be fat. "Buzzie" should be fat. Short. Ugly. But Buzzie is none of those. Not exactly handsome, but certainly not ugly.

When I stand, my dress clings to my ass. I pull it down while his stony eyes seem to carry out a cold calculation of me. I feel perspiration on my lip, despite the freezing temp.

"So, you Olivia?" he says.

I nod, extending my hand.

Loosely he takes my fingers, before letting go and plopping on the bar stool. "Lemme see your résumé."

My heart races upon the request. I reach in my purse, fishing around, as if it will produce an imaginary document. Strangely, I'm wishing for a call from John. I could use an excuse to think. I shuffle through my purse, feeling my wallet, lip glosses, and a pack of fruit chews. Then I scratch my chin, thinking to myself, *What in hell am I doing here, really?*

"Hey," he says, tapping my shoulders. "I'm just messin' with ya."

Breathing a sigh of relief, I smile. "I didn't think to bring one."

"Why not?" Buzzie raises his hands. "You think I run a crappy business here?"

I shake my head vehemently. "It's nice. I've just been out of the workforce for a while. Betsy only asked me to apply this morning –"

"So, you got any experience? Waitressing or bartending?"

"Not exactly. But I'm a mom. Waited on kids for the past ten years."

Buzzie tilts his head. "You got any *real* work experience?"

"I worked in the marketing department for a small newspaper. Designing print ads."

"The creative type, then?" Buzzie puts his head in his hands as if he's bored.

I sit up straighter, crossing my legs, aware of my skirt sliding up. His eyes don't budge though. "I liked the job. Only quit to stay home with the kids."

"Kids? Well, I ain't supposed to ask you none about that stuff. So, I won't officially ask you."

"My kids are with their father. In Minnesota."

"Okey dokey, then. What else you got to tell me 'bout yourself?"

Betsy's washing dishes behind the bar, looking straight at me, trying to hear everything she can. I'm torn. Do I really want this interview to work out? I turn back to Buzzie and land on his eyes. Hauntingly green. A few old scars are tunneled into his tan skin, next to his jawline. Maybe he's been in the military. Or maybe he's spent some hard time drinking in bars. Either way, I suddenly want this man to think I'm interesting. Go on, Liv. Be clever.

"Communications. I majored in communications. Minored in art." I pause, racking my brain for some interesting experience in my life that doesn't involve my kids. But I only note his tired gaze, wishing he'd at least blink. "Look. You could always give me a shot. If I don't work out, I don't work out."

"That's sort of a given," he says with an unsmiling wink. "Tell ya what? Show up tomorrow. Around ten. We'll go over the menu. Test drive a little lunch. You and me. Maybe mix a few drinks? Then you follow Betsy around. I'll *observe*. See if ya fit in. Sound agreeable?"

I nod and smile, feeling stupidly flirtatious, as if I'm back in college trying to get this guy to buy me a drink. When he juts out his lip and leans back, a wave of guilt fires through me as I consider three children in Duluth, sitting in a house, watching cartoons, drinking juice boxes.

Then I remember. The poop.

The washing machine. The vacuum in the closet.

The days I envied the vacuum in the closet. The poop.

I shake off the guilt.

After I thank Buzzie with another handshake, which he returns in a firmer manner than our introduction, Betsy leads me out of the bar. Her arms wrap around me, like a fifth-grade school girl. As soon as we step out, a flash of sun blinds my eyes.

"You're gonna be part of Majerle's family! I'm super duper excited."

I gently release myself, reaching down into my purse for sunglasses. Since my phone is on top, I grab it instead. The blank screen beckons me to power it up, so I do. I check the most recent message which says, *Figure it out.*

Not from Lola. John.

Glancing at the iron-wrought gate, I feel a trickle of sweat inch down my back. My knees feel unsteady.

Betsy takes my shoulder. "Honey? Everything all right? You look kinda sick."

I thumb through his previous messages – there are . . . twelve, all telling me how patient he will be. Patient. He became impatient at twelve.

"I'm fine," I say with a quiver. "Fine." Then I lift my phone to text him back. I'm a statue, poised to make my move.

Betsy rubs my shoulder. "Sweetie, I need to get back inside. We open soon."

Taking shallow breaths, I quickly read his messages over again and feel the possessiveness creep up with each post. Then I type up a message.

I'm coming to get the kids.

Before I hit send, Betsy pats me on the shoulder. "You're gonna be great here. I can feel it."

As she turns to leave, I stare at the words in my message. And just before I hit send, I remove my finger from the button. The black Majerle's sign towers over me, and a crisp realization enters my mind.

A plan. I need a plan first. I power off my phone and put it away for now.

Stepping away through the blurry crowd of faces – women, children, grandparents, families – I'm forced to squint. Spotty sunglasses annoy me, so I toss them in the next trash bin I see. The glare of the Phoenix sun makes my eyes water. At least, I think that's why my eyes are watering, probably making mascara run down my cheeks. Eventually I'll wipe it off to freshen my face. It's been a while since my face felt fresh.

Cradle Robber
By Daniel Brian Mobley
⟨⇒⟩

DANIEL BRIAN MOBLEY was born in 1983. He received an Associate Degree in Commercial Art from Nossi College of Art in 2003 and lives with his wife Crystal and their dog Presto in Springfield, Tennessee. In addition to writing short stories, he creates graphic novels. Daniel can be contacted at https://twitter.com/danielbmobley. Here's what he wrote about "Cradle Robber":

> Cradle Robber actually began as a subplot for a novel I had been working on. Lucero and Allie were never meant to be the focus of the story, but the more I wrote about them, the more interesting they became. Human beings develop bonds with one another organically, often without conscious thought, and this happens despite the prejudices of the society in which one lives. The story is essentially about putting the greater good over personal gain and the price that is ultimately paid for it."

⟨⇒⟩

We are Transcenders, sentient energy made flesh and blood for the purpose of finding, and aiding, the last human vessel of the Ethereal. They are the Corpse Legion, demonic creatures that feed on the vices of mankind. For as long and as deep as the oceans of the earth we have warred with one another. But now the endgame is upon us, and

> *only the Infinite can contain the hell overtaking*
> *the earth . . .*
> – Transcender Headmistress Melina

Allie could barely run anymore. The full moon sat high in the sky as the girl made her way out of the dark alley. Leaning against the brick wall, she doubled over and gasped for air. Her dirty-blond hair obscured her face: it was matted with sweat and clung to her forehead.

The beads of sweat ran down her cheeks as she coughed deeply and raised her head. It was nearly midnight. Her mentor – a man called Lucero – wouldn't wait for her much longer. It was too dangerous. She refocused and bolted for the large apartment complex across the street. A fence around the maze of buildings stood a good seven feet off the ground. Without breaking stride she jumped – clearing the height and landing hard on the other side.

As Allie rose to her feet, she thought she heard a moan. Slowly turning around, she listened, her muscles tensing. Only the wind answered. Goose bumps sprouted on her arms and chest as she stood frozen in the night. Praying that her speed and cunning had been enough to evade THEM, she crossed the grass that fronted the tenements.

Her head moved from left to right as she walked, listening for the slightest hint of movement in the darkness around her. Again she heard only the wind and the persistent, steady beating of her own heart. She crossed into the breezeway of one of the buildings, climbing the stairs. A young smoker passed her on her way down the hall to the next flight of stairs. The smoker, a tattooed man with ruddy skin, eyed her until she was out of sight.

On the next floor – the third – she slowed her pace. Each step she took slowly after that. Her lips moved, the whispers little more than short sighs. Nearly two-thirds the length of the hallway she did this – then came to an abrupt stop. She turned her head, running her fingers across the heavy door beside her. The numbers on the door read "313." Sliding her hand down to the knob, she twisted the handle and opened the door.

Save the light coming in from the hallway, the apartment was completely dark. Allie stepped inside and closed the door. The light vanished. She crept to the center of the room, the only sound her own coarse breathing.

"Mister Lucero?" she called out. There was no answer. She shifted her weight when she heard a loud rustling. "Who's there?" she called again.

"Who else would it be?" a voice answered back.

Lucero stepped from the left corner of the room, his boots thudding.

Allie smiled, wiping the sweat from her cheeks.

"I almost thought you'd left me!" she breathed.

"Not at all," Lucero replied. "I didn't break my back training you for the last seven years just to be done with you now."

Her smile stayed. She moved close, reaching out to touch him. He took her hand. As their hands locked, she gave his a squeeze. She stretched the moment, holding on longer than she should have, longer than ever before. Her breathing became elevated again, and Lucero let go, stepped back.

"Did you make it to the Well?" he asked.

Her smile faded. She knew he could sense her disappointment.

"Yes." Her voice cracked.

"Krator said we're in the right place to receive him. His mother, our sister, may resist us, but he's confident she'll give him up in the end. He said that unlocking his potential will not be easy, but essential to our mission."

"Without him, then, our mission is vain."

"Exactly."

Lucero laid his hand on Allie's shoulder.

"Without you, we wouldn't have the information to do this. Melina and I value your courage."

She laughed.

"I enjoy the thrill. It sure beats waiting around for those horn-heads to come kill us!"

He laughed back. Had it not been for the silence that followed, neither would have heard the bump from the ceiling above. They froze, listening. There was nothing – no sound – for seconds. Then . . . BUMP.

BUMP.

Allie's chicken skin returned. BUMP. BUMP. BUMP.

They moved closer, the mentor wrapping his arm around the student's body. The room began to shake and creak as the bumps grew louder. A grating chorus of moans echoed through the tiny space. Lucero held Allie tighter as she covered her ears. The voices cutting the air were not human.

BUMP. BUMP. CRACK.

Their heads snapped toward the last noise. In the upper corner of the room the wall plaster split. The ceiling began to part, asbestos falling, and the sounds of the moaning chorus rose. A viscous fluid – like the blackest blood – ran from the cracks in the walls. And then, hordes of cockroaches and spiders emerged from every crevice in the room. As the surrounding walls began to collapse, they formed a back-to-back formation.

Allie clutched her throat.

"How did they find us? I'm so sorry!"

As a pair of grotesque, hose-like arms emerged from the hole in the ceiling ,Lucero grabbed her hand and rushed toward the boarded-up window a few feet away.

"We have to get out!"

His body smashed through the solid wooden boards as if they were rotted twigs – Allie's scrawny-but-lean frame behind him. They glided across the moonlit sky, as if propelled by an unseen force. They cleared the length of the nearly eighteen-foot courtyard below them. Lucero's hand shot out, grabbing the roof of the adjoining building. At once, gravity pulled his body down and into the cold bricks of the wall. He snorted and then, without looking, snatched Allie up by her sleeve with his other hand, tossing her onto the roof's surface. Without breaking the motion, she rolled to her feet, grabbing his hands and judo-tossing him over her body and onto the roof as well. Instead of landing on his back, he tucked his feet beneath him, and they both made another seventeen-foot leap onto the next roof in line.

After landing, Allie turned to listen. She was startled at how fast they were pursued. She could hear the moans, the flexing of alien musculature as the monsters approached.

"Move!" her mentor commanded.

She turned to his voice, suddenly realizing he was already on the final building's roof. She crouched for another leap, and something grabbed her arm. As its shadow swallowed her own, she did not raise her head. There was no time for fear, or it would all be over.

Lucero dug his heels into the roof.

"Come on!"

Allie could smell the corpse stench of her enemy as it yanked her into the air, pulling her body toward its vom-it-filled mouth. She flailed around, trying to free herself from its grip. The monster raised her fingers to its jagged teeth. And that was all the time he needed. Pulling three metal stakes from the thigh holster at his leg, Lucero threw them at the monster's head and arm. Time slowed as the sharp weapons sliced through the air, glinting in the moon-light. Allie screamed, and then she was on the ground. The creature staggered back and screeched – its eye and arm gushing that blackest blood.

Allie jumped to her feet and then to the next roof, hav-ing learned her lesson. She sprinted and jumped, sprinted and jumped, until she caught up with her mentor. They turned to jump to the street below, but stopped. A mob of the demons surrounded the apartment complex. No escape.

Hellish sounds filled the night air. Clawing upward, spindly limbs stretched until the meager flesh tore. As student and mentor stood in place, the creatures pursuing them across the roofs were catching up.

"Oh, no," Allie whispered, her heart a jackhammer. Lucero turned to her, placing a dagger with a crescent-shaped blade into her hand.

"Take this," he said. "You must jump down into the fray. Do not stop slashing until you have made it past them."

She looked up at him with a terrible frown.

"Mentor. I don't know if I can do this."

"I will draw their attention the best I can. Do not stop. Do not wait for me. And you WILL do this!"

She bit her lip in response to his command, her fists clenching so that her palms bled.

"I will."

THEY were on top of them now, and her mentor pulled two flash-bang grenades from his belt in preparation.

"If I'm not at the rendezvous point when you arrive, assume I'm dead and return to Melina."

No more was said between them.

As she leaped down into the waiting mob, Lucero pulled the pin and flung one of his grenades onto the roof a few feet behind him. In a split second, the demons were upon him. The grenade exploded, filling the night with white light, disorienting his enemies.

They staggered around the rooftop, jabbing their sharp fingernails into each other as he armed and tossed the second grenade down into the mass surrounding the building. He then tossed another flurry of metal stakes, stabbing the creatures trying to flank him. As they collapsed at his feet, he pulled three more stakes from his belt, flinging them at another growing mass charging the rooftops. He listened to the mob below. Allie hacked and slashed her way through the dense sea of them, her face and clothes stained with entrails. The grenade Lucero tossed had gone off instantly, its blinding flash helping her carve a path of escape. Metal met bone and cartilage over and over again. She screamed as she swung her dagger through the air. The demons, much larger than her, slashed back at her shredding attacks, but only harming one another in doing so.

Making it past the fray and jumping the same fence she had cleared less than a half-hour before, she listened for any sign that her mentor was still alive. She heard only the chorus. Fighting tears she sprinted back into the dark alley, hoping he somehow survived.

⬅⇒➤

Lucero did survive. After making sure that Allie was nearly out of the mob, he turned back, fighting his way past those that still crowded the rooftops. He was able to jump down into the courtyard and escape by losing his foes through a carefully planned route through the city's alleys. It took him the better part of twenty-five minutes to elude his enemies. He couldn't allow himself to be followed back to the rendezvous point.

Exhausted, he hastened back to it – an old cafe targeted for demolition on Jefferson Street.

Sliding in through one of its broken windows, he entered, half-expecting her to jump into his arms. As he staggered around an old table covered by a dusty tarp, he reminded himself that he had told her not to wait for him. Realizing that she was halfway to Melina by now, he shook off the silly fantasy, smiling.

The important thing was that they survived the mission. That was all that mattered.

He had to believe that the mission was all that mattered. After all, he was twenty-four years her senior. Anything more than friendship between them would be controversial. And ridiculous. Not to mention despised.

Goodness! He had watched her develop from a girl to a woman, from puberty to full-blown maturity! She could never be any more to him than a surrogate daughter at best.

He knew no one, not even his beloved friend and leader Melina, would accept such an odd and distasteful relationship. But he could not deny what he felt during the events that night. He could not deny the burning passion that threatened to escape him every time her hand touched his. When he was with her, he felt no fear, only the need to protect her – at any and all cost. She made him feel as if he could do anything. He did not know why he felt this way about a girl that was young enough to be his daughter.

It was time to challenge some of the world's convictions and condemnatory judgments. It was time to throw caution to the wind. He decided it in that single moment: he was going to tell Allie how he felt about her. And to hell with the consequences. That was when he noticed the *blood*.

He breathed in deeply, his nostrils bombarded with the raw odor of body-produced iron.

He knelt, touching the floor. It was wet. He slowly rubbed the thick fluid between his thumb and forefinger. Indeed. *Blood*. He craned his head around, trying to pick up the slightest sound in the building.

He heard nothing save the beating of the wind on the closed windows. His chest became tight as he called out her name.

"Allie? Are you in here?"

He stomped past and around the bar counter – toward the kitchen – calling her again.

"Allie? Where are you?"

Entering the kitchen, he smelled odors of old grease and oils – remnants of a busier time – but the smell of iron was stronger. He walked through the kitchen in a daze, the random splotches of blood leading him onward.

He called out for the third and final time.

"ALLIE!"

The kitchen was T-shaped, and as he came to the top of the "T," the blood trailed to the left. He did not raise his head as he turned the corner. He knew what was there.

"I was wondering when you'd get here," said a weak voice. "I knew you'd make it. You always do, Mentor."

Lucero's body pumped with adrenaline and terror. His skin on fire, he knelt by his wounded student. Allie lay against one of the kitchen's lower cabinets, her skin pale and bloody. Her eyes drifted to his face, and he brushed her hair away.

"Where are you hurt?" he said. The words sounded like a cough.

She took his right hand, raised it, then placed it on her left side. Near her ribs. Lucero silently thanked God that he was blind.

"I was home-free," she began, as he ripped his shirt and began wrapping her wound. "I could've been halfway to Melina's by now, you know. But I wanted, needed, to see if you were okay. About a block from here, near the cemetery. It hid near that tall oak tree. I didn't see it. By the time I did, it was on top of me. It's *dead* now, though."

She winced as he cinched the makeshift bandage around her wound. The fabric was saturated within seconds.

"I told you to never look back," Lucero said. More coughing language. "*Never* wait for me!"

Allie turned her head away from him for a moment, making a chuckling noise as her breathing became shallower. When she turned back to him, her cheeks were stained with tears. Still, she smiled.

"You're the only reason I ever came this far. You've always been there for me, good or bad, rain or shine. You helped me become a woman. A warrior. And you taught me righteousness. Men like you save worlds, fight wars for the weakest of us . . ."

He gripped her left hand as she spoke, feeling the silk scarf that she clutched in her palm as he did so. She stared at the ceiling, seeing nothing. Her voice was smaller now.

"Just a girl, but I see what matters in this world. It's not money or weapons, power or fame. And I feel sorry for the people that will never know it."

Lucero held her close, Allie whispering her last words in his ear.

"I'm not scared, my everything. Not scared. You've always been my light in the darkness. Always my light –"

Her heart stopped. He stroked her face and then her hair, as her eyes fixed on the ceiling. He wept that night, not letting go of her body for an hour after she had passed. It would be another two hours before he would be able to bury her.

> *Many men kill themselves for love, but many more women die of it.*
> - Author Unknown

Black Pearl Earrings
By Randy Ames
⬥⬥

RANDY AMES is retired from the U.S. Air Force after a twenty-one year career. He lives on the Gulf Coast in unincorporated Bay County with his wife Claudia and a stubborn Welsh Pembroke Corgi named Bennie the Jet. He is interested in motorcycles and archery. Here's what he wrote about "Black Pearl Earrings":

> All of my other twenty-six short fantasy stories had the protagonist as a very good person. I thought it would be interesting to see if I could write a bad person as the protagonist.

⬥⬥

With a flick of her wrist, Kata brought her dagger to hand and moved in silence to stand behind her victim, a fair dwarven damsel absorbed in combing her long azure hair. Nary a sound did Kata make as she clamped her hand over the luscious mouth. In a single, fluid motion her other hand came up and slid the sharp edge of the blade across the muscled pale neck. Bright red arterial blood sprayed from the cut and turned the damsel's white linen nightgown crimson. Soon the young woman ceased her struggles and slumped lifeless in her arms.

Kata, as slim and finely made as her assassin's dagger, let her trusting victim fall to the wooden floor and rifled the nearby nightstand. The trinkets she searched for were proudly displayed and easily found: a pair of black pearl earrings. These she pocketed. Her sponsor wanted them as proof of the kill.

At the windowsill, the black-haired assassin grasped the thin, knotted rope she'd used to climb in. She let herself down hand over hand till her soft-shod feet touched the cobblestones, then simply walked away, leaving the rope hanging in full view. It no longer mattered to her. As she walked along the mist-shrouded lane, Kata listened for any screams that might indicate the corpse had been found too quickly. None came.

An hour later, Kata arrived at a table in an eatery of the upper class. Six large and proficient-looking men kept undesirables away from the building and the stable outside so that the gentry could comport themselves with dignity, away from bothersome scoundrels. Though she herself was a scoundrel, now that she wore a fine velvet dress Kata no more looked the part than the young woman she'd so recently murdered. She smiled and passed by the guards with no trouble at all. She took her seat. Now all she had to do was receive payment. But that itself was no easy task.

Being a freelance assassin was a dangerous business. She had learned that final lesson when she found her mentor hanging from the crow-infested gibbet in the town square. Without a go-between to handle the money, it was always a chancy business collecting one's fees. A client might forego payment and simply inform on you to the authorities; hence the meeting in a fancy place. The status quo was looked upon with great favor by the upper class and any of the gentry who broke the rules were frowned upon, even ostracized.

Kata's fine velvet dress was more than just a way to blend in with the eatery's wealthy patrons. And the provocative slits up each thigh did more than show off creamy white legs. Along with her flat-heeled shoes, those slits would let her run very well, should she need to. The one long sleeve on her left arm hid her preferred weapon, the slim black steel dagger.

She was ready. But where was her sponsor? She sipped again at the wine in the silver goblet. What would she do if he didn't show?

The first lesson of her mentor, which Kata kept close to her heart, was to be ready for any unexpected turn of events. But even as she thought this her sponsor sauntered into the tavern. His grin seemed plastered on as he made his way toward her table.

Calon was of middle stature and mean appearance. He was the son of a wealthy merchant, and upon their first meeting three days prior, she had known his type on the instant. Feelings of entitlement ran strongly through his veins instead of regal blood, but he did not let that interfere in his paltry machinations. He was petty and he was a bully.

Kata gave her sponsor a sweet, pleasant smile and held out a dainty hand. Calon ignored the gesture. He seated himself arrogantly, one arm over the back of the chair. Kata kept up the pretense of her smile. With a nod so slight that it was imperceptible to Calon she signaled to a specific serving girl. This girl was about twenty years old, had hair less black than her own, and had been a sudden replacement for a serving girl that had conveniently come down sick.

At Kata's seemingly normal request for more wine the serving girl approached at a bustle. Calon ignored her until she tripped over her own feet and spilled the bottle of wine on him. He stood abruptly and swore at her clumsiness. The serving girl rushed to his side and brushed at his vest with her scarf, apologizing impressively.

Calon pushed the girl away as the ever-alert manager came and forced her towards the back. Kata held her smile as people began to stare. Her sponsor looked about and, in bad grace, asked if she had what he wanted.

Kata indicated the small envelope made out of good parchment that lay on the table before her. "I have brought the items you requested. I would like to see my asking price now, if you please."

Calon smirked and turned to signal someone outside the front window. The door opened and a captain of the guard appeared within the frame. Candlelight glanced off his burnished breastplate. He came to the table and every patron hushed. They knew something was afoot.

The captain stood tall in his uniform and looked down upon the slim woman.

He nodded toward Calon. "An acquaintance of this man here was robbed of a pair of black pearl earrings after her throat was cut this night. He believes you have them and are therefore the murderer. I would like to take a look at that envelope by your hand, if you would please."

The captain was very polite, but also very professional. This was a man known for his honesty and incorruptibility. He waited for Kata to hand him the envelope.

Kata looked up at him with widened eyes. "But Calon here has agreed to purchase these earrings from me here tonight. They were my mother's, and it is with deep regret that I must sell them." She let her voice take on a fragile quiver that betrayed none of the irritation she felt. "We had agreed on a price of fifteen gold coins three days ago, right at this very table."

The captain would not be dissuaded. "May I see the envelope, please?"

"Captain," she begged, "are you saying that whosoever has these black pearl earrings in their possession would be proven to be this poor woman's assassin?"

The captain agreed and Kata handed the packet to the man. He opened the flap and poured the earrings onto his open palm. There they lay, wonderfully styled diamond earrings shining in the candlelight. The captain turned to Calon, who frowned. Confused, the merchant's son looked at Kata in disbelief.

"You see, Captain," she said. "Those are my dear, dead mother's diamond earrings, and would you not say they are worth fifteen gold coins?"

The captain nodded. He had not the foggiest notion that the diamond earrings were actually clear quartz, craftily cut, or of the going rate for either. They looked authentic and, therefore, valuable to him. He showed them to Calon. The merchant's son looked as if he were about to protest, but Kata cut him off.

"Now, Calon, do you have our agreed-upon price?"

Calon looked murderous, and as the captain turned to face him he barely regulated his ire.

Quietly, she added, "Maybe you should check your vest pocket."

Calon scowled but at her nod he did so, and his questing fingers touched something that should not be there. He blanched. He had not felt the black pearl earrings insinuated into his vest pocket by that clumsy serving girl.

With the evidence upon his very own person, he would most assuredly be behind the legendary stocks very soon.

"I'm afraid I do not have the agreed-upon price at this time." Kata watched her sponsor begin to sweat. She then nodded ever so slightly to her second conspirator, an example of the more handsome and nefarious gentry, at a nearby table. He stood and approached Kata.

Viscount Brisan enjoyed creating intrigue, much to the consternation of his elder brother, Count Norman. He detested merchants, though he favored the romantic conquest of their sons and daughters, and had jumped at the chance to ensnare Calon without actually getting his hands dirty.

The captain noticed the young royal immediately. He turned to look at him, as did all in the establishment.

The viscount smiled nonchalantly, brushing a wisp of his long brown hair from over his gorgeous green eyes and said, "Maybe I can be of assistance here, my good Captain. I could not help but overhear the young lady's plight and that the honorable man here could not pay the agreed-upon price. I just happen to have fifteen gold coins upon my person and would be happy to take the young man's marker in recompense, and then all will be well."

Calon seethed. He looked from Kata to the viscount and nodded reluctantly, a beaten man. Viscount Brisan produced a convenient marker from his waistcoat pocket and, with the captain as a signing witness, the transaction was completed.

Viscount Brisan handed the bag of gold coins to Kata, Kata handed the fake diamond earrings to Calon, and the captain handed the marker to Viscount Brisan.

Calon thundered out of the tavern. The oblivious captain saluted the viscount and followed. Kata smiled warmly at her debonair savior and thanked him most properly. The dining hall patrons returned to their meals, their drinks, and their status quo.

Kata walked out of the eatery with fifteen gold pieces – ten more than Calon had originally agreed. The fake diamonds had come to her at very little cost and, for his attempt to betray her, Calon was getting off easily from the point of view of a trained assassin.

Kata smiled to herself as she glided down the streets, away from the wealthy quarter to the modest place she called home. The greatest lesson Kata's mentor had ever taught her, before she died, was that the strongest bluff was to actually be holding the winning hand.